Dedicati

To Glendower Preparatory School for giving me the assignment in year 6 that inspired the first words of this novel.

Worldreader

Proceeds of book sales for Sardaron will go to World Reader, a global nonprofit whose mission is to help the world read. The organization provides students and their families with a free digital library available on e-readers and mobile phones, complemented with a suite of reading support programs. Since 2010, over 10 million people across 49 countries have read from their digital library of over 35,300 local and international e-books.

www.worldreader.org

SARDARON

First published 2018

Published under licence by Brown Dog Books and The Self-Publishing Partnership, 7 Green Park Station, Bath BA1 1JB

www.selfpublishingpartnership.co.uk

ISBN printed book: 978-1-78545-362-5
ISBN e-book: 978-1-78545-363-2

Cover design by Kevin Rylands
Internal design by Andrew Easton

Printed by CPI Group (UK) Ltd, Croydon CR0 4YY

SARDARON

TWO SISTERS. ONE CHANCE OF SURVIVAL.

ANNA PATTLE

.PROLOGUE.

Nevan

I stared dully down at the corpse.

The corpse of Eimana, her clothes shredded, face set in a furious expression of anger and passion. I was kneeling, my sword slipping out of my belt. I carefully adjusted it without moving my eyes from the woman's face, watching for any movement on her part. As if some small, desperate facet of my mind still believed that she was alive.

Her skin was lined with dirt and crusted with blood – it was sallow, the colour already fading out of it. Her hands were clenched shut, one holding a small dagger that gleamed silver in the fading light of the evening.

I could do nothing but stare down at her, feeling emptiness in my mind. Silence, as I tried to process what had happened.

A wisp of flame, spreading slowly upwards from the woman's arm, was the only sign of life. I stared at it as it slithered up her arm, leaving behind the smell of burning flesh and charcoal. Where it had moved, a black line marred the smooth skin of her forearm. It snaked upwards, heading towards her head, trailing ash and puffs of smoke. The flame was not controlled by her, but by the remnants of an enemy's power.

I simply watched as it slid onto her face, cracking and burning the skin that lay there. Furiously, I stared at the flame as it devoured her features. The flicker grew, engulfing her nose, mouth and eyes, until her face was a ruin. In my mind, there was only an imprint of what she had looked like. The only image I now had of her.

I stood, taking a deep breath, watching as the flame moved further and further along her body, leaving behind seared ashes. I watched, until there was nothing but a decomposing heap of ash and burning meat left. Around my fingers cruel wind whipped, ice begging to be unleashed on the flame. Begging at least to try to preserve the woman's body.

I clenched my fingers together, shutting out the urge I felt in my blood. The instinct to destroy the flame in front of me.

I stepped back, averting my eyes, knowing that I shouldn't be watching the flame, lest I give in to my temptations. What was done was done – there was no point in trying to fix it. Trying to fix her.

A sudden hand on my arm made me turn, startled. Remas, my second-in-command, stared at me apologetically, his hand now resting on my shoulder. The sight of his face made the first of the tears start to trickle down my face.

'I'm so sorry, Nevan,' Remas said softly. 'More than you can imagine.' I nodded weakly, brushing my eyes. I glanced once more at the corpse, sparking fresh tears to trail down my face.

My voice cracked, face crumpling, as I whispered, 'I loved her so much.'

Remas said nothing, eyes searching my face. 'I know you did,' he uttered at last, taking a deep breath. I longed for it to be someone else comforting me, for Eimana to have her hand wrapped around mine once more. I stared at her corpse, the flame finally extinguished. The corpse of my loved one.

'Come. It's not safe here. That flame might have come from one of the Firborn.'

I stared at him silently, wondering how he could be so crude. His face was twisted away slightly, eyes awkwardly darting between mine and the ground, the position of his body uncomfortable on the ground. I realised that with none of his family killed, he didn't know what to say to me that would make anything better. He didn't understand.

I said nothing. He took my silence for agreement and slowly led me over to our side of the battlefield, footsteps squelching through the blood and gore that decorated the sodden ground. The safe side.

For it was war we were fighting, a brutal battle that had led carnage to rage for centuries. Two opposing immortal sides, both fighting against each other in their desperation for survival. The Falcords – myself, my people, and my beloved Eimana, who were woven with the crisp wind at our heels and ice adorning our fingers – and the Firborn. The opposing people, ones that ruled with fire and merciless heat. Who had killed my family – and my friends.

The war was a desperate attempt by each side to win survival for their people – each side ferociously, viciously, determined to win.

For the people who lost… they were left with nothing but the scarce game that wandered their land – for the Falcords, just a few species of woodland mammals. The extreme environment we lived in, snow-covered mountains that embodied the spirit of our gifts, was cruel in its beauty, allowing only a few survivors to nourish themselves from its bounty. A bounty that was growing increasingly small as the population grew and wars were lost. Two, in fact, was the precise number of battles in which the Falcords had succumbed to the Firborn. Two battles set a hundred years apart – once a century the two sides converged to fight battle and then returned to their own lands.

The people who won the wars were gifted with supplies for survival by our ruler. Supplies that would just about last until the next century rolled around, when wars – we called them the wars of Meridian – would be fought again. The gifts included clothes, weapons, food supplies, and the necessary ingredients for survival in the harsh land.

I had experienced crushing loss a hundred years ago, when I had eagerly joined the Fydars (a group of Falcords who trained exclusively for the battles and who were known with reverence throughout the legions of the people) in hope of winning valour for my people. Unfortunately, we had lost, and had returned home dejected and angry.

After that, I had promised myself that I would dedicate my life to fighting, to becoming a legendary warrior like the rest of the Fydars. Only it hadn't worked out – I had met Eimana and fallen in love with her almost immediately. Suddenly, war wasn't my focus so much as being a good husband was.

Now that we had lost for a second time, I knew that there would be urgent talks on rationing our food and conserving what we had. A hundred years was a long time to be without plentiful food and means of survival. It was easier for us, however. We remained hopeful, because a hundred years… it was the equivalent for us of a few years of the life of a mortal.

And we – the species of superhuman who were split into two different peoples – weren't mortal.

We were considered immortal, our lifespans ranging from 700 years to over a millennium, depending on our lifestyles and how well-nourished we were. Many died of starvation in the village outside our camp, and mortality rates in children were high.

All for this war.

Before the wars, the Falcords and Firborn had lived together for eons, presided over by a true immortal. A god of sorts. All I knew was that his reign had ended when another god arrived from a different dimension and killed our previous ruler.

The new god, Sardaron, was the ruler of darkness and death. He rejoiced in the suffering of others. It was what kept him alive – the deaths of his people powered him further.

At least, that was the myth, woven around battlefields and passed on from generation to generation.

It was also said that this dark god had created a prophecy. The prophecy ordered wars to be fought every hundred years. The deaths that occurred were used to power the life of the god – but whoever won the wars also received all the equipment and supplies needed to survive the next hundred years.

The prophecy contained a curse that took two girls from Earth to fight against each other the result determining which side won. That was the most devastating part of the curse: the girl that lost would either be killed or be turned into a mortal once more.

I turned away from Remas, who was looking at me with concern still hovering in his eyes. He smiled ruefully and patted my shoulder once. His distance was to be expected; we had never been close, and I understood that he didn't know me well enough to know how to comfort me.

Anyway, I didn't want comforting. I didn't want sympathy. None of those things had mattered before, not when I had the attention of the only person I needed it from. Everyone else was irrelevant – extras in the scenes I had performed with Eimana, the spotlight seemingly on just the two of us. She was the only one that mattered.

I walked away from Remas towards the small tent that I had set up for the duration of the battle. It was small and discreet, and I pushed open the flaps to let myself inside.

In a corner, a small bedroll was covered in a blanket and a grey, worn pillow, and I plopped down onto the dismal bed, shucking off my shoes as I did so. I lay down, staring at the ceiling, staring at nothing.

Eimana was dead.

I sighed and rubbed my face. The shock of the moment hadn't sunk in. I felt distant from the event, as though it had happened to someone else.

For what felt like hours, I stared up at the ceiling of the tent, watching it sway gently as a wind rustled around our camp, the warriors calling across to each other as they moved around the site, caring for the wounded. We had precious few medical supplies left.

I couldn't stay here.

There was no point in my life on this dimension. No point without her. I knew that the endless years of fighting for survival would eventually kill me.

I could go someplace else – somewhere where I could start again. I knew exactly the place that I wanted to go. It was the place that Eimana had talked of so frequently with longing and passion in her voice.

Earth.

I got up, groaning over my stiff bones, and strode out of the tent.

I passed the circle of tents that housed the army, spotting the guard on duty.

I moved past the sleeping warriors, making sure not to catch the eye of the guard before I slipped into the dense green foliage surrounding the area.

They would never even realise that I was gone.

...

One week later

I stared at the huge cave, eyes drooping and dusty. Baleful and cavernous, my breath resonated into the darkness, the air crackling with a poisoned stench.

I stepped forward.

Small stones crunched underfoot as I walked to the back of the cave, eyes squinting in front of me.

'Hello?' I called out, staring into nothing. I hadn't realised quite how debilitating the loss of sight would be. The slightest sound throbbed in my ears, and my every nerve was on edge as I struggled to adapt to the situation. I was vulnerable here, alone.

The cave was set on a moor, the slight breeze shivering through the cool air as I glanced around me.

I was exhausted and alone, and this seemed like a good enough place to rest before setting off again in the morning.

Sliding my foot over the cobbled ground, I cleared away the excess debris and stones so that I had a clear patch of ground to lie upon.

Carefully, I sat, feeling the cold of the earth beneath and behind me as I shifted so that I was leaning against the wall of the cave.

My eyes fluttered as I gazed at the ground. Fatigue washed over me as I drooped, leaning sideways until I was on the floor, head uncomfortably resting on the dirt.

My eyelids were drooping, my breathing getting heavier as I gradually felt a drowsiness, almost like a drug, take over my thoughts. It was an uncomfortable feeling; as if someone was manipulating me in my loneliness and vulnerability. I was losing control of my thoughts, as if they were being manoeuvred by a puppet-master. My emotions were as real as they had ever been, however, as fear sapped my strength and made me unable to move, to sit up or even to open my eyes.

In the cloudiness of my thoughts, I saw the presence of a hideously scarred face; a figure monstrous and corrupt. A demon.

My conscious mind wondered if this hallucination could be the boundary that needed to be crossed to get to Earth, the rite of passage to a better world, the payment that needed to be made in order to access a life worth living. This, in effect, was Sardaron, the manipulator of lives and happiness, the most satanic figure of our realm.

In my sub-conscious mind, a voice whispered his name. My voice. The figure didn't reply but in my mind I could feel his eyes fixating on me, closing in as if he was about to pounce. He was supposed to be a myth, but yet was completely real in that moment as I felt his gaze burn into my face: judging me, evaluating my life as if it was nothing more than a trickle of water in the river of time to him.

'I want to leave Nzar,' I begged the mythical yet pervasive figure in my mind. 'I want to go to Earth. I have lost the only person I love and my request is the only trace of hope left for me.'

I felt the sound of my thoughts reverberating against the empty stone of the cave. It echoed into nothing before I had even finished the sentence. Yet the eyes and the hollow eeriness of the figure were staring into my soul, a feeling so uncomfortable that I felt paralysed. This control that Sardaron had over me was emotionless, restraining. I desperately wanted to be freed of his control but I was too afraid to do anything but watch.

Without warning, a burning vision radiated into my brain. I could see Earth and its brightness, light and happiness. I felt the raw emotion of love once again, teasing me in a cruel way to remind me of my devotion to Eimana. In the undecipherable image, I saw two prosperous children and the flash of the thought made me realise that I had been starved of such powerful love in Nzar, our minds and bodies broken as we trained to kill, kill, kill. My mind was undulating in and out of this force holding me still. I wanted to be on Earth so badly to experience this sense of love; a progression and reward of the love I had for Eimana. But as a cold wave of consciousness swept in, I remembered that Eimana was dead, her life finished. I would never have children and never experience fatherly love with her.

The pervasive power of this god seemed to cloud my mind again, as if to ask my inner consciousness a question, to make a deal with me. He forced an image in my mind of the children (two twin girls) but this time they were Syths fighting a war against each other. Precious, beautiful and immortal beings that were ruined by war and destruction. They were gone forever; taken by Sardaron in a mighty black wave that crushed them in a second. This image was so wicked and wrong that a small gasp erupted out my mouth, as I watched that golden life being quenched into oblivion. Sardaron's power crashed over my mind once again, offering me a choice: travel to Earth and live, with my children taken away from me, or stay here forever.

I whispered once more to create a wave of echo in the cave. 'I will offer my children to Sardaron…' I trailed off. My words came out almost against my will. My only thread of possible consciousness was that I would never have children. Eimana was dead.

With that, the choice was easy, and I would do anything to relieve my soul of his presence. Even agree to his deal.

I promised in that cave that those children would one day belong to Sardaron. Now all I wanted was to leave.

.1.

Kai

The stone of the small outdoor storage entrance smelled strongly of mildew and other foul substances. I wrinkled my nose in disgust. Next to me, Amber eyed the dank space doubtfully.

'Do you really want to go in?' she asked me. 'It's probably dangerous.'

I slid my gaze across to her, smirking. 'Don't tell me you're scared of a tiny little storage area that no one uses any more. Please. It probably only goes down to about five feet.'

Amber peered downwards, leaning over to examine the dimly lit gap. 'It looks like a family's old bomb shelter from years ago during a war or something.'

'Then it's probably as safe as you can get,' I said, shrugging. Amber rolled her eyes slightly but peered down again.

'I dare you. Climb down and look around,' I challenged her, intrigued myself. Amber sighed and stood back up, looking around.

We were standing in a tiny cornfield, the azure skies beating down on us. Our family cottage, inhabited solely by us and our mother, was several miles back, nestled on a small hill in the southern countryside. My twin looked back in the distance, as if she wished that we had never ventured out on this foray.

We had decided to spend the day wandering the areas surrounding our home; after all, it had been a stifling summer day when we set out, and we were unoccupied. The sole warning we had been given by our mother was to not stray further than the church a few hundred metres ahead of where we were now standing.

'I'd rather not,' Amber said, eyeing me distrustfully. 'I know you're going to do something to scare me while I'm down there. You've played your tricks too many times.'

'Who, me?' I asked innocently, half laughing. 'I would never.' Amber half smiled, but still didn't look convinced. 'Come on, lighten up!' I said to her, nudging her arm. 'Look, I'll do it if you do.'

'No, Kai. If something happened to us like it did Dad, Mum would never recover.' She looked around nervously before meeting my eyes. I stared at her.

Our father had died two years ago in a training accident at an army base on the northern side of the country. He had been severely injured and had been sent straight to hospital. He hadn't made it through the night, his death drawing ever closer as the hours passed.

I should know. I sat next to him for every minute of it, determined not to cry so that my last few images of him wouldn't be blurry and tear-stained.

He had held my hand, smiling upwards at my face throughout

every moment of agony that he was going through, his weathered face wincing every so often. I hadn't dared go to the bathroom or eat for fear that he would pass while I was gone.

So I had sat there, scanning his eyes, determined to look only at his face and shoulders, and not the bloody mess of a stomach he had left.

'You and Amber are my favourite things in this universe,' he had whispered to me fiercely. 'My strong, brave little girls.' I had sniffed then, gripping his hand so tight it had turned my fingers purple.

'Don't leave me,' I had whispered. 'Please.'

But he had. He had left me forever.

He had been my closest friend. Since his passing, I retreated more and more into myself, refusing to share my burden of grief with anyone. Amber had been there for me at that time, and it was why we were so close now. But I had been hurt for life – scarred.

'Why would you bring that up?' I asked irritably. 'It's not going to happen, and all you're doing is digging up old resentment and sorrow. Just do it.' I glared at her, angry. I didn't want to let my father's death stop me from doing the things I would have normally done. I didn't want it to change me.

'Fine!' Amber said, raising her hands, surrendering, and shrugging her shoulders. 'If you want it to make it a big deal… I didn't realise you were so touchy about it.'

I rolled my eyes, whispering under my breath. 'It's my own father's death – what did you expect?'

Amber turned from me, body frustrated. I knew that I had

been slightly irrational, but I didn't care. I was allowed to be – for a while more, at least.

Without turning to look back at me, Amber crouched down, trainers slipping against the loose soil as she cautiously made her way downwards. I watched from behind her, staring again into the grey darkness, taking a deep breath.

Focus on the future, I told myself. Focus on the right now.

Amber disappeared from view into the darkness, yelping slightly, and without hesitation I slid down after her, feeling the dampness of the soil as I entered the underground space.

A tarpaulin lining the floor of the cavernous space crumpled at the corner as I fell onto it slightly. In front of me, Amber was standing, arms crossed against the cold, looking around. Her face was an apprehensive combination of fear and curiosity as she reached forwards, towards where a stack of old crates lay. They seemed ripped open, as if someone had hurriedly opened them in desperate search of something. Leaning against the end wall of the space, it looked rickety and unstable, like it might crash if we so much as touched it.

'Should we look inside them?' I asked her.

'No. We've done enough. Let's go back up – there's nothing interesting in them, from what I can see anyway. Just old torches and batteries and stuff,' she said.

I ignored her and walked over to the crates myself, being careful not to trip over anything lying on the ground.

The crates were made of a pale wood – beech or ash, I guessed. They were covered in dust, the layer so thick that I could hardly see beneath them into the contents.

Amber was right, most of them contained old torches and discarded camping gear, but littered among the rusted items were old canned food products. I lifted the crates down from the pile one by one, nearly gagging as I found row after row of expired beans, fruit and vegetables, all in cans.

There were about five crates in the pile, and I had lifted three down when I saw the door.

Amber came up behind me and, as I turned to look at her, her hand covered over her mouth in shock.

'Quick – help me move the last two!' I said excitedly, rushing to push the last of the crates out of the way. She quickly went round to my other side to help, excited despite her initial hesitant fear of the darkness and isolation of the cavern.

Panting, I stood in front of the door, previously hidden by the wooden boxes. It was dark, wrought with a black iron that I was just able to make out in the gloom. I gingerly picked up one of the torches from a box, pressing the button.

To my surprise, a ray of light sputtered to life from the bulb. I pointed it at the door, stepping forward. I grasped the handle, shocked at the sudden cold that bloomed under my palm. Wincing, I pulled down.

'Kai! What are you doing?' Amber gasped, rushing to stop me. 'We don't know what's behind there. Yes, the door's interesting, but we should probably be heading back now anyway. What if this whole thing collapses?'

I looked at her for a long moment, letting the anger and defiance on my face shine through as I pulled as hard as I could, struggling to open the door.

It swung ajar after a moment of resistance, a scent of must leaking out of the tunnel I beheld behind it. The smell oozed its way into my nostrils, and I wrinkled my face in disgust. I glanced again at Amber.

'I'm going in, whether you want me to or not. Either come with me or leave. Your choice.' I said nothing more before stepping over the threshold, pointing the torch in front of me as if to wield it against an attacker.

Stones crunched against my feet as I walked, and I looked down to see thousands of tiny pebbles and shells, cracking as I stepped over them. I frowned. We were miles away from the coast. What were shells doing here?

A frustrated sigh followed close behind, and I heard the sound of another person's footsteps walking behind me. Amber had decided to come, then.

I stared ahead of me, fascinated, as I walked, spotting the end of the tunnel around a hundred metres in front of me.

Something brown, gold and green flashed under the gaze of my torch, and I walked faster towards it. Amber's footsteps sped up too, and I guessed that she didn't want to be left in the dark by herself.

After a minute of walking, I could see the wall clearly. I gasped as I beheld it, halting my stride as I paused to depict the huge tapestry hung from the top of the tunnel, resting against the partition.

The tapestry was covered with images that glowed under the light of my torch. I squinted as I looked closer, stepping forward slightly.

A huge king-like figure, adorned with emerald jewellery and a crown, stood on the left side of the drawing, painted in gold. His benevolent face shone with kindness as he looked across the painting. Around his feet sprung wildflowers, and tiny bodies danced in front of him, laughing faces on every figure. I shivered as I looked closer, the hairs on my arms rising as noticed the eyes of these people who seemed so merry.

Their eyes were painted in pure gold, the colour glistening with life. I stared for a long moment before glancing up again at the king, who was so huge in comparison to the people that he looked almost divine. A god, I realised. The emerald adorned figure was a god. Despite his kindly facial expression, in his hands he held a silver sword, glinting as it pointed towards something, his body braced for attack.

My torch swung to the right-hand side of the tapestry, and I heard a gasp echo from behind me. Amber was standing a few feet behind me, I saw, as I swung around to glance at her. Her eyes were fixed on the image painted roughly on the other side of the illustration, a figure of another creature crudely carved. Around it, the edge of the tapestry was blackened, huge words written across it.

SARDARON, it read. My eyes widened as I saw the creature below the words.

Wrapped in a cloud of darkness and obsidian diamond, a monstrous form stood, black dagger pointed towards that god who shone with gold. I backed away as I saw the face of the monster, and bumped into a motionless Amber.

The huge face was scarred all over, eyes seeming to watch

you wherever you moved. My breathing rate sped as I watched it, a fear so intense gripping my heart that I felt paralysed.

It seemed to urge me closer, my head pounding as I broke my stare to look at Amber. She, too, was staring at the figure, eyes pinned to its face.

Suddenly, she took a step forward, and I watched apprehensively as she walked ever closer to the figure. I followed her, once more intrigued by the whole picture.

The two gods fought, blades touching, while the tiny people danced around the golden god's feet.

I stepped in front of Amber, turning to face her. 'What does "Sardaron" mean?'

'I have no idea,' she said, eyes turned towards mine. 'Maybe that's its name.'

'Maybe,' I said, turning around again, so that I was once more facing the tapestry. Reaching out a hand, I brushed my fingers against the golden people, the tapestry seeming to glow where my hand traced.

I lowered my arm, marvelling at the beauty of the illustration, chills racking my body.

The painting seemed to shift as I watched, and my smile faded as I gasped in shock.

The darkness of Sardaron was moving.

Amber screamed as it started to crawl across the painting, glancing at me.

'What have you done, Kai?' she shouted, terrified. I didn't reply, simply staring at the tapestry in fear.

The obsidian travelled further, trailing across the image

until it had reached the tip of Sardaron's sword. Then it seemed to jump, sliding across the gold like ink in water. It travelled upwards, towards the golden god. I gasped as it spilled across into the god's body, polluting the vibrancy of it.

I could only watch as it formed the shape of a heart in the centre of the god's chest, darkness glowing as it settled.

I backed away, grabbing Amber's hand as I did so. My wide eyes met hers, and I whispered, 'We should go. Now.'

She nodded vehemently and we both turned away, glancing once more over our shoulders at the painting.

I tried to take a step forward, but I couldn't.

I cried out in fear, starting to cry, as I watched Amber struggle next to me. Her eyes, too, dripped over with tears of terror, as we both desperately tried to move our bodies forward, sobs echoing through the tunnel. My feet were pulled downward, as if gravity's strength had increased.

In front of us, a rip seemed to form out of thin air. It was dim, and I couldn't see it in that much detail, but I could sense a rippling darkness beyond it.

I tugged Amber's hand, pointing, my throat too dry to say anything.

We could both only watch as it started to grow, expanding with a crackling noise as it blocked the way out. I wept, clinging onto Amber as tight as I could.

What had I done?

The darkness beyond the oval rip seemed to flash with a bright white light momentarily, and I felt gravity release its grip slightly. Suddenly, another force seemed to take over, pulling me closer towards the rip.

Amber slid with me, both of us blinded by fear, desperately thrashing to get away from the hole.

My feet neared the edge of the gap, feeling nothing but air beyond where the dirt of the tunnel ground ended.

I felt a gasp from Amber as her feet started to slip over the edge, pushing against the force as hard as she could.

I could only clench her hand into mine as we both slipped entirely, falling over the edge of the tunnel into darkness.

.2.

The crash of waves jolted me awake.

I sat up, panting, eyes wide and staring, instinctively scrambling away from the sound.

Next to me, Amber groaned, shifting slightly as I leant over her. She turned her head, and I saw a small gash of red running across her forehead, the crimson liquid oozing gently out of it.

'Amber! Wake up!' I shouted, shaking her vehemently. She lifted her head towards mine, eyes blurry with sleep. I could see her mind start to whir as it dawned on her that we were no longer in the tunnel.

'Kai?'

'Get up, Amber, now!' I said again, panicking. 'We're not in the tunnel.'

She scrambled up, me close on her heels, as we both looked around in shock.

The cove we were sitting in sheltered us from the gentle wind blowing in our direction. The ground, littered with the same pebbles and shells that I had seen in the tunnel with the tapestry, sloped gently downward.

The mouth of the cave opened onto a sandy shore, grey sea lapping against the earth a few hundred feet away.

'Where are we?' I whispered, twisting to look in every direction. Amber lifted her hand to her forehead in shock, before wincing and pulling away.

'You've got a cut on your forehead,' I said, pulling her towards me, worried.

'Do you think it's infected?' she asked, eyes round.

'No. At least, not for the moment,' I said, examining the cut to check for yellow pus.

Our eyes met, and she recoiled away from my touch.

'What? What is it?' I asked her.

'It's your… just look for yourself,' she replied, pointing towards a few small rock pools that dotted around the sandy shore.

I walked over in trepidation, eyeing the sky as if something might fall out of it and attack me.

I stumbled on the rough rocks, using my hands to pull myself up to the largest one.

My reflection stared back at me from the water.

I looked closer, towards my eyes, until my nose was almost touching the water.

They had always been blue, but now they were sapphire. The colour faded to midnight at the core and seemed to spill into the iris, so that it looked as though I didn't have one. White flecks were dotted around the edge, like white powder in a snow globe.

I looked away, glancing back at Amber.

'Can I see yours?'

She nodded and walked up to me, climbing so that she too

was standing by the tiny pool of water.

I looked into hers, noting how they were a deep russet, hazel adorning the edges. The only way that I could describe them was, well…fiery.

Amber turned from me after a moment, bending over to look in the pool, an expression of deep confusion etched on her face.

I understood how she felt. We were apparently on a beach, having been transported here in some way.

The hole – or portal, as I should probably call it – had somehow transported us to this place.

My ears picked up on Amber's ragged breathing. I turned my head to where she was standing, as if frozen, staring furiously at the cool water of the pool. I looked at her in confusion, watching her eyes flicker with fear. She was no longer staring at herself, but at the body of water in front of her.

What was she so angry about? She was breathing heavily now, her nostrils flaring delicately as she watched the rise and fall of the rippling waves.

'Amber?' I asked curiously.

'Get away!' she whispered fiercely, chest rising and falling in a pattern that grew faster and faster. Suddenly, she screamed, a chilling sound of terror and pain.

'Amber! AMBER! What's going on? Are you all right?' I shouted, grabbing hold of her shoulders and yanking her away from the water to face me. Suddenly, her breathing stopped.

She was so still, I thought she might be catatonic. Scared, I shook her again.

'Amber, are you all right?' I asked again, a small sob slipping out before I could stop myself. Fear and fury mixed together in my stomach, turning it into a roiling mess.

'What was that about? Amber, talk to me!' I demanded. Amber remained silent, and I felt fear truly settle itself in my heart, throwing me into a blind panic.

'Amber, please, what happened?' I cried, wiping my eyes.

I was so scared.

I began pulling her away from the pool, hoping desperately that whatever had happened would snap if we were moving away. Amber walked with me as if it was a reflex, her face still blank. In her eyes, I could see the shock and fear of what had just happened but her body didn't seem to be registering anything but her wild emotions.

'Amber, I don't know what's happened to you, but we need to leave. We need to get out of this freaky place, find a town nearby. We can't be that far away from home… maybe if we find someone they can help us.' Amber said nothing, and I glanced at her worriedly. 'But Amber… that hole took us here. And unless we find it again, we might not be able to get back.'

…

I spent the next hour walking in silence, picking a random direction to follow in the hope that it would lead us to somewhere we could find help. As we travelled, Amber's silence seemed to devour the sound of our footsteps. We were passing through a glade a while away from the beach when Amber finally spoke.

'Help me.'

I turned, looking her in the face before promptly throwing my arms around her and looking her in the eyes.

'Amber! What happened? Are you all right?' I pulled back to see what she was talking about, what she needed help with.

Amber's face gave away nothing, but her hands shook as she said,

'I was… afraid. Of the water, of the cold. It was irrational, but I felt as though it was pulling me into its grasp with every second I looked at it. But I couldn't stop. I couldn't stop looking, even as this… anger threatened to consume me. I had the urge to smash the rock to bits, if only to release the water.'

I stared, lost for words, wondering if she was extremely ill – or worse, hallucinating.

'But… it's just water,' I said, confused and more than a little fearful. I chewed on my lip as Amber stared at the ground once more. I studied her, how her face was now pale and grim. The events of the past few hours had shocked and confused both of us, but this unexpected reaction was pushing her to her limit. I could see the whites of her eyes around her pupils, and the lingering fear flickering there. Putting my arm around her, I led her again across the land, being careful not to step on anything that might set off her reaction again.

'We'll work this out – whatever it is,' I promised, my eyes caught by the movement of a sparrow darting above us. It circled once, twice and then flew off to the south. Amber's uneasy look echoed my own as we reached the safety of a copse of trees surrounding the shore. 'You were probably just in shock from seeing your reflection, not at the water itself,' I said, more to myself than her, thinking of seeing a doctor as soon as we got home. If what she said was true… I walked on, determined not to think about it.

'Kai – I'm not sure that this problem *can* be solved,' she whispered, eyes frantically darting all around us. 'I know that it wasn't my reflection. I *know* it! And I don't know… I don't know whether it will happen again. I'm… I'm scared, Kai.'

'So am I, Amber. Whoever did this, or *what*ever did this… it isn't funny. We have to find the nearest sign of civilisation,' I said, grasping her hand more tightly. Would we ever find anything though, considering where we were? I pushed my doubts away. We had to be somewhere around home.

The trees whispered gently, sunlight filtering undisturbed to reach the springy moss that squished like a sponge beneath my feet.

Ahead, I spotted a tiny rabbit darting in between the bushes, attempting desperately to free itself from a snare that had been placed there. As we approached, it squealed with fear, and I placatingly put my hands out to calm it.

I stepped forwards to help remove it from the snare, eyes looking back towards where we had come from.

I felt the snap of a trigger as I stepped into the area, ropes snapping as I was lifted off the ground. I thrashed and screamed, Amber's cry of shock consumed by the trees. Opening my eyes, I found myself dangling from a tree by a huge net with tentacle-like ropes. I shifted desperately, but I couldn't move a single limb. I panicked, my breathing flipping as I tried to stand up in the net, or at least sit, and found that I couldn't. I started crying in fear, screaming desperately at Amber to help me. She didn't answer, and I called her name again.

'Amber!' I glanced down at the forest floor.

It was not just Amber in the leafy clearing with me.

A low laugh reverberated against the air as a man stood, grinning wolfishly, on the ground. His crude, dark hair was ruffled slightly in the breeze as the wind picked up, his rough clothing barely moving. His shifting brown eyes, a rich chocolate in colour, assessed us with a hard stare. I stared just behind his shoulders, where a quiver full of arrows sat. The feathers flashed strangely in the light of the sun, looking almost like flames as the man adjusted his stance.

He didn't look like a normal human. There was something… off about him, something that screamed danger.

Scanning the man again, I noticed that he was dressed for winter, not the mild summer weather we were in the midst of. His brown fur-lined tunic was topped with an overcoat that fell to mid-thigh. The ends of his leather pants were tucked into his dark boots, polished to a fine gleam. He noted my stare and stared back, eyes furiously burning into mine. I looked away quickly, so scared that my heartbeat seemed to be a singular thrum of sound.

He whistled, and a ring of similarly armed men stepped smoothly out from behind withered trees.

As one, they pointed their arrows directly at Amber.

They formed a circle around me and my sister, who was now standing directly below me, terrified. I knew that one wrong *look* from me would send one of their arrows straight into my sister's rapidly beating heart.

The men behind Amber stepped forward menacingly as she began backing away towards them in her haste to get away from the overdressed young man. He shifted his stance again, as if he had all the time in the world to be standing there. When he looked up, his brown eyes had turned fiery with violence. Their colours, similar to Amber's, seemed to glow brighter as he stared at her.

'All we want is for *you* –' he said, pointing at Amber, 'to come with us. I promise that you will be safe and well-looked after.' He carved a smile at me as I snarled through my terror, enraged, not believing that these men could do such a thing. The most important question was…Why?

The man took a step closer to Amber.

And another.

And another.

Fear washed over me as I realised that these men *were* deadly serious, that they would take Amber. Were they the ones who had transported us here?

I began shouting, thrashing in my net as the man stepped forwards and held out his hands towards Amber. With a gasp, I realised that amid my chaotic thoughts, I had failed to notice that Amber had fainted, probably with shock, and was slumped against a tree stump.

The man hauled her up by her arms, slinging her over his shoulder as if she was no more than a sack of rice. He grinned at me, knowing that I was powerless to save Amber from him and his comrades' grip. He saluted me cheerfully, but I could still see the glint of viciousness sharpening his look. He whistled again, and he and his men paused for a moment. I watched in confusion and fear as they seemed to glow for a moment, before slowly rising above the floor, as if pulled by strings. They rose higher, shooting into the sky, vanishing from sight within seconds, leaving me on my own in a seemingly deserted forest.

.3.

Laboriously, I spent the afternoon slowly climbing out of the net, watching as the sun started gilding the trees. My nails were bloody stumps by the end of it, but I managed to haul my body up the thick rope connecting the net and the tall oak tree. It took fifteen minutes to shimmy down the tree after my exhaustion of climbing out of my trap. By the end of it, I lay on the grass, staring at nothing, chest heaving, and felt my heart slowly cracking open, tears flowing out instead of blood, cascading down my face. I had to find her. I would follow them, go in the direction they had left by, and not stop until there was no hope that I could reach her. The men had somehow flown away, but that simply wasn't possible. No man on Earth had ever managed true flight.

Unless this wasn't where I thought it was – that it was somewhere where such things were possible. That it wasn't Earth, and when that hole had sucked us in, we had been taken to a different dimension.

I pushed the ridiculous thought away, knowing that sorrow and confusion were warping my common sense.

I became aware of my surroundings when the golden light faded into darkness. It was not night time yet, as the sky was only a deep ocean blue, but it sent shivers down my spine to think of what creatures might be lurking out in the forest. I couldn't bring myself to move, the shock of losing Amber still haunting me. It was only when I heard a low growl and snapping of branches near me that I hauled myself up, and managed to climb up a few branches into the canopy of a tree. With every movement, the bark ripped against my skin, and the leaves desperately flung themselves at me, flinging pollen into my eyes as they brushed against my face. My body heaved with racking sobs as the realisation hit me that I truly was alone, with absolutely no concept of where I was or what I was doing here. Amber's capture had left a hole in my heart, that had been healing over from the moment my deceased father had ripped it open, when his white-clad doctor had told us that he wasn't going to make it through the night.

Tears blurred my vision as my shaking muscles clung on tight to the thick tree branch, silent tears echoing through my body. I retched and leaned over the side of the bough to empty the contents of my stomach onto the leaf-littered ground.

I continued quietly crying for the night's duration, only ceasing when an uneasy sleep pulled me from this strange land.

...

I awoke at dawn, my tear-crusted eyes blinking blurrily at the bright morning sun. Emerald leaves lazily waved, blocking out the worst of the sun's rays. The setting was so peaceful that I almost believed that yesterday hadn't happened.

I frowned as I thought about the brown-eyed man who had stolen Amber from me. How had they managed to surround us like that? Most importantly, why did they want Amber? Why her and not me?

My mind feared the worst, and uneasy dread filled my thoughts.

Thinking of the rabbit we had been chasing, my stomach rumbled. I hadn't eaten for too many hours, and I felt as if I was going to faint at any moment. I thought of the meagre breakfast I had had at home yesterday morning, a place and time that felt a million miles away.

I slid off the branch slowly, cursing my stiff limbs. On the forest floor, I stretched and shook out my legs wearily. Today I would start to follow the men south, and maybe forage or catch some food while doing so. Resolved, I started walking.

...

After two hours of trudging along in a direction that I wasn't even sure was where the men had flown, I found some berries. They were purple and ripe, but didn't look like anything I had seen before. I decided to take a chance and just take a bite out of one, to see what they were like. I picked a handful of them, and sat underneath a tree to try them. The succulent juice trickled down my chin, and I almost rolled my eyes with pleasure, deciding that they must be safe to eat. Gathering as many as I could, I put them into my pockets before plodding on. The trees were dappled and bright, the grass becoming progressively sparser as I travelled. I noticed around midday that the trees weren't the ones that I had seen when I was with Amber. These were colossal pine trees, filling the air with the comforting smell of their leaves. There was also the occasional birch tree mixed in, but those became harder to see as the day progressed.

I grew weary of walking after the first day. When you are surrounded by nothing but peridot-coloured leaves, the occasional squirrel, and trees, boredom takes over. I also felt peculiarly faint and had to rest my hand on the thick trunk of a towering birch tree to steady myself more than a few times. Mid-afternoon on the second day, I began to feel dizzy, and wondered if somehow the fruit had had a negative effect on me. I gasped and sat down as nausea roiled in my stomach. I sank onto the forest floor, keeling over, and succumbed to darkness for a few desperate seconds, panic the only feeling in my stomach.

With a fog in my mind, I rose from my position on the mossy floor, glad that my short fainting episode had lasted only for seconds, instead of minutes, or worse, hours. Groaning, I started walking, stretching out my arms as I did so. The nausea and dizziness faded away slightly, but were quickly replaced by a pounding headache that followed me for the next hour.

The shine of the leaves in the trees faded to a singular, dull pine colour as the terrain grew colder. I foraged further, eating only the purple fruit, which no longer gave me stomach illness, and a mysterious yellow fruit which looked like a strawberry, only it grew on a tiny tree that I had found one day. It was bitter but refreshing, and I collected as much as I could before carrying on. Hunger seemed to be the permanent feature in my stomach, but I couldn't risk eating more than a few berries at a time, because I might need them if there was no other food around. I was rapidly weakening, and I knew it. Every day I found it harder to start moving.

Only once, I saw a magnificent stag leap across my vision, and I stared at it, hunger tightening my throat. I knew that it would be pointless even to try and chase after it, but for the next few hours my mouth watered uncontrollably, and my thoughts kept returning to the direction it had been travelling.

On my third day of wandering through the tundra, I saw a small pond that seemed clear of life. Up until now, I had licked leaves for their moisture, and ate a berry if I felt faint from dehydration. I knew that I couldn't go on much longer without more water, and my relief to finally find a pond was overwhelming. I peered into the water suspiciously before drinking. My gaunt face stared back at me, eyes hollowed and cheekbones too sharp. In only a few days, the lack of food had reduced me to a version of myself so pitiful I was having trouble walking sometimes.

I drank the water gratefully, splashing it all over myself in the process. Looking around, I searched for something to carry it in. Nothing. I stood unsteadily, glad to have the slosh of water in my stomach. I began to trudge on again, feeling only a little rejuvenated.

I was no longer surrounded by moss and grass but by brown, dead plants. Once I saw a sprinkling of snow atop a log, and wondered why Amber had been brought in this direction if the arrogant man with ruby-feathered arrows found mild summer weather so cold. Maybe he had been preparing for this if he was dressed so warmly. The towering plants faded to slightly smaller pine trees that were good protection from the rain should it choose to pour down. I wandered on in a daze, never stopping in one place for more than a night. My sleep was fitful and jerky in the treetops, and I tossed around so much that, every night, trying to hold on to the branch I was sleeping on was almost impossible. I rarely got more than an hour's sleep, exhaustion hounding me wherever I went. Not to mention the beasts that I was sure I heard prowling around me every dusk.

I was getting worried for two reasons, I decided, as I woke up on my fourth day in the wilderness alone. Firstly, my fainting was getting more frequent, and I was unconscious for longer periods of time. I was also worried that I was just walking aimlessly, Amber possibly having been taken in a totally different direction. What if the men had doubled back in their flight, just to confuse me?

The days bled into each other, but it wasn't until a week had passed that I felt that someone was following me.

Now, pausing to scan the woods beneath a withered pine tree, I started to feel real fear. I could tell that the beginnings of a fainting episode were just about to start, so I sat down to resume my watching of the silent trees. My legs were so weak I had only been able to move in a slow shuffle, but I felt adrenaline pump into them as I sensed something approaching me.

Shadows seemed to gather beneath bushes, under trees, and

behind rocks. The ground was now lightly covered in snow, but I didn't feel all that cold, perhaps due to the fainting and mild fever I had developed. I stared fearfully at the sky, which was now beginning to roil with thunder. A splitting crack whipped around me, and the air in front of me seemed to waver, changing colour as something… something formed out of the wind and rain and thunder. A hole, dark and gleaming.

Five men appeared through it, shoulders broad and muscled, faces impassively cold. Shocked, I jerked backwards, fingers shaking uncontrollably with the freezing temperature. It was the same kind of hole that I myself had travelled from when I had fallen down the hole.

However, only four of them looked like men. The other was clearly the leader, his merciless cyan eyes resting on me long enough for me to see the thrashing power within each. His copper skin glowed under the weak, buttery sun, which was slowly sinking, drowning under the weight of the approaching night. His raven-black hair matched the necklace hung round his neck, which was a glowing onyx. Although a boy in appearance, only a fool would ever have called him anything less than a warrior. I scrambled up, staring at them all.

The boy stared at me with no emotion on his face, before his mouth opened to speak.

'Don't move a muscle.'

.4.

The boy's striking eyes seemed to shred me to pieces as I stared at him and his followers, absolute fear coursing through my already chilled blood, freezing it over. Although I was rooted in place, my mind began to work furiously, adrenaline sending my heart into a frenzied overdrive. My eyes shifted east and west, to either side of the direction he had come from, and the boy tracked my movements, two of the men shifting so that they blocked the way. Only sprawling forest greeted me, but to the right I thought I could just make out a mossy cave in the far distance, an easy place to hide. Except, of course, that these people might very well have excellent sight in the dark. Scanning the men once again, I realised how difficult it would be to escape their grip if I went in either direction. Which left me with only one other option.

Glancing at the setting sun, I sagged, body leaning forwards, compliant and weak. As if sensing that I had given up, the warrior stepped forwards eagerly.

I turned, my hair brushing the boy's face as I whipped it around, facing southward. In the same moment, I started moving.

My muscles burst into a sprint, dodging round the tree I

had been sitting under, towards the only direction unguarded. Shards of ice seemed to pierce the inside of my throat as my breathing turned ragged – days of malnutrition had reduced my strength to almost nothing. The men quickly overcame their surprise and charged after me like a lion pack after a nimble dik-dik deer.

There was no chance of me escaping unscathed, not with five men against one girl who was severely malnourished. At least I had given myself a head start. I might be able to climb a tree onto a branch that they could not reach me on, and use their size as an advantage to me, instead of a curse.

This maelstrom of thoughts barricaded into me as, blond braid thrashing against the grip of a cold, humourless wind, I saw my chance. A tall pine tree with low boughs came into sight as the men chasing behind me closed in, their legs pounding against the ground. At the edge of my vision, I could see the swinging arms of the boy-warrior as he came closer, herding me as if I was indeed nothing more than prey. Muscle corded his arms and legs, and I knew that there was absolutely no chance of walking away without injury if it came down to hand-to-hand combat. The tree neared, and I knew I would have to slow down to some degree, or risk either splattering myself against the trunk or jumping up onto a branch and not being able to get a grip before falling off again. There was only one chance to get this right.

Approaching a tree while dodging several others, trying not to fall into enemy hands, and running at high speeds all at the same time was not the best combination of things I could do. I slammed into the tree, reeling back as blood spurted from my nose. Without giving myself time to think about it, I jumped. I heaved myself onto the first branch, close enough to the strange warrior that he could have touched my toes with his hand if he had reached out. Instead he gripped the branch below tightly, and hauled himself upwards. I rocketed through the tree, the easy-to-reach branches scratching my face, arms, legs as I pulled myself towards the higher, thinner branches. The other men sounded like they were waiting at the bottom – I realised, with a jolt, that the boy had to be the lightest one and would almost be able to reach any branch that I could.

I darted towards a thin, light branch I could see, which I could reach if I was a step higher. I jumped, almost slipping, and grasped the branch bodily. It was nearly too light to hold me, and it creaked when I went any further than a foot out from the main trunk. The boy had reached a thicker, parallel branch near to mine, not so close as to be able to touch me, but still close enough that he might be able to leap across to my branch.

With a grunt, he swung across, landing roughly on my bough.

Splinters went flying as the branch seemed to cave in on itself, an indent forming. For an agonising moment, everything seemed to slow down. I stared at the cruel young face of the boy as I slowly tipped backwards, arms flailing, into thin air.

...

People say that your life flashes before your eyes just before your death, but that's a lie. All I could think about was the frosty cold, the hollow moan of the wind, and the burning anger that surged up towards the warrior as I fell, wishing I had more time for the living, and furious that this was all the time that I had left.

. . .

I didn't touch the ground.

A swoop of wind, and I was in the warrior's arms, flying steadily over the trees. I thrashed, trying to free myself from his grip, but he gave me a look that said that if I even tried, he'd drop me. We arced up, hitting the wind, and I fell, limp, against his arms, shock the only emotion coursing through me as I went through the events of only a minute ago. Rallying my energy, I glanced at his feet to find what I'd been suspecting to be the transportation of his flight. The boy was moving in the same strange way as the man who had taken Amber, seeming to push himself against gravity, bending it to release him from the ground. Looking behind his shoulder, I saw that he, too, had a quiver of deadly arrows, all tipped with gleaming blue feathers that seemed to glow frostily in the weak light.

We shot away to the north, the unsettling effect of this boy's flight making me almost regurgitate the meagre berries I had eaten today. The boy was staring off to where we were headed, and my beating heart froze in fear of wherever we were going. Observing his cold face in a quick moment, I noticed that, somehow, it seemed like a mask – as if, underneath it all, I could see a glimmer of joy, of enjoyment of riding the crisp winds. A small part of me shrank away from this heartless killer as I watched his eyes swirl dangerously. Even the way he flew was predatory.

'Who are you?' I asked him. 'Why have you taken me?'

He sighed, and I looked at him again, only to quickly glance away.

'I'm Faolan,' he said. 'One of the Falcords.'

'Why did you take me? Please, put me down!' He ignored me. 'How dare you take me like this?' I asked, trying my best to put on a fearless front in the hope that he would be intimidated enough to put me down. It was highly unlikely that it would happen, but I had to try.

'We're counting on you,' he said to me, almost absent-mindedly. 'I assume another girl was with you, and she was taken by some other men?'

I nodded hesitantly.

'Well, those men are our greatest enemies – the Firborn. In a few weeks, we will be forced to fight each other.'

'Forced?' I asked quietly, still scared.

He nodded. 'Yes. It is not our choice to take you, or to fight. But it is something that we are commanded to do every century. Which is why I can only apologise to you for what has already happened.'

I said nothing, pure shock vibrating through my veins.

Fighting. Battle.

And I was needed.

I tried to relax in his arms after a couple hours of flight, knowing that I should at least try to rest in preparation to escape when we landed, but I was sure he could feel my racing heartbeat underneath my grimy clothes. Clothes which were now stained with freckles of blood and ripped in several places from my desperate clamber up the tree. Once again, a fruitless attempt to escape. I sighed through my nose, feeling the cold bite my face.

The snow-capped mountains in the distance seemed to stretch further away from us the nearer we flew. I had not noticed them when I was travelling in search of Amber; partially because my thoughts had been on her, and partially because the trees had blocked my vision. Now that I had time to look around, I was observing just how stunning the surrounding landscape was. Although I feared these men, it didn't put me off the thrill of wonder as I spotted a massive lake, leading into a river that wound its way around the trees, seeming to ebb and flow continuously as I stared at it.

We stopped underneath a cluster of huge fir trees, their sinewy arms lacing around each other as the men, who had dropped behind to trail us, set up camp. One had looked on the verge of introducing himself, even taking the steps to shake my hand when I approached him, only to be silenced by an icy, withering look from the leader.

The small tent I would have to myself for the night was barely big enough to fit someone half my age. The others were to sleep in tents only a foot bigger than mine – I almost felt sorry for them, but then I caught myself as I remembered how the silent ringleader had nearly made me plummet to my death, despite the human-like encounter I had had with him afterwards.

The six solitary tents, huddled in a circle, seemed so sad and defeated in the wind that I was glad to get away to one of two log benches sitting opposite each other in the middle of them.

For dinner, we had a measly snack of bread and cheese, along with the few remaining berries I had salvaged from my pocket. I even offered some to Faolan, my bravery coming to the surface. Bravery was my shield in my darkest times, protecting a heart that had become cowardly and fearful of letting anyone in. He simply shook his head as I sat back, disgruntled, on my log.

'Don't we need to make a fire?' I asked curiously after several minutes of silence as the others ate. Surely we needed heat on a cold winter's night like this one, I thought, as the weak sun bathed the edges of the trees around us in a pearly glow before fading completely. The boy just looked at me, distaste coating his expression, and shook his head.

I trudged back to my tent, tired and more than a little upset. Collapsing on my bedroll, I was startled to find that it was extremely comfortable. I curled up in a ball, disoriented and confused by my situation, and fell asleep crying softly, knowing that my chances of escaping from these peoples' grip were narrowing like a closing window.

...

The next morning, I opened my eyes slowly, scared of what I

might see or what might happen when I awoke. To my relief, it was only the white of the tent canvas that greeted me.

Getting up, I realised that I desperately needed to wash my filthy clothes in the lake we had stopped by – and maybe try to leave by swimming along the cold river I had spotted yesterday. It depended on my ability to get past the wicked, fast current that swept even the strongest of water creatures downstream. Fortunately, Faolan stepped out of my way with a nod of his head when I asked him whether he would allow me to bathe in the water. I wondered what he would do if I tried to run, or rather swim, away. How would he even know if I had gone? Coming to think about it, I realised that he probably had someone *watching* me while I bathed. I shuddered. I would bathe in my clothes.

I slipped down to the bank of the river, eager to wash the journey from me. The grass was slick with mud, my feet slippery with it as I toddled my way to the edge of the water. For support, I grabbed hold of a bush on my way there, but the sting of it as soon as it touched my hands was enough to make me let go immediately. Wincing, I pulled away and reached the edge of the water.

I dipped my feet in, the freezing current refreshing. I waded in up to my waist, enjoying the feel of the current pushing and pulling at me, occasionally slipping on a smooth rock. Fully clothed, I swam hard upstream for the edge of the lake, cursing myself for not entering the water there instead. I tugged against the unforgiving current that threatened to lash me against the rocks like a broken toy, and succeeded in gaining a few inches. Deciding just to get out and walk to the lake, I started swimming back for the edge of the river, careful to not cut myself against anything that could hurt me. I gripped a huge boulder and clung on to it as I heaved myself out of the water.

What I saw beyond it made me slither back in again.

Faolan was standing, arms crossed, obviously angry with someone half-obscured from my vision by a tree. In the blackening night, I wondered what the man could be saying to make him so furious.

I craned my neck, ears straining to hear what they were talking about. Disappointed, I only managed to catch a few words.

'...No! We only have a few days left!'

'I know – but I wanted to ask you if you were keeping track of how long we'd spent here. Our time must surely be up soon...'

'...Stop pestering me...I'd estimate a few days at most...'

The subject of Faolan's anger muttered something that I couldn't hear.

'The girl...definitely seems unruly...precious. We can't waste an opportunity like this!'

Frustrated, I realised that they were talking about me. I tried to go even closer, sticking my head out from the top of the bank, but the men were already moving away in the direction of the tents, still talking in low voices, their feet padding softly as they stepped.

Keeping my head angled down, I got back in the water and swam for the lake again, suddenly not so desperate to clean my clothes. Clambering out, I started shivering violently, but not with cold. No, it was the fear of these men, their plotting and kidnapping of me, that made my blood boil and my insides churn with relentless terror.

I walked slowly back to my tent, passing two sentries who were watching me curiously. I didn't pay them any heed.

Ripping the openings to my tent apart, I slipped inside, water dripping off my hair as I looked onto my bed. My feelings of fear once again rose to the forefront, and without thinking rationally about it, I decided that I was going to leave right now. I didn't care if they saw me, I didn't care if they chased me. I would run as fast as the wind that had slashed against my face on the way here.

I carefully gathered the bedroll and sleeping bag up, tying it around my waist before leaving the tent.

My exit was silent and unnoticeable. At least, I thought so.

I heard shouts coming from behind me and I took off running towards the trees. Footsteps and cries followed me as I howled in desperation, frantic to leave.

A rough hand grabbed my elbow before I had even run a hundred steps, and I screamed in frustration and fear. Tears started to well up, but I quickly blinked, pushing them back down. Thrashing like a wildcat, I tugged against the iron fist holding me in place.

I twisted to find Faolan holding me, an almost sympathetic look on his face, even though I could also see frustration. With as much effort as it would take to lift a sack of grain, he slung me over his shoulder and started running back to the camp. I pounded my fists against his back, trying to dig my sharp nails into his skin. He paid my efforts no heed, and before long we were back where I had started.

He put me down, but started dragging me to his tent. I thought for one terrible moment that he was going to beat me or something like that. He must have seen the look on my face, and let out a small laugh, chuckling despite his exasperation. In confusion, I stood still when he released my arm once we were inside his tent. He motioned for me to come forwards, but I started speaking instead, eyes flashing with the force of my anger and fear.

'Let me go, you savage! Why did you take me? Please, will you just give me some *answers*? I heard you talking!'

His eyes tightened as he heard about my eavesdropping.

'I told you – we need you to fight, unfortunate as it is. When we arrive at our destination, I'll be able to explain more. There's nothing more I can say,' he said, hands palm up as if to express his words.

I only looked at him for a moment longer before I retreated from his tent, walking swiftly towards my own.

I was so confused, and so alone.

.5.

I spent the whole evening lying on my back, staring up at the yellowed side of the tent.

I was burning with self-righteous anger. If Faolan thought that I would be content to settle for scraps of information, like a dog after a chewed bone, he was wrong. I was about to go back there, to that cramped tent, but I had more pressing questions resounding in my head.

Why weren't we leaving? Surely we should have been where we were meant to be by now. Unless the camp was waiting for someone to join them. Or it was permanent.

Shuddering at the thought of living in a tent with only these five men for company, I turned over and fell into a fiery sleep late into the night, my dreams laced with violence.

When I awoke, I heard someone shout to pack up, we were on the move! I grunted and quickly sat up, still half asleep, wondering at the commotion. A wave of dizziness washed over me, and I remembered the short fainting fits that were now occurring daily. I almost had to lie down again, but managed to stay in a sitting position.

Stepping out of the tent into the crisp, cold air, snow crunching against my feet, I found that my theory from last night had indeed been correct. Someone had arrived. A tall stranger with a flowing cape and an ivory hunting bow was chatting animatedly with one of the sentries, black boots shining. I frowned, thinking that he certainly didn't look very imposing, with his youthful eyes and crop of chestnut hair. His face was full of mirth, but there was also a type of emotion – anger, maybe – lingering there that I couldn't quite put my finger on.

The only reason I knew that Faolan was behind me was the low cry that came from his lips at the sight of the stranger. Without hesitation, he ran forwards, strange power almost lifting him off the ground, and hurled himself into the stranger's arms, both of them grinning ecstatically as they greeted each other like long-lost brothers. When the stranger caught sight of me, his expression saddened and he turned to ask Faolan something, to which his face darkened dramatically.

I approached carefully, still watching them.

'I'm Angus,' the stranger said as I opened my mouth.

'Please,' I said desperately. 'You have to explain what's going on.'

'There's a reason… why you were brought here,' he said carefully, stalling. He, too, was cautious of what he said. 'You'll understand when we get home. However, none of them' – with this he waved his hand at Leader and the sentries – 'are allowed to say too much to you because you were travelling, and it might have put you under too much stress and shock. But maybe… I could answer some of the questions you have until we get home?' He said 'home' as if it was mine too, which was somehow both galling and comforting, although I knew it shouldn't be.

'Please.' I tried not to sound too desperate with Faolan still watching me tensely, his cyan eyes, which I now noticed were ringed with silver around the swirling vortexes, flicking between me and the newcomer, Angus, intensely. I was still half angry at him, but now at least I understood why he hadn't told me much.

Angus led me over to my tent, and we sat down together on opposite ends of the bedroll, me eyeing him warily as he tried to shuffle closer. He laughed when he saw my expression.

'I only want to talk,' he said. 'You must have questions for me – but I can't answer any about the girl – your sister? – who came with you, unfortunately.' I sighed and rubbed my eyes. He had said that he didn't want to shock me – but what kind of news did they bear that would send me into such a state? I looked at him again. I wanted answers – frank and plain.

'Where am I?' I asked.

'You and I are both in what is known – to us at least – as Etrais, the inter-land between our two planets.'

I stared at him.

'Think of it like… a parallel dimension. I say planets, because they are realms, worlds apart. For example, this planet, so to speak, is Etrais.

'And… where is… why did you take me?' I said, fumbling for words as I tried to process what he was saying. Angus shook his head sadly, as I focused intently on the answer to the question I had just asked him.

'I'm afraid that I can't tell you any more than I'm assuming Faolan already has. You will find out when we get back home, to Nzar.

The shock of hearing those words caused a ringing in my heart and a dizziness in my head. The ground rose up to claim me as darkness filled my mind, my body overcome with yet another fainting fit.

I awoke to Angus pressing a warm cloth on my forehead, and murmuring something to the men outside, who were ready to leave, but who needed to pack up my tent.

'Kai, I want you to know that this may be confusing, but we are running out of time. The longer we stay here, the longer and more frequent your fainting will get. I forgot to mention this before you had that episode, but because we are in the planet in between Nzar and Zio, the air we breathe is half made up of air that is toxic for us but easy for the Firborn to breathe. The same goes for them. Our air is toxic for them, so neither side can stay longer than about a week and a half. With training, the length of time that you can stay here increases.' Seeing my confused expression, he added, 'The Firborn are the men who took away Amber, back to Zio, another realm. We are the Falcords, the opposing group to them, who live on Nzar.' He looked outside to where the rest of the men were waiting impatiently, Faolan among them.

'And is he the leader?' I asked, pointing to Faolan.

'Who – Faol? He is a skilled general in our army,' Angus said. 'The others won't really be spending any time with you on

Nzar, so unless you really want to know who they are, I don't think it's worth the time telling you about them.' I shook my head.

I got up, heaving myself onto my feet, Angus helping me. We stepped outside the tent, my legs still a bit shaky. To my surprise, Faolan looked to me with something resembling kindness in his gaze. Friendship. I stared back, and the look quickly vanished.

I noticed for the first time the true colour of the arrows in Faol's quiver. This morning, when Angus had first arrived, I hadn't been paying attention to the deadly weapons covering my sight of his back, something which I should have been keeping my eyes on. But as I glanced around now, I saw that everyone had a quiver of arrows, all of varying shades. I wondered what they were for as I admired the colours of each, a palette of blue feathers behind every man's back. I noticed that not every blue was the same. Faolan's were so dark they were almost black, the hints of midnight blue only shining in the light. A couple of sentries had ocean-blue wings, while others ranged from glacial blue to midnight. Angus's were a steely blue-grey that matched his eyes.

Smoothly, Faolan stepped forwards and picked me up. We rose into the air, my stomach jolting as we travelled higher and higher, heading north once more. I wished it was Angus carrying me instead, just so I could ask him more questions.

The land grew faint around us, a white-speckled universe that had no apparent end. However, this was not what I was thinking about as Faolan carried me, Angus in front and the other men behind.

Amber was on her way to Zio? I wondered what the people who had taken her, part of the Firborn, were doing with her. How did they even know which girl was on which side? I stared desperately downwards, utterly confused and lonely. How did Angus think – pleasant as he was – that I was just going to accept what he said without question?

I supposed that I would, anyhow, if only because there was no other choice.

.6.

We flew and flew, until Faolan's breath became laboured rasps and I had to be switched with Angus midair. I was quite happy with this transition, since it meant that I could continue questioning him. He seemed serious, the lines of his face drawn together in an expression quite unlike the one I had seen on his face when he had first caught sight of Faolan. It was an expression of concentration, mixed with sadness and determination. I wondered what the issue was.

I turned back to *my* issue. I still didn't know exactly why I was here and if Angus was lying, then I had absolutely no idea what was going on. Irritation, fear and desperation gnawed at me behind my mask of cool nonchalance.

The mountains rolled into a craggy cliff edge as we approached them, invisible power carrying them smoothly through the air. I was opening my mouth to ask Angus a question when we suddenly dived, a ninety-degree plummet that caused a breathless scream to shoot out of my mouth. This was all too much.

The edge of the cliff approached, the sheer drop off it making my heart curdle with terror. Narrowly missing the edge of the grey stone that made up the mountain's edge, we shot downwards, wind clawing at my hair, before we seemed to pass through a thick wall of enveloping static air, causing my hair to stand on end. We had obviously arrived at some sort of base camp, as in between the trees I could make out rows of orderly tents.

I stumbled in shock at the base now in front of me, as Angus set me down gently and strode past me to scout the camp with Faolan, making sure that no one had infiltrated it while they had been gone. They carried no weapons as far as I could see, except for long, elegant silver swords and the feathered arrows slung over their shoulders. I doubted that they would use the arrows – they seemed precious, and carefully crafted for some other purpose.

I watched Faolan and Angus approach one of the further tents together, swords held in front of them. A wind seemed to ripple from somewhere near them, a probing, curious breeze that touched me gently. It seemed to rush back to its master to tell him who I was the moment it reached my skin. I stared with interest at the general and the newcomer as they looked at each other silently, stepping into the tent in a single step. They were completely unified, a solid, impenetrable force that I doubted any man would easily walk away from on a battlefield.

The camp was set up in an orderly way, the tents in a row, forming a square. In the middle of the square I could just make out a huge table, wooden benches surrounding it. It was protected from the wind and rain by a marquee-style canvas tent. In every direction I could see huge, thick pine trees covered in snow and frost. The ground, too, was a labyrinth of ice, frost and snow, piles of it, feet high, blocking some of my vision.

Turning back, I walked towards the base of the cliff, its stony silence seeming to echo as I moved closer. I put a hand on the grey slab of granite, and hissed with pain as what seemed like a tiny lightning fork electrocuted my fingers, making me jerk back. I stared up, remembering the solid wall of air that had swallowed us when we had flown in. This must be a type of shield then, I mused, wondering how it worked and why they would need it. Were there animals roaming around here untamed? Or was an enemy force waiting to attack? From the way the men were scouring the camp, I knew that enemy forces were the biggest danger on their list. Maybe it was those Firborn they were talking about.

I trudged to a felled tree, sitting down. Fear had spiked my pulse, setting my blood running desperately through my body. Looking around carefully, I watched the others search for danger, their whole bodies poised and tensed to attack. Nothing seemed to be amiss, however, and they reassembled together by a large tree that towered over all the rest. It was apparent that they knew this camp well, from the way that they examined every nook and cranny. Angus beckoned for me to join them, and I ran over, breath puffing in clouds as I breathed out in fear.

Reaching them, I saw that Angus and Faolan were standing in front of the group, ready to talk to them.

They started chatting, but I thought that there was no point in trying to talk with them – I was going to leave tonight anyway.

I had decided this on the flight with Angus, when his silence on the topic had infuriated me. I had considered going with them, using their shelter and protection, but I knew that they would only drive me crazy – and they clearly wanted me for this battle of theirs. Besides, I had to find Amber. Frankly, if these people wouldn't explain their motives, then I wouldn't explain mine either. Uncomfortably, I shifted on my feet. Getting away from these men would be the problem. After that, I would easily be able to travel south again, towards Amber. All I had to do was keep the mountains behind me.

While Angus was talking, Faolan had been watching his men with a cold scrutiny. I could feel his gaze flicker over me, lingering as he stared at my face, assessing me. I glanced up to find him walking over to me, and stood straighter. I thought he was going to say something to me, but he breezed right past me to talk to the man who I had overheard by the river. I was fairly sure that this man was his second-in-command. I stepped away, smoothly slipping behind a tree before heading away. Some small part of me wanted to hear their conversation, but I already had something to plan for. I needed to get back to my tent.

Despite that, I desperately wished that I could know the full story of why I was here, because if I pretended to cooperate with them, they would expect me to be complacent.

The reek of my clothes dragged me back to where I was, the trees bending and leaning towards me. Even after I had washed them thoroughly in the lake, the dirt in my jumper and jeans had refused to fade, the stain of a few days' travel etched permanently on them. I would have begged at Faolan's feet if it meant that I could have a hot, steamy bath and clean clothes.

Approaching my tent, I saw that it was indeed much larger than the other that I had stayed in on our journey here. I assumed that we were staying here for longer than our journey had taken. Passing the tent flaps with barely more than a ripple, I took in where I would be staying for the next few days, as I had heard Faol say. Aside from the bed, there was a tiny table, an extraordinarily small chest, and a nightstand with a sink, somehow equipped with running water when I turned it on, even though there were no pipes connecting it to anything. A small stool sat before the chest. I turned my eyes to the actual mattress, topped with downy pillows and a thick quilt, sitting in the middle of the tent. I could have cried with thanks as I toppled down onto it, eyes slowly closing. The calls of sentries to one another kept me from completely drifting off, but I was content to lie there, eyes shut.

I was pondering on the sheer comfort of the tent – why would I need such unnecessary luxuries? – when someone pushed through the tent flaps, bending their head to get through. Angus. I tried to push down the small flutter of disappointment I felt when I caught sight of his face. I would have liked to try and get some answers out of Faol. I sat up as Angus approached to sit on the small stool that sat in the corner of the room. His steel eyes hardened slightly as he looked at my face. I was surprised; normally Angus would have been friendly and charming, like he had been since we had met this morning. I frowned, and he noticed. The look in his eyes loosened, and he rubbed his forehead tiredly.

'I'm sorry – the stress of the past few days, and the stress of what will happen in the next few, is quite overwhelming.' I stared at him curiously.

'What's happening in the next few days?' I asked, eager to see if he would give me an honest answer. I almost felt bad for him as I watched him struggle to answer me. Despite the stress he and Faolan had put me through, they hadn't been unkind to me.

'Do you remember a dark hole seeming to suck you into it – and then arriving here?' he asked me. I nodded slowly. 'Well, that was a portal. We still have to reach Nzar. There is a special portal that we have to go through to get there, but… it may be painful for you. We only have a few days left before all of us could suffocate from the lack of breathable air.'

'When will we leave?'

'In about three days – we must go then, because the opportunity will close, and won't happen for another hundred years.' My interest sparked at this.

'What could be so important about me that you're hiding all these secrets? Why is there a *war*?' the words burst out of me as I sprang up in the bed. I was surprised at myself, at my own anger. Angus, too, seemed surprised, and more than a little irritated.

He rolled his eyes, irritation burning his handsome features into something much uglier.

'Kai. Please, do not shout. Calm down! You'll find out soon enough, so stop asking, all right?' he said.

Standing up, he left the tent silently. I stared after him, even more confused than I had been before. These people obviously thought that what they were saying was true, or they were *very* good actors. I reckoned that the former was probably the most realistic theory. I lay back on my bed.

What was this portal he was talking about – and why would it be *painful*? I shuddered. There had to be a way out of this. A single mention of a portal wasn't going to answer the million other questions sizzling into my brain. This whole camp was too much for me, and I needed to get out. Now. I covered my face with my hands tiredly, noticing that some of the muscle had returned to my body after three days of being fed relatively well. I would have to face the threats of the wilderness with only my own wits, but staying with these men, if only to get food, was driving me insane.

And I had to rescue Amber.

The dusky sky darkened to the colour of Faolan's arrows as I formed my plan, spending the rest of the day perfecting it. I didn't even come outside for dinner, only peeping my face out to see if what I'd thought about the sentries was correct. It was.

I carefully examined the tent, looking inside the chest, underneath the old rug on the floor, and on the underside of the table and stool. The only thing I could find of any use was inside the chest – an old, curved knife. The rest of the items in the chest – some shirts and tunics, thick trousers made for fighting and wilderness exploring, and a pair of boots, I put on, glad to change out of the festering jumper and jeans I was wearing.

The new clothes shifted against my skin, light as silk even

with their thickness, as I bent to pick up the knife, my silver-blonde braid sliding over my shoulder. The boots were slightly too big, and my feet slid forwards ever so slightly as I walked, but they would have to do. At least the rest of the clothes were a perfect size.

In my hand, the knife was cold, burning my fingers onto the hilt. It seemed comfortable there, and I decided that I would keep it. Thinking of a name, I decided on Tholan. It seemed to suit the blade somehow, with its wicked curve and elaborate handle. I twirled it in my hand admiringly, gazing at the hilt, which I thought was made out of pure silver. I wondered what the actual blade itself was made from. I hoped it was something incredibly strong, like steel or titanium – but if it was made of steel, I would have to be careful that it didn't rust.

Footsteps outside the tent made me slide the knife quickly under the mattress. I hurried over to the nightstand, pretending to wash my face as Faolan entered the tent.

His footsteps stopped a few steps away from me. I turned, and saw him gazing at my clothes, his flickering cyan and silver eyes full of an emotion I couldn't place. Anger, perhaps. Or sadness. But not at me – when he looked at me, I thought I saw his eyes flash with something resembling hope, but the look was gone in an instant, replaced by the usual indifference. He nodded at me, saying,

'I really am sorry, Kai. I just wanted to come see why you weren't at dinner.'

What I was going to say wasn't the truth, but he didn't need to know that.

'I'm sorry I wasn't there – I just… needed a moment alone.' He nodded in understanding, saying nothing more.

'Well… goodnight.'

'Goodnight.'

He strode out of the tent a moment later.

When I was sure he was gone, I put a hand on my hammering heart, relieved that he hadn't been able to tell just how nervous I was. If this was going to work, no one could know.

.7.

Angus

I watched the girl all evening. She was hiding something, just like I was. She didn't even emerge from her tent, where she was holed up, for dinner, and I was forced to eat with Faol and his commanders. I had to put on a mask when I was around him. The boy didn't know a thing about dealing with these girls – he was only a few hundred years old, and had spent most of that time with his winged forces in the far north.

My cloak snapped behind me, the wind at my heels as I strode back to my tent, hidden in the heart of the territory. Yes, the girl was harbouring a plan. Well, she would see just how far it got her when she realised that the shields around the area would fall only under the command of the Survivors of Meridian, the name given to those who had not died in the wars against the Firborn. Every hundred years, wars raged between our two peoples, and many were slaughtered. I had Firborn blood on my hands, just as they themselves did. A ripple of wrath spread over me at the mere thought of those conniving liars, setting my heart pounding in my ears. The instinct in the Falcords meant that whenever they talked about, approached or even thought of the Firborn, they felt the urge to kill them on sight, no questions asked. The same instinct was felt strongly in the Firborn against the Falcords, so there was never peace between the two peoples.

I was so concentrated on the thought of the Firborn that I slammed into Faol on my way to my tent. He grunted and pulled back as I swore viciously, my nose having hit his jaw. I noticed that his tracks led away, towards Kai's tent. He must have just visited her, although I couldn't think why – it wasn't as though he could talk to her. I looked at him questioningly, half wondering if he was there because he was attracted to her. He noted my expression and scowled.

'Angus, the only reason I was in her tent was to check that she was still there – I'm not some besotted moth towards a flame!'

'Whatever floats your boat,' I said distractedly.

He only rolled his eyes at me before walking away, back to his tent, situated near the girl's. I merely continued on, whistling quietly to myself as snowflakes began to fall around me.

I took in the scenery, looking for the perfect natural screen. The trees were the perfect plant to hide behind – they were thick and dark, and the sheer quantity of the prickly pine leaves meant that it was impossible to see through them to whatever was happening beyond. This could prove to be both helpful and a hindrance. I would have something to hide behind, but I wouldn't be able to see what was happening unless I stuck my head round the branches, exposing myself.

But it was the only plan I had – and I needed to spy on that girl.

I needed to see what kind of person she was – whether she would resist the rules about to be imposed on her by the Falcords.

If she did… there would be consequences.

.8.

Amber

From the moment the dark-haired man had approached me, I knew that there was every likelihood that I wouldn't see Kai again – ever. The man's eyes, the same colour as the tilled fields that farmers plough, were watching me as we moved forwards. We flew, me resting in his arms after fainting just before my capture, with him checking my forehead every half an hour. His body was hot, and I wondered if he himself had a fever. No normal person could have a body temperature that high without having a serious illness.

We stopped to walk on the terrain a few hours later, when the men apparently became exhausted from flying. The man noticed me looking at him, and smiled as we walked. The vicious person from before had faded away entirely, leaving a warm, gentle young man. I knew that I was meant to be angry and fearful of him, but there was something about him that was irresistible.

I smiled cautiously back at him, and his eyes brightened.

'I'm Amber,' I said, intrigued to know this man's name.

'Helmon,' he said, evidently surprised that I would willingly talk to him – after all, he was the one who had left my sister in a net. We moved on without saying anything more.

It was only when I felt the gaze of his eyes on my face that I again looked at him. I was about to ask what the matter was when he jerked back, a roar erupting from his mouth as a dark hand gripped his throat.

...

Helmon

I was able to tell, even from across a clearing, that this girl walking next to me was fiery. She seemed to burn with some internal flame, but I hadn't been able to get a closer look before we took off. Asleep, she looked nothing but peaceful - kind, even. The blind rage I had felt upon seeing that Falcord girl was unlike anything I had ever experienced, and I wasn't able to pay much attention to the auburn-haired young woman that I now carried in my arms. I was sure the girl would hate me for what I had done to her sister. To my surprise, she engaged in conversation with me when I spoke to her, seemingly unconcerned. She had even walked without complaint or resistance when we landed.

We were walking when they approached.

If I had been paying attention to the scenery, I would have sensed the attack from behind. Pain ripped through my head, followed by a sharp agony through my right arm, and I twisted with difficulty, turning my head to see who my attacker was.

Five Falcords hovered behind us, death written all over

their bodies. My men were still scouting far behind, catching up to us. They wouldn't get here in time to save me. *Faolan*, I thought, staring at the glowing cyan eyes of the leader. Even on Zio, we had heard of the legendary warrior who prowled the northern lands of Nzar. He flew downwards as I desperately tried to take to the air, head throbbing with pain. He grabbed my shirt, hauling me towards him. I grabbed Amber, lifting her off the ground too as we all rose higher. His teeth were inches away from my throat, and I knew he was trying to stifle the urge to kill me right then.

'Where is our girl?' he hissed, jaw clenching.

I didn't say anything, struggling to breathe as we reached a height of a few hundred feet. I managed to look down to where Amber was slowly but surely slipping out of my grasp. He noticed her finally, after I tried to shout that she was *falling*, and helped me to grab her before she did so, body trembling from the urge to kill such a threat to himself and his people.

'I don't know – we found both of them together on the western edge of the Neowald river. We left the other girl in a net…' I hissed in pain as Faolan clenched my shirt and the skin below, tightly enough to leave a bruise, when he heard those words.

'You know the rules of the Prophecy! How could you?' Faolan snarled the words, eyes brimming with hate. I could see now why he had been known for his magic, sensing the thrumming power radiating from him. The silver in his eyes turned so fast and violently that it seemed that the true colour of his eyes was constantly shifting. He almost seemed inclined to dig his knife harder into my arm, but saw my pale face and reconsidered. He let go of us and ripped out the knife, sending jolts of agony through my body. He rose in the air with his commanders as they swept themselves away, cold as the Northern wind itself.

I spiralled slowly to the ground, Amber tightly in my grip, trying to prevent freefall. We hit the ground roughly, me stumbling as darkness formed at the edge of my vision. Amber helped me to sit, her russet eyes bright with concern. Shouts sounded around me, and I thanked the Creator that my men were here to help me. Neil, my second-in-command, rushed forwards, hissing in outrage at the wound he could see was seeping blood. I gasped as dizziness swirled around my head. He retrieved a bandage from a small pack on his waist, and wrapped it gently around the wound on my arm – and the one on my head, where Faolan had grabbed me forcefully enough that he might have broken a bone. I arched my back in pain at the contact, and a low snarl slipped through my teeth. Onyx eyes wide, Neil gave me a quick check for other injuries before standing, offering a hand to help me. I gripped it and stood, the wound in my now crimson head ripping and tearing with every stride I took. My arm was already healing over, the blood clotting, and I was weak with relief that the knife hadn't hit the bone. But I knew that with my condition, it would be days before I could even attempt to take to the skies. It meant that we would have to trek the rest of the way to the camp before the portal opened – a tight schedule, since it would only be open for half an hour, and we had to make the journey on foot.

I scanned my surroundings, assessing how difficult it would

be to travel without flying – since I would have to concentrate on it, having a head injury meant that I might lose focus at some point and seriously injure myself.

Short, stubbly bushes were dotted sparsely across the land, the ground cracked and withered like the face of an old crone. For water, we had some in our packs. I eyed Amber warily. I didn't know how she would react to water – maybe I could ask her? It would be dangerous for her to touch it if she was severely reactive – in past wars, the mere touch of water on an Elder's skin could cause near insanity.

She was huddled on the ground, obviously in shock at the quick turn of events that had led to her almost being dropped from hundreds of feet in the air. I hobbled to her slowly. She turned, and I found her eyes to be full of flames as she directed the source of that anger to the skies above us, watching for any sign of the Falcords.

...

Amber

I heard near-silent footsteps behind me, and twisted to find Helmon staring at me. The wave of pure white fury directed at the attacker in the sky rose again as I glanced to his injury, and then to the azure skies above us, checking that the men didn't return.

Helmon was grinning weakly, and I felt my heart thump strangely at the smile, even as I was angry at him for having the nerve to laugh in a situation like this.

Strands of my auburn hair travelled the wind to rest on my brow, and I tucked them behind my ear as Helmon said, 'It's not that bad. At least no one was permanently injured.'

'That doesn't excuse what happened.' I glared at him.

'I can see you're going to be a delight to deal with when war is upon us, if you react that much to a little encounter.'

I glared at him, but asked as my insides curled in fear, 'What war?' if I had to be involved in a war when I didn't even know where I was…

'Come – sit with me. I will explain everything.' He led me to a small boulder and we both sat on the smooth, warm surface. He told me of the planets, of why I was fainting, and the dangers of touching water.

'Did anything happen to you around water when you were alone with Kai?' he asked, after learning her name.

'Yes – we had gone to a lake to look at ourselves when I felt this… anger – but you're right, I felt the edge of insanity gripping me at the same time. I didn't want to tell her that, because she was already concerned enough.'

He nodded gravely. 'I'm afraid you must have quite a severe reaction to it then, if even looking at it caused you problems.' He looked at my worried face. 'It's all right – some Syths before you have had the same reaction, so we have the proper equipment to deal with it.'

'But *why* is it happening?' I asked. 'Kai didn't seem to have a problem with it.'

'No – she wouldn't, because she's a Falcord. We are the

Firborn, the fire-wielders. They are the opposite to us, and are the bearers of gifts including ice, snow and wind – and therefore water in general. There is a curse surrounding our two sides… which you will find out about when we reach Zio. The way you are able to tell if a Firborn will react badly to the Falcords' magic – or the other way around – is if they can feel this insanity. It means that you are more vulnerable, but also that you have special abilities. I don't have anything special about me, because I don't have these abilities – I'm fine to touch water, drink it and look at it. You do have something special, and although we don't know exactly what it is yet, most of the Elders in the past have had powers of flame. We do not know what yours will be, or how powerful it will be. The rest of us lads –' he motioned to the men talking together a few feet away '–don't have special powers. Some on Zio possess them, and it's fairly common, and they manifest themselves in the form of heat and flame.'

Gawking, I stared at him, watching his eyes to see if he was telling the truth – even though he was earnest in his explanation, and seemed to be a truthful person. He was right about the water, though. I glanced at my hands instead, thinking of the magic that I had now discovered I possessed.

'So will I become an Elder?'

'Maybe. You may not, because you may not survive through what the Elders survived through, or live for long enough to properly be considered one of them. For now, both you and Kai are known as the Children of the Prophecy – the Syths, as we call them.

'Can one of you show me your powers?'

'Unfortunately, none of us is allowed to display any of our gifts in front of you until we get to Zio. What we were told by our Elders was to not overload you with information, or shock you – sorry if all of this is too much at once. Anyway, none of us is especially powerful.'

In front of us, the sentries had finished the plan they had made while we were talking.

We stood, and I said, 'Thank you. For telling me.'

His eyes crinkled in a smile as he nodded his head and extended his arm. I took it, and we started walking southwards towards the camp that he had told me about. The men behind us fell into formation, the one called Neil walking on Helmon's right. He eyed me with surprising hostility when he saw my hand on Helmon's forearm. I looked back, surprised at his unfriendliness. He only continued walking, back a bit stiffer than it had been a moment ago. Helmon seemed oblivious, and continued to chat with me as we walked on.

'We're about to go to one of two camps, which are the only places on Etrais that you can get to either Zio or Nzar from. This is because of two portals that are situated in both of the camps, which are only activated once every hundred years,' he said, filling me in on the details of where we were going and why. 'Kai probably won't know as much as I am about to tell you until she gets to Nzar, because the Falcords tend to be much more… cautious with information.'

'Why are you not the same?' I asked.

'We were given a letter by our Elders, who you will find

out about. I can show you the instructions they gave us, but I have to follow them, I'm afraid. They gave us strict orders on what to do with you until we get to Zio.' He drew a yellowing, crumpled piece of parchment out of his pocket. Handing it over to me, I saw that neat, elegant words were written on it. I read them intently, interested and a little frightened at what these unknown Elders had written about me.

Helmon,

The safe capture of the new girl is your top priority. You and your men must be prepared to lay down your lives for her if you happen to run into danger. Remember to keep her warm – she won't have the same protection as you. When you get to Zio, we will be waiting eagerly in the Eastern Forests, by the sparring rings. We'll come get you as soon as we can, but other matters are also extremely pressing at the moment.

Good luck.

Yina

I stared at the paper. *Be prepared to lay down your lives for her.* Helmon was looking at me, and I glanced up at him, raising my eyebrow at the words. He was willing to die for me, just to get me back to Zio, where Yina, one of the Elders, was waiting. I could see that he would do it, too.

'Thank you,' I said quietly.

'There's nothing to thank me for yet.'

'I know… but thank you for being prepared to do it.' My eyes were shiny and I desperately blinked. 'No one has ever been willing to do that for me, except for Kai.' He nodded, and we continued forwards.

'Are you cold, by the way?' he asked. 'Firborns get cold easily, even in this climate.' I shook my head and handed him back his piece of parchment, which he stuffed back inside his pocket.

'That's how you treat a document written by the Elders?' I grinned weakly, trying to push past the feelings of gratitude that had now formed a bridge between us. He chuckled lightly again, the sound merry and bright.

I wasn't listening to him, just staring at his face that glowed as the sun shone on it, casting his brown eyes with a golden sheen as he talked to me. I couldn't believe that he was actually willing to lay his life down for a girl he barely knew. I frowned slightly, uncomfortable with the idea that he might do so soon, if we came into danger. It wasn't until his smile faded that I paid attention, realising that he had said something and was now waiting for a reply.

'Sorry, what?' I asked, a sweep of red rising from my throat to my cheeks.

He either didn't notice or was too polite to comment, but merely said, 'I asked you what your life was like back where you live.'

I hesitated. I didn't normally like to share the story of our family because it prompted pity from those who heard it. I looked at him and sighed.

'You don't have to tell me if you don't want to.'

'No… it's not that I don't want to tell you, it's just that I don't want or need pity from those who hear it. When I was still a child, my father suffered from battle injuries and… passed away.' It was still hard to get those words out.

Helmon helped me climb over a long, flat boulder. He looked at me, promising that he wouldn't act any differently around me than he had before, giving me his condolences, watching me in that way of his. I decided that maybe Helmon was the right person for me to confide in, and opened my mouth to tell him my family's story.

'We lived in a small cottage in the country with our parents – but we could only afford to live there because my father was in the army. When… when he died in war, we were given compensation money.' Tears pricked in my eyes, and I had to stop speaking. My father had been the sole source of Kai's joy, and even though I hadn't been that close to him, when he died I saw Kai drift away from everyone, building up a wall that no one could penetrate. No matter how happy she seemed when she was talking to you, her eyes never lost their haunted look. She hadn't let anyone else in – at least, not in the way she had let him in. I didn't tell Helmon this, but merely walked in silence with him beside me. When I dared a glance at him, his eyes were soft with sadness. I hated myself for getting so emotional about it, and I hated that his silent understanding was just what I needed. I continued after another moment.

'So… my life back at home was definitely not what a normal child had. In a way, it meant that we were not bothered by anything else happening.'

'What about your mother?'

'My mother… was for me what my father was for Kai. We were very close, so much so that Kai was often left behind,' I admitted, glancing at the floor. On some occasions, I hadn't been the best sister. 'My mother loved both of us, but Kai was so different from us both that it was hard for my mother to ever see eye-to-eye with her. I often felt trapped between the two of them. Kai was very much like my father was, and I wondered why my mother married him if she didn't have anything in common with him. Opposites attract, I guess. What about you?'

'All of us on Zio are born of the Elders. The earliest men were already there when the first Elder arrived, so after the initial shock of arriving, they settled into life quickly. They got married to the men, and started families. To their shock, their many children were all males, even though they had many in the hope that one would be a girl to carry on the line. And now, thousands of years later, they are still males. Things might not be going well for us in terms of our numbers yet, because our newest Elder hasn't completed the ritual of Omricrit yet, which is the same as marriage for you, except that the two people's souls are joined permanently, and they can never have another person for their partner.'

I furrowed my brow, taking in what he said. If the Elders had all arrived like I had… and he said that I might be one of them if I survived…

'Do I have to do what they had to do – with the Falcords?'

He nodded gravely, his chestnut hair blowing slightly in a warm air current. 'We all do.'

My chest tightened at that, thinking, while Helmon was

getting patched up, how I had heard one of them mention war a while ago, but I asked, 'So how many of you are there now?'

'Around five hundred.'

'In a thousand years, your population only ended up being five hundred?'

'It's not to do with giving birth or anything like that – we can reproduce as easily as you humans. You'll find out everything from Yina and the rest of the Elders soon.'

I felt worry lace itself through my heart. War. That's what made a population fall. War and famine, although these men looked perfectly healthy.

'What do you mean, "*you humans*"?'

'We – both the Falcords and the Firborn – are the Ylvares, but in your terminology, I think our description matches that of a man – mostly.'

'So what am I? Human or Ylvar?'

He hesitated before answering.

'I'm not sure.' I knew that he was lying, but I let it go. He probably couldn't tell me.

'So… the men we ran into back there…' I said cautiously. 'How will they find Kai? They can't possibly search the whole Western side of the river!'

'When the two girls first arrive, they both are dropped in roughly the same area – as you know. However, when one of the Syths gets taken, the other will probably try to follow. To prevent this, each has a spell wrapped around their footsteps when they arrive. As soon as the Firborn Syth is taken, the Falcord Syth can only travel in the direction that her heart knows it belongs. North. If she had been taken first, you would have travelled south, because that is where you subconsciously know is the best place for you. This happened to make the search easier for one party. We have an agreement with the Falcords that we will get our Syth first, and they will stay up north until their girl finds them. Usually the girls are dropped in roughly the same place, so it isn't that hard to find them.' I blinked at this overload of information, and he looked down, apologetic.

'Sorry. I know that all of this is very new to you.'

'It's all right. I don't mind it at all, but you have so many different names for things that I don't think I'll be able to remember them all! But… I'd like to hear more about where we are going, and what the portal does.'

'The portal… is the way to transport us to Zio. It only opens a few times every one hundred years: once, in Zio, where we fly through it to arrive here, and a second time, on the way back, with you. It only opens for about half an hour each time, so we need to hurry to the camp if we are going to make it on time. It opens at the last possible minute to give us lots of time to find you – but it also means that even our training in surviving in this half-breathable air is failing. For you… the fainting fits you have will become much longer and more frequent, because you have not had the same training as we have. If we had been flying, we would have been halfway there by the time nightfall set in. At this rate, we won't be there for a few days, if not longer.'

We both looked to our right, where the sun was almost beginning its descent.

During the time that Helmon had been talking to me, I had been looking at the way Neil was tersely assessing our surroundings, muscles tightening as stress lined his body. Every so often, he would look across at us, a pained expression flitting across his face before it quickly vanished when he caught my eye. The agony I saw there took my breath away the first time I saw it. I watched him carefully from then on, watching to see what had caused it. Every time he made to glance at me, I quickly looked up at Helmon, feeling Neil's glance burn onto my face. He knew I had been looking at him, and he knew that I was aware of this, but I still pretended I hadn't, arranging my face to make myself look deeply interested in the rather one-sided conversation I was holding. Finally, I dared another glance at him when I thought he wasn't looking, only to find him returning the look. The pain on his face quickly melted away to smouldering anger when he looked at me. I got the impression that if Helmon hadn't been standing there, Neil might have said the seething comment I could almost see boiling behind his lips. Fear curled around my stomach, almost tightening it to the point of pain. Helmon continued telling me about the portal, and I started paying attention, realising that this was important information. The next time I looked at Neil, he was staring off into the distance again, lips pressed tightly together.

I spent the rest of the hour wondering why he was in so much emotional pain, and why he had been so furious at me. However, I couldn't wonder about it for long, because we stopped for a water break a short while later. My parched throat had closed up a long time ago, even though all of the warriors seemed to be fine, exchanging words with each other as we walked in the midst of them.

Stopping by a small tree, withered like the rest of the land, the men slung their packs off their shoulders, but didn't take anything out. Instead, they quietly continued chatting to each other as Helmon drew me away from them to have a word with me. Neil seemed inclined to follow, his body leaning towards us as his muscles strained with the urge to come too. After a second, he seemed to think better of it and turned to the rest of the commanders, contributing to the conversation with a quick comment. He looked back over his shoulder at us in frustration. Helmon saw him and made a placating gesture with his hands before shrugging, turning and walking with me a little distance away from the other Firborn.

My apprehension grew as he twisted to face me. His face was deadly serious as he said, 'We have stopped for a water break, and given your reaction to the sight of it, it might kill you if you touch it.'

My shocked, scared face reared back as I took in what he said. I opened my mouth but he put up his hand to signal that he wasn't finished yet.

'The way you have to drink water is complicated, but I think you can manage it. You must learn almost immediately – water is a necessity for all of the Ylvares, I'm afraid. Even the Firborn.' He took a deep breath before speaking again, watching my face intently. 'You cannot see, hear or touch water, so to drink you must close your eyes and sip from a container that will be covered in cloth. Instead of drinking from the lip of the container, there is a straw attached so that the liquid can go straight into your mouth and body, the only places where it cannot affect you.' I nodded mutely, my mouth too parched to speak. He led me back to the others, where he retrieved something out of his pack. I squeezed my eyes shut as he approached, as he had instructed me to do. I could almost sense Neil staring at me as Helmon pressed something squishy into my hand, covered in a rag. I lifted it, feeling dread as I felt the water slosh around in the container. I felt someone tug at the straw, pressing it into my mouth. I blindly drank the warm water until I was sucking the remaining air in the container, and opened my eyes when I realised that it was finished. The other men had already finished their drinks, and quickly packed them away as we prepared to move away again.

The landscape around us was also preparing – but for night. The few animals that were present – mostly birds – were quietly chirping in the withering trees where they had started to roost. We continued on quietly, all of us watching nervously for danger as night time approached. Even the near-silent, desert-like plain we were passing through seemed to fall still as darkness finally encroached on us after hours of walking.

Mid-step, I yawned, shaking out my swollen, aching feet before continuing forwards. Several of the sentries had taken to the skies a while ago, circling around us to scan for anything amiss in the landscape. I had watched them make great sweeping motions in the air as they circled until, bored, I again started watching Neil, who was back beside me and Helmon. Gone was the pained look from before – only a faint worry covered his eyes as he watched the moon rise slowly. When he turned his head to face Helmon, the intense agony from earlier returned. I wondered whether he looked like that every time he looked at Helmon, and why he seemed so resentful of me. What was the matter with him? Did Helmon know? He certainly didn't seem to, quietly humming to himself as he strolled beside me, steps feline and graceful. For a moment, I was reminded of the vicious creature I had first seen in that clearing with Kai. The unending fury radiating from him then had taken the breath from me before I fainted. The man walking beside me now, arm brushing mine, was so different from the furious, deadly one I had witnessed that it was laughable. Helmon, too, was watching both the sky and the land around us for a danger I wasn't aware of. What was out here? While his demeanour was relaxed, his hands in his pockets and his lips whistling merrily, there was a cloud of worry that seemed to stoop his shoulders and press fear into his eyes. I could tell that he was trying to act casual when there was clearly something wrong. I wished that he would just tell me what it was, instead of acting as though there was nothing to worry about. His face revealed nothing, and I almost sighed in frustration. Their worry was contagious, and I found myself scanning our surroundings for any hint of danger, even though I had no idea what we were looking for. Out by one of the sparse bushes, a flash of movement caught my eye. I looked to see the shrubbery shaking gently. Wind or beast? I had no idea what the size of the danger was, or whether it was even alive.

Turning to Neil, I asked him politely, 'Why are you and

everyone else so worried? Is something going to attack us?'

His face twisted in disdain as he looked at me slowly, flicked his gaze up and down my body as if to say, *and who, exactly, are you?* and then slowly lifted his eyes to mine. The loathing in those onyx eyes bored into mine, before he twisted his head away again.

Disgust and anger burned a hole through my stomach. He couldn't even deign to *answer* me! Why did he hate me so much? I turned away, making it clear with my stiff posture and clenched fists that I wasn't going to take his behaviour. I smiled venomously at him from over my shoulder, and turned to Helmon.

'What is everyone so worried about, Helmon?' I asked sweetly.

'I'm really sorry, but we can't tell you, in case it shocks you in some way.' His face was distant, and he didn't even look at me as he answered. Anger, mixed with hurt that he thought I was the kind of person to hide from a fight, had me glaring at him. A cough from my other side had me turning back from Helmon to Neil, who smirked and then gave me the exact same smile I had given him a moment ago. The look almost screamed, *told you so.* I narrowed my eyes at him and gave him a withering look, wondering why I had ever felt sorry for him.

I walked on, not speaking to Helmon, feeling lonely for the first time since he had approached me in the clearing. Hurt gnawed at my insides, churning like the thoughts swirling in my head. What had I done to make Helmon act the way he just did?

Glancing sideways subtly, I saw that Helmon and Neil had their heads bent together, talking quietly. A pang of jealousy hit me as I saw Helmon flash a quick smile at something Neil had said. I was so surprised at the feeling that I stumbled in my steps. I barely even *knew* Helmon! More confused than ever, I moved away from them. I continued walking onwards about a hundred meters away from the pair of men, furious that they hadn't even noticed my absence yet. The cracked ground seemed to lead on forever, my footsteps a dull sound in my ears. The cobalt sky was tinged with rose, a vibrant orange flashing through from time to time as the sun continued its descent.

I didn't notice anything was amiss until utter silence coated my ears.

I looked around suspiciously at the trees, noting the absence of birds in any of them, and the lack of even a single whisper of movement. Checking the ground, the trees, the bushes, the sky, I saw nothing.

No presence of life.

Nothing.

Wait – there – was that an animal? I peered into the large bush quite a way away and saw that indeed, a coarse, sandy-coloured tail was poking out of the side of the bush. Well, at least I knew now that there wasn't anything too serious to worry about. Anything hiding behind a bush that size couldn't be dangerous. Still, where was Helmon?

I watched the tail carefully as I strode a few steps closer. It twitched, waving gently, and vanished behind the bush. I scanned the bush from where I was for any sign that it was still there. Why was it hiding in the first place? If Ylvares were so rarely here, why was the creature so frightened of us? The men wouldn't have had time to attack animals to eat because they had to get to the camp.

I ventured a few more steps towards the creature, a dour smell punching me squarely in the face, forcing itself up my nostrils. I was now only a few feet from the bush, and there were still no signs that the animal was even there any more – but where could it have possibly gone?

I leaped forwards in a sudden movement, twisting so that my head could see behind the bush.

No creature greeted me.

What? Where did it go?

I looked under the bush carefully, lifting branches to check for a burrow. The ground was cracked here too – a little less than the vast expanse surrounding me, but still cracked.

I was examining the ground and the land beyond it when a warm gust of humid air breathed on my neck. The warmth was much too humid for a desert-like environment, but I couldn't notice the difference, because I was swelteringly hot. The breeze paused, continued, paused, continued in a rhythmic way. I furrowed my brows and slowly turned. A wet panting sound filled my ears, washing my heart in an ocean of dread.

Swivelling my eyes upwards and bracing myself, I saw the huge shadow of a creature standing over me. Distantly, I thought I could hear Helmon's panicked voice shouting my name. I paid no attention, terror dimming all senses that weren't focused on the huge creature in front of me.

I could see that its pointy nose and massive upright ears were similar to those of many desert mammals that I had learned about in my terrible schooling. The beige colour of the animal blended in perfectly with the landscape, its smooth fur caressing the skin of its back. The tail that I had seen before was short and stubby compared to the bulk of the rest of the creature. How had it been able to hide behind a bush so small?

The animal crouched, its brown eyes glazed over with hunger. My eyes met its own just as Helmon – or was it Neil? – shouted my name again. The muscles on the predator bunched as it prepared to leap, all the while maintaining eye contact with me. The domination in the stare had me cowering like a useless fool as I slowly started inching back, back, back, desperate not to be eaten.

The immense creature snarled, its sharp fangs bared as it tracked my movements with an eye like a hawk. I stilled and focused my breathing, not daring even to blink in case it lunged forwards to grab my neck in its dribbling maw.

We stared at each other, and it readied itself.

It leaned back, muscles straining.

.9.

Kai

I twiddled my thumbs, crouching low on my downy bed as I watched the moon rise. Its light would make it easy for me to see where I was going, but also easy for others to see where I was headed.

The moon was a hanging orb in the centre of the sky when I finally had the courage to walk the few steps to the edge of the tent. Looking back behind me at the bed I was meant to be sleeping in now, I realised that I had forgotten a crucial detail of my plan. I ran back over, making sure to keep my footsteps light and soft. The blanket was thrown back on my bed, exposing the fact that I wasn't there, for everyone to see. Glancing over my shoulder at the flap of the tent, I checked that the sentries standing mere feet away from the entrance of my tent hadn't noticed anything. They would soon, probably when they came in in the morning to wake me up – but a few hours were enough. Ever so carefully, I teased and wheedled the duvet and my pillows into something resembling a human shape facing the side of the tent opposite the flaps.

Bringing out Tholan, I weighed it in my hand before

slashing it down in a quick sweep towards the side of the tent. The fabric ripped loudly, and I silently cursed as I jumped back into bed in case the soldiers came in to check what the noise was. Facing the rip, I tried to cover it with my hands as much as possible, the faint moonlight illuminating the line etched by my blade. Hopefully it would be big enough for me to squeeze past into the cool night air beyond.

A faint crunching of footsteps had me freezing up, my eyes clenched tightly shut, trying to make my body look relaxed and resting. I breathed in and out deeply as two people – probably the sentries – entered the tent.

After pausing for a few moments, in which I clenched my pillow so hard that my knuckles turned white, the sentries decided that whatever had caused the ripping sound was not coming from my tent.

They left, their footsteps slow, as if they were reluctant to let me out of sight. I let out a silent sigh of relief and, after waiting for a few more tedious seconds, slipped out of bed cautiously. I was careful not to creak the frame – I had spent the better part of an hour this afternoon carefully inspecting it to see which parts of it I wouldn't be able to lean on.

Standing, I risked a second to spare a quick glance in the direction of the sentries. No noise came from where they must be standing, but then again there hadn't been any noise during the better part of tonight. My hair shone silver in the light of the moon, and I prayed that it wouldn't be too noticeable in the darkness. I was wearing grey fur-lined clothes and dark, flexible boots, which would help to blend me into the shadows.

Creeping around the side of the bed, I pressed myself against the edge of the bed and the tent, curling into a ball. Holding one edge of the flap with my hand, I slowly lifted it, cringing as moonlight flooded into the tent, illuminating the bed. I peered outside against the moonlight, trying to see whether there was anyone out there. Frustration clouded my senses as I spotted Faolan, sitting with his back to a tree, mere feet away.

The moonlight silhouetted the side of his face, making it nearly impossible for me to see if he had spotted me. I frantically started trying to back up, but quickly realised that I was well and truly stuck in my position, and the only way to move would be to go forwards. Faolan didn't notice my quiet curse, followed by a shuffling sound as I edged closer to the gap. He sat as still as a cat, looking up at the moon.

At some point in my struggle of trying to creep forwards as silently as possible, I noticed that he was examining the stars intently, an expression of slight sorrow on his face. I almost felt sorry for him, but his sadness was the perfect distraction from what I was going to do. While I was slowly moving centimetres closer, I pondered on the reason for his expression and finally reached the very edge of the slit that I had cut.

A sharp, vicious wind seemed to whip around me, settling at my very bones. I shivered violently, unable to prevent a small chatter of my teeth. Faolan's head whipped around, staring at me straight in the face. I inwardly groaned, keeping as still and silent as possible. The wind intensified, slashing at me cruelly. The hairs on my arms rose, my lips turning blue. Another chatter burst out before I could stop myself, and I gritted my teeth together to prevent it from happening again. Too late, I realised, as Faolan shifted stiffly, rising to brace his hands on the ground as he rose to his knees. He jumped to his feet in shock, and I could see the whites of his eyes as they widened in disbelief. However, he didn't make a motion in my direction, and I thought that maybe somehow he didn't think that I was going to escape with him now there. I hesitated, asking myself the same question, and decided that I had to see my plan through. If Faolan knew that I was trying to escape, he would make sure that tomorrow I would have twice as many guards surrounding my tent, circling it like sharks after a seal.

He ventured a step closer, anger now burning across his features as the wind raked across his hair. He crossed his arms, and I thought I started to hear the soft pattern of raindrops. Silent as snow, lightning arced in a grimace across the sky. A few seconds later, a thunderous boom sounded as the impact of the strike reached us. I stared wildly at him, rain now blurring my vision, watching to see whether he would attack. He did nothing, only stood, clearly furious at my gall to escape when he, Angus and the rest of the sentries needed me for whatever sick agenda they had.

I took a deep breath, preparing myself, and darted out of the tent, fast as the lightning above us.

The wind was a wild hum in my ears as I took off, not waiting to see whether Faolan was following, or how far behind he was. Like I had planned, I headed north-west, rocketing through the dense foliage.

On my way, I thought I saw the edge of a red cloak snap

behind a tree, and veered left in my fright. Could Faolan somehow be ahead of me? Pounding footsteps followed in my wake, and I knew that whoever was behind the tree was not Faolan, but someone else. Risking a glance over my shoulder, I was shocked to see Faolan only a foot or so away from me if he reached his arm out. With a desperate cry, I veered back right and pumped my legs and arms faster. My throat had become painfully clogged with the cold, my breath coming in ragged gasps as I bolted through the trees like a cheetah. Déjà vu flashed through my memory as I remembered another scene just like this, only without the painfully hard raindrops and flickering lightning.

I could hear Faolan shouting above the rain that poured like a torrent all around us, and I slowed for an instant before carrying on. An instant was enough for Faolan, however, and I could feel the tip of his finger brush my snapping braid. He continued shouting, his voice becoming hoarse from trying to force me to hear it. Even at the top of his voice, the words were indistinct, muted by the roar of the rain. I couldn't make out what he was saying as I plunged towards the electrical barrier-shield that was drawing ever closer.

...

Angus

I peered at the girl, her sodden clothes, and the elegant knife at her side as she streaked past me. The edge of my red cloak slashed at the wind, and I tugged it into my side as Kai glanced once at the tree and ran on. The sheer panic in her midnight eyes had me looking around again. Where was she going? Was she trying to escape? Faolan must have discovered that she was missing by now, if the sentries outside her tent had noticed anything amiss and alerted him. I grinned wickedly as I spotted Faolan, feet away from her, chasing the girl with a determined look on his face.

This was all going very nicely indeed – the girl was exactly the kind we needed for this war. Ruthless, impulsive, and not afraid to go against anyone who challenged her. She would need training, though, and I would have to gain her trust.

Strolling back to camp, I didn't once worry that the girl would ever escape.

...

Faolan

I sprang through the trees, hot on the heels of Kai as she desperately tried to reach the protective barrier that surrounded our camp. I had seen her fascinated face when she had touched it earlier, and pondered the reason for her curiosity, because nearly all of the Syths before her had been afraid of touching the boundary. I supposed the magic of the barrier must have worn off slightly – part of the boundary's magic was to instil fear into whoever went close to it.

We had almost reached the barrier now, and I knew that

the game was almost up. She couldn't escape, so I didn't need to catch her now. Initially, I had thought that she was going to hurt one of my commanders, as I had seen the silver dagger strapped to her waist. Thankfully, that hadn't been part of her plan – she could just as likely have injured herself as one of the commanders, and she probably knew it. She was running like hell towards the shield, and I fell into place behind her as I saw the crackling mass of electricity loom in front of us.

Kai didn't hesitate before practically diving into the shield. A hoarse cry came from her throat as a barrage of shocks tunnelled into her body. Her hair started sizzling dangerously, the whites of her eyes showing. I could almost see the white-hot sparks shoving themselves into her heart, her body convulsing. Slowing, I frantically pulled her away from it. She tore her wrist from mine and pounded on the shield, a silent river of tears flowing down her pale cheeks. Thunder cried overhead, an echo of the girl's cries as she frantically tried to leave.

I gently grabbed hold of her wrist again, twisting her to face me. I was about to tell her that she was going to die if she kept hitting the barrier like that, but she didn't seem to care as she hissed viciously at me. My mouth snapped shut in shock at the savage gleam in her wet eyes. She snarled once again, and I could already see that her eyes were changing, brightening, glowing, as she stared at me. I stepped back in shock, almost stumbling in the snow and moss. She was about to use her powers for the first time – something she didn't even know that she had.

Desperate for a way to get her to stay focused on me and not on the wall, I sent a flash of ice for her.

I could tell from the way her eyes flared that she was shocked at what I had just done. *Control, discipline,* I thought to myself, willing the wildness in my nature not to take over like Kai had almost let hers do. I paced forwards, watching as she shrank back slightly.

I lunged forwards, but she was nimble. She jerked back, fear alighting in her eyes, ice gathering at her fingertips involuntarily.

I stood there in front of her for what seemed like an age before I made my final move. Taking the slight advantage I had, I glared viciously at her, stalking closer. I needed to bring her back to the camp, and I needed to do it without resistance. I hated the fact that I was going to have to frighten her more when she already had a haunted gleam in her eye, but it was the only way to make her go back to the camp.

...

Kai

I glanced at the weak rays of sun, slowly filtering through the mountains, as I decided that I had nothing to lose.

Faol stood, his glowing silver eyes narrowed, as I knelt before him baring my teeth in an attempt to make him back down.

Making my eyes glint viciously in the early morning light, I stared down the person facing me, his white teeth flashing in a reflection of the light bouncing off the snow. I knew that he wouldn't kill me, because he had captured me for a reason, but I still felt fear creep into my frozen heart.

'Please,' I gritted out, teeth clenched, in a final effort to staunch the attack.

Silence was my only answer as the boy drew back, gathering ice at his fingers.

He hurled it towards me; the last sound I heard was my unearthly scream, echoing through the snowy woods.

...

Faolan

The girl screamed as I hurled an icy spear at her, giving away our location to any who were awake at this time in the morning. Fortunately, the sentries didn't normally get up until the sun was fully in the sky, so we had some time. Still, Angus might have risen earlier.

I didn't want anyone to know that Kai had tried to run away because I feared that they might do something to her to constrain her further. Lock her up.

In all my years of training the Syths, I had learned that if they were shackled now, forced to stay where they were, they became defiant and started seeing us as the enemy. By giving Kai space to roam, she might be more cooperative with us. She would hate me for what I was about to do, but at least she wouldn't dislike the other commanders.

Unconscious, Kai's face was peaceful, muscles relaxed for

once. I guessed that the only time she ever let down her guard was when she was asleep – when she woke, her features seemed to be etched in a hidden sadness that lingered beneath the surface of her eyes. A wariness – and fear.

I carefully picked her up, her head shifting as she lolled against my arm.

I ran slowly, feet making deep imprints in the snow as I struggled to carry her all the way back to the camp. Normally, I would have reached camp in a few minutes by flying, but having her in my arms made me feel uneasy.

Flying might wake her – and others might catch sight of us. No, better to walk, slow as it might be.

I sighed, frustrated at the slow pace I was forced to move at.

The girl's hair, tied back in a loose braid, bumped against my back with every jolting step I took, swinging back and forth as I careened through the awakening forest.

During the time she was in my arms, I wondered how it was that she had been able to use her powers. Normally, it took Syths a great many days of practice even to spark ice into creation by accident. She was certainly unusual, I thought. Her personality and quick temper meant that she wasn't someone who easily took orders.

She seemed determined to carve her own path.

After what seemed like a lifetime, I saw the light of the sun cresting above the horizon, casting the ground in a sparkling sheen. The light made it easier for me to see the beige rooves of the tents, rising up off the ground. Nearing the camp, I saw all four of the sentries up and about, Angus talking animatedly to them as they went about fetching water and food from our small underground storage cell. I would have to get Kai back to her small tent without being noticed, and before one of the men thought to wake her.

I knew that they would take precautions to keep her locked up if they saw us. Not even my orders would stop them. Their urge to protect would be in overdrive. I just hoped that at some point Kai would realise that what I had done was for her sake.

Prowling over to the nearest tent, I slid behind it, hoping that none of the guards would come to fetch something from inside. I doubted it, but I still had to be cautious.

I jumped as a small bird flew past, chirping into my ear. To my horror, Kai slid off me in a smooth motion, still not conscious. She slumped to the ground, head sticking out beyond the side of the tent for all to see. I inwardly cursed and rushed to drag her away before anyone could notice. I would only have to pray that no one walked behind this tent before I had time to cover up my tracks.

I heaved Kai upwards once more, muscles bunching, as I slowly moved around the side of the tent, peering out to see whether anyone had noticed me. Fortunately, I didn't think they had, because they were all still talking quietly. I had no doubt that they had noted my absence, and assumed I was off hunting for food or something like that. They couldn't have noticed that Kai was missing because they would be in a panic if they knew that she was, and would have tried to contact me already. One of the sentries stood, stretched and yawned, and picked up a knife to start dicing the apples we were to eat for breakfast. Remembering that the girl I was roughly dragging was armed, and having seen the weapon, I quickly pulled the knife out of where it had been sheathed by her waist, making a mental note to check her tent for any more weapons.

A man sitting around the makeshift benches suddenly let out a burst of raucous laughter at something Angus had said, and I used the opportunity to slide the girl quickly across the gap between two tents as the men looked at each other. Thankfully, her tent was the next one over, so I only had one more tent to cross.

The girl mumbled softly in her sleep, a lock of her hair that had come loose falling across her face as I jerked her forwards. On silent feet, I crept forwards, peering once again around the edge of the beige tent. It was all clear as far as I could see.

Darting forwards, I crossed the final gap between the two tents just as I heard Angus say, 'Well, I'm going to see whether Kai's awake yet. Tell me if you see Faol coming back – we're low on meat and we need to make the rest of breakfast quickly.'

I desperately tried to move Kai around the side of the tent before Angus saw us. The entrance to the tent was facing the soldiers sitting together, but I remembered that she had cut a slit in the side of the tent with the knife that I was now awkwardly holding. I lowered the girl towards the slit, hoping that it would be relatively easy to push her through.

Poking my head through the hole, I saw that Angus had just started to walk away from the men sitting on wooden benches, and was approaching us rapidly. Thankfully, the tent was quite far away from the central working space, so I had about a minute to dump Kai in her tent before Angus arrived.

I tried to push my whole body into the tent and found myself stuck with the dead weight of Kai positioned in my arms. I put her on the ground, turning back to the gap. I would go in first and pull her in after me.

In what seemed like an hour but was probably only a few seconds, and I managed to haul myself through the gap. I turned to Kai, and saw that there was no way I could pull her through without her using her muscles too. If she was as limp as this, she was never going to be able to slide past the awkward angle of the slash. I silently cursed her for cutting it so small.

I pulled her arm towards me, fitting it through the gap easily. The hard part would be her head, I thought. With grunting and squeezing, I managed to get half of her head through the gap, squishing her nose in the process as her arms took up most of the space. I cursed again, and looked around to check where Angus was. He had almost reached the tent flaps and I gave a violent tug on Kai's body, and her head and chest slid through the slash. I frantically began lifting her legs into it just as Angus reached the lip of the tent. I dumped Kai by the side of her bed, hating the fact that I had to leave the knife too in my rush, and dashed off into the snow back through the gap before Angus could see me.

Once in the woods, I realised that I would have to make up a story about why her head was bruised, and why she remembered me hurling a ball of my power at her. I could say that she must have fallen off the bed, and dreamed that I hit her. That would have been a fitting way to explain her injury, I thought.

Remembering that I was meant to have been hunting this whole time, I scrambled into the trees to find an elk, thinking that when I returned, I would have to have a word with Kai in private. Obviously, she would know that it wasn't a dream. No dream is as vivid and lifelike as what she had been through.

The trees seemed cruel today, their leaves whipping viciously against each other, the snow harsh and unwelcoming as my thoughts returned to the mission in front of me: as I remembered that tonight, the portal was going to open for the first time in a hundred years.

.10.

Amber

All I could think about was the reeking smell of the fox as it jumped, the stink of carrion on its breath as it surged forwards to snap my bones.

I shut my eyes, bracing myself for the inevitable, tears leaking out of the corners of my eyes.

No growling filled my ears, no crunch as I became this animal's lunch.

Only footsteps, and a grunt as someone hurled themselves towards me –

Then a whine and a shriek as I opened my eyes in shock – only to find Helmon grappling with the fox, hands fisted in its fur as he tackled it to the ground. I gasped in shock and screamed his name, but Helmon only drew out his knife and slashed forwards in a vicious, elegant sweep, cutting the head off the animal entirely.

I looked away, disgusted and distraught, as blood squirted onto the ground, onto Helmon's clothes, and into the dry air.

I sank to the ground, shock reverberating so strongly into my heart that all I could do was sit, stare, blink, breathe.

Helmon had just saved me, even when he had been injured.

I owed him the debt of my life for killing that animal.

The sounds of the background faded into silence as my head clouded with the enormity of what he had done.

He had saved me.

...

I shivered, in absolute shock. The only words that came out of my mouth were *thank you*, over and over again.

I whispered them to the breeze that swept past me, drying the sweat forming on my face.

Helmon rushed to me, and I tried to say the words louder so that he could hear. Instead, I choked on them, throat so full of emotion that all I could do was look at him, eyes shining with tears of gratitude, mouth wobbling. Throwing my arms around him, I held onto him tightly, his initial surprise wearing off quickly. He folded his arms around me hesitantly and then leaned back to peer into my face intently.

'Are you all right? Did it hurt you?'

I smiled weakly, my overwhelming relief making my knees shake like a new-born calf. 'No, I'm fine. You... you saved me. Thank you so much...'

He waved my thanks away, acting like it was an everyday event.

'Please. It was nothing – don't worry about it.'

'But what about your arm?' I asked, looking over his right shoulder to where the stitches had ripped, blood now oozing out of the wound. He grimaced, and I watched him, concerned.

'I'll live.'

'Helmon, you can't just brush this off! It's a serious injury!' my voice raised as I inspected the slash of blood against the tanned skin of his forearm. It was deep and ragged, the blood drying quickly in the hot air that swirled and eddied around us.

I looked further over Helmon's shoulder, no longer focusing on his wound. Neil was standing by the corpse of the animal Helmon had slaughtered, watching me.

He looked from Helmon to me, eyes flicking so fast from him to me that I couldn't see them clearly. He had obviously seen me give Helmon a hug, as he was standing with his fists clenched, back ramrod straight. He narrowed his eyes furiously at me, and I backed away a little, a tendril of fear piercing my heart. Stalking forwards, Neil stood close to me as he, too, examined Helmon's wound, running his finger over it with gentle hands. He frowned, looking at the torn stitching, ignoring me completely, and addressed Helmon.

'I think I can patch that up relatively quickly. The portal opens tomorrow and I'm not sure we'll have time to get there with the pace we're moving at. I wonder…' he mused, even as worry clouded his sharp onyx eyes. Helmon turned and looked at him questioningly, worried too.

Without saying a word, Neil gripped him under the arms, maroon arrows swinging on his back. He jumped upwards, beating dust from the parched ground. He grunted and started to lift Helmon into the sky as I watched in amazement. The muscles in his arms strained as he started to rise higher.

Even though Helmon had carried me quite easily, it seemed that a Ylvar weighed significantly more than a human. The positioning of the flight was also awkward and painfully heavy, because Neil couldn't lift Helmon into his arms like Helmon had carried me – his injuries made it impossible. Instead, Neil had to carry Helmon at the end of his arms.

Despite all of this, Neil seemed to be managing, and I squinted my eyes against the insistent glare of the sun to watch. Shouts of surprise reached Neil's ears as the other three commanders finally approached, back from their scouting mission, flying forwards in surprise at what they saw in front of them. Neil turned in midair to greet them eagerly, and they all began descending towards me a moment later, moving in elegant, smooth motions.

It was only when they landed that the other commanders noticed how pale my face was, how Helmon's wound had been torn open again, and how his blade was now crusted with dried blood. They looked at each other and then us, confused.

'Some kind of wolf or fox species tried to attack Amber,' Helmon said. 'Luckily, we managed to kill it before it could – but my wound has ripped again.' The commanders murmured, eyes darting around nervously as they, too, started watching for more signs of danger.

Smoothly, Neil started speaking, eyes lit with an idea.

'I was just trying to see if we could carry Helmon – one of you could carry the girl,' – I opened my mouth indignantly at the dismissive way he talked – 'but with his weapons and weight, Helmon would be more difficult to carry, obviously.

I was thinking… if two of you helped me carry Helmon, one could carry *her*.' I raised my eyebrows in disbelief at the way he seemed to talk about me as if I wasn't standing right next to him. One of the commanders piped up, silencing Neil.

'But what about our scouting?'

'One of you can fly ahead with the girl while we're further back with Helmon to make sure nothing else happens to him,' Neil said, glancing at me for the first time.

'But the whole point of the scouting is to protect *her* from danger –'

'It doesn't matter!' Neil cried, some emotion seeming to spill out of him.

The commander looked rather taken aback, and Neil seemed to regret it an instant later, but only turned to Helmon once more. 'Helmon, are you all right with us carrying you?'

'Yes, but I did rather want to be able to keep an eye on Amber while we travelled… but I suppose, if it means we'll get there faster, we can travel like you said.'

'Great. Let's go,' Neil said briskly. He glanced over at me again, hostility covering his eyes like a mask. I rolled my eyes, ignoring him completely as I turned to one of the commanders who had approached me.

'Are you going to carry me?' I asked, and he nodded, motioning for me to come closer so that he could lift me into his arms. I did so, leaning awkwardly towards the ground as he lifted me up. Once in his arms, I shifted slightly, trying to get comfortable. The other three commanders, including Neil, gathered close around Helmon. Moving carefully, they held him by the legs, arms and chest, carefully avoiding his wounds, and making space so that they themselves could carry their supplies.

Glancing at the sun, beating down hard on us from above, I estimated that we had around six hours of flying before we would stop for the night. I almost groaned. Even though I wasn't the one who was doing the work, sitting for six hours straight was almost too tedious to contemplate. When I was flying with Helmon, the time passed in a blur, our conversation easy and engaging. With this commander… I could already tell he was uncomfortable with being the person who had to carry me.

The other men were all ready to go, and we rose into the air smoothly. I looked down at the ground dropping further and further away, and then up at the face of the sentry holding me. His face was impassive as he looked across the landscape, his nondescript features blending in with those of the other sentries. I sighed, turning my thoughts to Kai as we travelled further across the terrain.

I knew that I should be going out of my mind with worry and fear of these men, and no doubt Kai was, but… there was something about Helmon that made me feel comfortable around him. Natural. If someone else had been in his place, I was sure I'd have tried to escape by now.

Kai must be wondering, like I was, why we had been taken. If Helmon was right, and Kai wasn't going to be told much, then she must be at her wit's end, I thought, watching the cracked ground flow by me, the gaps in the soil like tiny rivulets.

I was sure Kai had tried to escape, but the thought of her

doing so made tremors skim down my spine. Was facing wherever we were going better than being stuck, alone, in the wilderness, about to die from lack of breathable air? At the very least, I thought that the men who had captured her would have told her about the problem with staying in Etrais for so long.

The thought of Kai being taken hostage by those cunning-eyed men who had been so vicious to Helmon made me want to shudder. The leader of their group had had such a glint of cruelty and violence in his eye when he had looked at me – but there was another emotion there as well, one that had shocked me completely. Fear. There had been a glimmer of it, hidden beneath the rage and sheer viciousness of his stare.

Watching the ground below once more, I thought back to the last time I had seen Kai's face. It had seemed a lifetime ago, but was in fact only a week and a half. Her face had been sympathetic of the rabbit she had tried to free, but wary. Frightened. Scared of whatever might have laid the trap. The image of her already gaunt face haunted me whenever I closed my eyes, her face etched behind my eyelids.

The hours passed in uncomfortable silence as I listened to the soft voices of the men, until finally, a shout from Neil up in front of us roused my brain from the sleepy stupor brought on by the sun.

'I think this is the best place to rest for the night. Sunset is approaching, so we need to set up camp for the night before continuing tomorrow.'

Looking down, I saw why Neil had chosen this spot to rest in.

A small cluster of trees had somehow managed to survive in

this barren wasteland, and I thought that maybe a dried-up oasis had supported the trees here until the scorching sun had finally evaporated it. About four or five trees rose up from the small patch of greenery around them and I saw the emerald of grass underneath the billowing overflow of branches and leaves.

We started descending slowly, the commander's arms around me as we dropped to the lush ground beneath us. It seemed to take an age, and I glanced across at Helmon to see how he had fared throughout the duration of our trip. His face was wan, and I looked over, concerned, as we arrived on the ground.

Landing, I stood and walked over to where Helmon was being placed by Neil under one of the massive, sprawling trees. I came closer to them, my dusty boots rubbing off on the grass as I moved. The smell of acacia hit my nose a moment later, and I breathed it in deeply as I arrived at Helmon's side, Neil walking off for a few moments to fetch something.

Helmon sagged a bit, body leaning as his arms drooped to the ground. Normally, they were tensed, ready to grab weapons if he needed them, but now they fell flat, the muscles relaxed. I glanced at the wound, brows drawing together as I noticed that the blood hadn't stopped flowing and that Helmon had a glazed look in his eye and a sheen on his forehead.

He didn't say a word to me before slumping against the trunk of the huge tree, head carefully shifted so that it wasn't pressed against the rough bark. I slid down next to him, daring to reach up a hand to feel his forehead. His skin was burning hot, and my hand recoiled.

I called over to Neil, to where he was setting up camp for

the night, and he reluctantly came over, ire cutting his mouth in a cruel line. I steeled myself to talk to him.

'I think Helmon's got a fever – his forehead is boiling. You need to stitch up his wing – and quickly. It might be infected, but I don't know how or what could have got into the cut.' *Damn that Falcord*, I thought, thinking back to the attack that had rendered Helmon unable to fly.

Neil glared at me, saying, 'I know perfectly well what I need to do. It is not your place to question how we are caring for one of *our* warriors.'

He turned back to the rest of the men, striding over to his bag. I simply stood, seething, fists clenched. Watching, I saw Neil bring out a small pouch from his bag of supplies, and come back over to the acacia tree under which both Helmon and I were sitting.

The bag was made from a brown leather of some sort, and looked well worn. From the way Neil handled it, it must be a cherished possession. He untied it and reached inside, retrieving a needle and thread that he placed beside him on the grassy ground. Helmon gulped, and I echoed the sound. Neil only looked down again and pulled out a small vial of liquid, which I guessed was a drug to render Helmon unconscious.

Neil tipped Helmon's head back and opened his mouth. Letting a single droplet of the liquid splash into his mouth, Neil stood, picking up his needle and thread while doing so. Approaching Helmon's other side, I watched Neil inspect the wound as Helmon slowly sank out of consciousness. With brutal efficiency, he quickly disinfected the cut with some pungent alcohol that I could smell from feet away. Not wanting to witness the actual stitching itself, I got up, bracing my dirt-crusted hands on my knees while doing so. I turned and slowly walked over to where several tents had already been constructed by quick, skilled hands.

I offered to help one of the commanders in making dinner, an offer he readily accepted. We cut and diced mouth-wateringly ripe fruit, and I helped him skin the animal we were having for dinner – a small desert hare one of them had caught when they had gone scouting. We also had some shrivelled roots of a plant that looked decent enough to eat but smelled atrocious. After taking a whiff of them, I gagged and quickly went to set up the eating area, which was three wooden benches surrounding a ring of stones. After placing a woven bowl in the place that each man would sit, I went back over to where Neil was just finishing his stitching on Helmon.

Neil glanced up at me as he put his needle and thread away, scowling. I went past him to Helmon, and knelt beside him. The burning heat on his forehead had been reduced to a slightly more normal temperature, and some of the colour of his cheeks had returned. I sighed in relief, even though Helmon's eyes still drooped listlessly, the brown dulled from the bright shine they had been before.

The sun started a slow descent over the line of trees that shrouded us from the rest of the desert. Gathered by the tents, the men who I had helped to prepare dinner with started setting up the food to be eaten. Helmon was asleep in his tent – but the men said that he would be awake in time for dinner, and I was thankful that finally, his wounds would be healed.

I took a seat on one of the wooden benches around the ring of stones, wondering what they were for. Were we going to make a fire? It certainly seemed cold enough, the hot desert air rising up and away as the sun moved over the horizon. Someone approached, and I looked over my shoulder to see Neil. After he had finished the stitches on Helmon's wing, he hadn't said a word to me before stalking off in the direction of his tent, situated near Helmon's. It was I who had to half drag, half carry Helmon to his own tent, before unceremoniously dumping him onto his bedroll, he wincing at my crude manoeuvring.

And now, as I watched Neil walk towards the ring of stones in the centre of the log benches, I felt a hatred for this man who had treated me as though I was worth no more than the dusty desert dirt beneath his gleaming boots.

Even so, I still watched as he stood by the ring of stones and carefully placed logs inside it that had been neatly stacked beside one of the benches. With meticulous hands, he finished placing the logs and held out his hands in front of him, staring deep at the log pile. I sat up straighter at that. Helmon had said that some of the Firborn Ylvares possessed embers of magic in the form of heat. It only sometimes manifested itself directly into flame, he had told me, but the heat itself was enough to start the fire.

A look of intense concentration passed over Neil's face as he squinted at the wood in front of him. The air around the logs seemed to be wavering, I saw, as Neil appeared to do nothing more than use his eyes to stare in front of him. Slowly, I saw the wood start to smoke, and Neil lowered his head after a moment. On his face was an expression of extreme triumph as he looked across at me.

I guessed that the feat of lighting the fire hadn't been hard because of a lack of power – no, it came from the control needed to heat only the wood and nothing else.

A flicker of flame appeared at the heart of the log pile, and I felt myself drawn towards it, transfixed. Its shining light and twisting column of heat was like staring into the face of your happiest dream and your worst nightmare, the beginning and end and eternity in the middle.

Come to me, the flame seemed to whisper. *Come.*

I stood slowly, my stiff limbs aching dully. I only sensed it faintly, my mind wholly fixed on the living entity I front of me. I took a step, then another, then another, until I was standing with my toes in front of the ring of stones. A pulse seemed to echo through the lick of flame, spreading slowly as the logs caught fire.

And when the fire was a roaring beast, a living creature that encompassed my vision, I reached out my hand towards it. It leaned towards me on a whisper of wind, and my fingers came so close to touching it that I could feel it almost tugging on my hand, begging me to feel it under my palm.

A sharp tug on my elbow drew me away from the purring beast in front of me; instead, I was twisted to face Helmon, who was standing on shaky feet, face pale and wan, smiling at me. The tug of the fire behind me demanded that I turn once more, but I ignored it and smiled back at the person standing in front of me, ecstatic to see that he was at least partially healed. His eyes were no longer drooping – they were glinting in the dying light of the sun as it finally disappeared over the horizon to our west. So happy was I to see him awake and feeling better, his fever vanished, that I didn't notice Neil creep up on my other side, silent as a cat. I jumped when he spoke, making him cast a sly look at me, pleased to know that he had frightened me a little. I glared back at him.

'The sentries want to know how long you think it'll take for us to reach the portal tomorrow,' he said.

'It'll probably be most of the day, since they'll be carrying both me and Amber. We might not get there until nightfall, which is worrying, because it opens then. We'll have to leave at dawn if we want to make it there on time.' Neil nodded, striding off to the rest of the commanders. I faced Helmon again and motioned for him to sit on a log. The other commanders started approaching with bowls of food, and I helped them to place the meals around the benches.

I helped myself to a bowl of food and brought one over for Helmon. Sitting down next to him, I handed it to him and he accepted it gratefully, breathing in the delicious smell. He dug in immediately, and I raised a mouthful of food to my lips, looking over to make sure that Helmon was eating a plentiful amount of food.

After I had finished my bite, I scraped more food onto my fork while I asked him, 'So… how did your people come to be on these… dimensions – or should I call them planets?'

The other commanders sat up straighter from where they had been lounging on the remaining logs, talking between themselves.

'Either is fine. They correlate to mean the same thing,' he said, glancing at the fire, at the heat I could still feel radiating into my skin. 'In regards to how we came to exist... It's like asking you how humans were created. Most people believe in evolution, or some kind of god. On our planets, some of the more superstitious believers think that all life on our planets was formed by a Creator, who holds something called the Quill. Anything wished for with the Quill will automatically be performed on our worlds and peoples. According to old documents and some of our more superstitious warriors, the Quill fell into dark hands – the hands of our Creator – when he first arrived here. It is said that he lives in the heart of Etrais – but again, that's merely superstition.'

He paused.

'"The Creator" is simply a title given to anyone who owns the Quill. The current Creator is said to be a death-god, someone with a force of magic so mighty and dark that if anyone were even to see him in the light, without the cloud of darkness and magic wrapped around him, they would die of sheer terror. Anyway, the legend is that the death-god, whose name is so feared that even to say it is a bad omen, needs death to fuel his life. He can only live off of one death for so long, and therefore many people need to die in order for him to be sated. What is life for one person is simply a meal for him. To ensure that the death in our lands would never cease – or at least come often enough to keep him alive – he surrounded our planets with a curse...' He stopped speaking as Neil, sitting across from him, gave him a sharp look.

'Sorry, Amber. I've already said too much,' Helmon said to me, and we continued eating.

I wanted to tell him about the tapestry that Kai and I had seen before we were taken, but kept my mouth closed, still pondering on what he had told me, that the god was merely a myth – a fantasy created by some cautious warriors.

After a while, I finished my food and put my wooden bowl on the floor. I stared at the fire, half watching it writhe and twist, half mulling over the tale that Helmon had just told me. It was just superstition but there was something… chilling about the story, and the way that Helmon had told it made it seem that the Creations of this death-god weren't something pleasant, if people had to die – or be killed – to fuel the god.

'Can you tell me the name of this god?' I asked Helmon once he had finished too. What if it was indeed the same as the tapestry, and the name written there?

'As I said before, it is believed that to invoke his name would be to call death upon yourself – not that I believe that. If you really want to know…' he looked at me doubtfully, and I nodded, eager to find out.

He leaned over until his face was inches away from mine, and then motioned for me to turn my head. After doing so, he whispered into my ear so softly that only I could hear. Across the fire, Neil's face was pure resentment, but I didn't care. The name Helmon spoke sent ice skittering along my bones, and I could have sworn a wind encrusted with darkness and cruel, brutal pain swept past as he uttered the word.

'Sardaron.'

.11.

Kai

I spent the whole day trying to convince Angus that what Faolan had done wasn't a dream, but an event which had actually happened.

'See! My head is bruised from where he tried to kill me!' I cried to Angus, vehemently pointing to my head. He sighed, putting his hand against his forehead, clearly tired of hearing my story *again*.

'No, Kai – you got that from when you fell off your bed last night, as I found you myself,' Angus said.

'You have to believe me,' I said desperately, a half-choked sob coming out as I said the words. 'Faolan is a dangerous savage! Please, please help me!'

Angus shook his head, sighing, and sat down beside me.

'Kai, I promise, it was just a dream. You have to trust me, ok?' I stared at him.

'Okay,' I whispered, too upset to disagree. When I remembered the magic I had wielded earlier this morning, I remembered feeling powerful, as if I could do anything. However, I was frightened out of my mind, and when Faolan came back from wherever he had gone – presumably to hunt for something to eat – I would stay far, *far* away from him. And when this portal that Angus had talked about opened, I would seize my chance. I would run, but by then they'd already be swallowed up by it, gone forever. They had told me that the air wasn't breathable, but I had been managing just fine so far, with only the occasional fainting fit. I could only hope that I wouldn't have one of these fainting episodes when we were about to go through the portal, because Faolan or one of the other commanders would simply thrust me through the portal, and I wouldn't have a chance to escape.

Determined that that shouldn't happen, I sat on my bed silently. Angus patted me on the shoulder consolingly, and I flinched at the touch. He looked at me as if he understood and believed my story, but I could tell from his eyes that he didn't. Not at all.

When he got up and left the tent, all I did was lie there, silent tears flowing out of my eyes. Why could no one believe me?

I quickly brushed them off as someone else entered the tent, boots scuffing on the floor.

I sat up in shock and horror as Faolan sat down beside me.

I scrambled backwards, a scream coming from my hoarse throat. I dived off the bed and tried to take a step towards the exit, but a fierce wind whipped around me, buffeting me so that I couldn't move. I whipped my head to him, eyes dilating in fear. I cried out as the wind formed a hard barrier across the flaps of the tent. Had Faolan done that? I was on the verge of a breakout – this boy was too frightening to comprehend.

He certainly didn't seem frightening, though, as he continued to calmly sit on the bed, hands out in a placating gesture.

'Please, Kai. Listen to me. I really do understand why you're upset, but I had to do it – for your own good.' I paused in my frenzy of trying to escape from the tent that had now become a trap, and took in what I was seeing.

Faolan looked up at me, silver and turquoise-green eyes beseeching, hands making a pleading gesture. I guessed that he was trying to say sorry for what he had done. His raven-black hair glinted like the necklace strung around his neck in the dim light of the tent. His apology was no excuse, and I wasn't even close to forgiving him for what he had done to me; I edged only slightly closer, not taking my eyes off him. He gave me an apologetic smile, white, straight teeth gleaming, before getting up from the bed. He smiled again, almost as if to prove that he wasn't going to hurt me. He edged around me carefully, as if I was a doe he was trying not to scare off. The wall of roaring wind vanished as he came closer to it, and he strode out of the tent quickly, looking back once to scan my face.

Fear was the only emotion he saw – fear, and a hint of shock at the sheer power he had just displayed, the elegant stride and roiling wind that seemed to drift at his heels. I collapsed on the bed once more, staring at nothing, trying to calm my racing mind.

The next few hours passed in a blur as I thought about Faolan and his powers, wondering how I would ever get past them if it came to a fight. Hopefully, I could slip out of their grip as they vanished through the portal, but there were so many variables to consider that I had no idea how I was ever going to escape, find Amber again, and get *home*. The very thought of it exhausted me.

What if Amber herself had been taken through a portal by the time I reached the place where she had been? Surely she was looking for me too – the Amber I knew would never willingly let anyone capture her!

Reassured that we would find a way out of this together, I lay back down, unwilling to go outside for fear of seeing Faolan again.

Miserable as I was, I couldn't help but appreciate a drift of snowflakes as they spun past the rippling cut I had slashed with my knife. They gleamed, a swirling song of the wilderness – an icy, honed gift sent from the sky. I hadn't paid attention to the snow and ice before – I had been too focused on what had been going on around me, but now I probably had a few more hours until we had to leave.

The twisting beauty of the current of snowflakes captivated me; I was drawn in by a force I couldn't quite name, and I could almost feel each individual snowflake as if it was a part of me, flowing freely into the crisp air. I sighed as the small snowflake shower ended, a breezy wind blowing past to split the remaining flakes up.

Glancing behind the tiny droplets of frozen water, I saw one of the sentries move past my tent. I knew better than to try to escape out of the rip again; Faolan would be watching constantly.

I felt the weak sun shift throughout the afternoon as it moved across the sky. I did nothing except watch the dance of light and ice across the ground, spilling playfully over the snow like a river.

Someone coughed outside my tent at one point and I had a feeling that they were subtly trying to let me know that they wanted to talk to me. I ignored whoever it was – Angus, maybe – and continued staring at the side of the tent. They stopped a few minutes later and I blew out a breath I didn't know I'd been holding.

I waited for the inevitable moment when a man would call to me that it was time to go. I didn't know if that moment would be in the next minute or in the next day. I knew that it couldn't be very far away, because Angus had told me when we first met that we could only survive two weeks here without the proper air to breathe.

I mulled over the reason for their capture of me as the light faded slightly; it was only when the sun sank over the tops of the trees that someone entered my tent.

It was Angus, and he spoke to me from just inside the entrance to the tent.

'Kai, we're packing up, so you need to come out of the tent for a little while.'

I sat up straight, silvery blond hair mussed from being on my bed for so long.

'Why, where are we going?' I asked, already knowing that I wouldn't get a proper answer.

'We're going to Nzar now, but you need to come outside in

order for that to happen.'

I stood, figuring that it was better to act complacent while Angus gripped my wrist and led me outside. The cold air hit my face, numbing my nose and turning my ears red. The end of my tunic flapped against my thighs as I walked into the throbbing wind – a wind made by Faolan? I wondered as I was pulled forwards.

As a group, the men started packing up my tent efficiently, and I looked around the clearing to see nothing but melted patches of snow where theirs had been. The benches around which we had sat had been carefully arranged to look as if we had never been there, but I didn't know what they could possibly want to cover up their tracks for. There was no one else here.

A while later, Angus stood with me as the men finally finished their job and shouldered the bags containing our supplies.

Approaching us, they walked quickly, Faolan leading them, his copper skin stark against the snow.

We moved forwards, Angus handing me over to two of the guards as he shouldered his way to the front with Faolan. I rolled my eyes, annoyed that Angus wasn't going to talk to me and answer my questions about how we were getting to Nzar. Presumably, we were going through the portal now, unless that would happen at another time.

I doubted that Angus and Faol would assume I'd be cooperative – they would have their eyes on me as we travelled deeper into the snowy woods, staying inside the circle made by the electric lightning barrier I had tried to hurl myself into.

The trees seemed dull and listless today, even in the twisting wind that yanked on my hair, tugging my braid back into its embrace. I scanned the woods for any sign of danger as we moved, hoping desperately that a creature would appear, and that Faol and Angus would have to fight it, leaving me with a chance, however slim, of getting away.

I had no such luck and as we moved I could feel the sand timer of my options slowly trickling away. I needed more time, but I could see that I was almost out of it as Faol halted in a small clearing that barely fit all our bodies and bags.

Beyond us stood the newly-opening portal.

It was no more than a hole in the air, a floating presence that you could just about see through. I watched it form, the space, which had been air only a moment before, seeming to glow before a golden light burst through, laced with the icy smell of snow-topped mountains. I had watched it open until I could see the black void beyond. You could only fit your hand through, and I wondered how we were supposed to travel through a rip that size. It seemed to draw us closer, and I gazed at it from a few feet away, even as I was planning my escape.

The two sentries that had been holding me stepped forwards towards the beckoning abyss, and in my fear I wondered if their land was cloaked in darkness. Faol sauntered up to me and I shrank away from him, hating myself from acting so pathetic and cowardly. He gripped my hand tightly, and his ice-cold fingers enclosed mine. It was not a romantic gesture; it was a warning not to misbehave. I reached towards my other side, the tips of my fingers brushing the cool hilt of Tholan. I would be prepared to slash it at him, I realised, as I stiffened, body bracing against any attack on his part.

As one, the first two sentries reached their hands into the hole, vanishing from sight immediately. I gasped, shocked. I started shaking my head, desperate to escape that fate. But then Angus stepped up with the third sentry and they placed their hands into the darkness. They both vanished from the clearing until it was just me and Faol in the trees together. I looked at him and there was only kindness in his gaze. I was so shocked that I stepped towards the hole unwittingly. He dropped my hand and approached me. I stood stock still as he stood next to me, waiting for him to attack, poised to run. If I could only check exactly where the rip was –

Turning back to the hole for a moment, I risked a glance at it –

A violent shove from behind made me cry out as I fell forwards, hand hitting the rip as I did so. I felt the cool air beyond the hole, and I screamed as I felt my body just… leave the clearing.

The abyss was dark and brutal, the pain ragged and vicious as I screamed again, this time in pain, falling into what felt like thin air. A weight dragged onto my back, the feeling uncomfortable and prickly, but I ignored it, the agony too tremendous for me to focus on anything other than itself. The darkness eddied around us, a swirling abyss of vicious, unending horror. My eyes widened as I desperately tried to see what was happening, but the darkness was impenetrable and cruel in a way I had never known.

Directly below me, a small circle of light formed, like water at the bottom of a well. I fell towards it, unable to stop myself, limbs flailing. The circle brightened and grew larger as I fell, and it was impossible to stop my body as I smashed into and through it, the strange weight on my back fading away as I did so.

Bright blue sky greeted me as I shot through the circle, and I blinked my eyes against the light. The wind as I fell made tears run down the sides of my face into my hair, and I could hardly see in front of me due to the blurriness.

I was screaming as I fell, the wind rushing past me in a whisper of glee against my skin as I freefell for the earth, now far below me.

A triumphant cry of joy echoed above me, and I managed to turn my head beyond my shoulder to see Faolan dropping through the air at the same speed I was. There was only ecstatic joy in his face as he fell, and he loosed his battle cry again, meeting my eyes. He looked at me, grinning like a fool and, despite the terror of my situation, I felt a small smile curve along my lips at the sight of his wind-mussed hair and wild eyes. I turned my head again so that it was facing the ground once more, and gasped at what I saw.

Snow-capped mountains faded away into the distance, the rest of the land a wild tangle of pine and fir trees. More mountains formed a rough circle around an enormous crater of land, filled with trees and clearings. I could see an enormous hawk sailing below me, and I admired its glossy feathers as I tumbled past it. I suddenly laughed out loud, the sheer beauty of the landscape filling me with a joy I had not known in a long, long time – despite the fear I was in. Faolan's chuckle echoed mine, and I turned my head to find him next to me, probably having out-flown the speed of gravity with that strange gravity-defying force to get where he was now. Strands of my hair whipped into my face, and I spat them ungracefully out of my mouth as I grinned again. Faolan's arrows in their quiver fluttered behind him as he tucked them into his back. Surprised, I noticed for the first time that he had no bow to fight them with.

Far, far, below me, I could just about make out Angus and the sentry he had travelled in with. They seemed so small, like tiny ants, I thought. So insignificant compared to the beauty of the landscape.

We had, by now, begun to approach the tallest of the ring of mountains surrounding the land, and I reared back with fright, afraid that Faolan wouldn't catch me in time for me to splatter myself onto the snow.

He was shouting at me as we fell, and I strained to hear him over the roaring in my ears from the merciless wind.

'Pull up!' he shouted at me. I looked at him in confusion, scared that I would do something wrong – wasn't he supposed to catch me? Unable to get me to understand, Faolan pointed desperately at my feet.

'PULL UP!' he screamed again, at the same moment that I finally felt it.

It was like a faint tickling sensation, a sensation of being everywhere and nowhere, as free as the wind. It seemed to curl around my body, supporting me slightly as I moved swiftly towards the ground.

My clothes fluttered loosely in the wind, the sensation tickly but slightly uncomfortable. Looking at my back, I saw that I, now had a quiver full of arrows on my back that hadn't been there a moment before. They were long, and elegant, tipped with a feather of royal blue, specks of gold dotting them.

I screamed as I fell, jerking back. I tried to speak, tried to *think* around the shock. But I couldn't – and I felt darkness around the edges of my vision as a fainting episode approached – not from lack of air, but from sheer shock at the two things that had happened.

Breathe breathe breathe I thought to myself. *Think.* I tried to command the strange feeling around my feet to pull me up, but only managed in slowing a little. The sensation was strange, like using a muscle you didn't know existed. True terror gripped my heart like a vice, slowly squeezing as the top of the mountain rushed out to greet me.

I looked across at Faolan in terror, and he shouted, 'LIKE THIS!'

He closed his eyes, a small smile spreading across his face as he started to stop falling, soaring away. He rose far above me, sailing instead of falling. I desperately tried to copy his actions, feeling panic crushing my senses.

In one motion, I freed the feeling of gravity pulling you down, letting myself be ejected from it, feeling the new sensation flex and support me, tightening as I soared up, up, up and away from the mountain, gliding past it. My relief was so profound that I almost fainted again but there was a hand at my shoulder and I shakily looked up at Faolan. He grinned down at me reassuringly and I glared at him, furious that he had very nearly let me die.

'HOW DARE YOU?!' I said to him, shouting over the wind. He had the nerve to grin and shrug.

I commanded my power to bring me closer to him, and felt his as it spread a little, speeding him up. The sensation was strange, like someone touching your arm if you have goosebumps, but they only touch the raised hair, and not the skin itself. You can feel it, but at the same time you can't. I shuddered against the uncomfortable feeling, and concentrated hard to move a few feet beside him. He banked and swerved towards me, grabbing my arm. He stopped flying downwards and hovered in midair, holding me with him. I winced as my arm was nearly yanked out of its socket, he holding my wrist to make sure I didn't fall. I focused, trying to force the wind at my heels to bring me to the same position as him, as I struggled to get into a more comfortable position – and ended up failing miserably.

The wind had died down since we weren't flying downwards, and I looked at Faol's flushed features clearly for the first time as we hovered a thousand feet above the ground.

'Are you all right?' he asked, and I gaped at his audacity. Without leaving me time to answer, he carried on, half holding me up. 'We need to land soon down at a clearing, but landing is one of the more difficult parts of flying – using gravity and the wind to your advantage, so you might not get it right, which is why you need to listen carefully. When you reach about twenty feet above the ground, let the wind carry you up slightly. As you're a beginner, you must drop a bit, and then carry yourself upwards in a hover – like you're moving two steps forward, and then one back, all the way until you reach the ground. I'll be helping you, and I'll show you how I do it in a minute. Are you ready?'

I nodded, a bit breathless, and he flashed me a smile. 'By the way, I like the hue of your arrows – it is very complimentary to the shade of your eyes.' I stared at him in surprise at the compliment, and he stopped speaking.

I almost gave him a small smile, but then remembered that I was meant to be terrified of this boy who had done so many terrible things to me. Somehow, though, I couldn't quite bring myself to be angry at this moment, and so I simply started flying downwards, stooping and flipping into the air once I thought I would be able to keep myself in a glide. A joyous whoop worked its way out of my throat as I did so and Faolan laughed brightly. I felt that I could be quite good at flying – just as soon as I got over my remaining fear of landing and takeoff.

The air rushed past, probing and curious as I let myself freefall for the ground. I snapped my power out, sliding smoothly through the air, using the wind to help speed me along. However, I could feel the remaining strength in my power come close to giving out as I tried to access more of it. I would have to practise using it. I was exhausted after exercising this... ability so much when I had never used it a day in my life. I approached the ground rapidly, barely controlling gravity, to save my energy for landing.

Huge trees encompassed the frosty grass, and I marvelled in wonder as I approached. Faol swept in front of me and approached the ground. He banked, slowing. Merely feet from the ground, he glided smoothly onto the grass and came to a perfect standstill next to the other sentries and Angus, who had already landed. I gritted my teeth, steeling my nerves. How did he manage to do it so perfectly?

Continuing to fly down, I tried to bank correctly, but instead a current of air flipped me, and I quickly ended up falling, back facing the ground. Trying to flip myself around, I tucked my arms in and twisted, but only succeeded in turning myself slightly, gravity now taking over once more.

Remembering what Faol had said about flying upwards, I sent a strong wind pushing me upwards with the remaining strength lingering there. I stopped falling quite as fast, but I couldn't stay in my position forever.

With everyone on the ground watching me, I slowly dropped a few feet, hovering after that with a single gust of air. I repeated this again, my body almost giving out once I had reached the final few feet above ground. From there, my newfound power vanished as quickly as a breeze dies down, and I fell the last little distance, landing on my feet.

I tried to stand, but the shock of what had just happened meant that I was unbalanced, and I toppled over. Strong arms caught me before I could fall onto my back and potentially crush one of my arrows, which were close to spilling onto the snow. I looked up to see Angus and Faol holding me, and I quickly managed to stand on my feet, signalling to them that they could let go. Immediately, they released me and I gazed up at the sky, towards the portal we had just fallen through. I shuddered as a memory of the pain of that place flickered through my body.

The portal itself was merely a tiny slash of darkness against the azure skies, and the rest of the men and I all turned to watch as, slowly, that speck of darkness grew smaller until it vanished completely.

I sighed, despair once again clouding my brain like a fog. How was I ever going to find Amber again? If Angus was to believed, we were at opposite ends of the solar system, which itself was on a different dimension than Earth. There was no possible way for me to go back.

The men were all watching as a lone tear slid down my cheek, and I furiously brushed it away as their faces turned sympathetic – even Faol's. I turned away from all of them and dropped to the ground, realising that I would probably never see any of my family again. Not my mother, who had snapped at me the last time I had seen her, and would probably be going insane with worry after a week and a half without us. Not Amber, who I had watched being taken off by a group of Firborn to an unknown fate. I desperately wished that I had been given the opportunity at least to say goodbye to them, because I had no idea if the portal would open again, if Amber would even leave Zio, and whether we could get back to Earth again. My shoulders slumped, the shining feathers of my arrows seeming to dull slightly. I supposed I would have to cooperate with these men now, since there was nowhere for me to run to, and I was on their home turf.

Slowly, I forced my aching muscles to stand, feet still buzzing slightly with the ecstasy of flying for the first time. My bleak expression was noticed by Faol, and he walked up to where I was standing, the others subtly turning away and talking among themselves. He gave me an apologetic look, but it didn't begin to cover the fact that he and his men were the reason that I was never going to see my family again. I glared at him, and he turned away, respectful enough to not push it. I stared at the sky, blinking back tears, small sobs coming in ragged gasps as I tried to compose myself.

Still staring at the sky, I noticed that the sun had only just risen, but we had jumped through the portal near to the time of sunset. I must have travelled for a longer time through the portal than I'd initially thought. When I was in there, I hadn't paid attention to the time, just to the pain that had seemed to shred my soul to bits.

I took a deep breath and slowly gathered my spirits. Turning, I took a step in the direction of the men, knowing that from now on my feet would not walk the path I would have chosen for myself, but the path already laid out for me, covered in traps and snares and creatures of my worst nightmares.

.12.

Amber

We awoke at dawn, Helmon coming to wake me in the tiny tent I had been given for the night. He peered in through sleep-blurred eyes, and I could see the profile of his face outlined in the grey light lined with gold.

Silently, I got up and crept to him, moving out of the tent. We stood outside on the dewy grass while the other sentries quickly packed up my tent. I offered to help them, but they shook their heads kindly and continued with what they were doing. Helmon talked to me quietly about the portal, and how we were going to travel through it, while the other men worked. I nodded, not fully understanding, but reassured that I would probably understand when I saw the portal for myself. We set off soon after, the sun gilding our small oasis in golden light that shimmered along the tree boughs.

In the air, I was, to my extreme displeasure, forced to be carried by Neil. He had looked no happier than I at the choice but couldn't complain. Helmon was the man in charge – Neil was simply his second-in-command and so had to obey

Helmon's orders. Besides, if he had complained, Helmon would have asked him why he disliked me so thoroughly. The answer seemed to be a secret that even I didn't know, and one that would probably never be revealed.

The air was stiflingly hot, even as we flew higher into the crystal-clear sky. The trees shrank away, a stray bird darting between them. I watched it until the trees themselves were mere specks in the distance and then I sighed and focused on the journey in front of me.

As we travelled, I wondered about how Kai was doing, and where she was. I had always thought her to be someone suited for the winter environment; she seemed to love freezing weather, and all of her favourite animals lived in winter climates. When we were small, I'd be curled up by the fire, reading on a cold winter's night. She would be out there in the snow by herself, simply enjoying the beauty of the scene, playing in the snow alone.

I also thought about whether we might have found each other if only I had tried to escape. If she was alone, wandering the wilderness by herself, looking for me… I shuddered at the thought. If I *had* escaped, would we now be looking for a way home from Etrais together? I felt bad, my thoughts gnawing away at my mind.

Focusing on something else, I thought about the chilling story that Helmon had told me. The death-god, Sardaron… was he part of the reason I was here? If there was a curse of some sort, why were girls from Earth taken if that planet wasn't involved in this curse?

My thoughts stopped abruptly as Neil, holding me in his arms, pinched my forearm. I swung my head up to him, mouth open as if to say *"hey!"* He merely looked down at me, bored and spoiling for a fight.

I obliged him, and hissed, 'Do *not* pinch me!'

Ignoring me with only a smirk forming along his lips, he continued on flying forwards, hands uncomfortable on the backs of my knees and my arms and back. I clenched my fists, about to lose it. Neil was really getting on my nerves, with his snide comments and rude attitude towards me. The reason for his dislike was impossible to guess – I hadn't done anything to him and had barely spoken to him. If the reason for his dislike was that he didn't like me for who I was, then he had every right to think that, even though he had so little to judge me on. I rolled my eyes, frustrated beyond belief. His aggravating personality grated on me as the hours passed – the expectant silence that he exuded and the small smile he kept in place when he remembered to make it. Like he purposefully wanted to irritate me.

Even while I was thinking about him, I was conscious of the fact that even though we were well into the afternoon, we didn't seem to be near anything of importance. The withering shrubs were few and far between and I had no idea how Helmon and the sentries knew their way around at all. The area that we were passing through now seemed exactly the same as the one before and I glanced down at it, bored by looking at the same landscape for so long.

A shout from behind us made Neil slow and we turned as

Helmon, carried by the other three sentries, approached.

'We really need to hurry if we're going to reach the portal on time – it opens in three hours and we won't be there until twenty minutes after that! This is one of the most important jobs of our lives so, please, let's fly there at full speed.' Everyone nodded, including me and we shot away once more, the breathing of the men faster and more urgent than it had been before.

I breathed hard too as I realised that my suspicions had been confirmed about us being late for the portal. I wondered if it had ever happened before, and what happened if it did. I knew that if you stayed here for too long, you would eventually die due to the lack of breathable air. I cringed, shuddering even to think of it.

Neil had by now placed a look of worry along the lines of his face, and I was relieved that at last he wouldn't be irritating me any more.

Over the course of the next two hours small, scudding clouds formed along the edges of the sky and I looked at them in wonder, amazed that clouds would even form in a desert. We didn't stop to admire them, however, and they were quickly far behind us.

Once, I had looked down and thought I saw a beige animal, the sandy colour exactly the same as the one which had attacked me. I cringed in Neil's arms and looked away.

The next time I looked at the ground, it was gone, and I sighed in relief. Even looking at it had made me so anxious that my hands had been shaking violently. Neil had smirked once again and I had ground my teeth in annoyance afterwards.

I spent the rest of the afternoon wondering where the portal was, and worrying that we wouldn't get there on time. By the beginning of the evening, my heart had begun to pound with fear, and the faces of the men around me echoed my heartbeat. Helmon called from behind,

'Stop! We're here!'

'Are you sure?' Neil asked Helmon from where we had twisted to face him. 'It doesn't look like where we came from when we arrived.'

'Of course I'm sure!' Helmon snapped, and Neil shrank back. I desperately wanted just to go and travel through it, and to stop wasting time talking here.

Neil nodded at Helmon, but instead of flying down to the ground where I'd assumed we would go, we started flying upwards. I clenched on tightly to my shirt in fear as we rose until the ground was far beneath us. The sky seemed like an endless blue abyss, and I was confused, wondering where, exactly, the portal was.

Once we were so high up I could barely see the tops of the bushes, we stopped flying upwards and shot a few feet forwards, to where I finally saw it.

The portal was merely a tear in the sky, a small hole that looked as if it had been abruptly carved by a sword whose owner had been in a hurry to create it, and I gaped as the swirling darkness beyond that seemed to beckon. We hurtled for it, and I saw with dismay that it was closing; the hole was slowly becoming smaller and smaller. I desperately gasped as Helmon and two of the sentries came forwards, the hole growing smaller with each movement they made. The third sentry came towards me and Neil, but my attention was too focused on Helmon to notice.

The three men put their hands into the rapidly vanishing hole and quickly disappeared, Helmon sparing a quick glance at me over his shoulder before vanishing in a gleam of golden light. We shot forwards, and I grabbed tightly onto Neil as the hole became as small as a medal without the string attached. The sentry beside us widened his eyes, keeping beside us as we leapt forwards. I saw the hole shrink again, the darkness fading as it prepared to close.

I lunged out of Neil's arms, desperately trying to reach the portal as it began to close completely. As I leapt, I twisted so that my hand was in the portal, but I was facing Neil and the sentry. In a moment of blind panic, I grabbed a hold of Neil's fingers, grasping them tightly as we vanished into a well of dark despair and pain, the portal closing shut behind us.

...

I reached the other end of the portal, back burning, skin contorting with pain, but was surprised at what I found at the other end. Instead of being thousands of feet up in the air like I had been in Etrais, I was only a foot away from the ground. I fell through the portal hard, still clinging onto Neil's fingers as I tumbled into Zio for the first time.

Looking up in awe, my first impression of the place was that it was like one massive volcano that twisted and turned on itself like the many curling rivers of lava that flowed down the side of it. I gaped, transfixed by the image of this colossal force that seemed to pulse with life and light. Woven into the craggy sides of the volcano were crevices and shelves that looked like footpaths for people to follow.

Away to the east was a mountainous range of volcanoes that bubbled and gurgled violently and I saw deep ravines with lava flowing at the bottom instead of water. Further away, I thought that I could just about make out trees and underbrush where the spitting lava had ended and green things had started to grow.

My body seemed instinctively to turn towards the main volcano, as though my heart knew that the mountainous path towards it was the trail that my footsteps were meant to follow. As if, even though my mind still reminisced over the home I had left behind, it knew that this place was truly where I was meant to be.

So absorbed was I at staring at this wondrous place that I didn't notice the sound of someone crying until they let out a keening wail. My ears pricked, and I twisted, dread already forming a knot in my ever- tightening stomach.

One of the sentries was kneeling, back curved and shaking, staring desperately at thin air, where the portal had vanished. Sobs choked out of his throat and salty tears carved a path down his face, sliding down the column of his throat as he looked up. I didn't entirely grasp the situation until I had counted the number of people standing with me, not including myself.

Four.

The number clanged through me, making me start shaking

my head slowly as the realisation dawned on me. The other sentry, Helmon, and Neil were all pale-faced and drawn, their bodies seeming listless and haggard.

I searched desperately for that fifth head, for that man who had dropped behind Neil and me to make sure that we made it safely through the portal. I searched, and could not find him.

I dropped to my knees, Helmon casting a look at me, and recalled those last moments when I had grasped Neil's fingers when I could have grasped the sentry's. My head was pounding, and I thought that this had to be a mistake, we couldn't have – *I* couldn't have – left someone to live out their final few days alone, before lack of sufficient air killed them.

'No, no, *no*,' I moaned, tears already pricking in my eyes. That sentry… whose name I didn't even know. Who had selflessly sacrificed himself to make sure that I made it across safely. The image of my fingers reaching towards Neil's played over and over in my head while I heard a quiet whispering kind of sob coming from the mourning sentry.

I didn't know what to do with my hands, my arms, so I crossed them firmly across my chest, hugging myself as I rocked back and forth on my heels.

I should have saved him.

The thought stayed with me, like a dark wind, persistent and unwanted. I should have saved him – should have grabbed his hand too as I twisted. I had thought that he was reaching to put his hand through the portal, about to travel through with us.

I sat, my knees too weak to support me, and felt a strange weight drag me back so that I toppled over, head hitting the hard ground beneath me.

Struggling, I pulled myself upwards, still dull with the weight of what I'd done to that sentry. I looked over my shoulder, surprised to find that my guilt overcame my fear, and I stared with no emotion at what I saw hugging my shoulders.

The quiver of arrows were the same hue as the boiling lava behind me, the feathers crimson and sparkling in the light. My eyes stared, but my mind didn't process it. I didn't care that I had somehow been given these for some strange purpose; didn't care that this place was everything I'd ever dreamed a home could be.

All I felt was the savage tear of guilt in my stomach, the stain it drew on my soul.

Silent tears coursed down my face, lining a path through the grime coating me. The sentry was merely a nameless, faceless man who I didn't know, who hadn't even tried to grab my hand before placing himself in his own grave.

A muffled cough from behind me had me turning to face Helmon, who was standing behind me, having walked the few feet from where he had been dropped on the ground with the two sentries. His face showed nothing but sorrow and I echoed it as I stood, looking at him squarely in the face. I took a deep breath, preparing myself.

'Amber.'

I looked up in surprise from where I had been staring at the floor. Helmon's face had shifted from sorrow to concern, and his eyes flickered as he looked at me.

'Whatever you may be thinking and were about to say, I can

promise you that whatever happened back there, you were *not* the reason for this.'

I desperately wished that what he had said was the case, but I knew that it was my fault.

'Helmon – you don't know what happened! I grabbed Neil instead of the sentry at the last moment, and now he's as good as *dead*!' my eyes sparked with fresh tears at the thought.

'But Amber, what were you going to do? If you had grabbed the sentry instead, then it would be Neil who would be facing that fate.'

I glanced over to where Neil was, for once, being supportive – he patted the grieving sentry's back consolingly, and seemed to be doing so sincerely.

Bile rose in my throat as I thought about all the times when Neil had ignored me or been rude to me.

'Don't you see?' I asked Helmon. '*Neil* is the one who should have been left behind. Him, with his snide comments and rude behaviour!' I stopped speaking when I saw the slow-forming expression on Helmon's face.

Disgust.

I was shocked – Helmon had only ever been polite and friendly to me.

'You don't get it, do you?' Helmon said, and his tone pierced a shard of hurt through my heart. 'Even if Neil was that way towards you, it's probably because he's used to having me as his best friend, and on the journey here I was talking to *you*. Just because someone doesn't like you doesn't mean that they're a bad person – doesn't mean that they should be subject to someone else's suffering. If someone doesn't like you, then you accept it – don't take offence that not everyone in the world adores you!'

Anger was becoming a prominent feature in his face, and I reflected on just how quickly our conversation had turned for the worse.

He was right, though. Even if I thought that there was nothing for Neil to hate in me, he probably just didn't like who I was – or was jealous that he no longer spent as much time with his best friend.

I took a step away from Helmon, and he gave me a hard stare before striding back to the others. I realised that with Helmon angry at me for saying the things I had, there was practically no one I could talk to. I was all alone and I looked once more to the magnificent volcano in the distance before walking slowly towards the sentry, who was crying.

'I am… so sorry,' I said softly to him, putting a placating hand on his shoulder gently. He was still facing towards the air where the portal had closed, and now he turned to face me. His eyes were red-rimmed and hollow, and the loathing in them washed over me like a wave.

'Do *not* touch me,' he hissed savagely, and I backed away, tears of frustration and hurt now eating at my eyes, trickling down my face. I rubbed at them angrily, creating red marks on my cheeks. Neil saw the drops on my cheeks, but said nothing, instead looking at me in the eyes for a few seconds almost sympathetically, before turning back to Helmon and the second sentry, who were huddled together, talking.

I decided that quite obviously, I wasn't wanted here. Everyone seemed to hate me, so I began slowly making my way backwards, walking in the direction away from the volcano. Desperately, I wondered where I was going, what I was doing – and decided that I didn't care.

My arrows hung from the quiver slung on my back, and I tried to lift them up in an attempt to travel without them banging against my back.

As soon as I had taken a step in the direction I was heading, I heard someone call out to me from where they were standing.

'Amber!'

The voice came from Neil, who, as I turned, I saw facing me, he having stepped a few feet away from his comrades. 'Where are you going?' he asked, his voice unusually concerned.

I only looked at him for a moment before turning once more away from the volcano. Neil said nothing more, and I assumed that he'd given up when I started walking again.

I had only been moving my feet forwards for about a hundred feet when I heard footsteps behind me, approaching fast. I sighed and moved my feet faster, determined that no one should be able to see my tear-streaked face. I sniffed hard, hoping that whoever it was would give up and leave me alone.

The person came around to my left side, and I looked across to see Neil, walking calmly beside me. His face was serious, but there was no hostility on his face. None. Too shocked to form words, my body halted, and Neil paused with me.

'Amber,' he said, addressing me by my name, instead of "girl" or "her" like he had when talking about me to the others.

I looked at him in surprise and more than a little wariness. He sighed and ran his hand through his dark hair, seeming uncomfortable with what he was about to say. 'I have to… apologise for my behaviour on the way here.'

I stared at him, the dried tears on my face pulling at my cheeks. What was he doing? Why was he *apologising* when he clearly hated me? I decided that I was too confused, too upset, too *lonely* to care.

'It's fine. I forgive you. It's my fault anyway.' I said it dully, the pounding of my head throbbing with every breath.

'No. It's *not* fine.'

The blank expression on my face must have prompted him to say something to explain, because he said, 'Look, I was jealous of you. Of you, and your obvious connection with Helmon. You see, he's always been my best friend – through everything we went through. He was *always* there for me – always.' Neil's eyes had taken on a clouded look, and I knew that he was reminiscing over the past. 'When you arrived, Helmon was so distant that I thought I'd done something wrong. You and he were like this,' he said, crossing his index finger over his middle one in the sign many people make for good luck. His onyx eyes were wide and searching as he looked at me. 'I hated you for that. For being able effectively to remove my closest friend from my life in a matter of days. So I was spiteful. I was mean – and I apologise sincerely for all of it, Amber. All of it. And I was wondering – can we just start over?' He scanned my face for a second, gauging my reaction. 'Can you forgive me?' he asked tentatively.

After a minute, I gave him a small smile and nodded, eager to wipe the bad memories from both of our minds now that I knew the reason for his hostility. He, obviously relieved, let out a breath and smiled back, extending his hand for me to shake. I accepted it, feeling the warm, dry texture of his skin. He let go after a minute and gestured in the direction of the others, who had now turned, watching us.

'Shall we?'

I nodded, but inwards, my stomach was sinking as I contemplated the fact that almost everyone in Helmon's group hated me. Exhaling a breath I didn't know I was holding, I started walking back in the direction of the others, my footsteps unsure and faltering.

Neil linked his arm with mine and pulled me encouragingly forwards, looking back at me. I figured that seeing what they had to say to me was worth knowing – it would be good to know exactly how much they, as individuals, despised me for what I had done.

While we were walking, I asked Neil, 'What was his name? The sentry's, I mean.'

Neil nodded, opening his mouth to answer. 'Thark.'

I nodded my thanks and continued on, careful not to let myself start crying again.

Trudging along with my head held down, I didn't realise that we had arrived back by the vanished portal until the tips of Helmon's boots appeared at the top of my vision. I looked up nervously, afraid to face the expressions of the men.

To my surprise, only one man looked like he hated me, and

that was not so much *hate* as it was thorough dislike. The sentry who wore *that* expression was the one who had uncontrollably started weeping at the loss of his comrade. The other, facing the first sentry, wore a concerned expression towards his friend. I looked at Helmon last, afraid to see what his was going to be. When I finally looked, I didn't see hate there at all. His brown eyes were only full of distress as he looked into my face. My relief that he didn't despise me for what I had said and done was staggering. I felt my knees tremble as he approached, Neil coming around from my side to make our conversation a circle.

'Amber, are you all right?' Helmon asked. I stared at him, surprised that he could have forgiven me for what I said so easily. He seemed to have heard my thoughts, and explained. 'Even though I don't agree with you about what we were talking about, it doesn't mean that we can't get along otherwise. Besides, you seemed to have sorted it out.'

I nodded, desperately trying to put it behind us. 'I'm fine, thanks. I was wondering if that volcano is where we're heading?'

It was Neil who answered, and I turned slightly to face him better.

'The volcano is, yes, where we are going soon. First, however, we must wait for our leader to arrive – Yina, the oldest and wisest of the Elders.' I felt a spark of interest at the name, the letter Helmon showed me snagging in my memory. Neil spoke the name with reverence. 'She is my mother,' he said, and I looked at him in utter confusion. To my surprise, he began to laugh at my expression, and Helmon chuckled as he, too, beheld my bewildered face.

'How can she possibly be your mother? Surely she's too old, since I remember you said that she came here centuries ago at some point, and you're so young…' I trailed off.

Neil and Helmon finished their cackling and looked at me seriously.

'There is one important detail that I have been directly ordered not to tell you. Yina herself will explain our story, and why we captured you in a minute,' Helmon said.

Head whirling, I sat on the dusty ground, feeling the grains swirl beneath my fingers in the slight breeze.

I didn't know how long I sat there, staring at the ground. So much had happened in such a short space of time that it was impossible for my brain to keep up. I didn't pay attention to Neil or Helmon, who were both talking quietly, casting the occasional worried glance in my direction.

I was shaken back to reality by a joyful cry that echoed through the land. I twisted to see Neil staring off into the distance, an expression of such ecstasy on his face that I looked to where he was gazing.

A ridge on the edge of the land we were standing on dropped away into a valley, which then rose back up towards the volcano in the distance. It was over this ridge that I saw three figures emerge, arms flailing slightly as they climbed upwards. Why they didn't just fly, I had no idea. Unless they couldn't – like I couldn't. Or could I?

One was old, back hunched, withered face gleaming with light and joy as she spotted Neil. Yina, I thought, watching the old woman emerge. The two other figures followed behind her, their lithe bodies easily tracing her footsteps. One was a middle-aged-looking woman with long brown hair and a tanned complexion, the arrows on her back a chocolatey colour with red tinges. Her face looked familiar, and I realised that she reminded me of Thark. Scared, I thought that she must be some relative of his.

The other was dark-skinned, her hazelnut eyes stark against her skin as she approached. She was young, only a little older than me and so beautiful that I simply stared at her as she came closer, small body moving with the dexterity of a mountain cat. The arrows on her back, I saw as she came closer, were exactly the same shade as mine, the lava colour gleaming as she strode forwards.

The crone crested the ridge, and I saw her walk steadily forwards, gaze fixed determinedly on Neil. Looking back, I saw Neil rush forwards in a burst of colour and happiness. I watched him sprint, legs pounding as he raced to reach her.

They came closer and closer, until I saw Neil fling his arms around her, holding on tight. The old woman patted his back, laughing. Her eyes twinkled with happiness, and I suddenly wished that I had a bond like that with someone.

One of the sentries ran forwards to greet the middle-aged woman, and I saw him kiss her on the lips, whispering something into her ear. They must be husband and wife, I thought, noting the protective stance of him around her. I looked away, thinking that their relationship was something private, and that I shouldn't be watching.

Helmon and the remaining sentry walked forwards with

me, the young woman's face lighting up as she spotted Helmon. She jogged forwards, smile stretching as she did so. Helmon walked faster, a broad grin stretching across his face as they reached each other. I felt a strange flutter of disappointment in my stomach as I saw Helmon laugh and embrace the girl happily. She looked just as pleased to see him, I noticed, a sour feeling in my stomach. I continued walking however, the remaining sentry next to me.

The hazel-eyed girl flicked her gaze over to where we were awkwardly standing, some space away. Her eyes met mine and I saw excitement flicker there. She pushed herself away from Helmon, who turned to watch as she walked towards me slowly. As she came closer, I felt a tremor of a distant power echo through the ground, curling around my bones.

Reaching her, I got a good look at her stunning features as she held out a hand for me to shake, greeting me while doing so. She had incredible eyes, I thought, watching them flicker over me, wondering if I was going to accept her hand. Her high cheekbones and braided hair only added to her beauty. I stared at her nervously before accepting her hand, feeling the calloused skin against mine. She smiled at me, revealing her slightly crooked teeth against her skin.

'Hello,' she said, her deep voice rich in sound. 'I'm Nuru – and this is Yina, and Emeze. We are the Elders. What is your name?'

'Amber,' I said, my voice sounding high and nasal compared to hers. She nodded as I glanced over her shoulder towards the others.

The woman called Emeze was standing alone, back

hunched, hands covering her face. Her hair twisted and turned in a swirl about her face and I thought I could hear choked sobs coming – muffled though they were – through the hands covering her face.

Neil, Helmon, and Yina were gathered together, the two other sentries talking quietly to each other. I saw them all turn to face Emeze, Helmon opening his mouth to say something. Yina placed her finger on his mouth, effectively telling him to be quiet. He obeyed. And shut his mouth, instead looking pityingly over at the woman.

'Where is my son?' Emeze croaked out, voice ragged. We all stared at her, saying nothing. I was too afraid even to move, worried that she would immediately blame her loss on me. '*Where is my son*?' she yelled fiercely, and several among us jumped. Her eyes were wild, the green of them shining with tears.

Yina came forwards, stepping around Neil to approach the woman. She put a hand on her shoulder, murmuring gently in her ear. The woman flinched and threw Yina's hand off her, utter rage coating her expression. Yina seemed unfazed however, and said something else softly before coming back around Emeze to rejoin Neil.

I simply stared as Emeze dropped to the ground, coating her knees in dust and grit. Her husband – who had grieved the most for Thark – once again started crying, coming forward to kneel beside Emeze. I had had no idea that they were a family while we were travelling, and now I felt guilt once again start to tear on my conscience.

Looking out from under her lashes, Emeze saw her husband join her once more and suddenly hugged him fiercely, taking him by surprise. His torrent of tears, however, only increased, and I had no idea how long we all stood there sadly, watching them cry before the woman once more got to her feet. She appeared to be trying to compose herself, the sentry holding her upright as she swayed. Hiccupping through her tears, her nose a snotty mess, I watched her take in a deep breath, sucking the fresh air around us into her lungs. A lone tear sliding down her cheek was quickly wiped away before any others could encroach.

Yina said nothing, motioning for me to come closer to her haggard form. I walked from where I was standing next to Nuru to the old woman, watching her observe me. Emeze and her husband stepped away from all of us, starting to talk quietly together in distraught tones, their shoulders still stooped with the burden of their discovery. Neil, Helmon, the final sentry and Nuru all gathered together to catch up and discuss what was going to happen next.

Nervously, I walked up to Yina, wondering if *finally*, I was going to get the answers to why I was here.

She walked slowly towards me on stiff limbs, and I quickly moved towards her too, reaching her side in seconds. We walked together a distance away from the others, Yina gripping my wrist to lead me. Surprised at her strong grip, I let myself be tugged along until we came to rest near to a large boulder, the smooth texture of it at odds with the rough, rocky land around us.

The lady's piercing eyes judged me, looking from head to

toe at my ragged clothes and defeated stance – the stance of someone burdened with the consequences of her actions.

She tilted her chin upwards, her gaze becoming softer as she took in the tired gleam of frustration and longing I was sure adorned my face.

'You want to know, don't you? You need to know – or you will quite literally burst with confusion,' she told me almost laughingly (despite the grim situation around us), and I nodded, eager for her to continue. 'Just like myself.' I stared then, not quite sure what she was telling me. She sighed, a sound of remembrance, and a faint smile ghosted across her paper white skin, stretching her lips. 'That was certainly a very, very long time ago. So long that I almost can't remember the events that happened after it. But I could never forget what the oldest of the Elders back then told me – it seems like an eon ago. No, you would never forget something like that.' Her gaze rested on me again briefly from where she had been staring into the distance, almost as if she could see her younger self, standing on the rocky ground a mere wingspan away.

'What… what did she tell you?' I whispered, the desperation simply to *know* so great that I almost leaned towards the woman as I spoke. Her gaze became saddened then, and emotions flickered in her grey-blue eyes, lined with wrinkles.

'You see, we have something in common. You, Emeze, Nuru and I are all women. Some of the few we have.' I nodded as she spoke, impatient for her to get to the point. She saw my look and smiled wryly. 'You'd better get comfortable, if I am going to explain everything now,' she said, motioning for me to sit with her, our backs resting on the warm rock behind us.

Near where we had landed, I watched as the men and women who seemed to be so interconnected with each other looked in unison over at us, their clothes rippling in the wind. They looked and turned away, seeming to know that something important was going on. I looked across at Yina, who was watching them with a protective look on her face, like a mother hen guarding her chicks. She twisted her head to mine, seeming to sense that I was looking at her and I twisted my head away quickly.

'First of all, I want to know what these arrows on my back are for,' I said to her, drawing her attention back to me.

'Think of them like… identification. Without them, the entrance to the volcano – where we are going – would not let you in. Every time you enter from the portals, you have to sacrifice a feather to the wall of the entrance. The colour of your feathers reflects you. We brought our arrows in case they –' she pointed to Neil, Helmon and the others ' – forgot theirs. Someone else can give up some of theirs to let you in.'

'What happens when you run out of arrows?'

'You won't – they are always replenished magically.' Magically? What was she talking about?

'So… can you tell me why I was taken?'

'Are you sure you want to know?' she asked me softly, and I looked at her for a few seconds, weighing her tone.

'Yes,' I replied, my voice coming out weak, not the confident sound I thought it would be. 'I'm sure.'

She nodded, seeming to settle, preparing to tell her story.

'If that is so, then I must start at the beginning, before even I was born. I must start with the story of Sardaron, our Creator.' My ears pricked at that, hearing the name Helmon had told me was forbidden to be spoken.

'Helmon told me about it – I thought you couldn't say his name?' I asked, shocked that the woman would do so in such a careless manner. Yina shook her head.

'We are allowed to say it without it supposedly bringing bad fortune to ourselves – women are, that is, because we were chosen by the Creator to come here.' I listened raptly, not quite believing what I was hearing but willing to let her finish anyway.

'Sardaron is the most feared name on both Nzar and Zio,' she said. 'And the creature that owns it is certainly worthy of its reputation. You see, before the current Creator, it was said that we had a god who blessed our lands, and all the people within. He had something called the Quill, which had the power to create, making animals, people and everything in between. This god was benevolent and our people rejoiced that he chose to settle at the heart of Etrais, setting up his home in the heart of where we lived.'

I frowned at that, confused. 'But the people don't live on Etrais – they could never survive there,' I said wondering if what Yina was telling me was true.

'Indeed. You are right – they no longer live in harmony on Etrais – but once they did.

'Anyway, the people themselves often went to visit this god, presenting gifts, which he would then turn into happiness by whatever power he possessed. The days of joy continued, the people content.

'But around a thousand years ago, a dark being arrived in Etrais. It was said that this being was another god, one emanating darkness instead of light. This god arrived at the heart of Etrais, right into the lair of our much-beloved god.

'That day, the greatest battle Etrais has ever seen took place. The dark god invaded our lands, and the people said that in that moment, the very grounds themselves throbbed with the power of the two entities. But battle is battle, neither ceasing to fight until one has surrendered, or been beaten.

'The day that darkness overtook our lands, the dark god plunging a tendril of terror into the heart of happiness, fierce shadows forming for the first time in millennia, all of the women fell to the ground, screaming. The tales told around campfires suggest that the women went stark-raving mad, plunging off cliffs, holding themselves underwater, effectively wiping their side of the population out before anyone could stop them. They took their children with them – but only the girls. Only women. That day is known as one of the grimmest in the history of our planets.'

I thought back to the tapestry, to the picture embroidered on it.

'To ensure that happiness never again ruled freely and that terror would plague us for our whole existence, the dark god, Sardaron, cast a curse over the land of Etrais. The two people, who had before lived together, found themselves brimming with hate when they so much as looked at their next-door neighbour. They had this urge, you see, to kill those despised people – and they had no idea why.

'Many were killed in those first few days of chaos, and nobody seemed able to work out what was going on. The air itself seemed repulsive, toxic even. After a few days, the remaining people found themselves fainting, keeling over when they least expected it. The hate of the other side intensified, and the two peoples started to split, moving away from each other.

'Seven days after chaos had taken control, the people were, for once, given something. Gifts. They were given them by the new Creator, who seemed to be testing out his Quill. These gifts ensured that the two peoples could never live together, for they are as opposed as day and night. They were the gifts of snow, ice and wind to one side of the people. The other side were given fire. Fire, and heat and light.

The people found themselves with these new gifts, and more. They had a strange power – which you now have – given to ensure that they could fly distances greater than any have flown before.

'The next day, the air became so unbearable to breathe that some started to suffocate. That was the day that the penultimate part of the curse was carried out. The two people were violently shoved, pushed through two holes in Etrais. These holes transported them to new dimensions – Nzar and Zio. The two peoples, who had given their races names by that point, were utterly confused as to why this was all happening. Confused, until the prophecy arrived.

'It arrived by animal. An eagle gave it to the Firborn, and a wolf gave it to the Falcords.

'The prophecy – more like a curse – demanded sacrifice. We are forced to fight a war with no cause and no escape. A war that leaves no victors, and no survivors; one which breeds hatred where love should spark. It was an order etched into stone by the death god, forged when Sardaron took control of our lands.

The prophecy stated that blood must be spilled. It had to be spilled, because if it wasn't, then this dark god that had entered our world would simply cease to be. He needs blood – rather, he needs death because it fuels his existence.

'Anyway, the prophecy was created to take place every century. It declared that from then on, the two people could not live their separate lives. No, war had to be fought between the Falcords and the Firborn every hundred years. However, the prophecy itself had no power over us but the Quill did. And so it was the Quill that Sardaron used to force us to fight each other,' Yina said bitterly, face etched in resentment. 'The Quill would bring supplies to the winner of the wars (which we named Meridian). Since the land wasn't as hospitable to animal life as Etrais had been, natural resources were limited. Living off the land was only just possible, the people merely scraping by – if they did so. But supplies meant food, weapons and other new equipment – clothes, shoes and so on. We needed the reward – we would practically die of starvation if we didn't have them.

'Whoever won that year's war would receive the supplies – supplies which were attained at a steep price. The war would take place on Etrais, the battles lasting a day or so, continuing for almost two weeks. We were transported there by magic, the portals opening to summon us together.

'The price of the supplies would be the death of our loved ones – because they fought each other, they were killed by the opposing side. The battles would continue until the two weeks were over, when we would return to our planets, many of us never returning at all. Since we didn't know the outcome of the war ourselves, we had to wait upon Sardaron to see if we were going to receive supplies. There is nothing more crushing than to see a lone eagle soaring towards you, no sack carried between its claws. It was able to carry the supplies because they could all fit inside the bag – a magic that Sardaron willed into being by the Quill's power.'

The old woman stopped speaking, turning to look at me from where she had been gazing – at Neil – while she spoke.

I was horrified. If all of this was true, what scars would it leave in a man's mind? However, a bigger question was probing at the surface of my brain, demanding to be asked.

'Where do I fit into all of this? How are you here, if all of the women killed themselves and their children?'

'The women didn't kill themselves – Sardaron killed them,' Yina said fiercely. I knew her anger wasn't directed at me, but at the source of the death of these people.

'But you still haven't answered my question,' I said. Yina nodded slowly, resuming her faraway look as she started speaking again.

'Women were needed. Since everyone was dying in the

wars, there were very few people left by the time the next set of battles rolled around; it was purely the survival of the fittest, the fittest being those with the strongest powers, which they had learned to wield like a weapon.

So two girls were chosen from Earth – ones who had no past dragging them down, who wouldn't miss their old life. Girls like you and me. I assume that you found a portal?' I nodded. 'It opened when it sensed your presence. And it led you here for a reason.'

Yina took a deep breath, and I saw her try to steel herself for what she was going to tell me. I sucked in a breath too, feeling a wave of anxiety wash through my stomach, tensing my muscles.

'The curse couldn't be carried out by just the Firborn and the Falcords – if it was, there would be no end to the war. The powers of the two peoples are roughly equal, so they could, quite literally, keep fighting forever, until they all died out – from suffocation or murder. And if they all did, then who would provide Sardaron with the deaths he needed to survive in the future? Others were needed to settle the score, otherwise when the two weeks of fighting were over, most would be dead, and Sardaron wouldn't know who to send the supplies to and wouldn't have deaths to supply himself in coming wars.

'So Sardaron looked, with his dark powers, over Earth. He chose two girls – girls so that the line of people could continue – and made sure that they didn't have many connections to their families. The reason for this was because if they weren't very close, they would choose… they would choose to accept the curse as it was, and represent each side in battle.'

I stared at her, horrified. What was she saying? That I would have to go to war, and against my own *sister*? From the way she looked at me almost fearfully, waiting for my reaction, I could tell that she knew I was going to disagree.

'No.' I said the word flatly, anger starting to take over from my shock. 'I won't represent the Firborn in battle – who do you think I am, that I would go head-to-head with my own sister?'

Yina seemed to deliberate, thinking of her arguments.

'Should I tell you why I decided to do it?' she asked me. I opened my mouth to snap out that *no*, I did not want to know why she did it, but she swept on and I realised that she hadn't been waiting for a reply. 'When I first arrived, all those years ago, and I was told the story of Sardaron and the curse, I had the exact same reaction as you. I didn't understand why people would ever think I'd willingly fight a war for a people I barely knew and certainly not against my sister. But what I didn't know then, and what I am telling you now, is that if I chose not to fight, people's suffering would be longer and more unending than if I chose to go ahead with it. Each side suffers, but none more so than yourself, knowing that maybe you could have been the one to end the suffering sooner, to provide your people with warm food, a shelter. Do you not want that?'

'No – you can't do that, twist my words so that it seems as though I'm the one in the wrong! The only way you could force me to do that would be to tie me to a post and drag me there, into the battle with you!'

'Please – I am begging you, please just consider it. Consider your choice and the consequences of it. Anyhow, I haven't even told you the full story...' she looked at me hopefully, but I could see a cloud of desperation over her head.

I sighed in frustration, but let her continue.

'There is a factor, which will affect you if you choose to stand for us and won't if you choose not to, which could be the deciding factor in your decision. The Ylvares are special in that although we look like normal humans in most ways, our bodies are different, improved; instead of aging like humans, our bodies take on a different process. Our lives are long, because we need as many people as possible to create more of us – by staying fertile and youthful – before the next war comes around. Our children age quickly, only taking about a decade to reach mental maturity, and another five years to have the physical body of an adult.

'Instead of aging like a human, we go through something different – a process in which our bodies stop changing, and we stay in the same skin forever. This means that old age does not affect us as much – and since our organs are not growing old and withered, we stay healthy. Our lifespan ranges from about six hundred years to a thousand, but some extremely powerful people exceed even that, living to almost one thousand five hundred years.'

I simply looked at her, mind blank with the enormity of what had just been said.

'How?' I whispered, numb with shock.

The old lady merely smiled faintly, looking down at the floor, not answering my question. 'But in each of the wars, something strange happened. The two girls were fighting each other, and one of them knocked the other over with a blast of her power. The fight was coming to an end, and amid the chaos no one actually saw what was happening – they only discovered it later. The girl who was struck down came back different. She was the victim of our curse – the eternal youth bestowed upon her when she arrived had vanished, leaving behind the mortal girl she had been before. This girl, having been defeated by the other Syth, found that after she had returned to her planet, she felt physically unchanged, as she was still young. She still had her powers.

'She wanted to return to Earth, but fell in love with a Ylvar and decide to stay here to be with him. She lived out the rest of her life – the same lifespan as humans – helping others recover from their injuries. She became a doctor to those who needed her – since she couldn't compete with them physically, she put her mind to work, learning about the ailments we, as a people, can suffer from, and the plants and animals that could help cure them. She died peacefully while sleeping at the end of her life, body within reaching distance of the herbs she had so carefully dried the previous day.'

'Who was the Syth fighting her?' I whispered, fearful of the answer, as if it might tear through my heart in its dreadful truth.

'My great-grandmother – a Falcord. She was a powerful Syth – everyone knew it.'

'And what about the mortal Syth? Who was she?'

'My great-grandmother's sister – one of the Firborn.'

I closed my eyes, unable to stop my hands from shaking.

This was exactly what I had feared. If even sisters could turn on each other, what hope was there for Kai and me?

'And what happens if Kai accepts this prophecy and I don't?'

'Our people will be annihilated – she will wipe out all of them.'

I sucked in a breath, the words she had spoken seeming to twist in the air around us, cruelly whipping at the shards left of my heart. This couldn't be happening. Kai would never turn on me, we were sisters! I tried to push down the nagging feeling that we were both stubborn, and would defend what we thought was right until the end. And if she thought that this war was something to fight for, then she would battle it out, no matter that I would be opposing her.

My head was so full of confusion and anxiety that I had to sit still, ignoring Yina for almost a full minute, to let my head adjust. She respectfully let me do so, but I had the feeling that she was impatient to say something else. What more could she possibly want to tell me?

I opened my eyes, squinting against the light, and scrutinised Yina. She seemed desperate, her form haggard and listless as she stared at me. Looking into her eyes, I realised that she had too much pride to beg me to join her cause, despite her obvious desperation for me to do so. She was stubborn, like myself. Just as I thought she would, she started to speak again, her words running over me like water over a pebble.

'The girls taken from Earth must all perform the Rite, a ceremony that is held to determine the fate of the new Syths. In it, you will make your decision. There is nothing I am hiding from you, so make your choice knowing both the benefits and the consequences. If you choose to refuse the prophecy… it was done once before, with catastrophic results. The girl remained with her eternal youth, but she was changed – her soul was taken from her. Some say that she was so heartless that it would have happened anyway, but others whisper that it was the dark god's doing. That as punishment for refusing his wishes, he sucked from her soul himself, leaving nothing but a shell behind.'

'So you're saying that if I do refuse, I will have my soul taken from me forever. In other words, your 'decision' is blackmail. My decision is to choose whether to save my sister and not fight her or save myself by defeating her.'

Yina withered under my fierce glare.

'I cannot pretend that what you say is not true. But remember, Amber, that we did not choose this way of life. It was not our decision, but Sardaron's.' With that, she stood, and I rose with her, realising as I did so that the others had vanished from where they had been discussing their plans. I looked around, glancing at the sky, and saw that they were flying some distance away, still chatting animatedly as they travelled further and further away from us.

'What are they doing?' I asked, my voice still shaky from what Yina had revealed.

'They're going back to that volcano over there…' Yina pointed to the massive volcano with winding paths of lava flowing down it 'and are going to tell everyone that we're here.' I glanced once towards Helmon, watching as he moved. My eyes darted over to Nuru, flying steadily next to him. Neil, flying on Helmon's other side, seemed more relaxed than I had ever seen him – as if being reunited with his grandmother had loosed a knot in his muscles.

I turned my head, turning to face Yina. The weight I had forgotten on my back dragged on my neck as I did so, reminding me of arrows behind me. In the chaos my brain had been going through, I had forgotten about keeping them safe, and some had spilled onto the ground. I picked them up quickly. Looking over my shoulder, I saw the crimson of the feathers on the arrows fluttering slightly in the wind.

'What are we going to do, then?' I asked, already knowing what the answer would be.

'We're going to fly into the volcano too – and greet the crowds waiting for us. Then I'll show you to your room, where you'll have two days to decide whether you want to accept the Prophecy or not. The Rite is on the third day, held at dawn.'

I stared at her in disbelief.

'How am I supposed to *fly* to the volcano?' I asked, incredulous that she would think such a thing possible.

Yina looked me over speculatively, and I tried to exercise my new power – of defying gravity – by myself. I rose slightly off the ground, gravity loosening only slightly around me. I gritted my teeth harder, pushing the weak power until it gave in, lifting me off my feet and into the sky. I was doing it! Looking behind me, I stared once more at the arrows on my back, scared that they would fall off. The glossiness of the feathers took my breath away, and I stared at them a second longer before looking back at Yina, who was watching approvingly. Sweat slid down my brow as I held my body up for a minute more, trying to exercise the power I had, gauging whether I could fly for long enough to reach the volcano. At long last, I couldn't hold myself up any more, and I flopped down to the ground, landing crookedly. I grunted, arms flailing as I regained my balance.

'Try lifting yourself up again,' Yina ordered, and I did so, seething with the effort of doing it again. 'Now rise – like this,' she told me, lifting her feet with ease and swooping upwards. The air from her quick movement whooshed past me, seeping into my clothes. I moved shakily upwards too, my movement much clumsier than hers. I glanced at the fast-retreating figures of Helmon, Neil and the others, worrying that I would have to walk all the way to the volcano from here.

Yina's voice brought me back to attention.

'Now repeat – faster. If you want, you can run up and then leap off the ground. Once you're in the air, let your power flow around you, directing it as much as you can until you're as high as I will be. From there, you'll be able to glide quite a distance without doing anything. I'll tell you what to do then.'

I anxiously lifted my body once more, wondering how her voice could sound so calm. She must have done this many times before, I thought, as she stood expectantly waiting for me to do as she had instructed. I gritted my teeth once more and thought about lifting myself up – with no effect. Remembering what she had told me about running and then leaping, I backed up and sprinted forwards again, arrows tucked tightly behind me so that they wouldn't act like a parachute and slow me down. I moved forwards quickly and leapt off the ground when I thought I was moving fast enough. In a smooth movement, I pictured gravity falling away from me, my power lifting and supporting me, lifting myself higher. With a thrill, I realised that I was doing it! I was actually succeeding in moving upwards in the sky. Quickly looking down below me, I saw Yina jump into the air as smoothly as a cat despite her age, her power working to bring her to my height. She quickly overtook me, flying so high that I wondered how I was supposed to reach her.

My strength was next to nothing, but I managed to stay airborne a few more minutes in the warm breeze, until I was almost level with her.

My head had become foggy, the ground further away.

The scenery seemed to spin underneath me, and I felt a vague sense that I was falling, but didn't fully focus on it.

My muscles pulled so badly on my back and legs, from tensing them so tight, that the pain was the only thing I could focus on but even that sensation was slipping away as a strange sort of darkness emerged from inside my head.

I knew that I was falling – could end up broken on the rocks below – but somehow, with everything that I had done… I couldn't quite bring myself to care.

.13.

Kai

It was night, and we had only just arrived at the 'base camp' that Faol had told me about, supposedly at the heart of the ring of mountains. I was nervous about what I was about to encounter, and my heart still throbbed with the sadness of losing my family, possibly forever. We trudged on through the snow, the light slowly sinking behind the mountain in front of me. The camp that we had approached seemed devoid of life, despite its picturesque looks. I let out a breath, stunned at the beauty around me, despite my sorrowful feelings.

The camp was so well blended with the surroundings that I hardly saw it when I was flying above – it was nestled into the crack between the two tallest mountains. Down below, near the pine-covered forest floor, was the heart of the camp, which was where we were now. As we had approached earlier, I had seen a line of buildings snaking their way up the mountain, seemingly carved from the snow, pine and rock themselves. They got fewer and farther between as the mountain rose, with only the occasional cave tent jutting out from the side. I wondered why some people would bother to live so far away from everyone else

– it must be hard for them to survive out there.

As we got even closer to the small group of tents, I felt for the first time the atmosphere of the place. A few warriors moved about, striding in and out of a huge tent that must have been used for holding councils and other gatherings. Young boys with dark hair and piercing eyes tumbled past, their bodies haggard but faces light. I turned my head around me, taking in the ribs poking out from bellies, the gaunt faces and hungry eyes. This was not a place for happiness – or at least, the people didn't have enough energy to celebrate. I saw a dirty, rain -streaked piece of clothing on a tiny washing line, and a slim man come out of his house to take it off.

It seemed as though the warriors were the only ones who were fed properly – perhaps they were exceptionally skilled at hunting. The townsfolk looked as if they could barely hold an axe.

'Is this it?' I whispered to Faol, not wanting anyone else to see my shock at the appalling conditions in which these people lived.

'No. We have to walk past this bit to get to where the heart of our community is. It can only be accessed from here.'

'Why is everyone so hollow-looking?'

'You'll see in a minute.' I winced at his frosty tone, reminding myself to ask him later why he seemed so upset. He had been moody all afternoon, despite travelling through a place that made me feel so clean that I had actually had a sparkle in my eye while walking. I was still afraid of him, but the fear had lessened. Our mutual joy of flying had somehow broken the animosity between us – to some extent. He was still not as friendly as Angus, but he had improved his attitude towards me. Sometimes, I still wondered why he had been upset that night that he'd caught me trying to escape. I looked at him now, confused as to where we were going. Once we had reached the back of the village, we would hit nothing but the rock of the mountain in front of us. Faol didn't say anything in response to my questioning look, however, and we proceeded onwards.

I watched the village with sadness, wondering how the lives of these children had come to be so miserable. I saw similarities in the features of the few, hungry children prowling the streets and the men beside me. The same haughty exterior was there, the same cunning look in their eyes. However abandoned and mistreated this place seemed to be, I didn't feel that it was the heart of the people, that this was where everyone gathered, had meetings, laughed and lived. It felt empty. I could feel the throbbing centre of the place echoing from in front of us. Somehow – I didn't know quite how – we were going into the mountain. Faolan stepped in front of me, Angus sliding behind. The rest of the men assumed positions by my sides, and I wondered what the formation was for.

We proceeded quickly through the streets, now making our way towards the back of the tiny camp. I saw in front of us the foot of the mountain – to my shock, there was a small opening in its side, evidently our way of getting through.

A cave – or rather, a dim little passage, seemingly meant for nothing but wind and stray animals to pass through – was where we were headed and I could feel the gloomy cold of the cave wafting past us as we began to get closer. Pausing, I looked back at Angus, who encouraged me forwards with a wave of his hand. I wasn't sure about this place, but I stepped forwards again anyway. Faol stopped in front of the mouth of the tunnel, and looked back at me.

'When you pass through here, you must give something of yourself. An arrow, taken from your quiver. An arrow of your choosing – every time you pass through here.'

I stared at him, surprised. Why did we have to do such a thing?

To indicate how we were to get through, Faolan reached for the inside of his quiver, to a long, elegant arrow, sharply pointed, the feather dark and gleaming. He took it out, and thrust it into the wall. To my horror, I watched it begin to *melt* into the side of the cave, the dark blue of it slowly vanishing into that eerie black I had seen before. The rest of the commanders chose one of their arrows to sacrifice, and I looked for one of my own. I chose one that was small, inconsequential, innocent.

I plucked it out, feeling the sharp pain of it on my palm, and placed it smoothly against the wall. When I released my hand, the arrow stuck there, and began to melt in the same way that Faol's had. The cave seemed to shudder, the air becoming smoother, cooler. Faol began to step forward and I followed him. As one, we proceeded forwards and the sight in front of me captured my breath. Beyond, there were huge stalagmites, their glistening, pearly wetness dripping onto the floor. They were stunning and my heart sped in wonder as I looked at them, reflecting the distant light from the sun as it began to descend fully. We walked through and I had to duck my head to avoid the huge spikes. I wondered where we were going.

I saw Faolan's eyes seem to glow as the darkness slowly became ever more present as we reached the end of the tunnel. It took us half an hour to walk through the tunnel and by the time we reached the end, my feet were aching.

Beyond, a sky full of stars and light glittered. I gasped, almost pinching myself to tell if this was real. Faol, Angus and the other sentries let out breaths, obviously appreciating being back here once more. Looking around, I could tell that this was the true heart of Nzar, the place where light and joy radiated. Also a place of hunger, as I saw a gaunt warrior walk past, his muscles (despite being thin) still bulging from his legs and arms. We were walking on a stony beach, the silver of the pebbles reflecting the moon. Beyond them, a huge midnight lake rippled softly, its waves rushing out to shore, pushed by some invisible tide. But what lay curling around the pebbles made me jump in fright as I walked. Purple smoke wafted softly around the stones, making them look iridescent. It had to be water, I thought, watching the vapor condense on a stone, which in turn set it glistening.

Ahead of us I saw trees, and behind us, the dark belly of the mountain, forming a semi-circle clearing, in which the camp lay. Massive tents, painted with a silver wolf above the doorway flaps, had busy warriors rushing in and out of them. They looked relatively well nourished, but I could see the echo of hunger on them. One of them was carrying a dead deer, its head rocking to and fro as the men carried it away to be prepared for the next meal. Other vegetables and plants were also being carried, the sight seeming domestic, the work of the team seamless.

I watched the men stop, turn and stare at us, their eyes inquisitive but friendly enough. Faol, Angus, and the sentries rushed forwards, desperate to get back to their comrades. I watched with a small smile on my face. They leapt forwards shouting to their friends, and greeted them roughly but happily, grinning from ear to ear.

Out of the circle of people, I saw a woman emerge, her sly face already looking me over. Shocked, I backed away a step, still near the rear mouth of the stalagmite tunnel. She walked towards me in dark leathers and a black tunic, the glinting thread embroidered on the tunic standing out in the moon's light. Her boots were black and were shining brightly. She stopped a few feet away from me and I stared her down, feeling dirty and inconsequential when compared to her. To my surprise, a huge grin broke across the woman's face, lighting her eyes. The rest of the congregation had turned to look at us, but were still talking with their neighbours at the same time. I tentatively smiled back, feeling the dirt stretch across my face as I did so.

'Who are you?' I asked in a small voice, scared to discover the answer.

'I am Tera, one of the youngest of the Elders.' She held out a hand for me to shake, and I took it, feeling confused. Who, exactly, were the Elders? I didn't say anything, waiting for her to speak instead. She motioned for me to follow her with her hand, and I obeyed. Together, we passed through the crowd of people, everyone staring at us as we did so. We walked across the pebbly beach to the frosty grass beyond.

Situated in the middle of the clearing was a tent and this was where I was led. She took me in, and I felt the cool flap of the tent as it brushed past me. Inside, it smelled softly of ylang-ylang, but that was not the thing that hit my mind first. The tent was huge, much larger than it seemed from the outside, and contained a kitchen, living room, bedroom and bathroom. All of it seemed to be mine and Tera turned to me once we were both inside the living room.

'Sit,' she told me, her voice as smooth as honey. I sat, and Tera told me many things – of Sardaron, the prophecy, and the Quill. What my role was in this dreadful war.

And I listened, thinking to myself, What would Amber do?

...

Tera couldn't be serious.

I truly, truly hoped that she wasn't. I didn't know her, but I prayed to whatever god that might be out there that this story she had told me was not the truth. What my role was in the war… I didn't know what to say.

How could I fight my sister? If I accepted, what were the emotional consequences? If I turned it down, would the people, looking so gaunt and hollow, be starved for another hundred years? Tera had told me that for the past three hundred years, the Falcords had lost the wars of Meridian. Despite this, I still did not know whether saying yes was the right decision.

I thought again of the brave Falcords who had journeyed to get me, and of the people living in starvation. Tera had told me that those people either had injuries that prevented them from being effective in a fight, or were not old enough to fight yet.

I couldn't say no to something like that – unless I was heartless, which I very much hoped I was not. I turned back to face Tera. She looked at me, her eyes and face impassive. I knew she desperately wanted my help – and also that even if I refused, she would find a way to win this war. I realised that I still had not told her my name.

'I'm Kai,' I said – but instead of nodding, Tera smiled.

'I already know,' she said. 'But what I do not know is your decision. The Rite will be held in two days. You will have that time to make your decision, be it refusal or acceptance of the prophecy. It is your choice.' She turned, her tunic swishing as she made her way out of the tent, long dark hair falling onto her back. I simply stared after her, mind whirling. How was I going to make such a major decision? I would never fight my own sister. Never. But when the lives of hundreds of people depended on me… it changed things.

I needed fresh air, so I went outside, walking past the embroidered side of the tent as I did so. It depicted a wolf howling viciously, teeth bared as it stared down a magnificent eagle.

Once back out on the moonlit pebbles, encrusted with purple vapour, I saw in front of me the midnight lake and the crowd of people still standing around it, talking with each other. One turned to face me and stared. I glared right back at him, daring him to come and talk to me. He didn't, merely turning back to his comrades so I could no longer see his face.

I walked silently across the pebbles, spotting Angus and Faol at the same time as they spotted me.

I stalked towards them, steps quickening, mind racing.

'What is going *on*?' I hissed, seething with anger. 'How DARE you drag me into something like this! I will *not* be used as your pawn for this war of yours! And if you think I'm going to fight my sister, think again.' The words came out in a rush, an imitation of my thought process. They both looked at each other, and I knew they had nothing to say. There was nothing they could do to persuade me to join their cause. Except for one thing.

'Kai – we need you. We need you to fight against the horrors that go on in these mountains during these periods of peace. We cannot let the children grow here with no food, no supplies. All we are asking is that you fight for us this one time. You fight, so that for the first time in three hundred years, our children can have the resources they need to be nurtured in a healthy manner. Please, Kai. We're begging you.'

Faol said nothing, his eyes distant and wary. I looked at him, and he met my eyes quickly before glancing away. Curious, I wondered why he was in a bad mood – why he wasn't saying anything. Maybe he had been punished for what had gone on that night in the woods. I looked at them both a moment longer, Angus still looking at me beseechingly, and I felt anger rise up.

'It is *not* my responsibility to be involved in a war of

someone else's making,' I whispered, voice cutting like a knife slicing down. 'It is not your right to force me to do something. Maybe in this planet it might be, but where I come from, it is not.' With that, I stormed off, resolving not to talk for them until the Rite, and to make my decision alone.

Walking towards it, the tent seemed welcoming, open. I strode past the flap, irritated with everyone. I remembered that I still had Tholan to rely on, and checked that it was safely in the scabbard on my belt. It was, and I breathed out a sigh of relief as I placed it in a drawer by my bed. I sat on the mattress, the feeling downy and soft. A moment later, footsteps crunched outside my tent, and I quickly glanced towards the doorway, where a dark head and tan face was poking through. Faol.

I opened my mouth to shout, but he spoke before I could – and said something I wasn't expecting. His face, for once, showed some emotion – a faint anger, flickering at the edge of his eyes.

'I agree with you.'

I shut my mouth abruptly, startled at his words. He watched me uncertainly, still standing in the doorway. I motioned for him to come in, and he obeyed, following me to the kitchen. I leaned against the counter while he sat at the table, chair scraping on the stone floor, not looking at me. I didn't know what to say – was he joking? Was this some ploy to get me to fight for him?

'What do you mean?' I asked eventually, staring at nothing. 'Why have you been in such a bad mood today?'

He was silent and I sighed, guessing that he wasn't listening to me. I began to speak again, running a hand through my dirty hair as I did so. 'I don't know how you expect me to make a decision like this – to fight against my own sister? I could never. And yet, when I think about those desperate people we saw on the way here, and the ones in this camp… I'm not sure what to do. I need advice. I wish I could talk to Amber.' I was rambling, talking more to myself than him, and didn't try to stop the stray tear that fell down my cheek. So much had happened in such a small amount of time that it was overwhelming. Lack of sleep and the feeling of loss had hit me harder than I had expected. 'To know that if I refuse I would be heartless is something I wouldn't be able to stand. But if I beat Amber, effectively shortening her life, I couldn't live with that either. I would be a monster to do such a thing.' Tears started flowing freely as I spoke. 'Why did you have to drag me into this?'

'Trust me, I didn't want to.'

I flinched as he spoke, the tone of his voice harsh and cold. 'Then why would you do it? Why?' I was sobbing now, my mind looking towards the decision I couldn't swerve, couldn't avoid. The decision to fight in battle for a strange people I barely knew.

'I thought… I thought that if you agreed, whoever you were, we'd have a fighting chance of defeating the Firborn – a chance to finally, *finally* provide my people with a better life. Every day, I see them wasting away. The game we hunt is getting scarcer as we rely more heavily upon it. Many go without adequate shelter, clothing, hygiene. Every day, I feel more ashamed to call myself a commander if I can barely impact a tribe of people into leading better lives. So… I did what I had to do. I tried to accept the prophecy for what it was. Some years, we would win, some we would lose. I knew that the fate of my people depended on it – on you. I told myself that you would have suffocated on Etrais anyway – and so I picked you up in the hope that you would agree.'

'I don't agree – not at all.' I said it fiercely, fresh tears burning across my face. I sniffed hard, and continued, trying to compose myself. 'The prophecy… it's more like a curse. It *is* a curse. And maybe it makes me a fool to say this, but I can't just accept it, fight, and move on. I want to *end* it – completely,' I said, the idea having been planted in my head the moment Tera had told me of the prophecy. 'No matter what life throws at me, I don't want to be the one going along with it. I want to be the one throwing things at people – changing the fate I was given.'

I stopped then, because Faol was staring at me, an emotion displayed so thoroughly across his features I was dumbstruck. It was hope, shining like a beacon in his cyan eyes. His mouth wasn't smiling, but I could almost see the faint grin beginning to form around his face. He started speaking when I said nothing, his words rushed but hesitant.

'You truly mean it – that you want to break the prophecy?' I nodded, now not too sure what was going on. Faolan stood, and I stopped leaning against the counter. 'Come with me.'

Surprised, I followed, uncertain of what we were doing. Half of me hated him still for what he had done to me. The other half was whispering, *He couldn't help it. He was not the one who chose you to come here.* I sighed reluctantly, tracing his footsteps across the pebbles. He was walking fast, the purple smoke seeming to reach and curl around his boot-covered ankles as he did so.

'Where are we going, Faol?' I asked into the night.

'You'll see.' He said it slightly curtly, and I was suddenly worried. In the darkness, I could barely make out his silhouette, the crescent moon giving little light to see by. I jogged to catch up with him and started walking by his side. Looking at the side of his face in the darkness, I started to feel properly scared. Was what I had said so bad that he was going to punish me for it? All I wanted was for my life to go back to normal – which was ironic, since I had always wished for a more exciting life.

I said nothing as I was led further away from my tent, the direction heading away from the stalagmite tunnel. The darkness around us was cool and crisp, brushing against my eyes gently as I moved. I couldn't tell what was going on – the darkness, together with his naturally impassive face, made him frustratingly hard to read. Up ahead, I could just about see the outline of what looked to be a large hill, pines surrounding it. I could smell their scent on the sharp gust of wind suddenly blown our way.

It looked to be a small hiding place, with a round mouth signalling the entrance. As we got closer, the ground started to slope upwards, making my muscles tense and cramp as the walk became harder. A few days of having adequate nutrition had not fully restored my body, and I was still painfully weak from the weeks spent roaming the land by myself.

Pebbles and smoke gave way to glittering frost and grass underfoot, surrounded by the occasional clump of water reed, clustered near the lake. Beside me, Faol opened his mouth, as if he was going to say something. I waited for words to come out but, instead, he simply shut it again. I merely concentrated on my steps, too tired to do anything else. My eyes were itchy and sore from the tears that I had rubbed away by the time we reached the small opening into which I supposed we were going. There was a light radiating softly from within, which I hadn't noticed before. In front of me, Faol entered through the hole, having to crouch and almost crawl through. I followed, the hole easier for me to slip into.

Inside, the first thing I noticed was the source of light that I had seen from outside. Glowing softly, a mass made of a mysterious white material hung from the ceiling, shaped like an icicle. As I reached my fingers towards it, I felt a temperature that was so cold it burned. With a start, I realised that it *was* an icicle, frost glittering gently on it as it gave out that unearthly light.

I turned away from it to examine the rest of the cave room, buried beneath the cave. I heard a soft trickling echoing from the back of the cave, and peered down to see a small pool, trickles of water draining into it from tiny waterfalls. The bottom of the pool was rock, as were the walls surrounding it. Tiny crystals gleamed brightly from where they lay embedded inside the rock. The rest of the walls were dirt, speckled with a kind of golden ore that made the whole cave light up when reflecting the cold ice. They – the walls – were covered in paintings, almost like a collage of images. I saw wolves lunging, eagles with burning wings screeching and a leash of darkness stretching around a young girl's throat. Flame wreathed her fingertips, and I stared at her for a moment. Other people clashed against one another in the background, red against blue, until it they merged into darkness. There wasn't a space in there that was free of colour; everywhere I looked, pictures and images adorned the golden-brown walls. There was a small bench embedded in the rock at the far end of the cavern, softly blending into the background. My feet were aching, worn out from today's walking and, seizing the chance to sit, I walked over to the bench. It was cool to the touch, and a shiver went into my spine when I felt it.

'What is this place used for?' I asked Faol, who was crouching by the pool. He trailed his fingers through the water and I impatiently waited for him to answer. I was still slightly frightened – of him, and of what we were doing here – but I didn't think that he would kill me now that he knew I wanted to break the prophecy. Anyway, he had practically looked hopeful when I had said it, back in my tent. He turned away from the water next to him and looked at me. Remaining in his crouching position, he answered my question.

'This place is a secret.' He looked up at the ceiling, at the icicle hanging from the ceiling. 'What we do here... we would be killed by other members of our people if we dared voice it, because it could have great consequences for them. Down here, in that village, the ordinary people live. They do not fight, because they cannot. The Elders will have to choose one of them to be their husband if they survive through the war. If all our warriors are killed in battle, they will be there with the Elders. But there are some of us – of both warrior and villager – who came into this world with a different vision of how things could be. A dream – to stop the wars entirely.' He looked at me then from where he had been staring at the ground. I could see fear and hope reflected in his cyan eyes. Fear – because now, I had the perfect weapon in my arsenal to warrant his death. But also hope, and I realised what he was asking. I had said that I wanted to free the people from the curse in the tent earlier – and so did he and others.

'You want me to help you stop the curse.' I stated it, knowing it was the truth. He nodded, and I blew out a breath.

'But you would need to give blood – to bond us together. Every member has to do it. If you were to join, you wouldn't have to do it now – you could do it after the Rite. Anyway, yes, we want to break the curse.'

'How would we do it?'

'By killing the Creator.' He saw the shock flaring in my eyes, and hastily added, 'Well, going to talk to him first, and persuading him to give us the Quill.'

'And why would he do that?' I asked, exasperated. It was illogical to think that the Creator would just hand over the Quill – his life depended on it!

'We're going to promise that if we have the Quill, we'll instruct it to make him able to live off something else – like plants. Maybe we could then return the Quill to him – but a fake one instead. He won't need to use it, and by the time we've left, it won't matter if he does realise it's a fake – without it, he can't travel to our planets.'

I shook my head firmly. 'It'll never work – you'll only get yourself killed. If I join you, we're going to have to have a change of plan.'

He looked desperate, brows furrowed as he looked at me pleadingly. 'Yes, I see your point, Kai – but it's the only plan we have. The only one that doesn't involve death. I've had enough killing! Can't we just resolve this peacefully?'

I laughed, the sound hard. 'If he's so dangerous and powerful, do you really think it's going to be that easy? You can't possibly be serious.'

'Well, what do you suggest we do then – if you're willing to join?'

I looked around the cave, considering his words. As I thought about the hope that all of these members shared, the hope that one day, the world could be a place free of pain – no matter how naïve that sounded, I wanted to be a part of it.

'I'll join.'

He positively sagged with relief, and I stood, stretching as I did so. Now that I had this weapon to use against him should I wish it, I had no reason to be afraid of him. If the other elders and warriors found out that *I* was involved, they couldn't do anything about it. I was needed for the war. I strode over to him, standing tall as I approached. 'I'm going to go to sleep – I'll help you think of a better plan tomorrow.' I wondered why he thought a girl – or anyone – growing up in the peaceful countryside would know the first thing about battle, and scheming. I gave him a bemused look as I left the cave, making my way down the hill into the safety of my tent. Above, the stars glittered, and I stared at them as I contemplated what I had got myself into.

...

I awoke suddenly, my breath clouding in front of my face. I had forgotten just how freezing it was in here. Somehow, it seemed colder than last night, when the air was clear and bright. I got up, the duvet stiff for some reason as I lifted it to the side. I frowned, and looked across at it for a second more. As I stared, I realised that today was the day of the Rite.

I had spent the past two days being introduced to the Elders with Faol and Angus, and visiting the different parts of the people's home. I had seen the cabins in which the rest of the Elders lived – located in the crags of the mountain looming behind us, they were accessed only by flight. Since I hadn't yet managed to become airborne again, I simply admired them from a distance. Many Elders that I had met were from generations ago – there were few from ages closer to my own.

Meeting the people of Nzar for the first time, I had been struck by an overwhelming sense of generosity from them. They gave flowers, smiled frequently, and constantly seemed to be laughing. They seemed unaware of the crushing effect the war was having on their people – yet I could see their gaunt bodies and ribs poking from their bellies. The warriors, camped around the edges of the bay where the pebbles wreathed in purple lay, were less friendly. They seemed serious; all had a hollow emptiness in their eyes where I supposed joy and life had once resided. I didn't blame them: all had fought in at least one war. Their purpose had been to fight off the attackers of the Syths while they had been blasting their power across the battlefield. Many had numerous scars dotting their faces, arms and legs. However polite they were to me, I could practically feel the exhaustion leaking from them.

They were tired of fighting; tired of the constant pain they had to live through.

The group that Faolan was a part of – the group willing to break the curse – they were the Fydar Rebels. Quite a few people were part of it, I discovered later that day, Angus included – which meant that I didn't have to pretend to him about anything.

The Elders that we had met were polite – distant, but still polite. We had gathered at the base of a huge pine tree to meet and discuss my options. I disliked almost all of them immediately; they were old and withered, their faces unforgiving. The only feisty one that I had met was Tera, who was the youngest of them all. She had accompanied us and was constantly joking around, a twinkle in her eye. She was close to Angus, who was good-natured and amusing – but it had been only yesterday that I had realised that they were betrothed to each other. She had a dirty mouth and was always poking fun at the other soldiers; I could tell that we were alike. I had only rarely seen the dark side of her – when we were walking together – and I had glanced across to see sorrow written in her eyes.

Yesterday, we – Faol, Angus, Tera and I – had taken a boat out into the middle of the lake surrounding the bay, into the middle of the stunning water. I had never felt such a feeling of wonder as I had then, with the sensation of the water and wind surrounding me, spraying up in great plumes to shower our faces.

That night, when we had been returning from the boat trip, I had looked around at the night sky to see the Northern Lights, rippling gently across the sky. I was stunned and had returned to my bed well into the night.

I had stared at the softly glowing greens, yellows and blues for so long that I had started to feel a strange sensation in my heart. A feeling that, no matter how soon it was after arriving here, made me feel that this place was home.

I brushed off the thought as I made my bed, feeling that a place formed out of war and killing could never be my home. I stood straighter as I realised that today I would decide for sure whether I was willing to go into battle against my sister.

Smoothing the duvet over the bed, I took a shaky breath. I started to tie my hair back, looking around the tent as I did so. I still hadn't made up my mind about what I was going to do – refuse, and I faced somehow losing my soul, which left me unable to help Faol. However, despite the advantages that agreeing to the rite brought, it still meant that I would be fighting against my sister – and possibly forcing her to give up the joys that came along with being a Syth. I swallowed hard and began to get changed, putting on the clothes I had been given when I arrived. It had always been the same – combat clothes, not dissimilar to those worn by people in the army back on Earth. However, this clothing was lighter, nimbler and more elaborate. It was a midnight blue, lined with silver around the edges of the sleeves. The ones I changed into were no different. A tight-fitting shirt, a flexible yet comfortable jumper to go over, combat trousers, leather boots that were durable, yet so light that I barely felt them, and a jacket.

Once ready, I sighed, stepping away from the bed towards the door, leaving my blue arrows by my bed. I knew I wouldn't need them for a while. I was slightly surprised that no one had come to my tent, because for the last two days they had. Just as I was thinking, a muffled cough came from outside and I quickly strode over, breath coming in clouds as I walked.

Lifting the flap, I saw, not one of my companions but an Elder standing there, one that I recognised from the meeting that we had had with them before. She smiled at me in a friendly enough way, but I could tell that she didn't like me from the disapproving way she glanced at me. When she spoke, her voice was quiet, but no one would mistake her for gentle. She had high, arching eyebrows, age curling around every plane of her face. I thought she must be at least nine hundred years old, judging from her looks.

'Come with me – the Rite begins soon.'

I nodded nervously and, stepping out of the tent, I followed her outside. We walked together stiffly, my hair brushing against my back as we did so. I looked at nothing, my eyes darting between one thing and the next as I tried to sort through my tumultuous thoughts.

'Where is it going to be held?' I asked her.

'In the mountain, where everyone else is already gathered. They are waiting for you to arrive – and once you do, we'll start the ceremony.'

'How far away is it?'

'Only about a fifteen-minute walk from here. We'll be heading inside the very mountain itself. The ceremony will begin by the whole congregation sparking a light of ice in their palm – I assume you've seen one by now.'

I nodded, remembering the icicle that I had spotted hanging from the top of the cave into which Faol had taken me.

'Then the oldest of our Elders will say the words that will lead on to your decision. Do you think you've decided what you're going to do?' I looked at her.

'No.'

She looked at me in surprise as I said this; she had obviously been the opposite.

'I knew from the minute I was told that I wanted to fight for these people that I had met. Even though we are not all friendly, Kai, we are all practically family. We protect each other with our lives and the bond that we form with each other is… it is what keeps us alive.'

'But what about the girl you had to fight?'

'My sister, yes. I thought I would be hesitant to fight her but it turns out…it turns out we weren't. We had had a fight the day we were taken from Earth and so I was defiant. I quickly agreed to fight – too quickly, I suppose. I knew later that I probably would have said yes anyway. I fought, and won. We never made up – and I didn't see her again until I heard that she passed away. She became a scientist of sorts – she helped to heal battle injuries and discover plant properties. Anyway, it made my decision easier.' I looked down at the ground.

'But how could you do it – bear to hurt your own sister?'

'It broke some parts of me to do it. I know she understood – after all, she too chose to fight. We… weren't exactly happy to do it, but we understood the cause. In that way, I suppose we were both quite similar.'

The old hag's face was contemplative, and I sighed in frustration. This person was of no help to me – she had been in a completely different situation when making her decision. We continued on, wending our way through the campground, around the fir trees that grew thicker in density as we travelled further towards the back of the bay. I looked around nervously, hoping that one of my companions would be there and not waiting in the mountain. I saw none of them and desperately wished they could be here to give me advice. Over the past two days, I had come to think of them more as my friends than my capturers.

We passed through a small clearing before entering a patch of woodland and my heartbeat accelerated. We were walking briskly and each footstep took us closer to the mountain looming in front of us.

We were silent for the duration of the journey, my mind frantically trying to sort through all of my options. There was no way I could come to a decision before we reached the mountain, I thought.

I was right – by the time we arrived, I was so confused with myself that I had no idea what I was going to do. Taking a deep breath, I followed the Elder in front of me into the space beyond. We followed the dark rock in a twisting spiral of a corridor until we came to a set of wooden doors at the end of the tunnel, wreathed in black iron. Pushing it open, the Elder gave me a small nudge to indicate that I should walk forwards.

The hall was cavernous but, filled with hundreds of the Falcords, it seemed cramped. I stopped as we stepped through the doors that led out onto a pathway, raised above the ground. Looking up, I saw a huge, glittering mass of ice shaped like a chandelier, the points frosty and beautiful in their complexity. The roof of the cave seemed to be carved intricately in swirling patterns, with the one side wall made completely from glass. Somehow, they had managed to chip away the piece of the mountain covering the view through the glass – I could see beyond it, out onto the bay, the purple smoke floating up, faint and iridescent in the morning as I glanced out onto the water.

I realised the whole congregation was staring at me, waiting for me to walk down the aisle to the Elder waiting at the end. I nervously scanned the crowd and immediately spotted Tera, her brown hair blowing lightly in the breeze filling the cavern. She looked at me seriously for once and I could read the message in her eyes – that this was my choice.

I remembered what I was supposed to do and put one foot in front of the other, slowly making my way down the pathway. It was shiny, and I guessed that it was made out of polished marble. How there could be such luxury here when in the streets of the village, children were starving, I had no idea. This must have been built sometime around the very first war, when the people were living in a time of plenty. I continued walking, my boots clacking on the floor. The eyes of the Falcords watched me as I passed, waiting to see what I would do. The speed of my heartbeat increased, and I let out a shaky breath. Still, I had not decided what I was going to do.

I realised that my time to decide was up as I finally reached the end of the platform and stood in front of the waiting Elder.

...

Amber

The woman in front of me looked up, waiting to hear the response to the question she had asked. Standing in the middle of a crater, the whole population of Firborn surrounding me, I knew I had my answer.

'I will fight.'

The surrounding congregation roared in answer, their deafening cheers echoing off the sides of the crater. I merely looked to the sky, wishing I hadn't been given this impossible decision – to fight against my sister, and defeat the Falcords in the war.

...

Kai

'Will you, Kai, fight for us, the Falcords, in the upcoming war, knowing the benefits and consequences?'

There was silence, and I fought for breath, my head

spinning. How could I say no, when the faces of hundreds were looking towards me, faces hopeful, bodies hollow with hunger? Silent tears trickled down my cheeks as I stared at the Elder in front of me. Her face, however withered, was alight with a hope I could not fathom. Everyone was shifting uncomfortably at my tears, desperately hoping that I would agree. I thought of Amber, the sister who had supported and loved me, who had been by my side for seventeen years. I thought of these people, starving for the opportunity to provide for their families, just like Amber had done for me. I took a deep breath, my voice cracking as I finally spoke.

'I'll do it.'

...

Back in the cavern where Faol had first told me about his aim to overcome the prophecy with the Fydars, I felt tiredness pulling on my bones. It was night and I was exhausted.

I had spent the day with Tera, who seemed to be my closest companion in the camp. We had gone to her tent after the ceremony and, surprisingly, I hadn't cried once. I had only felt numb emptiness where my tears had once flowed over. She had distracted me by telling me about the festivals held annually here.

Now, sitting grouped together with Faol and the other rebels, I put the thought of what I had done aside. Most of the rebels weren't here, because they were training for battle by themselves. The eyes of every person in this room were some sort of grey, green or blue. It was so distracting to see that it was the first thing I looked at when turning my eyes onto a Falcord. Nervously, I looked to where Faol was seated, opposite to me. He looked up, catching my eye, and started to get up, motioning for the others to pay attention.

'We've spoken, and it is decided that Kai, our newest Syth, will join the Fydar Rebels. Blood must be spilled to show your commitment and loyalty to this group,' he said, now addressing me. 'Please step forwards.'

I stood up, my bones seeming to creak as I did so. This had been a monumentally long day and all I wanted was to go back to my tent and sleep.

Stepping forwards into the middle of the circle, I was instructed to hold out my hand by Faol.

Looking around slightly anxiously, I saw Angus sitting with a few of his friends. He gave me an encouraging look and motioned for me to hold out my arm.

I looked back to Faol, who was waiting for me to do as he had said.

Fingers trembling, I reached out my left hand to him. He nodded, but did not unsheathe the knife sitting in his belt.

'Take out yours.'

In surprise, I reached for Tholan, the dagger that I now carried around permanently. In the light of the ice hanging from the ceiling, the silver hilt seemed to glow as I pulled it out of its leather sheath. The blade itself flashed as it reflected the light, and I handed it to Faol. Around me, I could hear the faint rustling of clothes as the people seated around me adjusted themselves, preparing to watch me.

'Are you sure you want to do this?' Faol asked me.

I nodded vehemently, pushing down the part of me that screamed not to make any rash decisions.

He stepped a bit closer, gripping my hand with one of his, while pressing the knife blade into the palm of my hand with the other.

I felt a searing pain as he sliced through the skin with the blade, the crimson dripping onto the floor. I hissed through my teeth, gritting them through the pain. He had sliced deep – I could feel the pain echo through my arm, into my head. I made to back away, but he continued to grip my wrist. I clenched my fingers into my palm in an effort not to start crying. The whole room was looking at me; I couldn't be seen crying – it was a sign of weakness.

Faol looked up at my face, and I saw a stranger reflected in his eyes as I stared back at him. I stiffened, thinking of how much I had changed in the past three weeks.

Glancing back towards my hand, I saw the blood now forming a small puddle on the floor of the cave. Eyes alight, the rebels watched it drip, until finally the gash started to clot. I drew my fingers away, cradling my hand. The congregation seemed to heave, finally moving positions from the eerily silent ones they had assumed.

Warriors stretched their limbs, and Faol announced, 'It is complete. Welcome to the Fydar Rebels, Kai.'

I gave a nod of my head, still wincing through the pain in my hand.

The congregation, having dipped their heads as Faol said these words, arose to their feet. Silence reigned as we all left the tunnel, the air seeming clouded with the words of the warriors, departing for their tents.

I sighed as, Faol walking a few feet away, I made my way back to my own new residence. My breath came in clouds, and I watched it as I walked. The night sky was breath-taking and silent in its majesty around me and I felt a small tear trickle down my face as I walked. My breath caught and I shakily sighed again, reigning in my feelings. Some steps away, Faol said nothing and after a while our paths diverged. He trudged away with no words to me. I glanced once at his departing back, as he slipped away to his own tent to sleep, but then turned away. I needed to be alone for a while – to be in some place where I could think.

Glancing around furtively, I scanned the area for anyone as I slipped past my tent. Although no one had said not to leave, I knew that everyone was expecting me to be in my tent soon, sleeping. I headed back, away from the bay, through a section of wood that lay behind my tent. Ahead, the mountains loomed, watching me as I travelled away from the mess of my actions. A fierce wind growled around my body as I moved and I felt my power of flight swirl, catching the air as it flowed around me. After a few seconds, the night settled again but the burst of movement made me wonder. Could I fly to the top of the mountain? My mind felt shaky and weak, and I knew there was only a slim chance of me being able to do it. I thought of what could happen if I was that high up and my power suddenly failed me. I shivered from fear and paused. This was a bad idea. I glanced once more at the peak of the mountain, desolate in its wintry backdrop, and turned around.

Ten minutes later, I arrived back at my tent, snow dripping down my back, tiny crystallised droplets in my hair. I strode to my small bed and sat down. I stared at nothing for a while, hearing only the faint shouts of the warriors in the distance as they laughed.

What was I going to do when the Elders wanted me to fight and the Fydar wanted me to rebel?

.14.

Tera

the vast space was ample for what we were doing. We were standing on the peak of one of the mountains surrounding the bay, the dark blue waters rippling gently in the wind far below us. Beside me, Kai stood staring out onto the water, the sky grey and dim above us. We were here to train with Faol and Angus, who hadn't arrived yet. I watched strands of Kai's light hair flow in the wind as she stared at the sea.

'I've never been outside of England,' she said suddenly. I frowned. Where was England? 'My home country – where I grew up,' she said bitterly, as if reading my confused thoughts. 'We rarely went on holidays – and when we did, we stayed near to our house in the countryside. Our mother always took us.' I remembered again that she had a sister, who I had never seen. 'Even with all the bad things that are happening right now, this is still incredible.' I nodded, keeping silent. Observing her for a few seconds, I saw her take a deep breath, pushing the thoughts out of her mind. She turned to me, making an effort to smile.

'So, what are we doing today?'

'I'm here to teach you about the Instinct.'

'The Instinct? What's that?'

'It's like a feeling, something that controls our entire existence. In the past, before we separated ourselves from nature, we flowed with it and did as it directed. When we started to evolve, think of new ways to do things, we started, unconsciously, to push back against it. As we grew further and further away from it we tried to cut it entirely out of our existence.'

'Why?'

'We don't know much, only that it happened thousands of years ago, and ever since then, we have been unable to communicate with the god that once ruled our lands – the god of peace and prosperity. That is, until he was killed by Sardaron, and our worlds were thrown into war.' Her eyes widened, and I could tell she was thinking about what life would be like if the Ylvares had never separated from the Instinct. She wouldn't be here, forced to fight for a people she barely knew. It was what I had thought when I arrived, four hundred years ago, young and headstrong. I had thought I would always find a way to come back home. But I had met Angus shortly after the war, and things had become more complicated. In the end, I had decided to stay – if someone ever managed to find a way to escape using the portals, it wouldn't be me.

Behind us, I could hear warriors running onto the field, yelling at each other, gathering to fight each other. I sighed, and turned back to the ocean.

'Why are you telling me this?' Kai asked, hair blowing in the wind. She was dressed in fighting gear, her combat jacket wrapped around her body. She looked troubled, restless, as if she hadn't slept for days, even though I knew that she must have.

'During the next few weeks, we'll be preparing for battle together. There's something that we haven't told you yet.' She closed her eyes, as if sensing that something terrible was coming. 'In battle, you and Amber will find each other at some point. It will happen because you'll be drawn together by the Instinct. You will fight each other until you find out which of you will be the victor, the one who will live for centuries. Once it is determined, either you or she will become mortal.'

Kai stared wildly at me, face terrified.

'You mean… I'll be fighting using those powers I had in the woods, on Etrais?'

I stared at her, confused, until I remembered what Angus had told me. She had tried to bolt – had run off to the border of the camp, and had had a run-in with Faol, in which she had exerted her powers slightly. I had to admire her for the effort, despite it not working in her favour. I was also curious as to what, exactly, her power had looked like, having heard a few things about it from Faol.

'Yes – but you'll learn to control it. When you use your powers, you will feel the Instinct more strongly than now. If you succumb to it, you will be nothing but a wild creature, with no thoughts except those to kill.' I shuddered at the thought, at how it had felt to have the Instinct come so close to taking over my mind. At times, I had thought it would be better to succumb than to fight this pointless war. But the thought of the life waiting for me ahead of it had got me through it. When

I looked back at Kai at last, her face was set in determination.

'How do I do it?'

'You have to use the Instinct – wield it to your advantage. When you want to use your powers, simply look inwards, and you will find it. Attach yourself to it, but be careful. Once you are using it, you have to flow with it, but be careful to always be thinking of it in a corner of your mind. If you let go of thinking of this, you will be pulled by it, into its grip, until you don't even remember your name any more.

'And there's something else important,' I said. 'All of our powers originate from our eyes. This means that as well as being our most powerful weapon, they are also our weakest spot. If you were blinded, you would be cast out by your people, as you would no longer have powers. This happens on Zio too. You can be blinded by the opposition's power firing into your eyes, or by a weapon.'

...

Kai

The next hour was spent with Tera, Angus and Faol, as we discussed the transformation that had taken over my body that night in the woods. Angus and Faol were there for the second part of my training – teaching me how to fight effectively using my powers as well as my body. Tera, having experienced it herself, was teaching me the matter of control and how to enter the state of mind in which I could control my powers.

It was difficult, especially since I had only fleeting memories of the time I had used ice and wind. Tera showed me how it was done, her gifts swirling and shifting as she fired them at target after target. I watched, transfixed, as Faol and Angus demonstrated too, their eyes almost glowing as they whipped up a storm of wind and hail. I backed away as all three turned to look at me, moving further towards the edge of the clifftop training field. I could see the people behind their deadly looks, but was relieved when they finally halted, shifting with the wind, smooth as a river flowing. They seemed connected with their gifts, I realised, thinking how elegant they appeared.

'Your turn,' Faol grinned, teeth sharper than I remembered, eyes silvery in the morning light. I shut my eyes and focused myself, concentrating on the flow of the earth around me, the wind in my hair, and the rustling of the trees behind me.

After standing peacefully for a few minutes, I felt a strange song rise up inside and I reached for it, wondering what it was. It curled around me, seeming to rush past on excited feet as it made its way through my body. It was a song of the wild, of nothing but the open mountain and sky around me. I realised that this must be the Instinct, and cautiously approached it, careful to not immerse myself fully as I imagined myself dipping into it. It was a strange feeling to do so, one of nothingness and fullness at the same time. Ever so carefully, I let go of my image as a person and became a small part of that joyful wildness, hearing its cry as I felt ice spark at my fingertips, where I had been staring with my eyes.

When I looked up, Faol, Angus and Tera were all watching

me eagerly. I was concentrated more on myself, on the clarity of my vision, on the frost now spreading outwards, up my arm and dripping off my limbs. I lifted my eyes to the target, judging it. Inside me, the Instinct reached up, its song becoming wilder, faster. I panicked, thinking of what Tera had told me about giving in to the feeling. I pushed against it, hard, and felt the air move around me as the ice melted away, vanishing as quickly as it had appeared. Disappointed, I turned to her, wishing I hadn't panicked quite so fast. The euphoria that accompanied the experience faded as I looked around. Tera was examining me with a critical eye, obviously thinking of what advantages I would have with my gifts.

'Evidently, you have both ice and wind. Against the Firborn, whose power is that of fire, you will sometimes be at a disadvantage. Whatever your sister's power is, be it simply heat or actual flame, sometimes your ice will melt under her influence. She'll be taught never to land on the ground, because that's when she will be the most vulnerable – because she won't be able to see well through the flame. However, since she'll resort to staying in the air, you can tire her. Wear her out, so that she will not be so strong and nimble. When that happens, you can snag her with either your powers or your body and bring her down with a single blow.' Her face was hard, and I winced at the mention of hurting my sister. I wondered what trials she had gone through when fighting in the wars as a Syth. 'You don't have to kill her – or at least, you might not have to. Sometimes, the only way for Sardaron to determine who is the strongest is for one to kill the other. However, if there is a clear difference between your skill sets, your positions will be quickly determined. This is what we hope for when battling. However, she'll be trained as hard as the Firborn can make her so that they win the supplies, so we don't know how strong she'll be.'

I thought of Amber, of her temper and determination, and knew that this wouldn't be an easy fight. She was powerful, judging from the short time I had spent with her when we both had been dumped on Etrais. Possibly powerful enough to beat me. I shuddered, and looked again at Tera.

'I need to see you move around with the ice and wind,' she said. 'I need to see your assets and how strong you are.'

I nodded, and reached for that curling sense of wildness. To my dismay, I could no longer find it. I waited, but the thoughts of harming Amber had pushed the song of the Instinct to the depths of my mind, where I couldn't reach it. I sighed and shook my head.

'I can't. Can we try again later?'

She nodded reluctantly, and I looked towards Faol, who was standing with his arms crossed.

'So…when the fight between Amber and me is over, will I have to fight the rest of the battle with everyone else?'

Faol nodded.

'There is a period of time in which the War must be fought. We cannot fight for any less time than that, but we can fight for longer, if the battle between the two Syths takes a while. The minimum is a week, but in every war we've fought so far, the battle between the sisters has taken place after that week, when only the best trained warriors are left. In the beginning, it is extremely difficult to find each other because there are so many other people fighting – but after a while the population thins out, until only the strongest survive.'

'What if someone kills me before I reach Amber?'

'Then they win the war.'

I looked to him, disgust prevalent in my gaze. Not at him, but at the sickness of this game that had to be played. My breath caught as I considered the costs of this war. I needed him to teach me how to kill other people – something I had never thought I would need to do in my lifetime. Faol understood my glance and offered a sympathetic one back, crossing his arms. He turned and I followed him as we made our way to the middle of the training field, similar to a football pitch in size. In the middle, a rack of weapons stood strong, glinting in the frosty light. Instinctively, I reached for Tholan, sheathed at my side. It had never been taken from me by Faol – I thought he would have taken it after I was caught in the woods on Etrais, but something must have stopped him.

'If you want to learn to fight, take one of these weapons. I suggest using a sword over a dagger to begin with – simply because slipping a dagger into their body will be harder, because you'll have to get close.'

I gulped, selecting a sword carefully. The one I chose was gleaming, the silver so bright I could barely look at it. It was simple, but elegant, not clunky or heavy at all. I could feel the nimble point as I held it in my hand. It almost felt alive – felt cunning and sly.

Faol nodded, drawing his own sword from another point on the board. 'This is your sword now – the sooner you get used to using a particular one, the better you'll be when using it in the future. However, we're also going to be using the dagger, which is also yours now.'

The sun was flashing bright above us as we trained, sweat soon slipping down my body as I went through the manoeuvres Faol taught me.

Next to us, I saw Tera and Angus walking away, talking fast.

'They'll come get you soon – to try using your powers again, and start exploring it.'

I tried to put the thought out of mind. Unleashing the burning ice that I could feel almost constantly in my fingertips now seemed difficult and scary. I decided that I much preferred the physical aspect of preparing for war.

Two hours later, my muscles were weak as I faced the archery target. It was shaped like a human, the red bull's-eye over the heart. In my hand, Tholan felt dangerous and unpredictable. Faol had just instructed me in how to throw the dagger at the target and I raised it, my fingers gripping tightly. The silver glinted in the corner of my eye as I aimed and then hurled the dagger at the target, hoping that it would go to the bull's-eye. The air whistled as I threw it, the weapon making a resounding thud as it landed on the target. I panted, brushing the hair out of my eyes as I looked at where I had thrown the dagger. It was embedded deep in the target, having landed quite close to where I had hoped it would go. I looked at Faol, who was grinning widely as he took in what I had done.

'Do it again. To the top this time.'

I went to get Tholan, legs almost giving out thanks to the brutal training I had just been through, in which I had had to run around the entire field twice in just a few minutes. I had been wheezing on the floor afterwards.

I tugged Tholan out of the target and walked back to Faol. Taking aim, I again hurled the dagger into the target. My throat was as dry as straw and I drew a gasping breath as I moved. The dagger landed side-on this time, exactly in the middle of the head of the target. I was grinning, I realised, even as I contemplated that the head I would be throwing this into in real life might very well be Amber's if we had to fight multiple times.

I would learn – or try my hardest to learn, I thought, to be undefeatable in this war.

.15.

Amber

I had spent the past week hated by everyone except for a few. Yina had managed to grab me just in time to save me, after I had fallen from the sky while flying all those days ago, but I had still been in a state of shock for the rest of the day. My head had been clouded and dark and I had slept for almost twelve hours once we had reached the volcano in the centre of the land.

My room was bright and lively, filled with a bed and wardrobe, flames burning in lamps on the wall.

In the following days, Emeze had given me a look of absolute loathing whenever I passed her, which I had never returned. She had every right to be absolutely furious at me, after all – I had chosen to let her son live out his last few days alone, without any means of survival.

Two days ago, we had held a funeral service for him, and I had spent the entire service crying. Emeze and her husband had been standing at the front of the crowd who had come to pay their respects, eyes downcast. We didn't have a body and had instead planted a gravestone with cacti all around the area where we had landed through the portal.

No one would forget him, Neil vowed to the couple, before walking with me and Helmon back to the main mountain of lava, which, I learned, was simply called the 'Volcano' by everyone.

Once arriving back there, I had gone with my companions to the giant hall, where all announcements were made but also where everyone ate. A flame constantly burned in the middle of the room, tables and benches surrounding it. We had eaten, the food filling and delicious. Guilty, I was reminded that the Firborn had been afforded the privileges of winning the wars for the past three centuries, and had plentiful food and supplies. The Falcords must have to catch their own food off the land, I realised while eating. And it was probably scarce, since they had been hunting there for so long. I had eaten my food with less gusto after that, simply watching Neil and Helmon engage in conversation with others who came up to them.

During the rest of the days, I had started my training with Yina, who was my mentor. She had told me about the Instinct, which I had had trouble finding at first.

Using my powers had been easy once I had found it, though. With Yina, who had a tremendous wealth of knowledge on the best ways to use flame, I had practised throwing balls of fire at targets again and again. I had let the flame direct itself, making my aim unnervingly accurate. We had practised with swords and daggers, parrying and attacking as she taught me different ways to use my weapon.

On the eighth day of living there, I had finished practising for the day, my muscles sore and throat dehydrated, and I went to the hall where I knew I would find Helmon, who finished his training at the same time as I did.

Entering the hall, I saw him immediately, his brown hair flashing. I slid opposite him onto a bench, and he smiled at me politely.

I frowned. Why wasn't he looking at me like he normally did? The rest of the time, he treated me as he would his best friend – me and Neil, that is.

I got the answer to my question a moment later, when Nuru breezed to his side and sat down next to him, a plate of food in front of her. My heart sank a bit.

A few days ago, Neil had explained that Helmon and Nuru were engaged to each other, due to complete the ritual of Omricrit – marriage – the day before the wars began. When I had heard it, something in my chest had squeezed, even as I was happy for him. I knew I was being irrational, that I had known him for little more than a week, but still… something pulled me to him. I couldn't explain it, and wasn't sure if he felt the same way, so I hadn't said anything.

Nuru examined me brightly, teeth flashing as she smiled at me in a friendly way. I grinned back. I really did like her – she was funny and compassionate. Which was why I had decided that I wouldn't admit that I might have feelings, however insignificant, for Helmon.

'How was training today?' Nuru asked, slipping an arm around Helmon's.

'Good, actually. I think I'm improving fast enough that maybe I'll have mastered throwing weapons accurately in a week.'

'When I was training, it took me *ages* to master my powers. My mentor would come back every day with singed hair and no eyebrows,' she said, chuckling. Helmon, beside her, was still watching me as I grinned back at her. I flicked my gaze to his, and he quickly looked to Nuru.

'Hey, Nuru, can you teach me some techniques?' I asked, suddenly interested. Her eyes lit up, setting them sparkling.

My heart twisted at such beauty, stabs of jealousy prickling into me.

'Sure! I can ask Yina, and we might be able to have a session together once I've finished teaching some other warriors,' she said eagerly. I nodded brightly, but my smile dimmed as Helmon said,

'Actually, I don't think that that would be a great idea.'

'Why not?' Nuru asked him. My own confusion echoed hers.

'Well… given what happened last time you mentored somebody, I don't think it's safe.' Nuru's eyes hardened at his words, at what he was implying.

'But she won against the other Syth a hundred years ago, right?' I asked, trying to calm them both down.

'Yes, but barely. I just… maybe you two should just train separately, all right?' Helmon said, his voice becoming brisker.

'What, you don't think I'm a good enough mentor for her? What do you mean, "barely"?

'Nothing! I just don't think you would be the best coach for her, that's all!'

Nuru's gaze became fiery as she said softly, 'Don't you

dare tell me whether I am good or not good enough to do something, Helmon.'

'I'm not trying to tell you that you aren't good enough! I'm just saying that maybe you aren't the best fit for each other!'

'And you are? I've seen the way you look at Amber – as if she's the only thing that matters to you,' she panted.

Silence.

'Go on, deny it. But we both know it's the truth,' she spat, getting to her feet, waiting for him to protest.

Helmon said nothing as she stood there for a long moment, his eyes downcast. Without another word, she stormed off, giving me a glance as she left. Her eyes told me that it wasn't my fault, that she didn't blame me, but…I still felt bad. Enough so that I got up to leave too. Helmon's brown eyes followed me all the way to the entrance, where I paused to look back at him. But he was already swallowed up by another crowd of merry people, coming to eat with their friends.

I turned and left the chamber, wondering if the mess of their relationship was my fault.

…

Half an hour later, I was curled up in my bed, belongings splayed out on the mattress behind me, as Nuru knocked on my door. I got up, groaning at my stiff muscles, and opened it to find her worried face peering back at me.

'I'm so sorry, Amber. I didn't mean for things to blow up at lunch today,' she said, looking at me in the eye. 'It's just that…

Helmon's been acting strange ever since he got back here, and I don't know what to do – I mean, we're getting married in three weeks!'

I opened the door fully, and gestured for her to come in. She gratefully did so, and plonked herself onto one of the low-lying chairs at one end of the room. I slid down onto one opposite her, bracing my hands on my knees.

'What happened? I mean, aside from lunch today.'

'He's just… I don't know,' she said, turning a weary face towards me. 'I just don't know. When we're alone, he seems fine, but as soon as you come along, he starts getting stressed out and uptight. He won't say a word to me.'

'Do you think it's because he doesn't like me?' I asked, now worried too.

'No – I think it's something to do with me, but I can't figure out what I've done wrong.'

She looked at me, her eyes desolate, and I reached forwards to grip her hand in mine.

'Don't worry, Nuru. Just talk to him, and maybe he'll understand, and explain. Tell him how you feel.'

She nodded, looking down.

'Sometimes I wonder… was this marriage even supposed to happen?' she confessed, face bitter. 'It just seems like every time we get past a hurdle and I think things are going well, we have another problem that needs sorting out. And it hasn't been only since you arrived,' she added, glancing up at me from where she had been staring at her hands. 'It's been from when he first asked me to marry him. I love him and I think he loves me too, but sometimes I think we would have been better as friends. And Neil… he was very against Helmon marrying me. He said it was too rushed, and that we should wait until we know we're the perfect match for each other. Sometimes I think we should have listened to him.' She spilled the words in a torrent of worry, and I had the feeling that she had been holding them in for a long, long time. Perhaps longer than she cared to admit.

I was still gripping her hand, I realised, and I let go, leaning back into my chair.

'Nuru – listen to me,' I said worriedly, wondering if those were indeed tears gathering at the corners of her eyes. I had been told that never once had anyone witnessed her crying – she was a stone-cold killer on the battlefield. To see her in this state was horrific. 'Whatever happened between you, you need to be honest about it. Tell him why you think the relationship isn't working the way you want it to, and ask him how you think each of you can change the way you do things currently. It will be all right,' I said consolingly, catching her wrist as she stood, dabbing her eyes.

'I just… he's been my friend for so long that I don't want to do anything to damage our relationship,' she said as I too, stood.

'Don't worry. Being honest won't damage anything – it can only help,' I said, sounding as unconvincing as I felt. Nuru seemed to accept it, however, and nodded in thanks before quickly leaving the chamber, leaving me to stare after her in silence.

...

Helmon, too, found me soon after Nuru. I heard his voice behind the door as he knocked. I didn't open it, but instead crept up to the door from my position on the floor, where I had sat soon after the departure of Nuru.

'Amber?' he said uncertainly, into the door. 'Can I talk to you?'

'I'm here,' I said, my voice loud in the silence that followed.

'I'm sorry,' he said, 'for what happened at lunch.'

'Don't apologise to me,' I said, surprised. 'Apologise to Nuru.'

He was silent, and I sighed. 'What are you sorry for?' I asked.

'I wanted to apologise for making things awkward between you and Nuru,' he said, more confidently this time. 'I think that maybe you coming here is a sign – that maybe things aren't meant to work out between me and her.'

I flushed, glad that he couldn't see my face as my heart rate increased. I hung my head, the words that I said next heavy and dismal.

'You can't think that, Helmon – you're just going through a rough period now, and things will get better.' I glanced at him, even as my heart was aching. 'You love her, don't you?'

He didn't reply.

...

I didn't speak to either of them for three days afterwards – not because I didn't want to, but because Yina was pushing me harder and harder to train. I complied, but I was distracted. I knew that distraction could get me killed on a battlefield, but I was wondering about Helmon and Nuru, and whether they had talked to each other about their issues yet. I thought not, because I sometimes passed them in the corridors when I was running to training, and they looked equally miserable. Or maybe they had broken up. I did not give myself time to mull over the thought, and what it might mean for me. I pushed that selfish part of me aside, and tried to concentrate wholly on the fire that I could now control easily.

Using the powers of the elements was the best part of my training, I thought, watching flame writhe on the ground, snaking towards the target I had set up. We had moved on from still targets, and were now practising with moving targets, stuffed animals and people who I had to engulf in flame. I was told to direct the flame towards the head first, as that was the most crucial part of the body – without the brain, the body cannot kill on a battlefield. I had been successful so far and was now aiming to move my flame onto living things.

I couldn't do it, I thought, staring at my target. Yina had chosen people to be my victims – something that seemed cruel and dangerous, but was in fact very safe, she told me. They would be protected at all times.

I was still in shock as I looked from my flame, a willing servant, to Helmon. My victim.

'Begin,' Yina ordered from where she was standing in

between us. I looked slowly at her, panic beginning to cloud my senses. What if I accidentally burned him? Or worse, injured him permanently? I knew that he viewed it as a training opportunity, but that didn't stop me from feeling worried on his behalf.

I stepped forward nervously, flame flaring in my fist as I did so. I hurled it towards Helmon, who was now running to the right. He seemed to be taunting me, I thought in annoyance, as he slowed, turning towards me with a smirk. He obviously wasn't thinking about what had happened a few days ago, when he had implied so much to me. And now he seemed to have forgotten about what he had done, and was facing me with amusement in his eyes. He was toying with me, and he knew it. The flame I had sent hurtling towards him a moment ago he dodged easily, and I cursed internally, face heating.

Yina nodded at him, signalling for him to attack back. My eyes widened. I hadn't realised that this would be an actual fight. He stepped forwards, and my temper flared again as he unsheathed his sword. I remembered that he didn't have powers, his skill at killing his only gift. I threw another ball of flame at his face, but he deflected it off the side of his sword and kept advancing. I growled in frustration, and he chuckled. Flame reared up, a wall, forming and flowing, that swallowed everything in its path. He soared up and above it, landing gracefully on the charred ground.

I felt angry at him, my pent-up frustration from the last few days of silence overflowing into the ground, into my hands. I slashed with claws of flame, and he ducked, punching his sword towards my exposed side. It scraped past as I rolled, grazing my combat clothes. I drew Narox, the dagger Yina had gifted me with. It gleamed as I threw it for his head. His hand snatched up, grabbing it by the hilt as it hurtled for him. He turned it towards me, and I backed away a step. He hurled the dagger low and I twisted to avoid it – but he saw my move coming. His sword was already there, pressing against my clothes. He had turned the flat side onto my body to prevent himself from stabbing me as he moved, but I still felt the sting of humiliation, as sharp as any sword.

I hissed at him, 'What's your problem?'

'What do you mean?' he asked, parrying the thrust I had made with one of his own.

'Haven't you and Nuru talked yet?' I asked, irritated. His face turned solemn and any pretence of amusement vanished.

'No.' He said nothing else, and only sighed when he pressed the tip of his blade to my throat. He had beaten me easily. He removed the blade, nodding at Yina, and walked away, ignoring my apology for snapping at him.

Yina walked up to me, footsteps slow. 'What's going on?'

I turned to her, sighing.

'I have no idea. He doesn't seem to want to talk to either Nuru or me – and his silence only makes me more frustrated.'

Yina watched him leave the area, disappearing around a bush towards the volcano.

'Give him time. I think he's deciding what he wants, and what's best for all of us. He was almost forced to propose to Nuru, you see. Everyone expected him to, and kept asking when it would happen. They were more like best friends than partners, which is why I don't think it was the best match. I told him to wait, but he said that he might as well – Nuru, too, had expectations thrown on her. She needed to provide an heir, and she didn't have any lovers,' she said ruefully. I said nothing, feeling the sick twist of jealousy in my stomach at Nuru. 'They would have been a handsome couple, but I think both of them were waiting for something more in a relationship. Something bright, sparkling, as Nuru once put it to me. But… I know that they do love each other. And if anything happened, they would be changed – and not necessarily for the better.'

'Do you think they'll get through their issues in time for their marriage?'

'I don't know.' There was silence as I saw a dark head move through the undergrowth. Yina said, 'You're finished for the day. Take a break.' I looked at her in surprise, nodding my head in thanks before walking away.

I watched the dark head emerge, before transforming itself into Neil, walking briskly towards me. I hadn't seen him much, as he, too, had been training for the upcoming war, but as his handsome face came closer, I realised that I had missed his company. We had become fast friends in the few days before the funeral of Thark, who still haunted my memory. He smiled faintly as he stopped, hands in the pockets of his trousers, but his eyes were impatient. He seemed desperate to leave, even though he had been the one to come up to me.

'What is it?' I asked.

'It's Helmon,' he said after a moment of silence, in which he seemed to be deliberating what to say. 'I ran into him while I was walking to training, and he said that he was going to end it with Nuru.'

My face froze. What? It couldn't be.

I echoed the thought aloud, and Neil shrugged. 'Why don't we go find out?'

I nodded uncertainly, wondering if Helmon would want to be approached after going through something like that.

'This all seems to be happening so fast. Is he sure about what he's doing?'

'I don't think it's happened quickly. For the past few years, their relationship has become… uneasy.' I stared at him, wondering what that meant. 'Come. Let's go,' he said, and we started walking back in the direction that Helmon had gone after his fight with me.

I turned back to see Yina looking back at us, her face alight with interest. I quickly turned back and walked away.

We stopped near the entrance to the Volcano, where underbrush abounded, and the dark rock seemed alive with power. There, we heard low voices, and Neil deftly slid behind a hedge, crouching low. I followed suit, and he pressed a finger to his lips. I watched carefully from behind the bush, sidling around Neil to get a better view.

In front of us I saw Helmon, talking earnestly with Nuru.

'Are you sure we should be doing this?' I hissed at Neil, who had crept up behind me.

'Don't worry, he'll never know if we keep quiet,' he murmured into my ear. I frowned at this, but turned my attention back to the distressed couple anyway, pricking my ears nervously at what was being said.

'What are you saying, Helmon?' Nuru asked, her lovely voice washing over me.

'I'm saying that maybe... maybe things aren't right between us, Nuru. Things have been going wrong for a long while, and I think that maybe it would be better if we took a break, thought about what we want.'

'You think we shouldn't complete the rituals of Omricrit?'

'Well, binding our souls together just seems so...*permanent*.' His brown eyes were searching as he looked at her. 'What do you think?'

Her amber eyes were wet with tears as she looked at him, her mouth trembling. They were obviously well into conversation by now.

'Did you ever even love me, Helmon?'

He hung his head for a moment, before looking at her in desperation.

'Of course – *of course*, Nuru. I've always loved you. But love... it can come in many forms. I think we both loved each other like siblings, and I don't know if I can ever care for you differently.'

'And what about Amber?' she asked, and I leaned forward, ears straining to hear what he said.

'Amber... I think that maybe we could be something. I don't know about her, but I know what I feel.'

'And what is it that you feel?'

'Something... wonderful.'

I froze, eyes wide.

She nodded, seeming to understand, her eyes still gleaming with tears. Suddenly, she flung her arms around him, tears flowing openly now.

'All I want is for you to be happy,' she whispered through her tears. 'Don't let me be the one holding you back from that happiness.'

Helmon was silent for a long moment, simply holding her in his arms. Finally, they let go of each other and Nuru sniffed, wiping at her tears. She smiled through the salty flow, while he took one of her hands in his.

'I hope that we can still be friends – like we used to be,' he said quietly. I watched carefully, startled to see tears on his cheeks too.

'Of course,' Nuru said, squeezing his hand once. He nodded gratefully and let go of her hand.

I watched very, very carefully.

And I saw what Helmon did not.

I saw her broken heart, her features that put on a brave front even when I knew she was screaming inside. She loved him – deeply. But she understood that he would never feel for her in the same way. And that momentous realisation hit her like a blow to the gut.

'See you later?' he said hopefully, choosing to ignore what was written so clearly if you looked closely. I watched him stare at her beseechingly as she smiled gently, hair blowing in the warm breeze.

Her tone of voice was even when she replied, even as there

was a slight catch to her words.

'Of course.' She nodded too, and turned away, sparing another glance at him before striding to the stone entrance of the main volcano.

I stared at Neil, our shock echoing between our faces.

'I didn't think Helmon would actually do it,' Neil whispered, dark eyes following him. We watched Helmon take a deep breath and stride away, taking off mid-step to fly instead.

When we were sure that he wouldn't see us, we stood, stiff legs aching. We stood in silence for a long time, before I glanced at Neil's face. It was downcast, his eyes clouded with sadness.

'What's wrong?' I asked, pushing aside my own feelings of shock, and a tiny flare of joy at what Helmon had said minutes before.

'Nothing.' His voice was hard. I turned to face him more fully, frowning at his tone.

'Neil. What's the matter?' I asked again, tugging him to face me as well. I was shocked to see a tear form at the corner of his onyx eye. He brushed it away roughly, shifting his feet with the movement.

When he spoke again, he looked to the sky in hopelessness. 'I just… when he told me that he was breaking up with Nuru, my first thought was of you – which was why I came to tell you. It seems I was right about that – about him loving you,' he said, smiling bitterly. 'But there was also this tiny hope that maybe… they were both breaking up because Nuru wanted to be with me. That Helmon wasn't the only one having doubts.'

I was frozen, staring at him in silence.

He laughed sadly at my face, dipping his head as tears started to run down his cheeks, dripping onto his shirt. I had never guessed – all this time, and I had never known.

'You love her?' I whispered.

He nodded, raising his head to look at me directly in the eye.

'For years.'

'Does she know?'

'I hoped that at some point, she might realise what I felt, and return the feeling. It became clear when Helmon asked her to marry him that she wasn't interested in other people – in me, but I still hoped. Even though it was irrational. But now… there can be no doubt about it.' He held my stare. 'But I still… it still hurts,' he said softly. 'It hurts,' he repeated.

I looked at him in desperation, wondering what I could do to help heal his heart. I knew that there was nothing.

He understood my look, and patted me on the shoulder gently, smiling a little.

'Don't worry. I'll move past it, eventually. It might be a while before I can talk about her… about Nuru,' he said, pain flashing across his face at the name, 'without feeling anything, now that I know that she loves only him. But don't worry, I'll find someone at some point. Or at least, I can only hope that I will.'

I nodded, tears coming to my own eyes. He laughed upon seeing them, teeth flashing bright in the light of sun. He shook his head as if to clear himself of his thoughts, meeting my eyes.

'Do you want me to tell her?' I asked.

'At some point, yes. Whenever you think the time is right.

She deserves to know.'

I nodded.

We smiled at each other, mine understanding, and his sorrowful, before he walked away into the desert, steps full of mourning.

.16.

Kai

It was two weeks into my training, planning with the Fydars becoming more difficult as time went on. There was always someone watching, something that put the group off having meetings in the woods next to the bay. We had managed to have two, in which we had agreed on nothing.

Everyone was arguing, myself included. We needed to think of a suitable plan in time for the war, which was to begin next week. So far, there were two main ideas: a few of us would go ahead to find Sardaron and try to persuade him peacefully to give us the Quill in exchange for benefits once he gave it to us. Of course, we wouldn't actually tell the Quill to do anything for him – we would simply kill him using its power.

The second idea was more drastic and risky than the first and I didn't like it at all. Some members said that with a whole legion of warriors (who had arrived from the north at this point) we would be able to take the Quill by force.

'He's a god,' Faol said flatly when Iren, who was introducing the idea, had presented it to him. 'Do you honestly think that a single legion of soldiers can defeat a force so massive?' There had been protests from the Fydars, who had thought that maybe they could, but they had quickly died down. Faol had a point.

'Idiot,' Angus had muttered under his breath. He and Iren had an unpleasant history – Iren was insanely jealous of Angus, and had tried to kill him in one of the wars. Angus, obviously, had hated him once the wars were over. It was why Iren had a massive scar running from his jaw to the bottom of his neck. Only the skill of surgery had saved him.

Iren had backed down about our plan then, but I could tell that he wasn't happy about it. He had given the four of us – Tera, Angus, Faol and me – vicious glares whenever he passed us. He was a pig, I had decided after a few days, when he had convinced almost half of the Fydars to try and threaten us into submission.

Tera had told me something that had changed my perspective on the warriors here completely. Instead of seeing them as comrades, I found myself sizing up each one when I talked to them, or passed them. This was because tomorrow I would begin my practise fighting.

I would be thrown against one of the warriors, chosen carefully by the Elders, and left to fend for myself. Whoever pinned the other first won. If I won, I would be pitted against a more skilled warrior. If I lost, I would be put against someone less skilled.

During these two weeks, I had become extremely close to Faol, often spending long periods of time with him when training. He taught me new techniques, and we talked while practising them. He told me about his life and where he had come from – he had been born in the village outside the bay, he told me, and had grown up deprived. Angus, who was the son of one of the few privileged families, had befriended him and taken him on a trip up north to see a warrior legion. While staying there, Faol recruited himself into their army, rising through the ranks to become one of the leaders.

I had told him about my life back in the country, but not in detail. Thinking about Amber and my mother was just too painful. He had seemed to understand, his cyan and silver eyes glittering in the frosty air as I toyed with my powers.

I was extremely nervous for the fighting that would take place soon: almost every warrior I met seemed huge and impossible to defeat – they had been honing their skill for thousands of years, ever since they were cursed.

I had spent the entire day before the fighting training furiously – I was determined to not look like an idiot in front of the Elders, who would be watching, as well as everyone else.

The morning of my first battle, I woke with a sick feeling in my stomach. I was so nervous that my hands shook violently as I moved into the bathroom. I knew that I had nothing to be worried about: I had trained hard and I was prepared. Even if I lost, nothing bad would happen to me, surely. Except for being severely humiliated.

I went to Tera for advice. She was dressing in her tent and I knocked on one of the wood beams by the entrance flaps.

'Come in.' I entered, and she twisted to look at me, warmth lighting her green eyes. 'Good, it's you. Come help me tie this bow, will you?' I obliged, moving closer to her to knot the ribbon around her waist. She was getting changed into the clothes that the Elders had to wear whenever there was an official ceremony, such as the battle tonight. I gulped, the clothes only a reminder of what I had to do. Tera thanked me and twisted as I spoke.

'Tera… what is it like?'

She knew what I was talking about. 'It's brutal. Savage. But in some ways, it's relieving. I survive through the killing by imagining the good that will happen if we win.'

'And when you were a Syth?'

Her face shuttered, fast as closing a door. 'When I was a Syth, I made some very, very bad decisions.'

I moved on quickly, sensing her discomfort.

'And what about the battle tonight?' I asked.

'You'll be fine. Anyway, all it is is practice for you until the real thing.'

I nodded nervously, thanking her before leaving the tent. I had to find Faol.

Over the past couple weeks, I had told him things that I had never told anyone, even Amber. I had told him of my father, whom I had loved so much that it had broken me when he died; of my issues with my mother; and my growing hopelessness about my sedentary life at home. It seemed that (although I was a good student at school and was on the first team for most sports) I had never really excelled at anything. Now I was on Nzar, and everything had changed – and it frightened me. It frightened me to know that every dagger aimed at a target would be aimed at a living, breathing person in real life. It frightened me to realise that I would do it – kill people – if it meant that my own were saved.

I shifted with the breeze.

My fingers swished against the fresh-fallen snow as I bent. Footprints led away into the snow – I knew whose they were.

I straightened and started to walk.

...

Faolan

I glanced at Kai, approaching where I was seated high up in a tree in the forest, watching the falcons soar in the sky above.

She shifted mid-stride and jumped upwards, midnight wind blowing gently as she made her way up next to me. I saw that her face was worried and I sat up straighter, swinging my legs off the tree so that they dangled in the air.

She came to rest next to me. I felt the wind from her flight shifting towards me as she did so. My own wind murmured in answer, rustling the leaves of the tree slightly as she came closer. She sat beside me, bracing her arms on the tree branch.

'I need advice, Faol,' she said, casting a worried look at me. I felt surprised – this was the first time I had ever seen her nervous. She always had an expression which was hard to read – because of the pain of her past, I assumed. Overhead, the sky darkened slightly, clouds coming together. I flicked my gaze upwards at the same moment as she did, and then looked back.

'What kind of advice do you need?' I asked curiously.

Her dark eyes were wide with anxiety as I looked at her face, noting the pallid skin and gauntness. She had been training hard, but the nutrition available to us wasn't optimal. The warrior legion up north had helped, bringing whatever they could to help feed the village and the camp by the bay. Still, food was getting scarcer – something you could tell from the haggardness of the warriors. It wouldn't last forever, which was why we needed to win these wars so desperately.

'If I don't win these battles… what will happen? I mean, do you think Amber will beat me when it comes to the real thing? If she does, what will happen to the Falcords? What if we die of starvation?'

The words came almost too fast for me to comprehend.

'Kai, if you lose the battle in the wars… no one will blame you. It is more a testament to how good our training is here than how skilled you are. Don't worry about it, honestly.'

I tried to push away the thought of Kai only living for eighty or so years if she was beaten, becoming wrinkled and stooped with age.

I knew it was irrational, but I wanted to hold her close for a moment, if only to comfort her. I didn't know how she would react if I did that, so I took her hand in mine instead, the caramel of mine covering her own pale skin. She looked at me in surprise, but smiled slightly. She shuffled closer, putting her head on my shoulder. I rested my cheek on the top of her head, smiling too, as snowflakes started to drop from the sky. I glanced up once more at the grey sky, watching the ice fall to the already laden ground.

'Faol...'

'Yes?' I replied, still watching the snow.

'I...I don't want to live in a world where you aren't there. Where Angus and Tera aren't there.' I stilled as she raised her head to look at me, snow dropping onto her hair. 'If you're all killed...'

'We won't be.'

'But if you are... life won't be the same. It will lose its colour.'

'Life will give you another colour – someone else will pop up who you could spend time with. Iren's available the last I heard,' I said jokingly.

She snorted, swinging her legs back and forth.

'I don't want to spend my life with Iren. I want to spend it with you.' She dared to glance over at me, evidently nervous about how I would reply. I smiled faintly, the look blooming over my mouth as I watched her fidget.

'You would?' My voice sounded hesitant, nervous. I cursed inwardly, thinking that I must sound like an idiot. She looked at me.

'I would. But only if you do.' She nudged my shoulder with her own, glancing back to the snowflakes. 'But if you're already taken, then I understand.'

'I'm not,' I said, still looking at her.

She breathed out, seeming to sag in relief. 'Good.'

I laughed, putting my arm around her. She gripped my hand, our faces now only inches apart. I leaned closer, watching her eyes flicker as I did so. She was nervous, I realised.

‘This is the first time I’ve ever… felt something for someone – ever,’ she admitted. ‘I don’t really know what to do.’

‘Don’t worry.’ I leaned forward until our brows touched, holding her close. ‘Don’t doubt yourself. Amber probably has… she’s probably as nervous as you are. When it comes to the battle between you, no one can predict the outcome. But just know that we all support you, no matter what happens.’ I leaned back, the thought of fighting freezing my heart over. ‘It’s a cold thing. The two peoples are so different that I sometimes wonder how we were ever one group of individuals.’

She nodded. ‘I grew up in a different situation – there were different struggles.’

‘Do you think that you would ever try to go back to Earth, like Tera tried to?’ I said it quietly, hoping desperately that she wouldn’t. She looked at me for a moment thoughtfully before sighing, breath clouding in the air around us. Her hair was now crusted with snow, but she didn’t seem to mind.

‘No – I don’t think so. It would depend on what happens in the war. If I lose… maybe. But if I don’t, then I think I’ll stay here. I couldn’t imagine telling my mother…’

‘Hey, you two!’ a shout from the bottom of the tree had us peering down to see who it was. Angus’s head emerged as he tipped it back to examine us. I quickly removed my arm from Kai’s shoulders as she shuffled away slightly, letting go of my hand. I coughed as Angus grinned. He hadn’t been fooled at all. Kai gave him a withering look as he raised his eyebrows at her, and I chuckled. She grinned at me, braid slipping across her shoulder.

'What's going on?' Kai asked as Angus jumped into the air, hovering a few feet away from us.

'The Elders want to see you. They have to discuss what will happen tonight with… everything.' The words soured the atmosphere in the space of a blink, and Kai looked down.

'All right. I'll see you both later – tonight, I expect.'

'We'll be cheering for you,' Angus said to her, and she gave him a thankful look before slipping off the tree to drop down, only to shoot back up above the trees a moment later. She glanced back for a moment, catching my eye before soaring away.

'So, when's the wedding?' Angus asked casually, sitting down next to me. I pushed his shoulder so that he tipped backwards, falling off the tree. He shouted as he fell, and laughed, head tipped back as he came back up. Despite myself, I laughed too, shaking my head in disbelief at his audacity.

…

Kai

The arena was huge, the Elders watching me as I examined it carefully, Tera among them. She glanced at me before following the rest of them around to join me. There were only about six of them, one of them asking what I thought about it.

'Does every Syth fight in here?' I asked, not answering her question.

'Yes – we made it ourselves.'

I nodded, flexing my fingers nervously.

'What are we doing here?'

'We wanted you to see this place, know where you'll be fighting when the time comes tonight.'

'Who will I be fighting?'

'We can't tell you,' Tera said apologetically. 'But honestly, you shouldn't worry about it.'

…

I walked slowly around the arena, sizing up my opponent as he came closer. He was massive, the sheer bulk of him enough to intimidate me into submission. He grinned at me, cracking his muscles as icy daggers grew in his palms, frost covering his hands. I knew it was just for show – we hadn't started yet – but I backed away nervously, glancing up, to where the Elders were seated, about half of the Falcords also there. Their faces were hard and I scanned the crowd for a familiar one. A flash of raven hair made me look to where Faol had moved to the front of the crowd. He was looking at me, grinning slightly, teeth sharp in the faint light.

I glanced back at my opponent, who snarled as he caught my eye. I breathed out, feeling the Instinct running through me. I succumbed to it, pacing the floor of the arena a second later with ice roaring around me. I heard silence ripple through the crowd as they watched wind sweep around me, heads turning my way. I simply looked at one of the Elders' impassive face as she looked at me.

'You will fight when I say so – and use both magic and weapons. You will fight each opponent twice, to thoroughly test your skills.' I dipped my head as my opponent – a beastly man called Ranas – did so too.

'Begin.' Her icy voice cut through the air, and Ranas attacked. He leapt, using his size to his advantage. I wasn't a small person, but my lithe body was only two-thirds the size of his. His weight came crashing onto me and I panicked. As he rolled on top of me, I swiped my dagger powerfully across his face, sliding deep. Blood dripped onto the ground as Ranas let out a feral snarl. I hurled him off me, legs thrashing with the effort, and stood, panting. He got to his feet, seemingly unaffected by what I had done to him. I backed away as he came closer, creating space between us. I circled, feet silent on the stone floor of the arena except for a faint clicking of the frost I created occasionally. He did the same, face now covered in red liquid. I winced internally, even as I tensed to attack again.

I sprang high into the air. I bared my teeth at him as he, too, leapt into the air. He didn't get nearly as high as I did, but instead swiped for my exposed underbelly with a long sword. I twisted, trying to avoid his attack, dealing him a blow around the head with hands now aching.

He ducked, and I growled in frustration, aware of the Elders watching.

He attacked again without warning, and I sprang off my feet into the air like a startled cat. He backed me into the corner, towering over me as he dealt swipe after swipe at me face, my chest, my back. I returned them, blow for blow, but I was already tiring. This power needed energy to keep fighting like this for so long.

As if sensing my fatigue, my opponent pushed harder than ever, attempting to displace my feet so that I tripped. I could feel the hard wall behind me as I stumbled, leaving the left side of my neck exposed. He lunged, seizing my throat in his hands, drawing blood with his dagger. He was panting hard as he held it against me – not hard enough to kill, but hard enough to signal that he was the clear victor. I stared at the ground as the Elders signalled for him to let go.

He reluctantly released me, and I hissed at him violently, eyes flickering with fury through my exhaustion.

I did not like to lose.

He backed away, grinning slightly, retreating to his side of the arena.

'Again,' another Elder said, face devoid of emotion. I complied, making sure that the Instinct was still a strong image in my mind as I did so. Ranas did so too, drawing his sword from over his shoulder in one hand while summoning wind in the other. It buffeted against me as I grabbed Tholan, stalking forward. I pushed hard against it, muscles straining with the effort. The rusty smell of blood stung my nose as I swiped the blade, aiming for his side. He parried easily. I knew my face must be covered with blood and grime, and found that I didn't care. I crouched, retreating, and eyed him from under lowered brows. He smirked, pausing slightly, as if knowing that he had won.

I smiled slightly as a huge ball of wind and glass-shards of ice formed behind his back, driving down deep into his muscles. He arched in pain, but pushed past the crimson now dripping down his shirt. He ran for me, ducking as I swiped, fighting to press the blade once again to my throat. I pushed my hand against the sharp edge to fend it off, drawing blood from my own body. I snarled in his face while he chuckled at me, swiping too fast for me to see it. I twisted, only to find his blade now lodged against my windpipe. I was breathing hard, facing the Elders. They looked on disapprovingly – except for Tera, who was watching Ranas with a hard look on her face – and sighed.

'It's over. Victory to Ranas,' one of them said. Ranas released the blade, stalking away, being clapped on the back by his friends. I glowered after him, before looking back at Faol, who was watching me intently. I glanced once more at my opponent, who gave me a smirk before sauntering away, and stared at the floor hard.

Faol landed next to me, hands in his pockets. He watched Ranas disappear around a corner, and I turned to him.

'Let's go.'

He nodded, and I turned, bringing him with me. We walked slowly together, him supporting me as I walked in a daze, exhausted from a single fight.

'How am I ever supposed to fight an entire army of Firborn if I can barely hold my own against a Falcord who isn't even high ranking?'

'You forget – I'll be there with you.' I glanced at him, eyes narrowing as he smiled arrogantly at me. 'Besides, I bet I could take on all of the Firborn by myself and walk out alive.'

I snorted disbelievingly. 'You wish. Knowing my sister... she'd never let you go. She'd probably tear you to ribbons by the time she was done with you.'

He raised his eyebrows. 'She sounds…savage.'

'She can be, when she wants to.' I glanced across at him, a small smile on my lips, realising what he was trying to do.

'Thank you for trying to lighten the mood, but I think it's better if I just go to sleep and get ready for tomorrow. It's late.'

He nodded, smiling. My heart warmed at the sight of it.

We said goodbye, and he wandered off with his hands in his pockets.

I looked after him for a minute, wishing I hadn't sobered the mood. I sighed and turned back, striding away with blood still dripping slightly down my skin, towards my tent, which was a while away. It was deep in the bay, not out in the woods here, but I wanted to walk instead of fly. I stuffed my fists into my pocket as I made my way along the ground, following the path that was worn into the frosty ground.

As I looked around, I noticed the frost glittering on the trees. I hadn't made very good use of my powers – something that I would have to remedy in the next battle. I moved away, feet trailing on the ground as I walked. I watched the trees pass by as I made my way to my tent, preparing myself for the next battle.

…

The next two days were chaos, as I trained in the morning, ate a dismally small lunch with Faol, Tera and Angus and then fought at night. So far, I had lost all three of my battles and life was becoming increasingly stressful. I pretended that I was fine with it but inside I was desperately worried about letting my friends down – especially Faol. They all looked at me as if I was valuable, as if I had a purpose among them. If I lost the war, I'd probably be an outcast. I wouldn't be treated badly by them but I wouldn't be alive for long enough to fight again. They would probably still talk to me but we would never be as close as we were now.

It was the fourth day of fighting and I was in the arena, facing Iren. I gulped as he grinned evilly, showing off his cracked brown teeth. I shuddered to think that at some point those teeth might be at my throat, his dagger right next to it.

'Begin,' the Elders ordered, uttering the same instructions that they had the past three days. I stepped forward, taking a deep breath, and summoned my power, watching as Iren did the same. We stepped around each other, exchanging blows, until we were both fairly battered. My right ear was cut and the blood stung my nostrils, itching as it dried. I ignored it, hissing violently at Iren. I would not back down this time.

I leapt on him, arms tensed as I moved, icy claws extracted from my hands as I dealt him a blow so powerful he stumbled, falling to the floor. I pounced like a cat, not wasting my opportunity, and swiped again and again until his back was a mesh of clawed hair and sticky blood. He howled in agony, but I did not care. He was fully on the ground now, desperate to get out of my iron grip. He shifted his head forward slightly and I realised what I could do. I snapped down, sliding Tholan against his neck, looking to the Elders as I did so.

The Instinct rose up, and I focused once again on that image in my head, worried that I would give in to it.

'Fight again,' the Elder said, a hint of surprise in her voice. I shifted and dragged Iren off me, hissing in his ear.

'Think again before you threaten any of *my* friends.' He snarled back, twisting his head to meet my eyes. I pushed him away and strode to my side of the arena, watching Angus, who was grinning with delight. I smiled back at him, eyes glinting viciously. I would pound Iren to the ground.

He hurled himself at me, and I sidestepped easily, summoning my ice. It frosted the ground, making him struggle as he tried to rise up to attack. I chuckled softly, drawing my sword again from its sheath. I attacked and he rolled to avoid my lunge, cursing me soundly. I merely smiled down at him before swiping, giving him an unrelenting force that wouldn't cease until he backed down. He raised up his hands, one against my onslaught, another to summon wind of his own. He pushed it towards me and I snorted under my breath. I cut a path through his current with one of my own, propelling myself forward. He was backed into a corner now, and I pushed hard to reach my sword around, finally placing it firmly against his throat. He met my eyes, his own glinting with loathing. I smiled down at him witheringly and turned away to look at the Elders. They were sitting in shock. Tera was grinning ear to ear, and I smiled faintly back at her.

'Victory to the Syth, Kai,' one of the Elders said. I reached a hand down to help Iren up but he pushed it away, curling his lip as he tried to stand, his back still a mess. I grinned and simply walked away, into the coolness of the night air.

The next day was harder and I gritted my teeth as I pushed

my sword against my opponent in the bitter cold. He was a fairly young man, with hard eyes and a thin line for a mouth.

I swore as his sword scraped my arm, drawing blood from deep within my arteries. I winced through the pain, cradling my arm slightly. The man's eyes gleamed as he watched me, moving forward to claim his victory. I had beaten him previously but this time it was harder.

I flung an icy barrier at him to prevent him from coming closer. He pounded his fist against it before flying effortlessly upwards over it. I willed it to rise into the air with him, so that he could never get past it. He growled in frustration, eyeing me like he would prey. I scowled back at him, running under a hole I created in the shield so that I was on the same side as him. I flew upwards as he turned, striking fast. He winced from the reverberation, dropping slightly. I pressed on, forcing him to move lower and lower, and to raise up his sword to defend against me above him. I slammed myself on top of him, sending us both tumbling to the ground. I quickly snapped my power to attention and soared upwards, watching him flail. Before he could break his neck, I grabbed him by the collar, shoving him against the ice wall with a dagger to his throat. There was silence, and then cheering as the Elders announced my victory. I let the man down, shaking his hand before walking off the battlefield, heading back to camp with Tera. She was smiling madly, laughing and gripping my hand tight. She looked at me with eyes bright, thrill prominent in them. Through my tiredness after a long day, I had grinned back at her, pleased with my successes, even if I had only had two of them.

...

The cavern was packed, everyone arguing as we all desperately tried to agree on a plan for that night.

'Let's take a vote,' Faol said, voice quieting even Iren, who glared at us viciously. Most of the members nodded, and Faol continued. 'The first plan is that a few of us will go, surprise Sardaron, and *peacefully* offer him a bargain. We will leave in the first battle, taking Kai's sister with us. If he doesn't co-operate, then we attack, using the Syths to our advantage. But only as a final resort. Tera, Amber – Kai's sister – Kai, and I will be going. Angus will be in charge of you here, giving you orders while the rest of us are gone. The second, *idiot* idea, is that we try to take him by surprise, pin him, and take the Quill.' Faol said it in such a sarcastic way that a few of the warriors chuckled. 'All in favour of the first idea?'

Hands raised slowly, some warriors raising theirs immediately, glaring at anyone who didn't. I grinned, watching as nearly everyone raised their arm. Iren, scowling in a corner, spat on the floor.

'Well, I think we've decided, at any rate,' Faol said lightly, trying to hide his grin at Iren's face. Without a word, Iren left, dragging a few others with him as he went. I laughed aloud as one of them pushed Iren off of him in disgust, sitting back down.

However amusing it was to see Iren get humiliated, dread still formed to think that we would be fighting the Firborn the day after tomorrow – and facing Sardaron a few days after that.

...

The last day was cloudy, the sky overcast as I stared across at my final competitor. Across from me, Faol grinned back, already getting ready to attack. I settled my stance and waited for the cool command despite my slight shock that it would be he who I was fighting. It was Tera this time who said to begin, and I smiled wryly at the hint of excitement in her voice. Everyone had been interested in how this battle would turn out ever since we had both flown into the arena, and they were cheering for each of us in small groups.

I shifted, moving forward in a fluid motion. Faol was there to meet me as I swiped and then darted back, using the spiky ridges of ice adorning my blade to push him back as I turned from his blow. We tussled, rolling over and over, until he was on me, weapon swiping for my throat. I heaved, pushing him off in a heartbeat, and sprang to my feet. He leapt high, matching my attacks with his own defence. He was the best of their fighters, I remembered, wondering how I was supposed to overcome him.

He leapt forward, both of us twisting together as we battled it out physically, seeming to forget our powers for a moment.

I finally ended up next to the wall, him backing me in slowly but surely. When I felt the stone at my back, I tensed, waiting for his attack.

He lunged and I leapt up high, soaring over him to land where he had been a moment before. He saw my move coming, however, and reached up to swipe at my belly as I passed over him. I cursed inwardly as gushes of blood began to spill onto the ground as his sword scraped my legs instead.

But now I was the one cornering him and he couldn't get away the same way that I had. I prowled forward, until we were nose-to-nose. His eyes were still that vibrant shade of turquoise blue, I noted, following where they tracked.

He looked down for a moment, and I flashed forward, slamming his head to the ground and quickly pinning him.

Fighting against him a second time would be harder than what I had gone through before. I was so tired already.

Even though I had more power than him, he was more skilled in using it, and would do so to beat me. I watched a powerful wind whip through the hair of the warriors, coming to rest next to Faol like an otherworldly presence. I watched nervously as it rose up, stirring other breezes to approach me. I summoned the ice that had frozen over my life for seven years, for a vicious, savage wind to curl around it, splitting and sharpening it. It fractured slightly as I raised it above my head. As one, we threw our powers at each other, magic rippling the air around us as they tangled with each other, trying to get around to their target. I charged for him, dagger slipping up to his chest as I ducked around his tornado of wind. Another buffeted me back, however, and I tried to push through it. Icicles with razor-sharp tips shot for his head, and he had to duck to avoid them, losing concentration. The wind died down for a moment, and I sprinted to him, tackling him to the ground. He pushed me off, grabbing his own weapon, and started to attack, a whirlwind of ice sharp as glass hurtling around us. I could barely see past it, to where everyone must be peering through to see what was happening.

I grunted in frustration, trying a different tactic. I let go, making him stumble forward, sword out in front of him. I slipped around, grabbing him by the side and shoving him to the ground, pinning his hands behind his back and blade to his throat.

'Victory to Kai.' The Elders sounded shocked. I watched Angus and Tera glance at each other, eyebrows raised, grinning in delight.

I removed my knee from where it had been placed on his back, and helped him up. The onyx necklace that he always wore was dangling out of his shirt, and he tucked it into the cotton quickly.

He smiled at me, linking arms as everyone came around to congratulate me, sympathising with him, making jokes about it. He didn't seem to mind that he had lost, had seemed pleased for me, actually. I supposed he was grateful that I *had* strength on the battlefield.

I was so relieved that the battles were finally over that I could do nothing but laugh and smile until my face hurt.

It was only when I went to my tent that I realised that the wars started tomorrow. Dread curled in my stomach, and I found it impossible to sleep.

I tossed and turned all night, finally getting up to leave. I needed fresh air and headed out, stumbling back when I saw a dark figure seated in the nearest tree, gazing down at me.

'Faol?' I whispered, and the figure beckoned for me to join

him. I quickly flew up, joining him in the moonlight.

We sat in silence, hands clasped tightly together, heads leaning together, until I sighed.

'I need to go think somewhere. Alone.'

He nodded, and I quickly dropped from the tree, heading to the edge of the bay.

...

I summoned a breeze, the wind rippling around my skin as I did so. I was standing on a rocky cliff, staring out to the vast stretch of water before me, contemplating what I had to do tomorrow. Possibly to kill Amber… I could not live with myself if I had to do so. At the same time, there was so much I wanted to do and experience in my life. I thought of Faol. If I could survive this, I had a life before me, ready for me to tread. A life of adventure, but also of killing and fear. I didn't know how tomorrow would turn out, how I would be affected.

Letting out a sigh, I jumped down from the huge rock I had leapt onto, taking one last glance at the moon, whispering onto the bay in the faint breeze. I turned, bounding into the undergrowth that surrounded me, my movements silent as I treaded through the pinewoods.

Ahead, a faint light gleamed, and I realised someone else was walking through the woods. Not someone. Two people. The one further away was hard to distinguish, but I recognised the one closer to me with a jolt.

It was one of the Elders, her robe swishing behind her as she walked, shoulders tense. She was probably just walking with her husband, I thought, reassuring myself. But it didn't look that way – I could see the other figure (a man, I had realised by now) making quick, jolting motions with his hands as if he was speaking passionately. Instinctively, I pricked up my ears to hear what they were saying. Their words were faint and hard to make out, so I wandered a little closer, careful to keep my body close to the trees in case they caught me.

'Thank you for coming to me. I'll make sure that they're punished accordingly,' the Elder said, and I stiffened. What were they talking about – or rather, who were they talking about? The Elder swung her gaze in my direction a moment later and stopped walking. I crouched into a tree swiftly, praying that she hadn't spotted me.

'Do you see anything? I could have sworn I heard a twig snap.' The murmur of the man next to her was too faint for my ears to pick up, and I silently cursed myself. Fool. Why had I even come to this point in the forest? I should have gone to the regular spot to meet with the Fydars and go over our plan for tomorrow one more time, instead of standing in the dark alone.

I glanced up at the moon, hoping that it wasn't bright enough to illuminate me. Thankfully, I didn't think it did, as I watched the Elder gradually relax again.

The Elder looked around suspiciously one more time before moving away with the mysterious man, and I quickly slipped away, bolting down the cliff nimbly. My head was whirling with questions about who the Elder was standing with and what they were talking about. Could they have been discussing me and my fight tomorrow? Had I done something wrong? I made my way back to the main camp, careful not to go down the path they had trodden.

Once back in the camp, I breathed the night air in deeply, calming myself down. Glancing right quickly, I saw the same Elder gather her power of gravity-defying flight as she made her way to the platform nearby. Once reaching it, she ascended it, and unfurled her hands from her sides. Raising them into the sky, she shot a jet of pure blue light into the sky, the ice glittering as it formed a snarling wolf. A gust of wind swept by as the Elder held the ice in its position, making sure everyone could see it. I knew the sign – Faol had told me once what it meant. The Elder wanted those closest to come listen to what she had to say.

It meant that she had a message – one to be spread around the camp.

I stood straighter, lifting my body to the breeze as I shot closer to the platform, weaving around a few others who were doing the same.

The Elders face was twisted in fury, I saw, as I approached, and prepared to land. She opened her mouth to speak, and I strained my ears to hear.

'I am holding a gathering in the cavern where the Rite is held. Every Falcord must attend,' I heard her say as I landed. 'We have been betrayed by some of our own community. A more despicable act I cannot imagine,' she spat, eyes dark and frozen with wrath. 'A group that call themselves the Fydars is planning to confront Sardaron himself. Such idiocy should, and will, be punished. I expect to see everyone in the cavern in ten minutes for a full briefing. Pass on the message.' She swept off the stage a moment later, flying towards some of the other Elders. It was all I could do not to drop down to my knees as the others around me started to whisper to each other, their voices both curious and fearful. I stopped breathing.

No, this couldn't have happened.

No, no, no. All our hard work, all our training and careful planning. It couldn't have been for nothing. I turned on leaden feet, my only thought to warn Faol. We had to know who had betrayed us to the Elders, when they *knew* that we would be punished for it. As fast as a light switch, my shaking despair turned to anger. When I found whoever had done this… their ending would not be pleasant.

I cooled my anger, turned it into something razor sharp and cold as the moon. Then I started walking towards Faol's tent, the night swirling around me as I stepped forwards.

…

Faolan

'We've been betrayed.'

I looked up from where I was sitting on the ground in my tent, sharpening a dagger. Kai stood some feet away at the threshold, holding the tent flap open with her hand.

'What? By who?'

Kai opened her mouth to answer my question, eyes

gleaming with fear.

Behind her, I could see warriors rushing to and from tents, whispering furtively to each other. Some looked scared, some curious, others angry. In the moonlight, there wasn't much else I could make out.

'Just come. The Elders want to see us in the cavern where I took the Rite.'

She motioned for me to run, and I quickly stood, brushing myself down. In silence, we both stepped out of the tent, and surveyed the scene in front of us. It was utter chaos as some soldiers ran and others made their way quietly to the cavern, whole bodies shaking in fear. In the dark, I spotted Angus, walking with his head held high. Beside him was Tera, who was looking around nervously. She glanced over at me and beckoned for us to join her. We ran over, dodging scattering soldiers, trying to remain inconspicuous.

'Someone's told one of the Elders about us – about the Fydars,' she hissed as we arrived, eyes wide with fear. 'They don't know who's in the group, but they're promising death for those who are. They're angry because they think that our plan to confront Sardaron will just get them killed.'

'*What*?' I said, shocked.

Angus pressed his finger to his lips, and beckoned for us to start walking.

'You'll know the details when we get there.'

...

Kai

The cavern was as huge as I remembered, its walls decorated with frosty patterns. On the platform at the far end stood one of the Elders, a few others grouped behind her. I remembered her from the pits, when she had selected Iren to be my opponent.

She had a sense of disgust about her, and was eyeing the crowd as if she already knew who the rebel culprits were.

The crowd went silent as she raised a hand to speak.

'We have discovered, through an anonymous source, that there is a rebel group operating within our community. They call themselves the Fydar Rebels, and have an aim that leads to the provoking of the Creator, something that will surely end in bloodshed and death. We do not know who is in the group, only that they are going against all our rules and ways of living. They are evil and only want to see the destruction of others. There are many ways to find out just who, exactly, is in this group, and after the first battle tomorrow, interrogations will take place. If anyone survives the first battle and is found to be the traitor, they shall be executed immediately.' This speech, given in an icy manner, seemed to still the room, causing worried glances. My heart sank and I closed my eyes.

Execution? It seemed so severe. I worried for all the Fydars who would now almost certainly be killed – a whole group of fighters. In front of us, the Elder swept out, the ice dissolving from the atmosphere as she did so. Many of the Falcords were trying to subtly exit the scene, and others were standing, as if frozen, staring in front of them.

...

'The plan has to change.'

The cavern was squeezed full, the arrival of the entirety of the Fydars almost too much for it to handle. Many were nodding their heads to my announcement, their fear written clearly across their faces.

'And whoever betrayed us... we'll find you. At one point or another.'

I gave a serpentine smile and turned to Faol. He stepped forward.

'My plan is that instead of having you all return to the camp for the night, you come on the run with us.'

A lone voice shouted out, 'We can't have hundreds of people traipsing into the middle of nowhere! It'll lead to disaster, surely.'

Faol looked impatient. 'I know it won't be easy, but we can do it. Since there are so many of us, it'll be easier to overthrow Sardaron – as Iren himself put it.'

'Actually, Faol... they may have a point,' Angus said, putting his hand on Faol's shoulder. 'It'll be easier if they just hide out for a week or so, wait until we get back before doing anything.'

Faol glanced at Angus, betrayed that he would go against him.

'Fine. But I choose who is in charge.'

The glowing lights on the ceiling flickered as a strong breeze swept through the cavern. No one shivered. I supposed, being a Falcord, we were immune to cold and frostbite and those kinds of things. Faol's cultured voice swept over my head, and I realised that I was so tired I could hardly stand. All the training, fighting and flying left me exhausted.

Finally, clapping, and voices getting louder, signalled that the discussion was at an end. I straightened, glancing at Tera and then Faol. They were talking quietly as the crowd walked past them out of the cavern.

Over in a corner, Angus too was in deep conversation with a stranger.

I walked past Tera and Faol, into the darkened night, wishing that dawn would never come.

.17.

Helmon

'Helmon?'

'Can you let me in?'

'Sure.' Amber's door swung open, revealing her anxious face. 'What is it?'

'Can I come in?'

She paused for a moment before opening her door wider to let me in. I took in the comfortable room, awkwardly standing in the middle.

'What is it?' she asked again, and I took a deep breath.

'I just wanted you to know that Nuru and I are no longer together – I told her that maybe we weren't right for each other.'

Her face was impassive, arms crossed over her chest, but I caught the flicker of shock at my words, at what I was telling her. Implying.

'I'm really sorry, Helmon.'

'No, it's completely fine. Well, it's not, but… I'm telling you because I wanted to know whether you would consider the fact that maybe… I like you.'

She met my eyes, her own wide.

'You do?'

'Yes.' She looked down, studying the floor, arms still crossed.

'I like you too, Helmon. And I want to maybe start something with you. But… if it means breaking Nuru's heart, I don't want to.' I squashed down any feelings, trying to bring more confidence to the surface.

'Nuru and I have spoken a few times over the past few days. She gets it, Amber, she really does,' I said, looking at her placatingly. 'She just wants me to be happy. And the only way I can be happy is if I'm with *you*.'

She watched me intently, still unsmiling.

'I don't think she does, Helmon.'

'What do you mean?'

'Well… I've seen the way she looks at you. The adoration in her gaze. She still loves you, no matter what she might say.'

She took a deep breath, longing seeming to cloud her vision.

'I would very much like for us to be in a relationship,' she said solemnly. 'But only if it's in a while – when Nuru is over her love for you.' She paused, watching me while I nodded, excitement fizzing deep in my stomach. 'Helmon, I have something else I have to discuss with you. Something even more important than what you told me.'

My heart cooled, worry freezing it over quickly.

'What is it?'

'I think… I don't want to kill anyone in the wars tomorrow. It's just too sick to think about. I couldn't stomach it.'

I felt ashamed. Here she was, worrying about pressing and urgent matters, while I was worrying about whether she liked me.

'I understand – if that's your choice, then you can act upon it, even though it will cause trouble in the fighting tomorrow. You simply need to defeat Kai, but you don't have to kill her – or anyone else for that matter. But can I advise you to not tell anyone? It will only cause trouble.'

'All right, I won't – but I just wanted you to know.' She faced me, holding out her hand. 'Shall we go to eat?'

I nodded, smiling once more. 'Of course.'

I took her arm, leading her out of the room.

She leant her head on my shoulder for a second, and we grinned at each other. Her face sobered as she looked over her shoulder at a passing figure some distance away. She squeezed her eyes shut as I looked on in confusion.

'Helmon, you should take Nuru into account before starting a relationship with me.'

'Why?'

'You have to consider that she likes you as well. And not just as a friend – as more than that.'

'I know – you said –'

'Just make sure you talk to her.' She turned, but apparently remembered something else. 'Neil loves her, you know,' she said, glancing at me once more before twisting slightly, leaving me with my jaw hanging open, staring at her.

...

Amber

He glanced at me before removing his hand from mine.

'I need to talk to him.'

I nodded, hoping that it would all work out well. They were close friends – I was sure nothing too severe would happen. I felt a flicker of hurt as he walked away without another word, leaving me alone.

...

Helmon

I opened the door to Nuru's room gently, the door creaking slightly as I stepped past the threshold.

She wasn't there. I frowned, looking around the brightly lit corners to check.

'Hello?' I said, peering around once more. I knew I had seen her come this way earlier – in fact, I had crossed her path on my way to see Amber. She had been near here, and I had assumed that she was going to go in.

I walked further into the room, stepping around the comfortable furniture that littered the space. I knew this room well – had spent a lot of time in it.

I peered out of the window in the far corner, watching as people milled about the ancient courtyard that had been built centuries ago. Many of the Elders were there, sitting on benches and talking nervously, faces clenched and tight. Everyone was apprehensive.

A flash of colour caught my eye as I twisted to look out of the far side of the window.

Nuru was standing on a platform at the far left of the courtyard, raising one hand to the sky.

What *is* she doing? I thought, watching heads in the crowded space turn to watch her. All knew who she was. She glanced up at the sky, and flame sputtered to life under her gaze. It curled into the air, forming a huge eagle, it's beak agape and screeching. She stared at the flame for a long, long moment.

I knew what it was for. Whenever there was something that needed to be discussed with the whole of the Firborn, a signal flare was sent into the sky. Those nearest would come running, flocking to that person, as they were to Nuru now, to see what she had to say.

I stared in confusion before turning from the window, hurrying out of the room and along the corridor in my haste to reach the courtyard.

...

A crowd was pressing together, the small platform barely keeping Nuru's head above the confused people.

The Elders climbed onto the platform with her as she looked at the crowd. Her face was bitter, eyes darting from one face to the next. No love – no compassion for these people. At her side, two slender daggers gleamed.

I rushed up to her, pushing past the mobs, as she started speaking.

'I've called this gathering because I have an announcement to make.' She turned to look at the Elders standing behind her. 'I want to leave the Firborn.'

Silence descended as I finally reached the platform and heaved myself onto it, panting. Everyone was simply staring. No one had done this before – and certainly not the day before the wars began.

An Elder chuckled softly, looking at her pityingly. 'I understand that it's hard to fight, but you're being a little irrational.'

Wet tears gleamed on Nuru's cheeks as she turned slowly to face me. The look she gave me sent a dagger to my heart, piercing it thoroughly.

'No. I'm not being irrational,' she said, only looking at me. The whole congregation listened silently as she continued. 'I hate this life – this miserable, wretched life, where you are forced to fight for no reason, when you are taken from the family, friends you once had and placed *here*, where everything is so different. I hate it,' she said, sniffing. 'And the man that I learned to love, who I thought I would spend the rest of eternity with, never truly felt the same way.' He gaze was penetrating on mine. 'And without his love – the only love I had in this putrid place – I have nothing. No reason to stay – even to live. I know that I couldn't sit here for centuries to come, watching his relationship with someone else blossom and grow. So I ask you again,' she said, turning to the Elders once more, 'if I may be allowed to leave this tribe – to roam of my free will through these lands, where I can finally live my own life.'

There was no hesitation in her eyes, even then, as she awaited the judgement of the Elders.

One stepped forward, face placating. 'You must understand that it's impossible. You are too valuable, your abilities too precious…'

'That's what it's always been about, hasn't it,' Nuru bit back. 'My abilities. Not about who *I* am as a person. If I didn't have any abilities, I think the words coming out of your mouth would be very different indeed.' She stepped back from them, edging towards the edge of the platform. 'So I guess I'll have to take matters into my own hands.'

She reached for the two daggers I had previously observed, flicking them free from their casing. My eyes widened as she raised both at the same moment, level with her eyes.

I knew what she was going to do – and so did everyone else. She wasn't going to plunge the daggers into her heart, but into her eyes, the source of her powers. If she was successful, when she pulled the daggers out, she would be uninjured. Uninjured, but permanently blind. Of no use to anyone – and therefore automatically exiled.

It was a rule that had been in place since the dawn of time, survival everyone's top priority. We had no room for those who could not fend for themselves in wars.

The Elders surged forward as she started moving, crying out to stop, to wait. The crowd gasped, shouts ringing out as many tried to grab her, to stop her.

She plunged the daggers forward.

I covered my mouth in horrified silence as she fell to the ground, screaming, her hands covering her eyes, streaming blood.

She had really done it – had really blinded herself.

The crowd rushed forward, many calling for medical supplies, for bandages.

Slowly, I walked forward, until I stood above her. Horror covered my features as I stared down at those lovely eyes. Those eyes which were now mangled and ruined.

'What have you done?' I whispered.

…

Amber

The dawn was bright through my curtains as I sat up, yawning slightly. I bolted upright as I remembered that today was the first day of the wars – the portal would open at midday, and we would then travel to a special valley, where the Falcords would meet us. I was already apprehensive, even though I wouldn't be killing, but the thought of fighting Kai turned my stomach. Perhaps my journey to get here had mellowed me.

I dressed quickly, wondering where everyone was. There was silence in the volcano-building, the distant rumble of lava the only sound. I grabbed my weapons and supply backpack, making sure that I had everything before running to the large window bordering my room.

I looked out across the desert landscape, immediately noticing the large cluster of people on the horizon. I opened the window and jumped out, wind whistling slightly as I carried myself to the others.

They were milling by the portal, organising themselves into ranks and orders, some shouting commands. I ran up to Helmon, who was standing next to the rest of his legion. I grabbed his wrist so that he swung around to face me.

'Where's Nuru? Did you talk to her?'

He looked at me for a moment that seemed to stretch for eternity.

'You… you didn't hear?' he whispered.

My eyes were wide as I shook my head. 'Why, what happened?'

'She's gone.'

I didn't understand. 'What do you mean, she's gone? Gone where?' I asked, panicking. My heartbeat fluttered as I scanned his face, examining it as if it was a book.

He took a deep breath. 'She was exiled yesterday evening. She decided… that she couldn't stand to live with me any more. With us.' He looked down in despair. 'She didn't want to live, fighting again and again, without anything to live for.'

'What did she do?' I said, my voice small and weak.

'It is very, very hard to survive, to live the life we do, on these realms. It is so miserable that only the company of others keeps you going, keeps you thriving. Without it, you are nothing.' I watched him as his eyes sparkled with newly forming tears. 'So… she blinded herself. Thrust a dagger into both eyes in front of everyone before they could stop her. She survived, but…' He looked at me. 'She's been exiled – something I think she may have wanted to happen. Without your eyesight, you can no longer use your powers. Therefore,' he said bitterly, 'your life is of no importance to the Elders – or to the war. You are cast out – if you can't defend your people, then you shouldn't be using up their resources. At least that's the principle that many warriors use.'

I was shaking, my fingers trembling like leaves. All I could do was flick my gaze over Helmon's face, my vision of him clouding second by second as I dropped my head into my hands, the first of my tears emerging. He pulled me to him, and I stood, weeping silently, my head tucked into his shoulder.

He leant his chin on the top of my head as we rocked silently back and forth. He was sobbing quietly, the warm tears dripping onto my hair.

'Did she really want to leave?' I asked despairingly. 'How will she survive?'

'I don't know,' Helmon said, voice cracking. I took a deep breath and stepped away from him, drying my tears as I did so.

'Find me in the battle, okay?' I said.

Why?'

'I just… want to do this together.'

'I'll meet you when we get there.'

I nodded, glancing over at Neil. He was watching Helmon carefully, and met my eyes briefly. Helmon saw where I was looking and skimmed his eyes over Neil's figure dismissively. He knew that Neil loved Nuru – and probably thought that if

Neil had told her, she wouldn't have done what she did. She would have felt wanted.

I sighed and slipped away towards the Elders, who were all gathered together.

I checked that I had everything I would need.

There was a glint of light ahead, and I craned my neck to look. The portal was slowly opening, its shining outline stark against the abyss inside.

I watched apprehensively as a murmur went through the crowd, the first legion stepping up. I watched Helmon, who was with them, as they all approached the small hole hanging a few feet above the ground.

The first member put his hand through the hole, and promptly vanished. The others followed suit, and I watched each body disappear until there were none left.

The second legion stepped up, preparing to do the same.

I watched until there was no one left but me and the Elders.

They all turned to watch me, making sure that I went first. I smiled nervously, reaching my hand through the portal into the painful darkness, anticipating the well of light at the end.

...

We had been marching for a day now, and my feet were so sore I could barely stand. Things had been tense with Helmon and Neil, but they were now walking side by side.

I was terrified. I was heading into a war, one that I would not fight in, all to win supplies, and provide Sardaron with the deaths he needed. How was I supposed to survive? It felt wrong to let this war happen, yet there was nothing I could do by myself.

It was freezing, the temperature slowly getting colder as we made our way into a huge wood. I thought that, with the bright sun, we would be warm but I was still shivering slightly. I thought maybe it had something to do with me being a Firborn, accustomed to heat. The Falcords would probably be sweating by now. I wondered briefly what would happen if I was to go to Nzar. Would I die of hypothermia immediately?

Time passed, until the sunlight was a golden glow in the distance, and we heard distant voices. My ears pricked, heart beating faster. Were the Falcords here?

We passed through a dense mass of trees, and rounded out to see an enormous glade, sun filtering through the leaves, making them glow. It was bordered by two steep hills, which sloped down on either side of it.

It was beautiful – and it was also going to be a killing field.

I stared across the field, to where figures were weaving through the trees on top of the other slope. They moved away, but I could faintly see triangles in the distance. Tents. They must be setting up camp there then, I supposed, looking back to our own Elders. They, too, were moving away, calling to others to help them. I trudged over, glancing back to the Falcords' side of the field. Three figures stood, looking at us. I saw one, who had raven hair, point across at us. The other two, one brunette, the other blonde, glanced our way as well. I stared at the blonde girl, who was swinging a dagger between her fingers as she listened to the other two. Kai?

She glanced my way again, but I knew she had not seen me. I turned away, heart twisted with anxiety, and followed the others through the trees.

...

Kai

I made my way out of the tent I had decided to share with Tera the next morning at dawn, spotting Faol immediately. He was standing with Angus, discussing battle tactics together. I gulped and moved past them, stepping through the trees until I could see the entirety of the battlefield. The Firborn were starting to emerge over the trees as well, organising themselves into their groups. I looked back to see the rest of the Falcords approaching, doing the same as the Firborn. I knew Angus had spent much of last night with the Fydars, telling them where to hide while we were with Sardaron. The Elders – apart from Tera – had been furious, and had been promising death to anyone acting suspicious.

The Fydars were gathered together, arms around each other, branches mostly covering them from sight. Faol strode over to them, clapping one over the shoulder. They grinned and let him into their circle.

I sighed, turning my attention back to the army amassing on the other side of the glade. We were almost organised, and so were they. I felt dread take over my body, the Instinct rising up as I watched them. The Quill's effect – to make the two people hate each other when sensing each other – was already becoming apparent. I pushed it down fiercely, turning back to the army, who were now ready.

I slipped into my rank, in front of the Fydars, Faol behind me. I watched through the trees, peering to see if Amber was doing the same. An auburn-haired girl was running from in between the trees, and my throat constricted as I watched. She walked up to a brown-haired soldier, saying something to him before moving to the front of the army. It was her. Amber was here.

I felt a tear escape my eye as I watched, and I wiped it away, still watching intently. Amber looked across at the man, and I could just about see the glint of her teeth as she smiled at him. I took a deep breath, looking away from her as I tried to compose myself.

Someone gripped my hand, and I looked back at Faol, who was watching the Firborn from close behind. He smiled faintly at me and I let go of his hand, smiling back.

I turned away as something in the air started to pull the two armies together. I tried to plant my feet in the ground, but the invisible force pulled me forward. I could see that the same was happening to the Firborn, and almost vomited in fear. I lifted my sword, Tholan sheathed by my side.

The war was beginning.

The two sides were silent on either side of the field, and I knew that everyone was preparing to shift. A whisper from the Instinct confirmed it and, as one, our army rippled, eyes glowing as ice and wind howled. I felt it too, watching the other army, who still hadn't moved.

Amber was observing our army, and stepped back slightly in fear as our power roiled around us. I watched a shudder pass through their army as they did the same, flames and heat appearing from where soldiers stood. As one, they all lifted off the ground, rising into the air.

I felt a call in the Instinct then – a call to fight, and to kill. I stepped forward slightly, afraid of the hatred that rose up as I watched the Firborn. The Instinct was taking over all of us – or rather, the curse was.

A screech from the Firborn made my attention snap back to them. A single leader had cried out, and the first few were beginning to take action. A howl echoed from our side of the field, and I understood its order. I bolted forward at the same time as the rest of the army, the Firborn doing the same, as the battle began.

...

The carnage was everywhere as I faced a handsome man, his eyes a bright, merry brown. I recognised him as the man who Amber had smiled at before the battle had started. A few moments before, when I had seen a blue-haired man and a man with a snakeskin quiver, I had been sucked into the Instinct. Too much so. I was on my way to find Amber, so desperate to reach her that I had killed them both. My shoulders already sagged with the burden of my guilt as I faced this next attacker. I attempted to dodge around him, but he blocked me with a shout.

He dived with his sword, and I batted upwards weakly with

Tholan, trying to fend him off. I felt my weapon snag on flesh, swiping down, and opened my eyes to see him flailing to the floor, a gaping wound in his heart.

I stared, watching as the life drained out of him. I moved on, glancing one last time at the man I had just killed, at the person who was now fading away.

I had to find Amber, and sprinted forward, making my way towards the Syth somewhere at the edge of the field. I felt a tug to her, as though the Instinct told me where she was. Around me, chaos reigned; blood, flesh, weapons and gore were everywhere as the two sides mauled each other to bits. I thought faintly of Faol, and of how he was faring.

At that moment, I paused, scanning my surroundings. A strange urge from the Instinct had me shuddering, my whole form shaking. Somehow, the Instinct was urging me to fly upwards. It gave a forceful push, and I complied, terrified of what was happening. A few feet away, I saw another form shift and rise up.

Amber.

I stopped dead before hurtling forward, dagger in hand to protect myself from the onslaught of attackers.

I watched her fiery head turn towards mine amid the blood and chaos and I sprinted over, hurling one of my daggers into the gut of a man who swooped aggressively towards me with his spear poised to strike. He was a middle-aged man with a fierce green eye, the other covered by an eyepatch. He went down with a screech, his blood squirting all over my fighting clothes. A bright auburn eye caught mine, and I saw a small tear trickle down the owner's face.

Amber's face.

I flew, not caring that my arm had a long, jagged wound in it that was leaking blood all over me from fighting.

She ran too, and it was all I could see. She looked older, her hair tied back, eyes flashing with happiness and sorrow, the two emotions mingling.

'KAI!' she shouted, and I caught her muffled words before a host of soldiers, each baring their teeth, shouting and snarling at each other, blocked my vision of her. Moments later, a golden figure soared over the heads of the soldiers and swooped down, ducking over and under arms and heads that were clashing. I felt a jubilant, overpowering sense of joy as she landed.

Before she could say anything, I crushed her into a hug, tears leaking down my grimy cheeks. I was finally with my sister again. I started sobbing, the events of the past couple months crashing through my mind. Tears poured down her face too as she held me, dripping onto my shirt.

I don't know how long we held each other, only that I sensed another presence find us among the fray. Faolan, I saw, as I looked over. He was shielding us, I realised, because others were starting to realise just who, exactly, was standing here. Both Syths together, the most powerful combination of people.

As I pulled away from Amber, I could practically see their mouths drool as they eyed us, probably thinking of the glory they would get from killing us. I stepped away from Amber, raising a hand to the sky. Above, a white light flashed as dark clouds gathered, similar to lightning. But this was not lightning

– lightning would seem merciful compared to this.

I had honed this trick – one Faol had taught me in our lessons together with Tera – for as long as I could. Now was the time to test it out. The light intensified, making the warriors around me squint. I panted as I felt the toll of the power used in making this.

Faolan watched for a few seconds before he had to turn back to battle. I held the ball, expanding it so that it became larger and larger. We glanced at each other, his cyan eyes stark against his blood. I turned back to the sky, and rammed the ice into the ground.

Smoke spread as the ice exploded, and I quickly covered Amber's mouth and nostrils. Behind me, I could already feel it taking place. Silence was starting to fall, and I glanced around to check. Soldiers were falling still in the area around us – but on the majority of the battlefield, the fight was still raging. I looked at the closest soldier to see the result of what I had done. I could see it in his eyes, now completely icy. I had frozen the vital parts of his brain and spinal cord in the smoke from the explosion, effectively paralyzing him. Because he had breathed it in, he was a victim to the ice. Along the muddied grass, frost glittered. The paralysis wouldn't last long – only as long as it took for ice to melt in the body – so we needed to move fast.

I grabbed Amber's hand, watching Tera (who had come running) and Faol come closer. Amber was wide-eyed as I assured her that no damage would come to her men. I signalled for Faol and Tera to run underneath us, to move away. We rose, our two powers entwining as we soared over the trees to a small clearing away from the battlefield. I needed to talk to Amber – alone.

I looked at her face, seeing nothing of the girl I had grown up with. She was different now, I reminded myself. She was not one of us. Inside me, I felt the strange urge rise up as I focused more intently on her. It was a deep, furious pull, one that called for blood to be spilled. I pushed down against it. Now was not the time for the Instinct to take over.

We landed silently in a clearing, sweeping our hair back behind our ears at the same moment. Silent tears still dripped down my face as I watched Amber. I had thought for so long that I would never see her again; actually to be with her was a shock.

'Amber. We need to go – tonight. We're trying to stop the prophecy, and are going to find Sardaron. You know who he is, right?' She nodded her head furtively, shocked at my frank words, eyes flickering between the four of us, Tera and Faol having arrived at this point. 'I'm really sorry, Amber. Men came at me, and I had to defend myself.' My eyes dropped to the ground as I confessed what I had done. I had killed men on the way to her – many men. Her voice was sharp when she answered, her demeanour changing as quickly as fire spreads.

'Who?'

I saw their faces clearly in my head, but I couldn't express them in words. It was too awful to think about. I stayed silent, already regretting my words.

'*Who*?' Amber said louder, voice becoming angrier. 'Tell me now, Kai.'

'A man who was huge and had blue hair…'

'Sefros.' Amber closed her eyes, burying her head into her hands. Shakily, I continued.

'A man with an eye patch on his eye, one with a quiver made of snakeskin, and one with brown hair and brown eyes.'

Her head snapped up, her eyes becoming glacial.

'What?'

'I'm so sorry, Amber.'

I couldn't meet her eyes, the shame too great.

'Helmon,' she whispered, tears once again filling her eyes. 'The brown haired man that you murdered was my… we were together.'

I gathered the courage to meet her eyes, and saw nothing but loathing in them.

'*You* killed him.' Behind me, Tera and Faol glanced at each other.

I was frozen, thinking back to the brown-haired man I had seen with her earlier. What had I done?

Her breath was coming in shaky gasps, and with a wobble her legs gave out, until she was sprawled on the grass.

'Dead.' She sobbed violently, shoulders shuddering. I could practically feel her sorrow and fury, directed at me.

I thought about what she had just said. She was seeing someone? I gulped, thinking about what I could say to make her feel better. From her red eyes, I knew there was nothing, but I still tried.

'How… maybe it wasn't him who I killed.'

'Is that supposed to make me feel better, Kai? I thought you were peaceful! *I* haven't killed anyone, have I?' She was shouting at me now, anger giving her the energy to stand. 'You killed him – the only person who has *ever* understood me. And now, thanks to you, he's gone forever.'

I started crying silently, understanding what I had done. A stinging slap across my cheek made me meet her eyes, her furious face in mine.

'How *dare* you shed tears over him? You don't even know him!'

I could only stare at her, the consequences of my actions clouding my vision, even as anger started to take over. What about my apology hadn't she understood? I had been honest, hadn't I?

'Well, at least I looked for you! I was so starved I could barely walk from travelling so far to find you after you were taken!' I said.

She stared at me, malice taking over her features. I knew that she wouldn't have done the same for me if we had been in opposite positions. Although we were close, she had always been the one at home on Earth to find an issue with me and leave me alone, spending time with our mother instead.

'Do you know what your problem is, Amber?' I snarled at her. 'You only think about yourself. All my life, everything has always been about you. It didn't matter what I wanted, because if you wanted it too, then you would get it. That's not love. I'm *sick* of you blaming me for all of your problems!'

'My only problem was *you,*' she said with quiet venom. 'But I put up with you. Don't tell me that that isn't love!'

'Oh, get over yourself, Amber.' I rolled my eyes, anger burning through the grip I held on it. 'You wouldn't have come looking for me if I had been taken first. Don't even try to deny it.'

'You know what, you're right. I wouldn't, because you would have only been another hindrance in my life, dragging me down with you!'

I glared at her, my teeth bared, as she raised a ball of fire in her fist, eyes wet with fury.

...

Amber

Helmon. It couldn't be. Whatever dark forces were out there couldn't be this cruel, for us to have been together for only twelve hours.

I faced Kai, her midnight eyes dark and sorrowful as she looked at me with pity and apology mixed with anger at my accusations.

I didn't want her pity. I wanted her dead.

In a flash, I remembered how Helmon had once told me the name of Sardaron, and how it was believed to cause death. It seemed that that legend had come true, I thought bitterly, as I watched the three Falcords. Kai deserved nothing but the endless pits of hell.

With a scream and a lunge, I attacked, a ball of vicious fire in my soul. It manifested in my palm and I hurled it at her. She dodged just in time to miss its fatal blow, but the underside of her wrist was seared as it brushed by. Good. She needed to burn.

She snarled at me as she produced a dagger from her sheath. It was silver, and so sharp I couldn't see its edge clearly. I retrieved Narox from its sheath, and faced her. Ice froze the very air around us, and I found it hard to breathe. Pushing past it, I hurled flames at her, the fire slithering between our bodies. Icicles grew from the grass as her power grew, expanding until I could tell its power covered the field we were standing in. She was extremely strong, I realised through my tears and fury.

She came at me, an icicle shooting through the air right towards my heart. I dodged it, the icy dagger going left of where it was intended to. Now enraged, I screeched, cruelty taking over my mind. I would *kill* her.

She panted as she looked at me. 'I see how it is. Let's settle this. Hand-to-hand. No magic.'

In rage, I watched her release the grip on the wind and ice around us.

She lunged, leaping high as she swiped at me with sharp fingernails. I swooped, trying to rise into the air. One of my clothing layers snagged in her grip, and I let out a bird-like scream as I was pulled down. I was pinned, and there was nothing I could do about it. Everything was over in a matter of seconds. It had been so easy for her to overpower me.

We both shifted at the same moment, her hands vice-like against my throat. I was choking, the world becoming a blur. The Instinct, which I had had trouble accessing before, was now roaring at me to run, telling me that this person was dangerous. I felt a clang through my body as a slight weakness travelled along my bones. I knew what it meant, even as darkness clouded my vision. Her skin was icy against mine as I glared at her, wet tears dripping down my face. A white flash made me close my eyes, and I looked away momentarily. When I looked back, I saw the reason for the flash, as I clawed at her hands. I could see a faint aura of blue light in the air above us, a few perfect snowflakes dazzling in the light of the buttery sun. I knew what these signs meant.

Sardaron had chosen his victor.

Kai.

…

Faolan

I rushed forward with Tera, yanking Kai off her sister. She looked at me, too far gone in the Instinct to register who I was. Amber's eyes were fluttering, and I heaved her into a sitting position against a tree. Tera held Kai, talking to her soothingly until she calmed down. I was frantic. We needed Amber to come with us – she was a Syth, and would be invaluable.

But how would she agree now, when they hated each other?

.18.

Tera

It was dark outside, the battle for the day ended. Tomorrow at dawn we would resume, but for now everyone was sleeping.

Over on the battlefield, I could see piles of the dead littering the glade. They vanished before the sun rose by some power of the Quill, so that we didn't have to do it ourselves.

The moonlight was blinding against my face as I walked next to Amber, holding her wrist tightly. Glancing to her other side, I saw Kai walking in the same manner, holding her seared wrist to her chest carefully. Her face was stone cold, and I saw her eyes glimmer with rage as she glanced over at me. She was still furious at her sister, I presumed. And Amber was equally angry with her.

The trees seemed to bend out of the way as a dark figure approached quickly, his silhouette tall. Faol, I thought in relief, glad that he had finally been able to sneak away with the Fydars. I frowned as he approached, noting the lack of soldiers with him. Maybe they were waiting for his signal. But as the figure drew closer, I saw that the dark hair, cyan eyes, and onyx necklace I had become accustomed to looking at were not present. Instead,

Angus strode towards us, his mouth parted in a slight smile, steely weapons hanging neatly behind his back. I smiled back at him through my confusion. What was he doing here?

Beside Amber, Kai stopped suddenly, yanking on Amber's arm. I stared at her, wondering what was going on. Behind us, the soft call of a bird indicated Faol's presence. A moment later, I saw a male figure soar over the trees, landing smoothly next to us. Faol, I checked, glancing quickly at his face. My confusion grew as Angus strode up to us, still smiling like that. As he moved closer, I saw that it was a smile of malice, of violence. A tinge of fear crept into my heart as I watched him stop in front of us. Why was he looking at us like that?

Pressing through the emotion, I rushed to him and hugged him – but his arms didn't come around me. His body was hard and cold against mine, and I frowned, and slowly backed away. Something was wrong here. Kai was standing in the same position, staring at Angus with a pallid face.

'Why are you here?' she asked him, fear now spreading over her features. 'You know that you're supposed to wait. There's something… I can sense that you're not the same.'

'Not the same? What do you mean, Kai?' I asked anxiously, staring at her. She backed away a step, pupils dilating with terror as she did so. I saw her image flicker, and realised that in her fright, she was close to summoning her icy power. Angus crossed his arms, opening his mouth to speak, but I cut in before he could, my apprehension getting the better of me.

'Angus, we have to leave. What are you doing here? Where are the rest of the Fydars? We need to leave to find Sardaron *now*, before the Elders wake.'

A cruel smirk spread over Angus's face as I watched him, and I began to shake my head. Who was this person?

'I'm afraid that won't be possible,' Angus said, his voice laced with venom. 'I can't let you do that – it would be very bad for all of us.'

'What do you mean?' asked Faol, his face hard. I could tell that he was eager to leave, and this hindrance wasn't helping. 'We'll call for you and the rest of the Fydars when we're sure the coast is clear.'

'You still view me as below you, don't you?' Angus asked, his eyes alight with rage. 'Still think that you're some high-and-mighty lord who can prance about doing whatever he wants.'

'Angus, you know that's not true,' I pleaded with him. 'What's got into you?'

'You'll never survive your encounter with him. I made sure of that,' Angus snarled at us, practically spitting. Shocked, I simply stared at this stranger. 'And even if you do, you'll be dead the moment you come back here. I made sure of that too.'

'You were the traitor who told the Elders about our mission?' Kai asked, eyes flashing. Between us, Amber stood stock still, staring at the ground. Her eyes were raw and glazed, and she dully glanced up at Angus. 'Why? You *knew* the consequences for that! What is your problem?'

Angus laughed loudly, the sound something terrible.

'You see, all those years standing in your shadow made me realise something,' Angus spat at Faol. 'I hated you. I wanted you – and the entirety of this race – to die, every time the wars happened. You all constantly made me feel inferior and like I was worth less.

'So I decided to put my allegiances somewhere else – somewhere where I was understood. A hundred years ago, I journeyed to find Sardaron. And I joined his forces, acting as his minion to tell him everything that you were doing and planning.'

Beside me, I saw Kai shaking her head, her whole form shivering. How could Angus have betrayed us like this?

'He knows you're coming. I told him myself.'

Amber's head snapped up, and she snarled at him violently, her character changing in the space of a second.

'How *dare* you! Don't you have a heart?'

He simply smirked at her, which only manifested her anger. A tendril of flame appeared in her fist, her fingers clenched tightly together. Beside her, I glanced over at Kai. She had fully given in to her anger at this point, becoming a prowling beast of nightmares. Her fingers twitched in the cool air as she stared violently at him. Our entire plan was to take Sardaron by surprise – and now it was impossible. He would be ready for us by the time we got there.

I felt the unstoppable instinct to kill rise up towards this Firborn as I watched the flame flicker in Amber's small hand. As I stared however, the flame grew smaller and smaller. As it vanished, I glanced at Amber. Her eyes were once again dull, her face clouded with loss.

I realised that she didn't care. She had lost her loved one, and nothing else mattered.

I looked at Angus, to the man who I thought I knew, who

I thought I loved. I saw nothing of the man I had fallen in love with now. His eyes surveyed me, and then passed over. Dismissing me – because he thought I had been too stupid to realise his true character.

He looked at Kai.

'And *you*,' he hissed maliciously. 'Always wondering the same question, over and over and over.' He laughed. 'Why were *you* taken? Why you, and not someone else from Earth?' His eyes glinted cruelly as he slid his hands into his pockets, drawing out a spherical object that glittered with crimson. He tossed it up and down in his palm, watching me. I was frozen, his words stamping me into the ground – paralyzing me.

'Well, I can tell you why,' he said.

...

Kai

In a smooth motion, Angus raised the ball above his head, eyes glinting as he eyed me and my sister.

'It was your father, Nevan, who ensured that you would be brought here,' Angus said, a serpentine smile curling onto his lips. 'That father who you loved so dearly was also the one who made you fight in the first place.'

I stared at him, heart hammering. What did he mean?

Before I could say anything, he hurled the ball onto the ground. Amber jumped, and we both moved back a little as a light flared from the sphere, curling around us.

Behind it, Angus's steel eyes narrowed, reflected in the light, as he watched our agitation.

'You see, your father's life on Earth was built on a bargain he made. Originally, he was one of us – a Falcord.'

I shook my head, backing away. No – what he said couldn't possibly be true.

'How?' I whispered hoarsely.

'His wife, Eimana, died in one of these wars. She was an Elder. Well – I'll let the orb speak for itself. It will show you their story.'

I fell to the ground as the orb nestled there began to glow brighter, an image emerging slowly, flickering as it came into focus.

I could only gaze into it as my father, a young man, came into the frame. My heart lurched as I once again stared at that face.

Beside me, Amber too dropped onto her knees, staring into the light.

The images flickered as they seemed to move – like a video.

It showed Nevan, dancing with a woman that glowed with happiness and light. He laughed, twirling her around. I gulped back tears as I watched him so happy.

The image changed to one of battle, similar to what we had endured today. A whirlwind mess of flailing limbs and steely weapons clouded the picture, my father fierce in the centre of it.

Then that too faded, and I was left with him standing alone on a sodden battleground, the corpse of the dancing woman lying beneath him. He put his face in his hands and sobbed.

Tears trickled out of my eyes, too, as I watched his mourning, sorrow lining his body.

'He decided that, similar to some others in the past, he didn't want to live with his people any more,' Angus said as the orb's image changed to one of darkness.

'So he travelled to find Sardaron himself – as you are going to do. But his reason was different,' he continued as a cave appeared, my father standing outside it. He ran his fingers through his hair, breathing out deeply, before entering, shoes stumbling on rock littering the ground.

The image in the orb faded, the light vanishing as quickly as it appeared. Angus stepped down smoothly, picking it up with one hand.

He tossed it to me, and I fumbled before catching it.

'Keep it – it's of no use to me now anyway,' Angus sneered.

'Why did he go to Sardaron?' Amber asked, voice small.

'To make a bargain with him,' Angus said nastily, watching us. 'He wanted to travel to Earth – a place Eimana had spoken of frequently. He wanted to start his life over.'

'And what was the bargain?' I asked, still reeling with shock.

'Sardaron told him that if he ever had children, they would be girls – taken to be Syths in a future war.' Angus grinned evilly as we glanced at each other. 'And Nevan, thinking that he would never have children, readily agreed.'

I put my face in my hands, shaking my head. What Angus said couldn't be true.

Because if it was, it meant that my father was a liar – had lied to me my whole life.

How had he stomached looking at Amber and me all those

years, knowing that one day they would be forced to battle each other out?

I pounded the grass, turning hate-filled eyes on Angus. We stared at each other. I felt an unending loathing rise up as I watched him. Not just at Angus, but at Nevan. My father.

I had thought, even as I was taken and my world changed, that the people I had known and the memories I had made were real. To find out that even your own father was not who he seemed… I felt betrayed. Isolated.

Because I realised one thing: if I did not have my family, if everyone was not who they said they were, then I, too, had no idea who I was.

…

Tera

A movement caught my eye, and I turned in time to see Faol suddenly lunge forward, a dagger poised between his fingers. Angus easily dodged it, eyes flickering with surprise, and Faol hissed. His eyes were glittering with loathing as he attacked again, fluidly moving Angus against a tree, where he would be trapped. Angus had no chance, I realised. Not against someone as powerful as Faolan. The boy pressed his best friend against the tree, sliding the dagger to his throat.

Angus's eyes glittered as he stared at Faolan. 'You won't do it,' he whispered, a small smile slithering onto his mouth. 'You can't bring yourself too.' A small chuckle came out of his mouth, his eyes alight with some inner emotion. He was crazy, I realised.

Looking behind me, I saw Kai and Amber sitting next to one another, both frozen in shock and anger, Kai holding Tholan. Her eyes were streaming tears, but she still held the weapon firmly. Waiting.

I looked uncertainly at Angus, thinking of the man I had loved for so long. And I watched as he let out another chuckle, provoking Faol to slide the knife harder against his throat.

Kai was scanning me, and I understood that she was waiting for permission – from me. Because he was my betrothed – so it was my decision.

I stepped aside, nodding my head slightly. Moving closer to Amber, I simply watched as Kai hurled the dagger like a missile, arm giving out just after she threw it. She turned away in the same moment, refusing to watch.

It whistled as it moved, until it found its target. When I looked again at Angus, Tholan was embedded in his chest, the ghost of his last laugh still etched upon his face.

Kai's face was lined with sadness, angry as she was, tears starting to spill onto her cheeks. She strode, clearly upset, over to me, Faolan still staring at the dead body next to him.

'What are we going to do now?' I asked, my voice loud in the silence. How could we have been so easily fooled? How could one of our best friends have been the one to betray us?

For as long as I had known Angus, he had always been kind and considerate. To find out that he was the traitor… my heart pounded as I mourned for the man I thought I had known. For the imaginary man who now haunted my mind, who I had fallen in love with. The body lying in the snow was only a reminder of what he had turned out to be, and I turned my face away. Faol was still simply staring at the corpse, cyan eyes intent and expressionless. I could see nothing of what he was feeling, but knew that he was distraught. Angus had been his friend for centuries. I forced my mind to focus, to home in on what we had to do, like I had done for years.

'What are we going to do now?' I asked again. 'Sardaron knows we're coming. Do you all think it's a good idea to still proceed?'

Slowly, Faol looked up from Angus's body, and I saw tears sparkle onto the grass. My heart twisted, and I stopped speaking. It was Amber who filled the silence with her voice next, the sound bitter and brittle.

'What other choice is there? You're all going to be executed anyway, so you might as well.' I stared at her in shock, noting her hard gaze. She was staring at Kai, and I thought for an instant that she was going to tackle her sister.

Kai, who had been looking at me while I was speaking, faced her sister.

She said to her, voice flat and emotionless, 'Going out there is a death sentence.'

Amber snorted, but half-heartedly. I could see the desperate mask she was trying to put on – a mask of nonchalance, when deep down she was hurting.

'Well, what else are you going to do? Sit around and wait for your death, or try to make something of your life?'

'I see that a couple of months have indeed changed you.' Kai's face was cold, her eyes glacial.

'We go on,' rasped another voice. The two sisters turned to watch Faolan trudge towards them, steps heavy. He glanced at me before fixing his gaze on Kai. She dropped her gaze and looked down, still holding the ball in her palm. She carefully placed it into a bag we had brought with us.

'Fine' she said. 'But we need a new plan.'

'Okay,' I replied, 'we'll think of one on the way there. First, we need to tell the Fydars that the coast is clear. Faol, can you tell them?'

He nodded at me and shot off into the sky. I watched his departing back and then turned my gaze to the grass, dark in the moonlight.

Angus was gone forever, and I had let it happen. He had done something terrible, but maybe there would have been a chance to come back from it – to redeem himself. Now I would never know. I sighed, watching the two sisters to make sure that nothing happened between them as we waited for Faol to come back.

A while passed, and we all stared at the ground in silence. I thought only of Angus, of all his good traits. I didn't believe that he was an inherently bad person, simply led astray.

Faol arrived back next to us a moment later, and we all started walking into the night, heading east in silence.

...

We had agreed to travel together for the duration of our trip, simply because it would be easier to defend each other if someone else caught us on our way.

We knew that Sardaron's lair lay in the east – there were documents littering the small library back in Nzar that all said the same thing. So we headed in that direction, careful to avoid detection.

The trees were brightly whistling in the morning breeze as we awoke on the first morning of our journey. Amber launched into the air, acting as our scout, and began to ride the warm air drifting upwards. She had spent the entire night shivering hard, while I was sweating under the weight of my thick fur coat.

It seemed that something dangerous was on the prowl, as Amber slid through the air only minutes after taking off, landing near us.

...

Amber

There was someone – I couldn't make out who, exactly – heading through the trees towards us. I swooped down through the foliage, careful not to go too fast, lest I catch their eye.

The three Falcords – Kai included – stopped what they were doing and shifted towards me as I landed, stepping towards them. I glared at Kai venomously, and then glanced at the other two.

'There's a figure heading our way – they'll be here in minutes unless we hurry up,' I said quickly. The three Falcords glanced at each other, communicating silently, and I scowled. They all seemed like such a unit – whenever I approached, they stopped talking, and just watched me.

If I was being honest, I had felt excluded ever since we set out – partly because of Kai, and partly because I was the only Firborn. They were so lucky to have each other, and I had lost Helmon *and* Nuru.

'We'll have to fly,' the one called Faol said. I watched him warily, wondering how we were going to do that without being spotted.

We all gripped hands, Tera's icy against my own. I winced, and we lifted into the air. We swooped low, heading over the rugged terrain. I could feel my heart rate increasing slightly as I contemplated what, exactly, the figure looking for us was going to do if he found us.

'They're below,' hissed Kai, pointing at the ground. She tugged on our hands and led us to the nearest tree, letting go to perch inconspicuously on a branch.

We followed her example, waiting quietly until the figure paused directly underneath the tree. I leant further forward, trying to get a good picture of the person.

It was a Firborn Elder, I realised with dread. They didn't know where I had gone and were probably searching for me. I gulped and backed up, moving quietly. The others looked at me as the figure stepped forward, scanning the area around the tree carefully. She seemed satisfied that we weren't here, however, and continued on, heading in a different direction.

We didn't dare speak until we were sure that she was gone and it was only then that we breathed out quietly, looking at each other nervously. We flew down, continuing on in trepidation.

...

Tera

The day passed slowly as we struggled past the towering plants and thick underbrush that hindered our progress. The sun was blazing above, and I was sweating so much that my face was throbbing. Amber seemed better, shivering less and less as the day went on. She was silent since the encounter with Angus, and had simply plodded on. Kai and she had exchanged a few clipped words, still angry with each other – which was nothing less than expected, I reflected.

We didn't dare fly, in case we were spotted by that figure searching for us again.

On our second day, we saw a ring of mountains, their snowy peaks bright against the backdrop of clear skies. I had been worried at dawn, when Amber had had her first fainting fit. We would have to get there and back quickly, I thought, if we were to survive.

The middle mountains had a grassy plain directly in front of their bases, and it was to that that I felt a dark presence calling.

'I can sense him,' I said to the others when we were scanning the plain from a grassy outlook high above. The others had said nothing in response, but I knew that they felt it too – the call of darkness, begging for blood to be spilled.

We cautiously made our way down the grassy slope, careful not to slip. There was a huge forest below, stretching almost all the way to the mountains. It stopped abruptly about half a mile away from the mountain base, as if the darkness was keeping it at bay.

We entered the forest a few hours after the sun had reached its highest point in the sky, and I immediately felt the relief of shade on my back instead of burning sun. Looking at Kai, I could see that she was sweating as much as I, both of us sunburned. Faol's burn was not as noticeable because of his darker skin tone, but you could faintly see a red tinge to his complexion. Amber looked no different, unaffected by the sun. She complained about the coolness of the shade once, and then fell silent again. She was thinking of Helmon, I realised, watching her every so often as the day progressed.

It was only a couple hours later that she sat down, rubbing her legs in fatigue.

'I can't go any further,' she said. Kai rolled her eyes, sighing. She was just doing it to annoy her sister, and was succeeding.

Amber was glaring furiously as Kai said, 'And now, *once again*, we have to make *another* stop for Amber, who can't handle walking on flat land for more than a few hours.'

'You know what, Kai? I'm sick of your rudeness. You know I can't help it,' Amber hissed, stalking off into the undergrowth.

'Come back! We need to stick together,' Faol sighed, stepping after her.

Kai waited with me next to a tree, picking her nails impatiently. I was eager to get going again too, thinking of our time limit.

It was only when a scream whistled like a ricochet off the trees that we looked up. Kai scanned the bushes, evidently looking for what had caused the shout.

'I think it's Amber,' she said finally. 'Something must have scared her.' She stalked off in the direction the scream had come from, following Faol's footsteps, and I followed.

We walked for another couple hundred feet, until we stumbled across a small pond, nestled between a group of trees. Faol was standing on the opposite side of it, desperately trying to grab a pale hand that was reaching up from the middle.

'Something – a hare, I think – scared her, and she fell into the lake,' Faol hastily explained, reaching as the hand disappeared under the water.

Amber was drifting in the small lake. It could cause insanity – like feeling fire could cause insanity for us.

Kai stared at the water, resentment lining her eyes. But without another word, she kicked her boots off, and jumped into the water after her sister.

...

Amber

I felt shock reverberate through my bones as the animal darted forward, and I stumbled backwards, toppling with a splash into the lake.

The water stung with painful, icy waves as I was dragged under. I could feel oblivion tugging at me, the insanity of the water beckoning me to succumb.

I pushed back for a moment, reaching out a hand for

someone to help me, but felt the water soak into my skin. I dropped my hand, trailing just above the water, hopelessness whooshing out of my body.

My lungs were on fire, the contact of the water so painful on my skin that I could hardly feel it any more. Tears leaked out of my closed eyes, leaking into the water. I didn't care about death any more. I didn't want to live without Helmon there – life had become a throbbing mess for me, and I didn't want to put it right. I just wanted it to be over.

I clenched my eyes shut tighter, waiting for death to finally claim me, but instead felt strong hands grab me by the waist and chest, pushing me upwards, towards the surface. I managed to crack my eyes open, a flash of blond hair floating past my face, enough for me to guess who had saved me.

I was dragged ashore by Faol, who pressed his hands down on my chest hard, releasing a gush of water from my stomach, which I vomited into the air.

The world was blurry and hard to see, and my skin itched against the pain of the water dripping from me. Tera, running around the lake, took her sweater out of her small bag, using it to mop away the water on my legs and arms. She wrapped it around me as I heaved myself up, shivering violently as I sat on a tree stump.

I had enough energy to stare at Kai, who was dripping wet as well, panting next to me. She had saved me – but I didn't want to be saved.

Tears dribbled down my cheeks as I glared at her.

'What did you *do*?' I asked, shouting at her, face crumpling with tears. She looked taken aback, and opened her mouth to explain. 'I didn't *want* to be saved. You should have let me die,' I cried at her, furious. 'You all hate me anyway – it's not like you care if I live or not. All you want is my powers to help against Sardaron.'

I laughed bitterly, meeting each of their eyes. 'Well, I can tell you this: it won't do a thing to stop him. Nothing will.'

They said nothing, Kai's face crumpling like my own.

'I'm…I'm so sorry for what I did, Amber. What else can I say?' she pleaded with me.

'Nothing,' I spat. 'Nothing you could ever do or say would make me forgive you.'

'I thought that if we got through this, we could make it home somehow together… but I see now that it won't be possible, if you feel that way about me,' she said quietly. She turned away, starting to walk deeper east, towards the mountains. Faol followed after her silently, Tera helping me up before she, too, moved away.

Alone, I let the tears drip down my face for a moment longer, before wiping them away quickly. I stepped away from the tree, travelling carefully around the lake before following them towards the mountains.

Towards Sardaron.

…

Tera

We spent the rest of the day walking silently through the forest, not listening to the birds cheeping happily in the trees. All any of us could think about was Amber's violent outburst, the hopelessness in her voice as she had said those words.

We prepared our tent about a mile away from the base of the mountains, where we could just make out a rocky cave at the base of a single, huge mountain. We had decided to approach Sardaron tomorrow, when we were fresh and ready to go. Approaching him now, while everyone was exhausted and snappish, was no use.

Kai stalked away to hunt us something for dinner, as the remaining three of us set up the three tiny tents for the night. One for Faol, one for Amber, and one for Kai and me. It was easier if we shared, since it meant we didn't have as many belongings to carry with us.

Kai returned a while later, holding a juddering rabbit in her arms.

We sat in silence as Amber moved away to cook the animal, making sure that the fire was obscured from our view.

A few minutes later, she returned, skewered meat on sticks for all of us. We ate it gratefully, glad that we could have cooked meat for once. On Nzar, we normally ate meat raw, purified by our magic.

We finished, crawling into our small tents as the sun finally set over the horizon.

I slept fitfully, body anticipating what was coming tomorrow. Beside me, crammed into the small tent, Kai was the same, often leaning against the side of the tent in a sitting position. I got up halfway through the night, sitting down next to her.

We stared at nothing until the first rays of sunlight filtered through the thin material of the tent, signalling that it was time to get up and be on the move.

My body was stiff, but my mind was racing as I helped Kai up, and we both headed outside. Breakfast – a few apples and cherries Faol had found – was a quiet affair, and then we set off again quickly, keeping our tense eyes on the cave at the edge of the grass plain, which echoed with that dark power that seemed to haunt us wherever we went.

.19.

Kai

We watched the huge cave across the grassy plains that we were passing through, the forest at our backs. I stared at it, apprehensive.

Tera was observing me, and I looked across to hear her say, 'This is it. Our one chance. Before we go… I just want to say to everyone that if things don't work out in there…'

'Let's not talk like that,' I pleaded with her, face placating. She nodded reluctantly. 'We have to trust that this *will* work out.'

Ahead, Faol was watching the earth-brown cave, made out of a huge shelf of rock. To me, it seemed empty, darkness looming within, but I knew that Sardaron was waiting inside like a spider for us to walk into its web.

We set off, all clutching hands as we made our way towards the Creator.

The cave was huge, much larger than I had anticipated, as I stared into the gloom. It was littered with rocks: huge boulders that must have fallen from the ceiling, I thought, as we all entered.

The roof of the cave had huge cracks splintering through it, and I shivered nervously as, slowly, we stepped deeper into the cave, the sunlight fading behind us as we travelled deeper into the large space.

I could feel a huge, looming presence waiting at the back, a place that felt a million miles away from the warm sunshine of the outside world.

The air was frigid, even for me, and I could see Amber's lips turning blue in the faint light.

'I see that you have arrived at last,' a hissing voice echoed from the back of the cave. I jumped, breathing hard.

'Yes – we have come to discuss something important with you,' Tera said bravely, inching closer. Amber's pupils were dilated with fear, her breath coming in hard, fast gasps. I knew she was on the verge of a panic attack, and glanced across at Faol. He was terrified too, I realised, watching him edge towards the source of the sound.

'I already know what you want to discuss. You want the Quill.'

'Well, we've come to bargain. In exchange for the Quill, we're willing to make a deal with you,' Faol said, his voice loud and clear.

A soft laugh skittered across the floor. 'You are in no position to bargain, children.'

'We know that – but please, step into the light, so that we can see you clearly,' I said, half scared of what would emerge from the shadows.

I felt the presence deliberating, and then there was a rustle as whatever lurked in the darkness finally revealed itself.

It was still gloomy, and I was glad of it as I took in what had stepped forward slightly. He was so large, his head almost touched the roof of the cavern and was encased fully in the darkness roiling around him as I stared. I caught a glimpse of his face and my blood curdled to see his scarred flesh, covered in pock marks and bruises. His eyes were huge, filled completely with darkness, and I shivered as he looked directly at me for a moment, before shifting his gaze to Faol. I could look at him for no longer than a few seconds before I had to move my eyes somewhere else, the fear that he instilled in my heart was so strong.

I spoke, trying to push past my agitation.

'We have something that might make you want to give us the Quill. All we ask for in return is the Quill – and we promise, we won't do anything to harm you with it,' I said.

'And what is it that you have that will make me give you the Quill?' He asked, voice partially curious. Faol answered him, voice meek and subservient.

'As you know, you have cursed us to fight wars every one hundred years. Of course, it must be frustrating to rely so heavily on the deaths of weak Ylvares when you yourself are such a powerful force.' The god said nothing.

'We know that you cannot wish for anything solely for yourself,' Faol continued. 'And therefore, you cannot wish it upon yourself. It would have to be done by another. We would wish that you no longer needed to rely on us for survival, no longer needed death to support you. You would be free of that burden.'

Sardaron sat still for a long moment, before a small smile slithered onto his lips.

'I'm afraid that that just isn't enough to convince me.'

'Hand over the Quill now – or we *will* attack,' Amber said defiantly. How she could speak like that to a god who so clearly had the upper hand, I had no idea.

Sardaron's face seemed to curl in on itself as his fury grew. His eyes darkened until they were charcoal black, and he roared his wrath.

'Do you think I'm so stupid as to give the Quill away to a few Ylvares who will only use it for my destruction?' he hissed, brown stumps of teeth showing. 'Get out.'

Faol stood down, brown boots planted firmly into the earth. 'Give us the Quill, and I promise that you won't suffer. All we want is peace.'

'But with peace, I won't be able to survive. Don't you realise that my death powers cannot be unbound by any spell, any magic?' He sneered, curling his lip as he examined us. Four insignificant people, who were either the destruction or salvation of their species. Tera, Faol, Amber and me.

'You have to at least let us try.'

The death god chuckled viciously.

'You think it's that easy? You think I have not experimented? It does not *work*.'

'You need us. Without us, you would simply fade away into nonexistence. Please, we beg you.' Tera stepped forward, holding her hands out placatingly as she bargained with the Creator. Beside her, Amber remained silent, but her eyes were hounded. She was terrified.

'Child,' he sneered at her, 'a death-god does not rely on a few long-lived Ylvar. If you are all killed, I could simply follow my dark power to the nearest source of life and settle there instead. If you were to make it impossible for me to leave by using the Quill, then yes, I would die. But that will not happen. Anyway, I rather enjoy watching you fight each other. So pathetic how you can't even resist the Instinct,' Sardaron mused, unaffected by our desperation. He eyed us once more, eyes glinting cruelly in the faint light. 'Leave *now*. Before I kill you myself.'

'Please.' My voice broke as tears welled in my eyes. We could not have travelled so far, risked so many people, all for nothing. It had been a fool's hope, but it was still a shot at freeing our people from this curse that had plagued the land for so long. We could not afford to fail, could not die fighting a pointless war…

The death god rose as we stayed motionless.

'I said, *get out*. Be grateful that I'm letting you keep your lives.' Foolishly, I stepped forwards, ignoring his words. 'I won't give it to you,' he hissed violently, but I spoke over his voice.

'Not until you give us the Quill.'

'*No*.' My heart twisted with fear and anger at his words.

He reared up, fury throbbing in the dark ball that he curled himself into a ball that then expanded and seemed to glow with some dark light. I could faintly see his face as he rose up, the darkness swallowing our vision of the cave.

'You have no idea what's coming for you. Since you seem so insistent on warranting your own deaths, I'll help the process along.'

I stilled.

'You Ylvares have forgotten the strength of my power – Angus, my minion, told me that I am now nothing more than a myth in the eyes of many.'

I dreaded his next words.

'I shall make a little… *visit*… in three days. To remind you all of who has power over you. And with me I shall bring an army. To silence you once and for all. Then I shall leave to another planet once you are all dead.'

I glanced around in terror, my eye snagging on something at the back of the cave. A painting – the same tapestry that I had seen such a long, long time ago – was hung on the back wall.

I could only look at it for a second before the sheer mass of him took over the space, and Faol started backing away. I followed, dragging Amber's wrist with me as she stared in absolute terror at the thing that Sardaron had become.

Tera was still standing, angry tears coursing down her cheeks, glaring resolutely at the dark god.

Above, I could hear the roof of the cavern shaking, shaking, as Sardaron grew until he was pressed hard against the roof. Shards of stone and rock came tumbling down, and I stared at the ceiling for a moment. A huge fissure was making its way across the top of the cavern as Sardaron slammed his head into it. Large fragments of rock fell down, the fissure spreading, spider-webbing outwards. It was going to collapse, I realised, and I started to move, still staring at the cracks. Sardaron pressed himself against the ceiling, encompassing the space. If I had thought he was huge before, it was nothing compared to him now.

Looking back for a moment, I could see Tera enveloped in a cloud of dust as a huge boulder dropped from the ceiling. Faol was metres away, and I shouted out as a fragment almost fell on my head, lungs burning against the dust and smoke.

'RUN!' I screamed, glancing back once at Tera before sprinting for the mouth of the cave. In front of us, the fissure grew, spreading wider.

Huge rock piles were already littering the floor, and I hurtled around them as the whole cavern collapsed behind me. I could see it falling away, the rocks almost breaking off at the same rate we were running.

I sprinted, pushing my legs faster, faster, fast enough to get me out of here. I could see the sunlight ahead – we were so close. So close to escaping.

I bolted for the light, for the land beyond, keeping my eyes on the entrance to the cave. Beside me, a tan-skinned head covered in raven hair appeared, flashing in and out of my vision. Faol. My legs nearly gave out in relief as he ran forwards next to me. A rumble filled the cavern as the entrance to the cavern started to collapse. An ear-splitting crack made me wince as I moved swiftly forwards, before I saw something falling.

Faol grabbed my wrist and I heard it give a resounding crack as he pulled me sideways, pain shooting up my nerves. Where I would have been running, a huge boulder had fallen, rolling away towards the entrance. I shot a glance at him, panting. His eyes were wide and tinged with fear as the silver in them flickered. I pushed on, feeling Amber sprint up behind us, falling behind me, to my left. I hoped Tera was next to her, although I didn't have time to look as we all shot around a cluster of falling rocks, and out of the cave, Sardaron's roar echoing around us.

The sunlight was blinding on my face as we raced onwards, until we were clear of any wreckage that might fall on us, racing to a few hundred feet away from the cave.

Slowly, we calmed our pace until we had stopped completely. Gasping hard, I fought for breath, the air of Etrais not enough to sustain my needs. Beside me, Faol was doing the same, and I kept my eyes on a lock of his hair, which had fallen forwards over his face, glossy in the sunlight.

I heard another person breathing on my other side, and turned to see Amber kneeling on the ground beside me. She slid her gaze across to me, and I saw nothing but despair in her gaze.

'I tried to grab her.'

With a sinking feeling in my stomach, I stood, looking around.

Tera was nowhere to be seen.

...

Faol

Darkness formed at the mouth of the cave, now far enough away that I couldn't see clearly what was happening. At Amber's words, I shot my gaze to her, as Kai was doing. Absolute shock coursed through my mind as I stared at her, and at Kai's wrist, now bent oddly from where I had seemingly broken it a few moments ago. She didn't seem to care as she fell to her knees, head bowing forwards.

We had left her behind.

Through her own pride and selfless courage, she had stayed, to try to convince Sardaron of our case, and had tried to take him on alone.

Warm tears dripped down my face as I let out a keening wail, head tipped towards the sky, salty tears trickling down my neck. Above, the sky darkened to a cloudy grey, warm drops of rain splashing onto my skin as a fierce wind ripped through my heart. The rain mingled with the tears on my face as I felt a roaring, icy abyss open up.

Not Tera. Not her.

Beside me, I felt a flicker of power form.

'Tera!' Kai's hoarse cry echoed through the wilderness, bouncing off the now collapsed cave. Gathering my energy enough to look behind me, I saw a small tendril of white light form as a figure clambered onto a huge boulder by the edge of the cave mouth. Tera.

Opposite her, on another boulder at the other end of the cave entrance, stood a ball of darkness, now so huge I could barely see the god writhing within it. Sardaron.

Fear curdled my blood as I saw a whip of darkness lash out towards her. She sent a white light out of her own, holding the darkness at bay.

Kai started sprinting forwards, still shouting her name as she raced now towards the cave, to save her friend. I saw tears course down Tera's face as she stared at the darkness before her. She cut a single glance at us, her eyes wide and filled with longing.

She knew that there was no way she would win against a god – that her time was almost up.

She shouted, 'RUN!' as she fended off another attack, tears racking her body. We started to move, and I understood what she was doing. She was fending off Sardaron, giving us time to flee before he turned his wrath upon us.

She sent a blast of power hurtling for Sardaron as he did likewise, and their powers fused, crashing through the land. She didn't have time to fully gather another bolt of white, icy light, before a wave of black came crashing down on her.

It swept over her, washing her away like she was nothing more than a breath of air. The white light in her palm was extinguished, leaving nothing but an echo of power.

I was sobbing as we ran, now sprinted towards safety. I didn't dare look back to see what Sardaron was now doing to her soul, how he would be feasting on it.

Tears trickled down my face, pulling at my skin. They stung the scratches and open wounds on my face, but I didn't care.

We fled into the forest, the roar of Sardaron shaking the trees around us as we journeyed back towards the camp.

...

It was three hours later that we finally felt safe enough to stop. The glade was quiet – peaceful, as we stumbled into it, exhausted from running for so long. Kai looked around, eyes flashing, and sat down, underneath a huge oak tree that was quietly murmuring to itself, holding her wrist tenderly. I followed suit, and Amber reluctantly followed, flopping down next to us. I carefully took Kai's wrist in my own, examining what I had done to it. It was lightly sprained, something that would heal in the next day or two, but it was still an inconvenience.

My heart was pounding in my throat as I contemplated what was going to happen.

Sardaron was going to raise an army to annihilate us all. It meant that we would have to be prepared – would have to unify our forces to fight back.

The Firborn and Falcords, whatever their differences, would have to push past the Instinct and try to work together against his army.

It was the only way we had any chance of winning. We knew when he was coming and, I thought, it would only take a couple days for him to be prepared and ready to greet us on the battlefield.

'We'll have to talk to the Elders and the two peoples, tell them what's happened, and ask if they'll join together. I suppose the Elders will let us live – after all, they could use the extra help when he comes,' I said slowly. The sisters both nodded glumly, staring down.

'We need the Quill,' Kai said. 'He'll bring it with him to the battle – I'm sure of it. He won't leave it unguarded.'

'Yes, but how are we going to get it?' Amber asked.

'We'll have to distract him,' I replied firmly, watching the grass shiver in a breeze, before glancing at them. 'Kai, you have to be the one to grab the Quill. No one will be looking your way. The army needs your guidance while fighting.'

She nodded dismally, glancing across at her sister. 'And Amber?'

'Amber will take care of the largest of the monsters with a legion of warriors, and clear a path for you so that you can slip around and grab it.'

'But what will the distraction be?' she asked hesitantly. I took a deep breath, making up my mind.

'Myself.'

'But we need you – you're the leader of most of the army.'

'I am – and that's why I should do it. Because I've got an army to control, Sardaron will be drawn to me – or I'll find him, and engage him. The warriors will be fighting by my sides – I'll be able to give them orders from where I am.'

'That sounds risky,' Amber said doubtfully. Kai agreed vehemently.

'It may be, but how else are we going to defeat him? At least this way provides a chance for our people.' They said nothing, and I knew I had won.

'He'll use the Quill to create the army – but he might think us inconsequential, and only create a small army. He won't waste all of the Quill's power on creating monsters – at least, that's what I hope. It means we might have enough to stop the prophecy there and then, but it's a gamble – a risk,' Kai said.

'Let's just try not to worry about it,' I said, reassuringly.

We sat in silence for a long while, and I closed my eyes, trying to direct my thoughts away from war for just another few minutes. On either side of me, Amber and Kai looked like they were trying to do the same.

Kai's face was furious, staring out at the thick undergrowth as if her gaze could tear it apart.

'What's the matter?' I asked, cracking my eyes open to watch her briefly.

'She shouldn't have died. It wasn't meant to go like that,' she said. 'I never imagined that this stupid quest would mean the death of a friend.'

Tera's face floated in my mind as I sighed, leaning back until my head rested on the tree trunk. Next to me, Kai was sitting silently, tears slipping down her face as she mourned for our friend.

'We should make her a grave – honour her memory,' I said hoarsely.

To my surprise, Amber nodded, and got up stiffly. She walked over to a huge branch of an oak tree, scanning it to check that it met her needs. She lifted a hand to the bark, and it sizzled, melting away under her palm. The whole branch toppled to the ground with a loud thump, and I stood with Kai, helping them both to lug the wood into the middle of the sunny glade.

Amber's hand shot flame outwards, precisely directing it to burn away the excess wood, until only a huge, cleanly cut wooden gravestone was left.

Kai held out her hand to a spot in the shade of the tree, and tussocks of grass flew out, taking dirt with it, ripped up by a fierce wind.

She lifted the huge piece of wood with her powers, and Kai placed it neatly into the rectangular hole she had dug. I looked at the blank slate.

'What should it say?' Amber asked me.

There were no words that could sum up her life – what she had meant to us. To me.

'In memory of Tera, who…who sacrificed her life to ensure that her people would survive,' I said, voice choked. Kai gripped my hand as the words were burnt into the gravestone.

Amber felled another tree, making a second gravestone quickly. This one she dedicated to Helmon, the man who had been killed by Kai. I felt almost sorry for her as tears dripped down her face.

We went to pick flowers, choosing bluebells for Tera and red hibiscus for Helmon. We stared down at the two meagre graves, all holding hands as we prayed for their souls briefly.

Then we walked away from the clearing, leaving the two gravestones side by side in the dappled morning light as we headed back into the danger waiting ahead.

.20.

Kai

We were exhausted as we started to recognise the plants around us, heading back into familiar territory. We had travelled fast over the past two days, barely stopping to rest as we desperately tried to rush back to camp in time for sunset, when the battles would be over for the day.

We had eaten virtually nothing, putting our physical needs behind what we needed to do.

And now, stepping cautiously forwards, towards the waiting Fydars, we felt the pang of those needs tug violently on our stomachs, cramping them up. I ignored the pain, pushing my way through a bush after Faol, watching his body shift as he slipped further ahead.

Murmurs broke out in front of us, and I saw the Fydars, approaching from a huge cave hidden from sight by towering oaks. They all looked relieved, dishevelled as they were. Many had a hungry gleam in their eyes, and I knew that they had probably eaten as little as we had. Many broke out into relieved sighs when they spotted Faol's face approaching them. Some started to rush in our direction as if to embrace us, but Faol held up a hand, his face serious.

Faol briefly explained what had happened as others started to question where Tera was. I watched their expressions change as he broke the news to them, dipping their heads in respect and sadness. A few, those who had known her well, started crying quietly, but soon rubbed their tears away, concentrating on what was being said to them.

Amber approached from behind me, having been lagging behind. Many lunged forward as the Instinct overtook them, wind raging around the clearing. Others held them back, but the whole army was now on edge. Faol motioned for everyone to follow him, and we walked as a single unit, a single being, towards the Falcord camp.

Once we were so close that we could hear the orders from the generals to the other warriors, Amber slipped away, glancing back at me once. She was going across to the Firborn, to tell them the plan without hostility breaking out between the two sides.

I watched the Falcords in the camp cautiously, wondering how they would take the news. I heard shouts as we appeared and Elders rushed forward, faces full of wrath at what we had done. I was grabbed violently by one of the older ones, and shoved against a tree.

'What did you do?' she hissed at me, eyes glittering. Behind her, the Fydars were wrestling with other warriors and Elders, trying to defend themselves.

'We found Sardaron,' I told her, trying to stay calm. 'We tried to persuade him to give us the Quill, but he got angry. He told us that he's coming for us, that he's going to raise an army to annihilate us once and for all – but we have a plan for him.' The Elder shoved me away, spitting in distaste.

'You fools! I knew this would happen!' I backed away, scared of what she would do to me, and turned to find Faol standing behind me, calmly watching the scene unfold.

The Elder turned to him, firing words into his face.

'You! I knew that this girl might be troublesome, but I've always had faith in you in following what I say. How could you betray us like this? Are you really so naïve as to think that a death-god would simply hand over the Quill?'

'I had no intention of betraying you. I simply want to end this prophecy once and for all, so that our two peoples can finally live in peace,' he said calmly. She laughed hysterically at his words.

'Boy, what you have done won't end the curse. It will only cause our entire species to be wiped out.' She said it flatly, and fear trickled down my spine, cracking through my bones.

Faol nodded his head at me, motioning for me to raise a signal flair on the battlefield. Across the small valley, I saw Amber looking across at me, waiting for the icy flair to shoot into existence from my mind.

I stepped onto the battlefield at the same moment as her, and we both raised our eyes to the sky. Flame curled into the darkening air around Amber, forming a giant eagle. At the same time, I hurled splinters of ice into the sky, forming a snarling wolf which I kept aloft with a gust of wind.

Slowly, the two sides stopped fighting and arguing among

themselves, watching us curiously. How could these two Syths be standing right next to each other in peace? They shifted towards us.

Cautiously, I motioned for the Falcords to stop some distance away from the Firborn.

'We need your attention,' I said loudly but clearly, the wind dying down in the valley so that my words could reach every warrior's ears.

Slowly, everyone turned their heads to watch me. With the eyes of almost a thousand people watching me, I gulped nervously, knowing that what I had to say would either make or break this mission.

'Amber, my sister, and I, together with Faol and Tera, two of the Falcords, journeyed to find the Creator – the death-god Sardaron.' The entirety of the Firborn army flinched at the name, while the Falcords eyed them strangely. 'Our aim, before we set out to find him, was to bargain peacefully with him, offering him his innermost desires in return for the Quill.' I looked around me, not wanting to say the words. 'We succeeded in finding him.'

The entire crowd fell deadly silent in shock, the abrupt gasps of some cut off by others as they strained to listen.

'Unfortunately,' I said, my throat tightening with tears, 'We weren't successful in our mission. We barely escaped, and not without the death of Tera, one of the Falcord Elders.' A tear dripped down my face as I spat the words out, hating how awful they sounded in the deadened atmosphere.

The Falcords stood silently. A few looked down in sorrow,

but the vast majority stayed immobile. Unaffected.

They had not known her like we did, I realised. All that most had seen was yet another of the cold Elders, faces stiff with disapproval. My eyes slid over the crowd, and a sob lodged itself into my throat as I realised that the only person to remember her like I did, to treasure her memory, was standing next to me. Faol.

Two people.

I was silent for a few moments, taking a deep breath before continuing.

'We fled into the forest, fearing his wrath. Before we left, he promised us that he would, in three days, create an army to kill us all – wipe out our species once and for all. He said that he would follow where his dark power took him, and find another planet to inhabit.' The two armies watched intently as I carried on. 'With this army rising, created by the Quill itself, we will have war on our hands in only a few days. The only hope of defeating him is if… our two armies join, and become one.' Outrage broke out between the armies, everyone shouting questions in my direction. I looked at Amber for help, and she quickly started speaking.

'We're not saying that you would have to fight side by side – obviously, with the Instinct, that is made impossible. However, we could become a united force.'

Silence.

'It's the only chance we have,' I said. 'Don't you value Tera's life? She died for each and every one of you. A person sacrificed themselves so that someday you would be the ruler of your own life. I don't believe that there's anything more I can say.'

There was a murmuring throughout the armies as people one by one began looking around, smiling slightly, nodding their heads.

They agreed.

'For those of you who know that you won't be able to control yourselves if you're too close to a member of the other army, stay where you are,' Amber instructed, face relieved. 'For those of you who think that you'll be able to push past it, and could team up together (a much more effective way to fight) please step this way.'

Around half of each army split off from the rest of the group, coming to stand together in the middle of the field. To my relief, no fights broke out as the two forces joined, and Amber nodded at me.

We split, the remaining Firborn and Falcords taken over by Neil, a man who had agreed to help Amber in the few moments she had been alone with the Firborn. I quickly spoke to the second-in-command of the Fydars, who took charge of the most Instinct-driven Falcords.

I slipped away, to find Faol, who was watching the two armies with hard eyes. 'We have to trust that this will work,' I said to him, walking over to the Falcord camp with him behind me. 'I have to tell you something. I was speaking to one of the Elders in Nzar a while back – the one that took me to the Rite – and she has some information that might help us. I didn't want to tell you before in case we never returned from Sardaron's lair. There are two books that were written just after the first

War of Meridian. One's written about the Quill, the other on the death-god himself. She says that maybe we could read them. I know it would be hard, with all the training that we'll be doing, but I thought that it would be helpful for us to know what we're up against.'

'Does she have the books?' he asked, face alight. I nodded, beckoning for him to come as I made my way through the camp to her tent. We linked hands, and I smiled at him, glad that I wasn't alone in this war.

...

We filtered through the pages of the books the next day as the three different parts of our now newly united army began their training, trying desperately to push past the Instinct. I felt it myself, tugging me towards the battlefield, but I pushed past it, determined that I would not succumb. Faol gritted his teeth, gripping the arms of his chair tightly as he sat next to me in the Elder's tent.

'Look,' I said with interest, sitting up slightly. 'This page has some interesting theories on how Sardaron came to have his dark powers.' I frowned as I scanned the text, Faol leaning over until his head was next to mine, and his blue eyes skimmed over the words quickly.

'It's just a theory though – and isn't saying much apart from telling us how the curse came to be,' he said, frowning.

'Yes, but so was the Quill – it was nothing but a myth, and yet it is indeed real.'

He nodded reluctantly. I knew the feeling. I didn't want to believe what the page said any more than he did, but I had to take it into account, even if it was somewhat doubtful. I took a deep breath, and read aloud:

"'The powers of the death-god are separate entities from the god itself. The benevolent god who used to rule the people of Etrais was greeted one day by a dark god, who arrived with the death-powers. They fought for ownership of the people and the land, the benevolent god trying desperately to defend the people he loved so much.

"'Most people believe that the dark god won the battle and took ownership of the Quill.

"'However, this cannot be true, as the Quill responded only to the touch of an Ylvar and the happy god himself – yet somehow, this dark god managed to key in to it so that he, too, could control it.

"'This suggests that perhaps the dark god was not looking to conquer a new land. He was coming because he wanted to be killed by that benevolent god, and finally be rid of the powers that he had acquired and the killing that haunted him.

"'You see, I believe that the dark powers of the Creator, Sardaron, were passed on to him when he killed the dark god who had arrived on that planet.

"'This dark power takes over your mind, forcing you to kill, change yourself and destroy what you once loved.

"'It is an interesting theory to work with, especially since it means that whoever next kills Sardaron could end up with these dark powers.'"

'We can't just ignore this,' I said to Faol, who had gone back to examining a page on how, exactly, to use the Quill.

'But what will we do with that information? If it's untrue, we could miss the opportunity to kill him once and for all.'

'Fine. But we still have to consider it.' He nodded, but I could tell that he had already dismissed the idea. I sighed, frustrated. If it was true, what were we going to do?

'Look at this,' he said, sliding the book over to me. 'It talks about the Quill's properties.'

I lifted the heavy book, reading aloud the text written neatly within.

'"The Quill is not an infinite source of energy – it too, becomes tired with the burden of creation. If all of its power is used, it takes almost a hundred years to recharge, as it slowly absorbs energy from its surroundings.

'"However, there is one way to quickly refill the Quill's power in an emergency, without waiting. One must give up one's own powers – be it fire or ice – and it is only in this way that the Quill will regain its energy.

'"It must be done with a blood sacrifice – simply dip your right thumb into your own blood and press it onto the Quill. You might notice it shimmering and then vanishing, as your powers are taken from you forever,"' I read.

Faol and I looked at each other, apprehensive.

'We wouldn't actually have to do that, would we?' I asked. He said nothing, staring at me nervously. I looked back down, and continued reading.

'"There is a way to regain your powers – once the Quill is

recharged, simply wish for them back. This would cancel out what you had just done, however, so it is advisable that you use the Quill for other purposes before waiting for it to recharge and then wishing your powers to come back. This would mean over a century of waiting, with no magical gifts.

"'The shape of the Quill is that of a golden feather, with a tiny sand-glass timer on one side. You will see that the timer has a blue liquid in it – this is its power.

Instructions for use…'"

I stopped reading and looked at Faol, who was watching me.

'Do you think that'll happen? That with creating the army, the Quill will run out of energy, and then one of us might have to sacrifice our powers for the greater good?' I could hardly picture myself without the icy wind and frost that I loved so dearly.

Faol shrugged. 'Maybe. It's hard to tell.' He sighed, blinking rapidly. I paused and looked at him fully.

'What is it?' I asked, scanning his face.

'It's not the same without Tera. I know that she would have a plan.'

'I know.' I said nothing else, other words seeming too insignificant. We sat like that for a few minutes, silence descending over the small space.

After Faol rubbed his face and sat up, I went back to reading, scanning the page eagerly, if only to distract myself.

"Instructions for use:

Lift the Quill upwards and align with your eyes, the source of your power.

Make your wish. You need to have a clear picture of what you want in your head before you wish for something. You can only wish for one thing at a time.

Blow gently onto the sand-timer, and watch the blue liquid fade away (if your wish requires more energy, it will drain more power)."

'Let's go – we'll meet with the leaders of the armies to discuss our plans later. Tonight,' I said to Faol, who nodded. My chair squeaked as I pushed it back and rose to standing, with stiff muscles.

We both left the Elder's tent a minute later, leaving the books behind.

It was midday by now, the sun partly covered by the huge trees covering us. We watched the armies going through training exercises, powers flashing as they were fired at each other, practising for the battle.

Over in a corner, a bright whiz caught my eye. I looked over to see Amber, coaching the army made up of both Falcords and Firborn, who were practising using their powers together. I watched her set up a target, and two warriors rush forward together. Fire curled around ice as they directed their powers to come together, hurling it towards the target. I watched in awe as golden sparks sizzled where their powers met, overpowering the target in seconds.

I turned towards them, Faol following, as we made our way down the hill to join in.

...

'Are you sure you want to do this?' Neil asked Faol, as we all sat in a circle together.

It was night, the armies gone to bed on their separate sides of the battlefield. We had only a single day of training tomorrow, before the battle, which would take place the day after that.

'I'm sure,' Faol said confidently, looking around the circle, although his eyes betrayed the nervousness I was sure he felt.

We were a small group of people, consisting of those who were in charge of organising the armies: Amber, Neil –who had Amber tucked securely into his shoulder – Faol, the Fydar second-in-command, and me.

We were discussing battle plans for the final war and Faol had just finished talking about the plan we had made in that glade where Tera's tombstone lay.

'And the rest of us? What will we do?' Faol's second-in-command asked.

'You'll be fighting with the armies. We're counting on you, because you have to tell them what to do,' Amber said from across the circle. 'And you, Neil. I'll be leading the army of the two joint forces with Kai. But it will be her job to find the Quill. We'll just protect her until she does.'

Everyone nodded at her words, including myself.

'Well then,' Neil said. 'Faol and Kai, you two will work out our statistics and numbers tomorrow morning, while we're training the two armies. I think we're all agreed on the plan. We'll tell the armies in a mass announcement tomorrow morning, before training, so that we know what exercises to do.'

We all got up, tired from the day's work, and stumbled back to our camps.

I found my tent quickly, stepping into it before promptly plopping onto the sheets. I dreamed of nothing, grey the only colour around my eyelids as I slept soundly through the night.

...

The next morning, I awoke, groggy but refreshed, and quickly got ready for the announcement. I combed my hair back and left the tent, grabbing Tholan on the way out. I strode towards the middle of the battlefield, noting who was present. Most of the three armies were already there, milling about, talking to each other warily. I could see that the centuries-old hostility to each other was only just starting to wear off, as they cautiously smiled at each other. The atmosphere was tense, and I knew that under the façade of civility was the broiling impulse to kill.

Neil stood at the head of the armies, hovering in the air as he waited for them to quieten. His boots glinted faintly in the sun's light, and the army slowly fell silent.

I quickly flew to his side, Amber, Faol and his second-in-command (a man whose name was Zytas) joining me mid-air.

'As you might know, the others and I,' Neil said, gesturing towards us, 'were discussing a plan for the final battle, which will take place tomorrow. We have decided that you will remain in your three groups for the battle.

'The Firborn-only group will be led by me in the battle – I'll be fighting with you, so make sure you hear my orders,' he said. 'We'll be positioned on the left-hand side of the battlefield, fighting Sardaron's creatures. We think that the death-god will be somewhere in the middle of his dark army. We're positioning the army of Firborn and Falcords combined in the middle – your joint powers are stronger than those of the separate ones,' he added. 'The Falcord army will be on the right-hand side, led by Zytas here, and will also be fighting the death-god's creatures.

'For those in the middle, led by Amber and partially by Kai, you have a particular job. Sardaron will be distracted by Faol here, who is one of the most powerful Ylvares we have. He'll be fighting him, so we have to act quickly so that Faol isn't fighting him directly for longer than half an hour. The middle group, your job is to clear a path through the carnage for Kai, who will be behind you, to slip through. She's the one who will use the distraction of Faol to snatch the Quill from the Creator. The reason why you have to clear a path is because she needs to be able to take the Quill without any monsters attacking her. Is everything clear? Does everyone know what they're doing?' He gave the speech quickly and efficiently, and the groups soon dispersed for training, the leaders with them.

When it was just me and Faol left, I gestured towards the Elder's tent. The Elder herself was with the others, fighting in the middle army. The books were where we had left them, on her table, and we walked slowly towards them, ready to calculate our odds and focus on tactics that we could use in the battle.

...

Faol sighed through his nose as, four hours later, our work was at last almost finished. It had been a huge effort and my stomach was grumbling violently by the time we were finished.

He fanned his face with a stack of papers, his writing neatly laid out on them.

'Kai, I'm worried about this.'

I glanced at him from where I was studying a layout of the battlefield, noting the stress lining his face.

'I know – we all are.'

'But we don't know how big Sardaron's army is. Wouldn't it be easier if I could go fly out there quickly, take a look at them, and fly quickly back?'

'No.' My voice was flat as I answered. 'You'll just be killed. It's pointless.' I hated myself for saying the next words, for appearing like I thought of him as a pawn. 'Besides, we need you for the distraction on the battlefield.'

'There are too many variables. What if the Quill doesn't have any power left, if we find it?'

'*When* we find it. And we have to trust that it will.'

'Yes, but how can you trust Sardaron?'

'I don't,' I said, irritated. 'I trust that he knows the value of the Quill, and that using it all up to create monsters is a waste against some inconsequential Ylvar – at least, that's what he'll think.'

He sighed in disagreement, and I rolled my eyes, turning to face him. 'Trust me, Faol. The Quill will have power enough left.'

'There's always the chance that it won't, Kai! You're the one who said yourself that we need to plan for all situations!'

'You're being irrational.'

'No, Kai, I'm not!' he said, raising his voice slightly. I narrowed my eyes, annoyed too. Getting into an argument was not a wise idea at such a critical time. 'We need numbers, Kai,' he said, waving a slim stack of parchments in the air. 'We need more information. How can we prevent ourselves from full-scale slaughter if we don't know how many warriors and Elders to send out onto the battlefield? What if all the elders are killed, and we have no one left to ensure the survival of our species?'

'You're being idiotic,' I hissed, exasperated. 'It's not going to happen, because, like I *said,* Sardaron won't use all of the power in the Quill. I know it.'

'I have to go out there.'

'NO, you don't. You're only going to be killed. You won't be able to blame anyone but yourself when that happens.'

I stalked around him furiously and left the tent. He seemed simply unable to see the point from anyone else's perspective. I stalked towards the training groups, approaching quickly. Amber saw me and reluctantly told me to join the group, resentment flashing in her eyes. I didn't care, simply immersing myself in training.

After a couple hours, when we were taking a break, I noticed that Faol had still not come to join the training exercises. I sighed, running through the exercise in my mind one more time before leaving to walk back to the camp. I flew towards the Elder's tent, thinking that he would still be there.

He was not.

I searched my tent, his own tent, every tent in the camp until I had stopped in the central area. Passing by his tent again to double check, I saw that his belongings were a mess, like he had grabbed a few things hurriedly in his haste to get away.

I closed my eyes, putting my face in my palms.

He couldn't have been that irrational to actually leave.

I sighed and stalked away to the east, the direction of Sardaron's lair, taking to the air to get a clearer view of the land as I travelled.

I had only gone a mile or so when I spotted a dark form running through the woods. Faol.

I swooped downwards furiously, the world tilting in a blur as I did so.

The trees scratched my face as I darted past them, slamming into his side as I did so. We rolled, him growling and desperately trying to get away. I shifted, pinning him swiftly. I snarled in his face, infuriated by him. We both shifted back, and scrambled to our feet.

'What were you thinking?' I spat furiously, and he glared right back. 'How could you not even tell me that you were going?'

'I'm going to get us some information, like we need.'

'*No*, Faol. We can't risk you. We need you for the battle.'

'So this is the only reason you're trying to stop me? Because you need me tomorrow – and not because you actually care for me?'

'That's a lie, and you know it,' I hissed at him. I grabbed his wrist and started dragging him with me, back towards the camp. 'What's your problem? Why can't you just accept what we have and try our best? Why do you have to risk so much every time you plan something?'

'What's that supposed to mean?' he asked, wrenching his wrist away from my hand. 'I can walk by myself.'

'Well, maybe if our mission before had been a little better planned, maybe Tera wouldn't have died,' I said venomously. His eyes froze over with fury, but he said nothing before stalking past me. I knew that he was devastated by my words, mostly because he actually believed them.

He thought that her death was his fault.

I trudged after him, knowing I had gone too far.

'Faol –'

'Leave me alone, Kai. Just go.'

'Please – I didn't mean it. I know it wasn't your fault –'

'Yes, but you still said it, didn't you?' he said cuttingly, turning back to watch me for a second. I stood hopelessly, expression pleading. 'Maybe you should think before you speak.' He turned away and walked forwards again, ignoring me for the rest of the journey back.

...

Faol

I walked back to my tent, Kai stalking behind me. She left without a word, striding off to her bed, only pausing to look back momentarily. I didn't meet her stare. After a moment of hesitation, in which her eyes flickered sadly from my face to the ground, she turned away. I watched her walk, stride despairing, saying nothing.

It was past sunset by this time, and I reluctantly put my supplies down, lying on my bed.

I found it hard to get to sleep, my mind racing, already picturing the worst things that could happen tomorrow. My eyelids drooped, and I struggled to keep them open as I thought.

Finally, my exhausted body tugged me into sleep, my dreams vivid and merciless.

.21.

Shouts awoke me near to the time of dawn, and I scrambled up, already in my fighting gear. I poked my head out of my tent, spotting Kai standing near to a tree with a few other warriors, talking with a hand resting on Tholan, belted at her side. She glanced in my direction, and our eyes met. She stared at me apologetically, but I skimmed my glance over her, still angry for what had happened last night.

Focusing on something else, I strained my ears to listen to what the warriors were saying. A few were pointing towards the horizon, where a dark blob was steadily drawing closer, spreading like oil over the land.

Sardaron's army was here.

The armies were hastily organising themselves, led by Amber, Neil, and Zytas. They assembled quickly, weapons and powers flaring as the army came so close that we could make out their features. Panicked shouts rang out across the clearing as people struggled to find an order in the surprise Sardaron had caused.

I slipped into the crowd, finding my way to Amber's side to examine their faces. I gritted my teeth against the urge to wrap my hands around her throat as I watched her turn towards me.

The monsters created by the death-god were huge, their dark bodies grouped together as they moved quickly towards us. Each wore a dark cloak, giving the impression that they were human in some way.

They were not.

They strode in our direction, mouths gaping wide. In their arms, darkness formed, writhing in and out of themselves. Their heads were monstrous, wispy shreds the only thing resembling hair. For eyes, there was nothing but milky white in their eye sockets. However, they could still see, I realised, as I watched the heads of many snap around to study the three armies.

My attention went to the death-god, the sight of him burning into my memory. This was the monstrous creature I would be fighting soon. Around him, glittering black crowded, like shattered black diamond. His face was scarred and crueller than I remembered it. I looked away, trying to focus elsewhere.

There was silence as the two armies came to a halt, sizing each other up. The two front lines eyed each other up, the creatures leering as they examined us, as if we were their prey. I cleared my head, forcing my mind to focus.

Just like I had for the past three centuries. I breathed deeply, clearing my body of any emotion I might have. But hard as I might try, the doubt and fear still lingered in the back of my mind.

Beside me, Amber looked just as tense as I felt and I smiled at her shakily, trying to reassure her.

'For Tera,' I said to her.

She glanced at me, nodding. 'For her.'

It happened then, as the other army started to move.

I screamed a battle cry, listening as it echoed off the sides of the steep hills around the battlefield. The Falcords roared in answer, Amber the only Firborn to know who Tera was, what she had sacrificed.

The other army roared too, charging down the hill like running ink. Our armies cheered as we hurled ourselves into battle, blood spraying as we fought the darkness that had ruled over us for a thousand years.

.22.

Kai

The battle was raging, the armies having been fighting for the past half a day. There was blood littering the muddy grass, weapons and corpses strewn about carelessly, and I almost slipped in the debris as I jumped upwards, hovering in the sky to examine the battle.

The Firborn army was fighting desperately against a huge crowd of monsters, flame flashing as they hurled it into the monsters one by one. They were tiring, I thought, watching them for another second. The Falcord army was having similar issues, only making slow progress through the mass of huge bodies they had to defeat.

The army of both Falcords and Firborn were ploughing through monsters as if they were nothing, hardly any being killed in the process. Sardaron himself was fighting in the middle of his army, just where we thought he would be. He fired darkness in all directions, killing warriors instantly. I watched as he was occupied by a raven-haired boy, his icy powers attacking relentlessly.

We weren't equipped to win this fight, I thought. The doubt

that I had been feeling for the past few days had exploded, leaving only icy fear behind.

If we weren't equipped, I had to find the Quill and Faol immediately.

...

I landed half an hour later, glancing about wildly in an attempt to find Faol. The army was indeed creating a path for me to follow where I would be protected from attack, but there was such chaos that I couldn't even spot Sardaron himself. Looking around, I searched for some kind of clue that could lead me to him and, hopefully, both the Quill and Faol.

I glanced at the ground, a black circle of stone catching my eye. I bent down quickly and picked it up. It was the smooth onyx necklace that I had always seen Faol wear, since the first day that I had met him. I clenched it in my fist, scanning the battlefield.

I scrambled up the side of the valley onto a ledge that jutted out slightly from the earth. I gripped the soil with my bare hands as I climbed.

The ledge barely had space for my feet to balance on and I pressed myself against the moss and grass. I scanned the crowd amidst the flashes of magic, seeing head after head in the myriad mass of shifting bodies. I looked in desperation to the far side of the battlefield.

It was carnage, and I saw three of Sardaron's creatures heading directly for me (despite my protection) at the same time as I finally spotted Faol. Sardaron was closing in on him, and had started to wrap tendrils of shadow around the warrior. White light blinded my face, and I was reminded of a very similar battle – only it was Tera fighting him.

I approached, careful to make sure that Sardaron wouldn't scent me as I came closer. With the smell of death all over the place, I doubted that he would be able to differentiate me from the crowd. I watched him as he moved in to attack Faol, realising that the scent of blood had sent him into a stupor not dissimilar to intoxication. He was drunk on death.

He was a huge mass of cruelty, swirling as he fired darkness in all directions. I ducked to avoid a shooting whip of it, and saw his quiver, lying on the ground, near to his feet.

Careless, I thought. Careless that he would leave it lying where anyone was able to take it.

I straightened, heart beating faster, as I spotted a golden feather inside it. The Quill. The world seemed to quieten as I stared at it. Our one shot at survival. I ran forward before I could talk myself out of it, sprinting as fast I could while still trying to avoid the darkness.

I approached, until the quiver was only ten feet away, then eight, then six. When it was close enough that I could see the golden letters embossing its side, I snatched it out of the quiver and stuffed it in my pocket, relief threatening to drown me. How had Sardaron not noticed?

I turned towards him, noting again how he was swaying slightly, eyes filled with a gleaming greed as he eyed Faol, who in his eyes was just another life to take.

I stepped towards them in the hope that I could help Faol.

He jetted ice ball after ice ball at Sardaron, a weaker version of what I had done in the battle against the Firborn. I knew that his powers were failing, that he was weakening.

Sardaron flung a strand of darkness at him, slightly carelessly.

The effect was still brutal as it slapped against Faol's chest, sending him tumbling to the ground.

I was enraged. My eyes grew red with fury and I envisioned a wall of pure steel and ice rising around me, tipped with barbs sharp enough to pierce through the heart.

A colossal ring of ice and snow appeared, and I sent it hurtling for Sardaron. It stabbed him in the calf, and he roared in agony, diverting his attention from Faol to me. Tendrils of fear shot for me, and I felt my heart quicken as they approached. I ducked as they swung past, but I was not fast enough. One stabbed me in the side, and I groaned before sinking to the ground.

Hesitantly, I lifted my shirt to see a small patch of darkness staining the side of my stomach, like ink dropped in water. I watched it swirl around, pain clawing at my nerves.

Returning my attention to the battlefield, I saw Sardaron turn from me. Bored. I had been easily defeated, and he was no longer interested. I could only spectate in utter torment as he made once more for Faol.

'No,' I whispered through my suffering, as I watched an icy dagger sent by the warrior disintegrate, followed by a wave of darkness from the god. It was only just halted by Faol, who I watched standing on a ledge, battered and haggard. He couldn't go on much longer, and he knew it. I yelled again, shouting for him to run, to try and escape.

Of course, he did no such thing, and I watched in horror as he attempted to attack Sardaron one last time. He lunged, dagger-sharp ice spraying as he tried to wound the god in any way possible. Anything to get away safe.

I cursed and scrambled to my feet, running despite the crippling pain in my side. I could hear Sardaron's laugh echoing through the battlefield as a huge ball of steaming fear and darkness rose up, hovering above the death god.

'FAOL!' I screamed, sprinting as fast as I could, dagger in my hand. He glanced once at me, consternation and hopelessness prominent on his face. I knew that look – the look that meant someone had given up.

'No, no, no,' I cried. 'Not again.'

Half-formed ice glinted in the faint sunlight as the huge ball of darkness crashed over Faol like a wave, leaving nothing but a few shards of frost behind.

He was gone.

I dropped to my knees, not caring that other monsters were now running for me, that I too might now be killed. Everyone had been taken from me. Everyone. I had no one left now, all of my friends killed in this mess that we had got ourselves into. What was I doing?

Tears trickled down my face, glinting in the sunlight. I was a damned fool, who had let her friends talk her into doing this. And now I was suffering the consequences for it.

'Not Faol,' I whispered weakly, bones giving out as gleeful monsters, scenting my despair, came charging for me. 'Anyone but him.' I watched the creatures come pounding towards me.

'Come closer,' I whispered. Take me. They slowed as they approached, as if hearing my thoughts.

However, as I shifted slightly the dark creatures were slammed back by an invisible wall.

I realised that Sardaron was rearing up behind me. He must have claimed me for himself, I thought bitterly. At least I would be able to see my friends again. I scrambled weakly away before my muscles failed me, trembling before I collapsed onto the ground once more. Lifting deadened eyes to Sardaron, I watched him come closer.

He lashed his power around me, the mass of onyx forming a dark cube. A cage. I watched it dully, not able to run, to hide. It crashed down on me, and I felt a laugh reverberate through the killing field.

I ignored the tears on my face and simply stared at the ground as dark shackles enclosed themselves around my wrists and pain lashed through my body.

I screamed, not hearing myself, losing myself in the pain of what the death-god was doing to me. Faint flashes were all that I could see of the battle still raging around me, knowing that we were losing badly.

My eyes rolled back into their sockets as torture settled into my bones, my body slowly frying from the inside out.

I was dying, I realised.

Dying.

.23.

Amber

I spotted Kai, thrashing with screams as her body was jolted with streaks of black lightning. Something twisted in my heart as I watched her. The murderer of Helmon. I saw Sardaron's exposed back as he focused intently on Kai. Playing with her as though she was a toy.

I knew that with him distracted, I could possibly sneak up from the side and slide my dagger, Narox, up through his ribs into his heart.

I deliberated, watching Kai judder as she roared with agony. Blood dripped from her skin, and I watched it bitterly. She was a murderer.

But she was still my sister.

I stared at Kai for a moment longer, stabbing one of the dark creatures who was about to tackle me with a smooth swipe. Tears still trickled down my face at the thought of Helmon, and I took a shuddering breath. She was my sister. I owed her for countless things over the years.

I launched into a sprint, mortal legs so much slower than the rest of the Ylvares. I grunted against the pain of my wounds, speeding towards Sardaron. My vision tunnelled, and the monstrosity was all I could see as I hurtled for him. I hefted Narox in my hand as I approached. Maybe I could actually do this.

I veered to the right as Sardaron turned slightly, still absorbed in my sister. I grimaced as she screamed in that unearthly way, braid thrashing against his power. Over to the west, the sun was setting and the battlefield was bathed in blood as I neared Sardaron.

Closer and closer I moved, until I was mere feet from him. I slowed, panting heavily, blade held upright. The Creator barely noticed me – I no longer had the power that I had had when I was an Ylvar. I shuddered against Kai's roars as the death-god tortured her, grinning, savouring her pain and suffering. He was unprotected, the other creatures fighting against the ever-decreasing wave of Ylvares.

I charged, sliding the dagger in a quick motion, slashing open the black cage surrounding her. Sardaron turned his attention to me, and I faced him, standing still. He hissed, baring his crooked, yellowing teeth. I stared him in the face, unafraid of anything for the first time in my life.

I brought fire, rearing upwards as I summoned everything that I had, every last drop of strength. He did the same, and I sent mine rushing for him – a distraction, while I slipped around it to his other side.

Before he could react, I slid the dagger around his chest, shoving it upwards. He tried to rear back, but the deed was already done.

It slid through his ribs, reaching the furiously pumping heart, stilling it into silence.

'NO!' Kai whispered, staring at me in terror.

Behind me, she was panting, struggling to stand, trembling arms still ensnared in those horrible dark shackles. I looked at her, and then at the now human-sized figure starting to slump to the ground, the ebony around him starting to dissolve. I stared as the darkness pulled back, revealing a face I had seen many times on the walls of the volcano, inked in centuries-old warriors' hands.

This was not the death god, but the god of happiness and love, who had ruled over the land all those years ago. I stared, watching as the darkness moved away from the body as if on a phantom breeze.

I stared at Kai, and felt a nudge against my feet. The roiling mass of darkness pushed against my toes, before entering my body. What was happening?

I stared in terror as it spread upwards, covering my calves, my stomach, until I felt it finally enter my heart as I backed away. There was a moment of silence in my veins as my mind tried to process what had just happened. And then I felt my heart twist, encompassing the darkness completely.

.24.

Kai

There was nothing I could do.

The snares around me tightened as I tried to face Amber fully. I could see her standing motionless, darkness writhing around her. What was going on?

I looked at the golden Quill, on the ground before me. It glinted in the sun's dying light as I twisted to watch Amber. Pain lashed through my side as the wound made by Sardaron opened once more, the dark stain there throbbing slightly. I gritted my teeth through the pain, and succeeded in twisting fully.

Amber turned to face me, and I stared back in terror as she opened a mouth with teeth long and sharp and watched me with eyes that were wholly black.

'Amber?' I whispered, too shocked to say anything else.

She laughed darkly.

'The girl you knew is gone,' she said, and I startled at her voice, at the darkness and cruelty drifting around it.

'Please, Amber,' I said desperately. 'Try and fight it.' She laughed but juddered slightly.

She and I stared at each other for a long moment, her body

still twitching. Adjusting.

Her eyes flashed as the brown colour returned momentarily, before the darkness took over again.

I tried to remove myself from the shackles, hands painfully raw against the hard material. I had no success, and could only stare at the monster in front of me.

'FIGHT IT!' I screamed at Amber desperately, who was approaching with her sword held out before her body, eyes glinting. On the rest of the battlefield, there were shouts as people started to realise what had happened.

The darkness wrapped itself tighter around her as she seemed to writhe against it. I could see that she was trying her hardest, but the power had faced opposition like this before, and knew what would happen. They seemed to be wrestling with each other as I desperately tried to free myself and reach for the Quill.

My chains were firmly fastened to the ground, and I tugged at them in vain, tears dripping down my face. I had to save her – whatever we had done to each other in the past was over now. All I wanted was for us to be together again.

The chains finally came free as I wrenched my hands from them, causing blood to be drawn from my wrists, gushing across my skin.

I picked up the Quill delicately with bloody fingers, watching Amber, who was still fighting against the ever-strengthening power.

It was golden, with a tiny sand-glass etched upon the side of it. I saw that the glass read that the power of the Quill was almost nothing.

I knew what I had to do. Remembering what I had learnt, I lifted the Quill in line with my eyes, making my wish, and blew a breath upon it.

The etching shimmered as the sand timer emptied completely, its power used up. I knew from the research I had done with Faol that its power took years to recharge – a full century, to be once again at its full capability.

Around me, silence filled the land as the two armies stopped fighting. I watched in awe and a little terror as the dark creatures that Sardaron had created drifted backwards, slowly turning from opaque to clear as their bodies slowly. There was a gushing breeze, and the remaining corpses were swept away.

It was over.

I watched the two sides – the Firborn and the Falcords – slowly look at each other, surrounded by their dead comrades, scarred and wounded. They looked across the battlefield and tears slipped down my face as I watched them rush together, embracing each other tightly. Many were crying, I saw, feeling what I had felt myself using the Quill.

The urge to kill, the one that had forced us to do so many terrible things, was gone – vanished. Vanished, as the prophecy faded away completely, leaving nothing behind. The air came clean into my lungs, breathable once more – for the first time in a thousand years.

I stared again at the Quill in my hands as the people, who had noticed us, began to rush forwards. I put up a hand to stop them, and they slowed, instead gathering around me. Amber was still thrashing, but the struggle was slowing. She was losing.

...

The light in Amber's eyes was fading fast, and someone in the crowd cried out to help her. I glanced once more at the Quill, a memory of the book I had read flashing through my mind.

I had been reading about what, exactly, the Quill could do, and had seen a tiny footnote at the bottom of the page that Faol had shown me. It was indistinct and hard to make out, but I remembered what it had said.

The Quill may be recharged by someone giving up their powers permanently. A blood sacrifice will transfer the powers from the giver to the Quill.

The thought echoed in my head as I grabbed the Quill, rising on shaky feet. The blood on my hands gleamed as it clotted, starting to dry in the warm air.

I stared for a second longer at the golden object in my hands, before slowly drawing out Tholan.

Behind me, Amber grunted, and then fell still. I cast a worried glance at where she was slumped on the ground.

I slid Tholan across my wrist, leaving a deep, jagged cut that left my head spinning with dizziness. I ignored the pain and pressed my thumb to the wound gently as Amber started sobbing quietly. The contact stung like nothing I had ever felt before, and I felt darkness threaten to wash over my mind.

I drew out my shaking thumb from the wound, and pressed it gently onto the Quill, leaving a fingerprint of blood over the sand timer.

A whooshing resounded in my body from blood loss as

Amber started to rise. I saw her eyes give in to the darkness, and desperately watched the Quill as the fingerprint I had made shimmered, vanishing a moment later.

The sand timer slowly started to fill, a blue light shining inside it as the power was restored to it. I clutched at my chest, feeling the ice, the wind and frost… feeling them melt away forever.

I held the Quill up again, wishing hard. I thought of the powers surrounding Amber, the darkness that swirled around her as she approached. I wished for it to be banished, thinking of how these planets were on a parallel universe to my own. I reached out, thinking of the power, and how it was now tied to Amber. I wished for it to reside on a different dimension – on another, empty planet residing there.

I opened my eyes, blowing a shaky breath on the Quill as my wish dissolved the power that had resided there, leaving it utterly empty.

I stared and stared, watching Amber.

Nothing happened, and a sob slipped out from my throat as I watched her once again try and throw the power off her, failing dismally.

I closed my eyes, not caring if my sister killed me, if I died. It hadn't worked.

…

I sat there for a long moment, eyes clenched tightly shut as I kneeled hopelessly on the ground.

I cracked them open as a rustling passed through the crowd of people, breaking out in furtive murmurs.

'Kai?' a voice croaked, and I slid to the ground, opening my eyes fully. In front of me stood Amber, face open and clear of any darkness. Her eyes filled with tears at what I had done and I stood, pulling her towards me. We were both crying as I hugged her tightly and she whispered quietly, 'Thank you.'

I pulled back to examine her, and the small crowd stood in shocked silence. A few clapped weakly but most were too absorbed in their own suffering to care much about us. They were wounded, with many of their friends and family dead.

'I'm so sorry, Amber, for what I did to you. What I did to Helmon,' I said, the words coming out in a rush. 'I know that nothing will ever be able to compensate for his death, and I don't expect it to. But I just wanted to apologise and tell you how sorry I am. 'Sorry. What a useless word,' I said dryly, shaking my head. It was such a weak word to make up for all the damage I had done to her.

She nodded slowly, taking a deep breath. 'I don't know if I can ever forgive you, but…I'll try.'

We simply looked at each other for a long moment.

'There's something that you need to know,' she told me hesitantly after a minute. 'I can't leave Etrais.'

…

'What? But…I freed you.'

'But I can still feel it – the power. It's still there. Not affecting me, but I can feel the bond between us. I know that I am as much a part of it as it is of me. Which is why I know that it would not be possible for me to leave Etrais. I am tethered here.'

'Don't you at least want to try to leave?' I asked desperately. 'You would have to live out your mortal life here. Forever.'

'I know I can't leave, Kai. I just know it.' I said nothing. 'But you'll be waiting for me, right? For when the portals open again in a hundred years, and the Quill is recharged. That way you can open them permanently, and live here with me. I understand that you need to go back to Nzar now, but… just don't forget me, okay?'

I sobbed, throwing my arms around her. She was still so young, I thought. The same age as me, but only seventeen.
She would never get to experience life in the same way that I would. She would forever be stuck here, left to carve out a living from the land.

'I would *never* forget you. I promise. But right now I need to leave. We need to go back – we wouldn't be able to survive out here without everything that we left back at home – and the Firborn too. The wolf that delivers the supplies has just arrived, I bet, and will be waiting for us. The portals are opening tomorrow, so we need to depart soon. But I promise, as soon as I can, I'll come see you.'

She smiled sadly at me, and I knew that this was probably one of the last times I would ever see her. I gripped her tightly, tears leaking down my face. She was all I had left.

'I'll be thinking of you,' I whispered in her ear as I hugged her. 'Are you sure that you'll be able to survive out here by yourself?'

'I'll manage,' she said to me. 'I always do, somehow.'

I tried to say goodbye to her, my words choked and tearful, but I couldn't form a coherent sentence. All I could do was clasp hands with her briefly, our fingers interlocking, before I had to go.

I walked slowly away, towards our belongings, now packed up. I started to move through the trees with the rest of the Falcords, the Firborn doing the same on the other side of the valley, and turned briefly to stare at Amber. She was standing on a huge boulder, waving frantically, eyes clouded with tears. I waved back, keeping the image of her, young and free, in my mind, determined never to forget it.

With that, I turned away into the trees, steps soft as I made my way home.

100 YEARS LATER

.EPILOGUE.

Kai

I bounded through the trees, legs pumping as I sprinted forwards before slowing. I could run forever, I thought – just for the sheer pleasure of it. I came to a halt, breathing in the air around me.

The trees were covered in snow, and I paused to shake a branch free of its residue, watching the white powder fall to the ground. I stared at the ground for a moment, longing washing over me fleetingly. Those powers that I had had so long ago were gone. I raised my hands in front of me, examining the green and blue veins running under my skin. They were like they had been for most of my life.

They were ordinary.

I knew it was wrong to wish for them, because it would be like regretting the sacrifice I had made for Amber, and the future generations that had been saved.

However selfishly, however, I wanted them back.

A horn blew and I glanced through the trees, back the way I had come. It was time to go. I sighed inwardly, dusting my hands off. I jumped into the sky, soaring effortlessly above the dark green forest as the horn blew again. Absent-mindedly, I glanced down at the side of my stomach, lifting my shirt to inspect it, something I had done every day for the past hundred years.

What looked like ink dropped in water, a stain marred the side of my stomach, the colour as dark as a moonless night. It would forever be a reminder of the life I had failed to save, of the raven-haired boy I had cared so deeply for.

I pushed the thought away, focusing on today, on now, as I had been taught to do my whole life.

Today, I would leave Nzar forever.

I had been preparing my departure for years, collecting everything that I would need for my journey and my continued life on Earth. I had said my goodbyes to the Fydars, who were up North again. I had spent the better part of twenty years by their side, learning how to be a warrior. I knew that never again would any of us need those skills, but I knew that I wanted to be as prepared as possible for my return to Earth.

Some of them, I would miss dearly.

Although I had loved my home in the desolate land, my mind had forever drifted to the possibility of returning back to Earth, thinking of my father and how he had done it.

I knew that there was no possibility of my mother being alive, but somehow… I had held on to a tiny flicker of hope that the magic of these worlds would allow me to travel back to where and when I was when I had been taken as a Syth.

My thoughts turned to Amber, my sister who had lived out the rest of her life on Etrais. I wondered if she, too, had passed away.

It was a thought I had forced myself to come to terms with long ago.

I knew I would never be the same person that I was. The deaths of so many of my loved ones had changed me irrevocably. I was saddened, suffocated by the materialistic wishes of those around me, even though I had a few of my own.

Today, using the power of the Quill, we would open the portals permanently. They no longer opened naturally, because Sardaron's curse was broken, so we would have to do it ourselves. No one was exactly sure how much of the Quill's power it would require to do such a thing. This had led to us erring on the safe side, waiting the full hundred years before we attempted it.

Thinking of the war, my mind drifted to the raven-haired boy who I had lost during that final battle. I often wondered what life would have been like with him by my side. Would I be leaving now?

My hand reached towards my throat, where the onyx necklace that had once been Faol's lay. Brushing my thumb over it, I felt its smooth coolness, the stone worn with use.

After the final battle, everyone had gone back to their respective homes and tried to move past what had happened. Our population numbers had been desperately low, and all of us had been wondering how we were going to carry on the population now that Syths were no longer being taken from Earth to fight.

Our answer had come exactly a year after the wars had ended, when one of the Elders had given birth to a child.

We were shocked to discover that this child, the first child to be born after the wars, was a girl. We had celebrated vigorously, throwing a huge party. After all, we could – we had won the supplies for it.

I stooped, flipping to the ground and gliding to a halt. Every member of the Falcords was gathered, preparing to wish me good luck. They stood underneath a glade of trees, wind whipping through the branches with the force of their magic.

I strode over to a huge fir tree, grabbing the bag of supplies I had left under it. In it I had packed food, my precious Tholan and as many books as I could find on the differences between Earth and Nzar. I had also brought a few things for sentimental value, things that I wanted as reminders of this life when I arrived back on Earth.

Walking back over to the crowd of people, I was shocked to see that a good few of their faces were streaming with tears. Watching them, I felt my own eyes well up.

I shook hands with everyone, hugging a few. The ones who meant the most to me were not here. I was slightly saddened by this fact but took a deep breath, composing myself.

Taking the precious Quill from my bag, I looked at the people once more. They had said that I should take it from this world for their own safety.

I had agreed, stowing the golden feather in my bag in case I ever needed it on my way home. I didn't know if I would be able to use it, or if its power would already be removed by the opening of the portals.

I held up the feather, staring at the blue sand timer on the side of it. It was fully charged.

I closed my eyes, thinking of what I wanted.

Home.

I made my wish before gently blowing over the feather tip.

A breeze stirred through the camp, gold dust beginning to swirl from the feather. It travelled to just in front of me, where it formed a gleaming circle.

As if it had been burned away, the oval shape ripped, revealing a gleaming darkness beyond it.

I watched with bittersweet emotions as the dark abyss appeared. The deed was done. It was time.

I took one last look at the people around me, at the life I was leaving behind. I smiled at them once more, and reached with my hand through the portal.

...

Two days later

I was trudging through the undergrowth, having flown until my strength failed me, and was now almost at the portal leading to Earth. Ahead, a sandy shore, covered in pebbles and shells, came into view. I walked towards it, marvelling at how small it seemed compared with how I remembered it. Tears flowed in my eyes as I remembered what had happened in a sandy cove further up: It was where we had arrived after first coming here.

I walked on, keeping my eyes on my surroundings. When I reached the spot where we had landed, I stared at the cave for a long moment, reminiscing over what had happened all that time ago.

Ahead, about a hundred feet away, I saw a dark, gleaming hole. The portal.

I strode forwards, eager to reach it.

It was exactly like the other portals and I stared at it before swinging my bag off my back. I knelt down, rifling through my belongings, checking that I had everything.

Pages fluttered in the faint breeze as I pulled out the old, decrepit book that I had used to find information about Sardaron. I sighed, prepared to throw it in the nearest river, and laid it on the grass, while I looked through my other belongings. It was the one book that I had brought just in case anything happened. Evidently, it hadn't, so I didn't need it any more.

I felt a cool sphere under my palm as I reached inside the bag and pulled out the glass ball Angus had given to me.

My father's story would forever stain my memory of him. I didn't want to remember him through his story but there was no other way to interpret his actions.

He had been a coward.

He had been selfish.

I stared at the glass ball, deliberating. Finally, I placed it back in my bag carefully. I would keep it, if only as a lesson to myself. I would learn from his actions.

When I looked back at the book, the page had flipped, onto one with a diagram of swirling darkness, twinkling lights echoing from in between the darkness. I picked it up gingerly, looking at the page for a moment, reading the text underneath the picture.

"The power of the darkness is what requires the deaths of

people; it is not the user who needs them, but the power itself. However, it is believed that the souls of those directly killed by Sardaron never truly vanish. Instead, they are sucked into the power, stored away after their body's energy is used up. In this way, it would be possible to retrieve the soul of someone killed by a death-god if you separated the power and the user. Resurrecting them would take an enormous force of power – the only thing that comes close to it is the Quill, the mythical object believed to have created all life on our planets."

I stared at the page, my heart thumping.

This could mean…Faol and Tera weren't dead.

They were simply trapped in the power of Sardaron.

I looked at the portal, wondering what I was going to do. I had dreamed for so long of going home, but… this was probably my only chance of finding them.

I had to do it.

…

Amber

My eyes squinted against the harsh light, mortal senses dull. Through the bushes, I could just about make out the figure of a girl, her silvery hair blowing gently in the breeze. The colour flashed though my memory, so familiar. Her steps traced the ground, face the same as it had been for the last hundred years. The same as it would be forever.

I watched her turn towards the land, the sea at her back, as she slung a bag over her shoulder.

Kai. My twin.

My hands, wrinkled with age, reached towards her, tears leaking from my eyes.

I moved as fast as my one-hundred-and-seventeen year old body would let me as I made my way towards her.

She started striding off, a look of determination clouding her dark eyes.

'Wait,' I whispered. 'Wait for me.'

THE END

ABOUT THE AUTHOR

Anna Pattle is a fifteen-year-old native of London who started this novel at age thirteen following inspiration from an English assignment she was given at her school. Anna is currently a student at Wycombe Abbey School and loves reading and playing sport in her free time. Sardaron is her first novel and she plans to keep writing more fiction in the future. Following Sardaron's publication, Anna hopes to share this book with young readers who are currently unable to access the reading materials which inspired her.